WICKED INTENTIONS

DISCREET COVER

SHANDI BOYES

COPYRIGHT

Editing: Swish Design & Editing

Cover: SSB Covers & Design

This is the discreet cover version.

WANT TO STAY IN TOUCH?

Facebook: facebook.com/authorshandi

Tiktok: https://www.tiktok.com/@authorshandiboyes

Instagram: instagram.com/authorshandi

Email: authorshandi@gmail.com

Reader's Group: bit.ly/ShandiBookBabes

Website: authorshandi.com

Newsletter: https://www.subscribepage.com/AuthorShandi

ALSO BY SHANDI BOYES

Lady In Waiting (Regan & Alex #1)

Man in Queue (Regan & Alex #2)

Couple on Hold (Regan & Alex #3)

Enigma: The Wedding (Isaac and Isabelle)

Silent Vigilante (Brandon and Melody #1)

Hushed Guardian (Brandon & Melody #2)

Quiet Protector (Brandon & Melody #3)

Enigma: An Isaac Retelling

Twisted Lies (Jae & CJ)

Bound Series

Chains (Marcus & Cleo #1)

Links (Marcus & Cleo #2)

Bound (Marcus & Cleo #3)

Restrain (Marcus & Cleo #4)

The Misfits

Russian Mob Chronicles

Nikolai: A Mafia Prince Romance (Nikolai & Justine #1)

Nikolai: Taking Back What's Mine (Nikolai & Justine #2)

Nikolai: What's Left of Me (Nikolai & Justine #3)

Nikolai: Mine to Protect (Nikolai & Justine #4)

Asher: My Russian Revenge (Asher & Zariah)

Nikolai: Through the Devil's Eyes (Nikolai & Justine #5)

Trey (Trey & K)

The Italian Cartel

Dimitri

Roxanne

Reign

Mafia Ties (Novella)

Maddox

Demi

Rocco

Clover

Smith

RomCom Standalones

Just Playin' (Elvis & Willow)

Ain't Happenin' (Lorenzo & Skylar)

The Drop Zone (Colby & Jamie)

Very Unlikely (Brand New Couple)

Short Stories - Newsletter Downloads

Christmas Trio (Wesley, Andrew & Mallory -- short story)

Falling For A Stranger (Short Story)

One Night Only Series

Hotshot Boss

Hotshot Neighbor

The Bobrov Bratva Series

Wicked Intentions (Katie & Ghost)

Sinful Intentions (coming soon)

1

KATIE

Fourteen years old…

*A*n annoying 'woo, woo, woo' drags me from my unconscious
state. I'm groggy, my head is pounding, and my mouth feels
like it is stuffed with cotton wool. I can't remember the last time I was
this thirsty. I drank at some point today, I'm sure of it, but you wouldn't
know that with how dry and scratchy my throat feels. My eyes are also
burning, but there's no chance to lubricate them since they're covered
so firmly with a rough, itchy material that blinking seems impossible.

"He-hello," I call out, my voice as weak and pitiful as I feel.

I've had the same group of friends forever, so my life experiences
are limited, but even with me attending an all-girls school, there's no
missing the scent surrounding me. Their deep, husky breaths are
telling enough, not to mention the grubby, mannish aroma in the air.
They smell like my older cousins when they leave the track after an
event—stinky and sweaty.

"Wh-where are you taking me?"

I cower when my question is answered by a painful backhand to the
head. With how much my skull rings in the aftermath of their assault, I

can't say I wasn't struck with a fist. The throb of bulging knuckles against my temples announces I was hit with the back part of their hand. I'm just unsure if they had their hand closed or open.

"Замолчи," snarls a deep, heavily accented voice.

When I bob my head again, ducking out of the firing zone before I'm hit for the second time, the sleeve of my shirt drags up the material hindering my vision. It isn't enough to announce to the men surrounding me that my blindfold is slipping, but enough to disclose that I'm lying on the floor of what appears to be a van of some type. The metal floor is scuffed free of paint, dotted with blood and housing over a dozen pairs of boots.

Oh God.

My stomach gurgles when my eyes land on my bound feet. The fact I'm tied like an animal isn't the shocking part. It is recalling why I'm wearing the hip-hop sneakers my mother gifted me for my birthday. I'm not meant to wear them out so they won't get wrecked before my dance concert at the end of the year, but I snuck them out today so I wouldn't look like a dork who attends a girls' school while walking to the local store with Blaire, my best friend.

Oh my God, Blaire!

I sit up so fast, there's no chance the return of my vision won't be announced.

Quicker than I can be pulled down by a brute with an ugly face tattoo, I scan the cab of the van, seeking Blaire. We were walking to get an ice cream, not a rare occurrence for girls our age who don't live in a town that's seen a surge in gang-related activities over the past two years, but something new for us. My father works in insurance, and along with increased premiums came a stringent set of rules.

No boys.

No non-school activities.

And definitely no wandering the streets alone.

I thought my father was being ridiculous.

I'm almost an adult, but now I feel like a fool.

The matching neck tattoos of the men surrounding me warrant his worry, not to mention the memories that flood my head when a white cloth is placed over my mouth and nose for the second time today.

I've been kidnapped by men with foreign accents, and I have no clue if my best friend escaped the carnage or if she is in one of the seedy white vans following us.

———

By the time I wake, the 'wooing' rotation of tires over asphalt is replaced by a much sterner and more deafening roar. It reminds me of the trip my family took to Cabo last year, except I'm in the cargo carrier with our dog, Pebbles, instead of in the main hull of the plane with my family.

Not wanting to be drugged again, I keep my head slumped while pricking my ears. We're definitely in a plane. My ears have the same weighted feeling they get every time I forget to chew gum during take-off, and there's a cold, too-high-in-the-sky briskness in the air.

I was out longer than I thought, or we've stayed on the East Coast because before I can roll up the bottom of my blindfold with the sleeve of my shirt, a familiar giddiness hits my stomach as the plane commences its descent.

I love the rush of takeoff, but landing makes me queasy.

It is fortunate my stomach is empty, meaning nothing but ghastly-tasting air bubbles escape my mouth during the quick descent.

Worry burns my esophagus when our landing is quickly followed by me being yanked onto my feet by an abrupt tug on my arm. Black military boots aren't the only shoes peeking out the bottom of my blindfold. There are several pairs of running shoes, high heels, and one lady is wearing a pair of red- bottom stilettoes. I would assume she was a ringleader if her knees and shoes weren't as scuffed as mine.

"Single file," shouts a thick voice in a deep foreign accent. "You will be directed left or right. Remain in your line." His hot breath fans my ear when he adds, "You don't want to know what will happen if you don't follow the rules."

I yank away when a calloused finger is dragged down my forearm. It isn't the touch of a gentle, kind man. It is deprived and violent, as villainous as the twists that hit my stomach when I'm told to veer left, and it steers me toward an argument between two men.

Their accents are different, but they have no issue communicating their dislike of each other with solely their tones. The deeper of the two is calm and collected, but the younger one, if you can call him that since he sounds kind of ancient, is full of silent mocking. He is goading the first man about his inability to control his sons and how his children would never step out of line in such a way.

"Rico is free-spirited. He—"

"Embarrassed you," interrupts the man with the same thick Italian accent as the owner of a pizzeria I frequent with my family. God, I hope I will be able to do that again one day. "He made a mockery of your name in front of our allies." I didn't realize you could hear a ticking jaw until now. "That is the last thing we need with the operative we're endeavoring to undermine. Henry—"

"Will be handled." The man with the dangerous tone lowers the volume of his voice a few octaves before adding, "As will Rico. By the time I am finished with him, he will not step out of line again."

Scuffling feet marching across asphalt and whimpered sobs are the only things heard for the next couple of seconds before the first man asks, "When?"

"Tonight." The abruptness of the second man's reply exposes he wants their discussion over. "After the shipments are organized." His Russian accent is more pronounced when he asks, "Even split?"

The Italian man hums in agreement. "With a ten-percent share offered to the Bobrovs as a courtesy for their help."

"Brilliant. It will keep Henry's focus on them."

"Exactly!" The first man snickers before I'm shoved into a dark room with more murmured whispers and whimpers than I heard on the plane.

"BLAIRE?" I murmur while circling the gathering of women sweltering in a large steel box in humid and sticky conditions.

I'm not sure how much time has passed since we entered what feels like a shipping container, but several women have passed out, and many more have banged on the container's walls with their fists, promising to do *anything* to be let out.

I've done nothing but focus on finding Blaire. I'm scared and frightened, but my father taught me that tears will get me nowhere. They only weaken me.

"Blaire?" I repeat.

"No," replies the lady I'm butting shoulders with. Her hair is a similar shade to Blaire's but shorter, so in my heart, I knew it wasn't her. I am just so desperate I had to ask. "But she may be in the other container."

My bewilderment is heard in my high tone. "There's more than one container?"

I can only see her from the waist down since her reply dipped my chin, but I imagine her nodding when a woosh of air rustles between us. "There are two. I was in the other one until... until..." Her words shift into a sob. "I shouldn't have saved myself. I've heard from the other women that Colum is a monster. That if you have the chance to pick, you should always go with the Russians."

"Col? Russians?" I'm lost, and my head is spinning with more than the effects of being drugged twice in a short period.

I work through a hard swallow when she answers, "The trade. We're being trafficked."

Before shock can set in, much less fear that I may never see my family again, I ask, "Do you know if there is a girl called Blaire in the other container? She is around my height with blonde hair."

"Is she the same age as you?" My brisk nod continues when she asks, "And a virgin?"

My nod isn't as purposeful this time around. Don't get me wrong, Blaire isn't as adventurous as me. It's just the direction of our conversation that has me swallowing razor blades. "We're close, so she'd tell me if she'd done anything like that. I don't think she's gone past first base."

I wish to God for my blindfold not to be so tight when the stranger replies, "Then she should be here. This is where all the virgins are."

I should take a moment to consider her words with more diligence, to let them sink in with the concern they deserve, but instead, I continue my search, confident I need to find Blaire before contemplating anything.

"Blaire..."

2

KATIE

Eighteen years old...

*B*laire was never found. I scoured every inch of the container I was housed in for three days with barely any food and water and spoke to every person trapped with me. There were a range of women from across the country, both young and old, but not a single Blaire.

For the past few years, I've sought comfort in the fact she must have escaped, and although I tried to do the same when the container's doors were opened with the assumption everyone was asleep, I'm still here, captive for several long months later.

I think I turned eighteen a couple of weeks back, but I can't be sure. Madame Victoria said I'll know the age I'm classed as 'ripe' as I'll be sold to my 'forever king.'

I've spent the last several years training to be his ideal wife. I was taught to cook, clean, and maintain a household with robust, energetic children under my feet. Most 'forever kings' already have children because they're usually onto their fourth or fifth wife before they seek Madame Victoria's services. They're at the age where they are desperate for order, but they don't want to be saddled down with the women who birthed their heirs and slaved over their meals for the past forty-plus years. They want fresh, young-blooded women who are too scared to make a move in any direction they haven't been granted.

Terrified women like me who know how horrible they can be to their own children, so they won't blink an eye to end a miserable existence with a flick of their wrist.

My first attempt to escape came at a cost. I stumbled onto a scene almost too ghastly to describe. I thought the stench in the shipping container was bad, but it had nothing on the smell that vaped from a room when I dashed into a mansion-looking house to seek help.

A young man was hanging from the rafters by a steel chain. The skin on his back was dripping past his naked backside, yet he was alive.

I don't know how he survived such a heinous assault, but my endeavor to help him thrust me into the path of a man Madame Victoria knows all too well. I guess I shouldn't complain. From the stories I've heard, half the women trafficked with me didn't survive their first year in the trade. Most of their deaths were from violence during sexual activities.

I'm still untouched.

Getting slapped over the knuckles with a cane, whipped for not making the corners of the bedsheets tight enough, and being forced to eat scraps instead of full meals seems like a walk in the park compared to what they endured.

My day is coming, but at the moment, I am as safe as I can be in a demented and violent world.

It doesn't stop me from peering out a rectangular box that was once a window, though, wondering what I would be doing if I hadn't been walking along that road at that specific time of the day.

I miss my parents and baby sister. I even miss Pebbles' stinky fur when she dives into the marshlands nose first, uncaring there could be an alligator waiting for her.

And I also really miss Mom's cooking.

Mashed potatoes just aren't the same when they're prepared

without butter and milk, and despite my active imagination, potato skins aren't wedges when they're not cooked and covered with dirt.

As I squash the boiled potatoes with a plastic masher, my thoughts drift to Blaire.

Is she safe?

Is she alive?

I honestly hope so, but I don't even know what day of the week it is, so my intuition isn't trustworthy.

"*Раб*, come." Madame Victoria's stern snap has me dropping the plastic instrument into the half- mashed potatoes and immediately spinning around. She is a taut, slim woman with killer black eyes and a stern hand. She is kind when you obey her every command, but if you cross her, don't sleep. She seeks revenge when you least expect it. A broom is her favorite weapon, closely followed by boiling water. "We have an important guest. Hurry." Her husky timbre is a mix of foreign accents. She is crossbred in all meanings of the word.

When I enter the main living room of the compound I've been held captive and brutalized in for the past few years, I take a stumbling step back. The man seated behind the coffee table is as old and arrogant as the many who've visited previously, but no number of hazy memories could conceal his sneer.

He is the man from the room, the one who gleamed while watching acid being tossed on the back of his ally's son.

He is my current owner—Colum Petretti.

"Stand up straight," Madame Victoria demands when Col rises from his seat.

My knees shake when he takes his time appraising me, the darkness in his eyes growing more evil with every second he stares. "Pure?"

Madame Victoria hides her disdain well. "Of course. As are all the women in this house." She circles me while pointing out my attributes like I am a precious gem about to go up for auction. I am far from regal. My body houses many scars from my inability to remember I am a commodity, and there is barely an ounce of fat on my bones. I am malnourished with lifeless eyes—two reasons I've most likely been overlooked the past couple of years. "Extensive training, magnificent culinary skills, and research indicate she will age well."

My heart patters in my chest when she hands Col a photograph. I only catch the quickest glimpse of it, but I will never forget my mother's ruddy cheeks and vibrant red hair.

A crack announces my increase in pulse didn't go unnoticed by Madame Victoria. Her hit is barely a slap across the thighs with her walking stick but firm enough to pull me into line. She hits hard enough to crack skulls. I've witnessed her strength firsthand.

"Your children are grown, yes?" Madame Victoria asks, her focus back on Col.

I breathe for what feels like the first time in minutes when Col answers, "Yes, but I am not seeking her to girth my loins." Bile burns the back of my throat when he murmurs, "Although tempted." He shifts his focus from my nipples strained against the dowdy white nightgown all women here wear to Madame Victoria. "I need her for a special project."

I've never seen Madame Victoria's interests this piqued, not even when one of the women gave birth only three months after arriving here. Usually, they're sold as virgins or brought here to rear children. Sophie slipped through the net. "Which is?"

I feel the size of an ant when Col's eyes snap to mine. After perusing me for several uncomfortable seconds, with a wave of his hand, I'm dismissed from the room.

With my heart thudding like it's never pounded before, I return to mashing the potatoes for dinner while staring out the 'window.' It is a bland and uninviting view when nothing but my murky shadow reflects back at me. The compound has barely any windows, and the ones it does have were boarded up with glossy silver tape many years ago. I haven't seen sunlight in years, and my pasty white skin makes my red hair even more vibrant.

I startle when Madame Victoria sneaks up on me unaware. "Leave that. You need to be prepared for sale."

"But..." This isn't the first time I've made this mistake, and although her retaliation for my disobedience is swift, I expect to feel the sting of her wrath for days to come. The men housed in every corner of this compound don't hold anything back when directed to intervene.

"You were told to do something, so do it," a goon sneers in my face, his spit hot on my cheeks.

"Yes, sir," I reply, my words barely audible since my focus is on not whimpering about the clump of my hair sitting by my now-scuffed knees.

He yanked me to kneel beside him as a reminder that I am *not* his equal.

I am his slave.

The next hour passes in a blur. My head is throbbing from where I was grabbed and forced to my knees, but I'm also feeling a little lethargic and sentimental. This compound is not the cute three-bedroom home I grew up in, but it is all I've known for the past three or so years. Leaving it is daunting, but even more daunting than that is the fact I feel a little homesick.

"Remember what I taught you," Madame Victoria murmurs from the only doorway in and out of this compound. "If you do, you will stay alive. If you don't..." She doesn't finish her sentence. She merely hands me a photograph that spells everything out in graphic detail.

Ivey didn't last a day outside these walls. She was killed by her new owner three hours after her auction, then returned like a broken doll.

I blink back the tears springing in my eyes about her cruel refund when the door next to Madame Victoria pops open. Guards flank the small opening, shadowing my face from the blinding sun enough to spot a row of dark SUVs lined down a dirt driveway several feet from the opening of the compound.

There isn't another house close by. Not a single one.

That's why no one heard my screams for help.

"Goodbye, ma'am," I stupidly murmur, my teachings beaten into me too fiercely to forget.

For the first time, Madame Victoria's harsh lines soften before she dips her chin in farewell.

My wish to vomit doubles when my slow trek over a heavily

manned threshold has me stumbling onto another conversation. This time, it centers around me.

"Are you sure she will entice him enough?" Since I'm not blindfolded this time around, I can take in the features of the man with a thick Russian accent. He is as old as my head imagined, but his hair is darker than expected, and his height is more substantial. "We need to make sure he is nowhere near New York state lines."

Col stares straight at me while replying, "He is already a registered bidder. She will lure him. She already has." He drifts his eyes back to his comrade. "Then Rimi will take him down."

3

GHOST

*W*hile tapping the end of my cigarette on its pack, I scan the senile yet still murderous men in front of me. Blue pills are no longer helping them, and they're too old to request a discount from the whores who regularly dirty their sheets, so they've resorted to this.

A wife for purchase.

Or maybe I should say hire since most barely last a week and come with a 'thirty-day-guarantee' all men in this room take advantage of.

They'll be chewed up and spat out before being replaced with a doppelganger lookalike. Only the ones with exceptional fertility and tasty cunts last a year. But still, by the time they give birth, they're replaced with a younger, fancier model.

Most of the men in this room could find their own virginal wives to train if they weren't so spineless. They don't know how to keep a woman in line. They're as soft and pitiful as the bounce of the woman's breasts who's being auctioned in cubicle number three. She is barely the age to breed, so the men bidding ten thousand a piece don't want her for a wife.

They want her cunt, and they want it bleeding.

"How much longer?" I ask Kirill, frustrated to have been dragged here while the waters are still extremely murky.

Rumors are circulating, and none of them are in the Bobrovs' favor. We have a target on our back, a fucking big one, but no one is listening.

"I don't trust these men," I murmur in Russian, my tone low enough to ensure no one from the Popov crew hears me. "Since when have the Petrettis and Popovs worked together? They're meant to be enemies."

"Enemies with the same objective." Kirill spins to face me, his age almost half of the men surrounding us. "To eradicate a mutual hierarchy."

I breathe out a husky chuckle. "They tried and failed, remember? Blood was shed for months when Henry caught wind of the travesty."

But you wouldn't know that since you ran to Russia like a coward.

I wonder if I said my thoughts out loud when Kirill's eyes narrow into tiny slits. I assume it is in response to my snipe but learn otherwise when they bring in the next lot of women to be auctioned.

Bland.

Demure.

Not a single interesting item up for auction.

They're either brain-dead from being beaten into submission or so fucking high on drugs they have no clue where they are or what is happening.

"If you want to fuck a corpse, we could visit the local morgue." I choke on the last half of my rile when the final member of the group of twenty enters the room. She is flanked by prospective bidders in under a second, and although she has the same manufactured walk and stare as the group in front of her, she is the only one to lock eyes with the people swarming her.

It is fascinating to watch a lamb enter a slaughter yard without the slightest quiver in her knees.

I've only ever seen such a riveting sight once before in my life.

When the redhead's eyes finally reach mine, a spark in them almost knocks me on my ass. It is a defiant glare that makes my blood pump faster and my hands sweat.

She is a challenge every man in this room wants to solve.

Including me.

Except there's one difference between the other bidders and me.

I never lose, and she is now of age.

4

KATIE

The evilness in the room is stifling, depriving the large space of oxygen. I feel sick to my stomach when I'm paraded on stage like my life isn't worth anywhere near as much as the men swarming me. I'm stared at with belittlement, poked and pinched without remorse, and then there is him. The blond-haired man at the back of the pack. Half of his face is shadowed by the poor lighting, but I can't miss that his hand is minus the bidding paddle most men are holding.

He watches me under the same set of hooded eyelids though, and although his stare is still startling, it doesn't have my skin crawling like the men hovering in close to get a prime spot. He is also at least half the age of the men surrounding us but still most likely a decade older than me. He looks uncomfortable like he is out of his depth as much as me.

As horrendous as this is for me to say, he is my lifeboat in a stormy sea, hence, my prolonged stare. I'll quiver if I continue scanning the room, thus not only increasing my bids but doubling the likelihood of me being purchased by a man like Ivey's 'husband.'

They want you scared.

They want you terrified.

But I won't give them the satisfaction.

I can obey orders and follow directions, but my fear is mine, and they will *never* own that.

My focus shifts from the dark and mysterious stranger at the back of the select group when a grumbled comment at my side speeds up my heart. "All guns are checked at the start of the auction. Even mine."

All guns?

Once again, I stray my eyes across the room, but this time, instead of locking gazes with the men who drooled at me as I was shoved by, I search their hips and ankles.

Guns have kept me in line for the past four years. I haven't seen a single man without one. They've become the norm, so to know a gun isn't associated with my presence at the moment has sweat beading at the back of my neck and my brain kicking into overdrive.

This may be my only chance to escape.

My eyes shoot back to the instigator of my new heart rhythm when "Katie?" faintly rumbles out of his mouth.

When our eyes lock, his throat works through a stern swallow, and my heart races.

He knows my name, which means...

No freaking way. He knows who I am!

"Help me. Please," I beg, my voice suddenly returned.

When his bright blue eyes snap down to the lock box his gun was just deposited into, mine drift back to the crowd. As suspected, my fear excites them, and it sends my bids into a flurry. They climb in ten thousand dollar increments until they reach an astronomical amount that announces I'm mere hours from suffering Ivey's fate.

"I won't conform to your ways. I'll never do what I'm told," I scream before doing the second most stupid thing I've ever done.

I run. Again. For the third time in my life.

This time, since my campaign isn't instantly upended by a man shoving a chloroform-soaked cloth over my mouth, I make it to the back of the gun-empty room with only a bruise or two from spectators trying to stop my flee by grabbing my arm.

I'm about to veer to the left when the man I locked eyes with for almost three minutes nudges his head to the right.

I shouldn't trust him. No one in this room is trustworthy, but for some reason, I do.

Seconds after veering right, I'm blinded by the midday sun. It is so bright and blistering it stuns me long enough for the man who tossed a hessian bag over my head a nanosecond after I crossed the threshold of Madame Victoria's compound to catch up to me.

He wraps his arm around my waist and yanks me back with force. I kick out and scream, but within seconds, the jab he hits my neck with has my arms and legs not complying with my brain. I'm conscious but am unable to move or speak.

I have enough drool pooling at the corner of my mouth to consider a diagnosis of brain damage, yet the bids still flood the auctioneer until I'm sold to a new owner then tossed into the sold pile so the next auction can continue.

"It's okay. Stay as still as possible. The sedative will wear off soon."

I tilt my head to the side since I can't trust my throat to swallow the slobber drowning my mouth and stumble onto the man who spoke my name earlier. "H-help."

He shushes me again before shifting his focus to my hands. I choke on my sob when he doesn't lessen their weightiness. He doubles it by circling zip ties around my hands and fastening them together.

"N-no, please." My second word is nowhere near as groggy as my first but still barely audible. "I want to go home."

"Your parents want you home too, Katie. They've never stopped looking for you."

I peer at him through glistening, tear-filled eyes. "Then help me."

"I'm trying." He glares angrily at a small hole between the molding and the roof before assisting me to my feet. "The hierarchies won't budge. We're outnumbered."

I shake my head so fiercely I almost vomit when he pushes me toward my old owner. Col is sitting behind a banged-up table, distributing women like corndogs at a fair. His gleam is as big as a clown, and he's hoarding his money as if it may soon vanish.

"She's ready for transport," the stranger who promised to help grunts out.

Col drags his eyes over my scuffed knees and white face before gesturing for my new owner to present. My face whitens even more when the man I was staring at earlier steps forward. He stands slightly back from a man with dark hair and an evil smirk, but he has as many eyes on him as the man handing over an exorbitant amount of cash for me.

Half the room's stares are in fear, whereas the other half are revered gawks. It could be the large scar down one side of the blond's face that attracts unwanted attention his way, but it feels like more than that. He has a haughty arrogance about him but in a demure, reluctant manner.

Could he be my savior?

Or will he constantly stand in the shadows that hide half his face?

If the gunfire that rings across the parade is any indication, I will never find out.

The blasts are deafening, but before I can swing my head in the direction the gunfire is projecting from, I'm pulled to my left by the man who bound me.

"We're taking heat," he announces while pulling me behind a pavilion the women were stuffed into after being paraded like meat at a cattle sale. "What do you mean it isn't you, Tobias? Then who the fuck is it?" I realize I shouldn't have run when he pulls out a weapon strapped to his thigh. "I can't hold back. We're being bombarded."

Bullets whizz over my head as wounded cries echo in the eerie carnage.

You can smell death and all the horrid bodily functions that come with it.

"I'm sending her out the west entrance. Get someone there." Before the stranger speaks another word, he plucks me onto my feet, drags me across the bullet-shell-riddled floor, then pushes me through the exit door the scarred-faced blond nudged his head at earlier.

The sun is just as blinding this time around, amplified by the amount of tear gas and smoke in the air. The building is on fire, but the parking lot is still filled with pricy vehicles.

"Aaren?" A man in a dark SUV asks when he pulls up beside the man who's playing both sides of the field and me.

When Aaren appears hesitant, the man behind the wheel murmurs, "Tobias sent me. She'll be safe with me."

Aaren's deliberation is cut short when a swarm of men heads our way. They're not associated with any faces I locked onto today, and they're brandishing a range of weapons.

After shoving me into the car, Aaren slams the back door shut, then says, "Take her to the safe house. I'll organize secure transport this afternoon."

5

KATIE

Twenty-two years old...

*S*ecure transport never came.

I was taken to a compound similar to the first one I was delivered to eight years ago, shackled to a bed in a room that only had a dirty mattress on the floor, then told my new owner would collect me soon.

Considering the amount he paid to purchase me, I thought he'd arrive within a couple of hours.

It's been over four years, and I'm still waiting.

Once again, I shouldn't complain. Excluding a handful of bruises for disobedience and a fractured rib, I'm still relatively untouched. Sexually, I am what Master Rudd likes to call a saint.

Pure in all meanings of the word.

I can't say the same for the women who live here with me. They're beaten and assaulted every day by men who come and go as they please. I know this because I patch up their wounds, offer them a shoulder to cry on, and nurse their children when they can't.

This compound differs from the one I stayed at with Madame

Victoria simply because some of the women here get to keep the children who aren't sold like their mothers once were. They have a range of health issues and live in conditions not suitable for children with disabilities, but it is better than the alternative.

At my old compound, they killed any baby born with the slightest deformity. Even something as simple as a cleft palate saw them murdered within minutes of birth.

The conditions are better here, but I live a boring, miserable existence. I'm forgetting the ruddiness of my mother's cheeks, my father's lopsided smile, and my little sister's once-annoying traits I'd give anything to be frustrated by again. I am miserable. So much so I get upset when Master Rudd's attention never fixates on me for longer than a few seconds.

He compliments me on the odd occasion but is quick to remind me I am not his to sully.

His standards are weird, considering he beds multiple women in one night. He has four wives, and between them, they have thirteen children, but that doesn't stop him from taking the occasional new 'slave' for a 'test drive.'

His last two wives only joined us last year. They were trafficked like the rest of us, but within weeks, they stopped fighting their fate and faced the inevitable.

They are as trapped as me.

I shouldn't want any man's attention, much less Master Rudd's. He's a vile, heinous man, but for some reason, I get jealous when he brushes his index finger down my nose before telling me to go to bed. He isn't a doting man by any means. However, when you've been starved for affection as long as I have, you seek it in any way possible.

If I could just go home, I'd feel different. But I can't. I'm stuck here for eternity.

And I hate it.

The thoughts in my head aren't natural. I've never been a negative person, and I have always seen the good in everyone, but a lot has changed over the last six months. I've been sick, both mentally and physically, and reached a point where I don't believe I will ever escape.

This is my life now, and I must accept that if I don't want my body covered with welts, scars, and burn marks. The ones I have now I can cover with well-placed trinkets and flowing locks. Others here are nowhere near as lucky.

"*Раб.*" I shift my head when Master Rudd enters the kitchen. "How much longer until dinner?"

Before I can answer him, a loud bang sounds from the living area of the compound. I would have believed Jace had fallen again if a silver canister didn't roll into the room and fill it with smoke. It is the raid at my auction all over again, except this time, they don't shoot, then ask questions. They ask questions, then shoot, and all their attention is focused on Master Rudd.

"I didn't touch her, I swear," he replies in English, even though the questions being fired at him are spoken in a foreign language. "I housed her and fed her as requested. That's it. I did everything you asked."

"If you're lying..." begins a tall brute of a man whose gun is pressed at Master Rudd's temple. It burns his skin since he used it to kill the two guards stationed in the living room. "We'll come back here and finish this." When he locks his eyes with mine through strands of sweaty hair fallen in front of his face, standing motionless like a robot at the side of the living room, he sneers a grin that seems more playful than evil before he shifts his focus to a man standing at his right. "Scan her." As a second brute heads my way, the leader shifts his focus back to Master Rudd. "Or perhaps I should take care of matters now. There's no way you didn't touch her. *Даже у Бога возникло бы искушение откусить от этого яблока.*"

I only catch portions of his sentence spoken in a foreign language, but it already had me worried before Master Rudd says, "You can check for yourself." He locks his eyes with mine. "Lay down, *Раб.*"

Almost trance-like, I move to a sectional sofa at the side of the now-cramped space and lie down. I'm quivering like a bag of nerves, but you wouldn't know that from the outside. The rod in my back has solidified over the past few years because it is the only thing keeping me alive.

"And get killed for deflowering his Mary." The brute cracks Master

Rudd over the head with the butt of his gun. "No thanks." After gesturing to the men around him to follow him, he lowers his eyes to me lying lifeless on the couch. "Come."

I snap my eyes to Master Rudd, then suck in air like my life depends on it when he nods his head to the man's abrupt command. "Go, *Раб*. We planned for this."

He may have always known I wasn't his, but his wives were never part of the equation, so why are they being walked out by men with blood splatter over their clothes?

"The men have a long trip ahead of them. Your wives will keep them entertained," the leader replies as if he heard my private thoughts.

"But the Bobrovs are never without women," Master Rudd complains, his voice the lowest I've heard it. It wasn't even that low when he suggested his first wife dye her hair and take my spot as a Bobrov bride. "And I've never disrespected him. Not once." When they continue without pause in their strides, his anger gets the better of him. "I should have bitten into her cunt and marked it so he'd never have a use for her."

My hand darts up to suffocate my sob when the ringleader's response comes in the form of violence. He shoots Master Rudd between the eyes, killing him instantly.

"Go to Mommy," I whisper when Jace remains standing at the side of the living room, staring at his now-deceased father. "Now, Jace," I shout when he remains frozen in place. He doesn't need that memory of him.

He's barely made it to the master bedroom when I'm stuffed into the middle car in a long line of SUVs. It's overcast today, so seeing the setting sun for the first time in years isn't as beautiful as I've imagined the past eight years.

Furthermore, I can't take my bewilderment off my surroundings for even a second. It's all so familiar, even with me not seeing it for years.

This can't be true.

I must be delusional.

There's no way they've held me captive in a town bordering my hometown for years.

The auction was held only a quick drive from my compound, and I arrived at Master Rudd's residence within minutes of being bundled into the back of an SUV by Aaren, but this route is familiar, and the scents are all the same.

We're at the docks my father took me to multiple times between the ages of eight and the day I was kidnapped. He had several insurance claims here that took weeks for him to sort through. I came with him because it was summer break, and I loved how the shipping containers were the skyscrapers of the sea.

I couldn't forget this dock if I tried.

When the SUV stops near a cargo ship that appears as if it was recently loaded, my eyes scan my surroundings. There isn't a shipworker in sight. Women, though, they're in abundance. They pile out of the SUVs tailing mine before being forcefully walked to the gangway of the ship without words needed.

Guns strapped to chests are demanding enough, not to mention our training. Most walk the same zombie walk I've seen many times during the past eight years. Their expressions are lifeless, and their shoulders are slumped. I can't tell if they're drugged or have merely lost the will to live.

Then there's the handful who haven't been taught the consequences of not following the rules yet. The ones who will enter the cargo ship with the blood of their friend splattered on their face because they were the slower of the two when they endeavored to make an escape.

There are no warning shots today.

No cruel tugs on their dirty locks.

Only cold-blooded murders.

As we enter the ship, most girls are directed to the lower levels of the deck. I'm grabbed and pulled to the left by the man who killed Master Rudd.

"You're a special order, and the swine down there can't be trusted."

The silence in this area of the ship is unusual. It is eerie yet thought-provoking at the same time. Offices sprout off the hallway in all directions, and every one of them is occupied by men in various stages of undress. Some have women sprawled out in front of them, others have their faces hidden between a pair of legs, and the rest have their backsides hanging out for the world to see.

It appears as if Master Rudd was right. The Bobrovs have plenty of women at their disposal, so what could they want with me?

My heart rate kicks up a beat when I'm yanked to a stop at the front of a door marked 'Captain's Hull.' Unlike the other doors in this corridor, this one is shut.

That doesn't mean the man who killed Master Rudd will knock before entering, though. He twists open the knob, shoves me into the room, and grunts, "Special order," before slamming the door shut behind him.

I'm half a second from spinning and fleeing before I recall how it ended for the women out on the docks.

I don't want to die.

I don't think.

Instead of sprinting how I really want, I dig my nails into my palms before slowly raising my eyes. At first, I think my new owner is sleeping. His head is flopped back, and his eyes are closed.

My assumption only lasts as long as it takes for me to recognize the gagging slurps coming from underneath his desk. Master Rudd's first wife made similar noises when she was forced to give him head while I sat across from them with my legs at the width of my shoulders and my undergarments removed. I wasn't allowed to look down—supposedly that was against the rules—but I was ordered to maintain eye contact with Master Rudd until his eyes eventually fluttered shut.

The 'game' was over not long after that.

Unsure of my new owner's rules, I try to get his attention without lowering my eyes past the partially exposed skin peeking out from beneath his crisp black dress shirt. It is undone to the third button and shows a light splattering of hairs across a scarred chest.

My faint cough alerts him to my presence. Not enough for one of his hands balled on his desk to stop his female companion's movements, but enough that he lowers his chin until it balances a couple of inches above his thrusting chest.

I choke on my spit when I recognize his face. He's the man from the auction, the one who nudged his head to the exit, except his eyes are no longer playful and calm. They're glassy and unhinged, like the white powder lines on his desk are the cause of their dilation instead of the woman kneeling between his splayed thighs.

While my eyes drink in the new scars covering a majority of the right side of his face, his lower to my dowdy and stained nightgown. It is white like the one I wore when I was auctioned but sullied and dirty —unlike my virtue.

Doubt seeps in that he isn't the knight I'm seeking when he unsuctions the woman kneeling in front of him, then dismisses her from the room like an unwanted toy. His cruelty doesn't surprise me. I've experienced it thousands of times in the past eight years, but it is the way he doesn't balk while exposing himself to me that has me stunned.

Master Rudd said he didn't want his penis cut off, hence his request for me to keep my eyes locked on his face. That is also why I've never seen a penis that doesn't belong to my father. Unlike the men holding me captive, my father is a kind, gentle man. He didn't flash himself at me. Our horror-filled three seconds was when I raced into my parents' bedroom Christmas Eve many years ago.

Santa was doing far more than kissing Mommy.

But this is full-frontal nudity where no amount of eye-locking will stop me from viewing a part of the stranger's body I'm striving to act unaffected by. It's too large to keep hidden and growing thicker and longer the more he stares.

I snap my eyes to his face when he growls out in a thick, gravelly tone, "Knees. Now."

"Ex-excuse me?"

I learned the hard way that manners aren't taught.

They're beaten into you.

"Knees," he repeats as he walks around his desk, exposing more of himself. "Now."

When he reaches me, the scent of his sweat-dotted skin smacks into me. It is mannish and pulse-quickening and has my stomach unsure of which way to churn. It should be revolting, but my senses are confused because I'm certain, for the first time in years, the quickening of my pulse isn't in fear.

With the light directly above us, he angles his head to shadow the scarred side of his face before raising his hand to my fiery red locks. "I've waited years for this. Don't make me wait a second longer."

Not speaking another word, he weaves his fingers through my hair, then uses the long, tangled knots as an anchor to tether me to my knees in front of him. He doesn't yank me down with the brutal violence I'm accustomed to, but it is very much a demanding do-as-I-ask hold.

His long, fleshy rod bobs when I'm positioned a mere inch in front of it. The glistening tip at the end could be blamed on the slurping noises I heard coming from under his desk only minutes ago, but it only formed once my mouth was lined up with the head of his cock.

A tremor I've never experienced before erupts down my spine when his thumb gathers up the bead and transfers it onto my top lip. His skin is calloused and sprinkled with the same white powder on his desk, but the smoothness of the droplet spreads across my lip with ease.

"That'll lessen the burn." His accent is one I've heard many times over the past four-plus years—thick, brutish, and Russian. "Now open your mouth like a good girl."

I'm scared as hell on the inside, but the fast opening of my mouth doesn't expose that.

I've been taught to obey, and obey I will.

"Push your tongue down. Give me more room. My cock is big, but I still want as much of it in your mouth as I can fit." Two of the bumps in his midsection twitch when I flatten my tongue. "Now breathe through your nose."

His head snaps to the side when a cell phone rings. He tries to ignore it by stepping closer, bringing his cock to within an inch of my mouth, but it immediately begins ringing again, this time with a different ringtone.

"Fuck." He drops his glassy and still-dilated eyes to me. "Don't move." He appears as if he wants to say more but doesn't.

Usually, orders like that are followed with a threat, and although I appreciate not having my life endangered again today, his expression when he snatches up his cell and squashes it against his ear feels super threatening.

"No..." He speaks in Russian, but I've learned a handful of small phrases the past four years. "What special package?" When he locks eyes with me, I career mine to the floor. "She is here... what?" Anger radiates from him, forcing every muscle in his body to pull taut. "That was not the agreement." His anger has him switching between Russian and English. "Этот гребаный ублюдок!"

As he continues his conversation, his anger grows—as does his dressed state. In three heart-stuttering seconds, he yanks on a pair of trousers and buttons up his business shirt to the top button. Then, after telling his caller in no uncertain terms that they're a Russian bastard, he yanks me to my feet and shoves me down the hall with the brutality I was anticipating only seconds ago.

6

KATIE

*T*he stranger's grip on my arm turns deadly when he stops us in front of a door one deck down from his. It is as shiny as the captain's door but has no name plaque.

The fight not to step back when the door is swung open is overwhelming. A man with a seedy gleam and even more sullied shirt drags in a long draw of his cigarette before his eyes shift from me to the man who is suddenly acting like I have cooties. "Ghost, to what do I owe the pleasure?"

His welcoming words don't reflect his depraved gawk. He looks greasy and perverted, and the instruments inside his room have me conjuring up murder scenes in the movies Blaire and I regularly watched over Halloween.

"He wants authentication," replies the man now known as Ghost, his voice low but still very much demanding.

The man with slicked-back hair and a cigarette hanging out of his mouth acts ignorant to who is the clear alpha in the room. "He?"

The temperament in the air shifts, turning from comfortable to downright roasting. "He..." Ghost shunts me forward two steps. "Who the fuck else requests authenticity by a *trained* professional?" The way he spits out 'trained' reflects he doesn't believe the title any more than me. "Do it quick. He wants authenticity before the anchor is disengaged." He forcefully walks me into the room, sits me on an unsterile-looking hospital bed, then spins to face the man who appears as if his every wish has been granted. "You have five minutes."

Certain he is the lesser of two evils, my hand shoots out to grip Ghost's wrist before I can stop myself. I don't want to be his lapdog who performs tricks for a treat, but my desire not to be left with this man far outweighs my concern Ghost will once again force me onto my knees the instant we're alone.

The 'doctor's' room smells weird. The sheet at the end of the bed is stained with blood, and the glove box under his instruments of torture is empty. And don't remind me of the gun on his bedside table.

I'm not safe here. Not at all.

Ghost's eyes flick down to my hand circling his wrist before he returns them to my face. With one three-second stare, they sober up a lot. He looks angry, even more than before, so the last thing I expect to leave his mouth is some kind of reassurance. "He won't hurt you." His accent is deep, almost terrifying when he adds, "Not if he wants to live."

Stealing my chance to voice my concerns, he exits the room, closing the door behind him.

"You need to lie back, bring your feet to your bottom, and spread your knees apart." I shake uncontrollably, my fear uncontained when the doctor guides me back while murmuring, "He let you keep your panties?"

I feel exposed when he drags down the meager scrap of material I scrubbed in the kitchen sink once a week at Master Rudd's compound. It was the first pair of panties I was permitted to wear in years, and I wasn't going to let them out of my sight for a second, not even for a proper wash cycle.

When the snap of latex overtakes the thud of my pulse in my ears, I slant my head to the side and focus on an awkward red splotch on the far wall.

"Nuh-uh," murmurs the gentleman wedged between my thighs when my legs instinctively attempt to snap shut. He's touching my vagina and spreading me wide with his fingers yet he expects me not to react. Is he insane? "Hmm. No hymen. He will be disappointed, but let's see if we can improve the odds of you not being fish bait before we sail across several continents."

My eyes widen when he stuffs an object inside me. From the length and width, I assume it is his finger.

When he swivels the fat digit around, wetness pricks my eyes and flows down my cheek before puddling around my ear.

"Oh hush," he mocks when he spots my tears. "We need to make room for his instruments." I feel more vile than violated when he adds with a whisper, "This will make it feel better."

Even being held captive since I was fourteen doesn't stop me from recognizing the section of my body he's trying to arouse with his thumb. He's stroking my clit in rhythm to the faint rolls of his hips.

I don't need to see his crotch to know he is hard. He has the same hungry glint Master Rudd had every time he made me watch him with his wives.

"You can still be a virgin even if you've orgasme—"

His reply is cut short by his door flinging open. It smacks into the drywall as fast as I snap my legs shut and sink my ear into the hard, leather bed. "Five minutes was too generous. You should be done by now." In the reflection of the empty paper towel dispenser next to me, I spot Ghost slanting his head and arching a brow. He barely assesses the situation for two seconds before he tries to work out the reason for the tension ridding the air of oxygen. "What the fuck did you do?"

I assume he's frustrated at me but learn otherwise when the doctor tries to act unaffected by his suspicious tone. "These tests are evasive, but the results are good. He will be pleased."

Before I can react, Ghost grips my chin and turns my head to face him. My tears have dried, but since my body temperature is at boiling point, I'm sure he can see the trek the salty blob careened down my face.

After returning his now-balled hand to his side, he cranks his neck to the doctor frozen at the side of my bed. "What *the fuck* did you do to her?" Ghost's voice is a roar, and it shudders my heart out of my chest, but before I can hunt for it, he grabs the doctor by the neck, folds him in two with a stern punch to the stomach then brings his face to within an inch of mine. "Why is she crying?"

"Sh-she's not crying." His eyes plead with me to back up his claims when he lies. "It's sweat. It is hot in here."

Ghost's icy blue gaze locks with mine for barely a second before they shift back to the doctor. Then even quicker than that, he snatches the gun off the bedside table, pushes it to the back of his skull, and fires one shot.

I inwardly scream when blood and brain matter splatter over my nightie, neck, and face. They turn vocal when Ghost loosens his grip on the doctor's neck, causing his slumped frame to land on top of me. His mutilated head flops straight onto the area he was trying to stimulate but failed.

When the blood oozing out of the wound drips down the crevice of my vagina, I scamper back before lifting my eyes to Ghost. He's not as white as a ghost. He doesn't appear affected at all that he just murdered a man. He merely stares at me, waiting for me to respond, so who am I to disappoint him?

With my brain shut down and my teachings out the window, I push on Ghost's blood-splattered chest, then make a break for it. I follow the path Ghost guided me through only minutes ago before racing down the corridor that shunted me back into his life, but instead of seeking the closest exit, I sprint for the stern of the ship. The boat is moving, so it is pointless heading for the gangway.

Ghost follows me, but he doesn't intervene, not even when I climb the railing to the top rung.

The wind whipping off the coast plays havoc with my words when I shout, "Don't touch me, or I'll jump."

He moves to the far left of the railing, balances his hip on the sea-battered steel, dangles his head so the scarred side of his face is hidden in the shadows of the moonlight, then folds his arms in front of his chest. "I'm not touching you." A haughty gleam flashes through his exposed eye before he asks, "But he did, didn't he?" His lips curve on one side when I shake my head. "You should have said yes, *маленький ягненок*. It would have saved you a year in hell."

When he pushes off the railing, I hold my hand out in warning. "I will jump."

My warning doesn't lessen his strides in the faintest. "I'm not going to pull you down. If you want to jump, jump." He strays his eyes down my body for what feels like the final time before he murmurs, "Letting you pick your exit could be the kindest thing anyone will ever do for you," then he leaves me alone on the stern of the boat, peering down at the temperamental waters that will swallow me under in not even a second.

7

GHOST

*U*ncharacteristic silence encroaches the dining room when a vision of white enters from the far left of the room. Grigori's blood has made her nightgown even more disheveled, and the wind whipping off the coast has tangled her vibrant red hair into grubby knots, but she can still stun a room into silence.

She has a face you'll never forget and a body you'd sell millions to feast on just once.

Three point eight million, to be precise.

When she entered my office, I thought the hefty knock my bank account took four years ago was finally going to be recouped, that years of carnage and sacrifices were about to be repaid in full.

I was a fool.

I kill for Kirill.

I maim for him.

Yet the one thing he knew I wanted more than a scar-free face he took for himself.

We didn't return to America to make amends with the comrades who stabbed us in the back four years ago by placing the blame solely on our shoulders. We're not even restocking the men's pride they lost after years of setbacks like it was announced before we set sail.

We came for her—the absolute meaning of perfection—and Kirill Bobrov's soon-to-be Virgin Mary.

8

KATIE

*Y*ou realize you value life more than you could ever comprehend when you choose to walk into a room full of murderous, vile men instead of plunging to death into an icy grave.

Ghost's eyes are the only ones I recognize when I enter the space bustling with over four dozen men, so I keep them locked on him while waiting for further instructions.

It is a long and tormented thirty minutes. He is testing me as he did earlier, aware I'll be even more obedient now that he's proven me wrong.

I want to live, and now that he knows that, he will play it to his advantage.

I'm certain of it.

The wind that turned my nipples into stiff, artic peaks has nothing on the iciness of Ghost's voice when he nudges his head to a chair across from me and orders me to sit.

When my feet remained glued to the floor, he mutters, "Don't make me ask twice, маленький ягненок."

When I scurry for the seat, many pairs of eyes follow me. I don't pay them any attention while slipping onto my wooden chair and folding an untouched napkin over my lap. It may seem pretentious to instigate the white-glove lessons I was taught, but the outside of this cargo ship doesn't match its opulent insides. If I didn't weave between many shipping containers on my way to the stern, I'd be none the wiser that we weren't on a luxury yacht.

"Only give her water," Ghost demands when a woman as young as me pours a thick red liquid into the glass in front of me. "And send her things to my room." As his narrowed eyes scan the full dining table, the number of hushed comments lessens. "No one will be game to drink from any well in my room."

The unnamed woman dips her chin in understanding, then makes a beeline for the closest exit. As I sip on the chilled water she poured for me, I eye the feast in front of me. I shouldn't, but it's been years since I've tasted red meat, and the mashed potatoes look like they've been prepared with butter and milk. They're super creamy.

"Eat, маленький ягненок," Ghost demands before downing a double shot of whiskey like it has all the protein he needs.

While licking my lips, I stray my eyes to the almost empty plates of the people next to me. Only steak grit and a handful of beans remain, but they'll see me through the next three or four days with barely the faintest grumble of my stomach.

My eyes snap front and center when a noisy clang hits my porcelain plate. After dumping a massive spoonful of mashed potatoes onto my empty dishware, Ghost picks up a piece of steak bigger than his hand and plops it on top of the generous serve. "Gravy?"

I'm too stunned to speak, so instead, I shake my head. Condiments are reserved for the men. We can't even borrow a sprinkling of salt.

"It will slide down easier with gravy." Ghost pours a thick brown substance over the serving for five in front of me like he's adding maple syrup to a stack of pancakes before he stabs a fork into the meat that's so tender it falls apart with only the slightest spear of a fork.

Unable to ignore the groans of my stomach for a second longer, I dart my eyes from the gooey chunk of meat to Ghost. "Wh-what will it cost me?"

The glint that fires through his eyes sends the twists of my stomach several inches lower. It is a weird and unusual sensation, but one I am certain I don't want to explore.

"I'm not hungry." My voice sounds foreign, almost accentuated with an accent I don't have.

I realize the light bulbs in half of the dining room were removed on purpose when Ghost's slant across the table unshadows the half of his face he doesn't want me to see. "You're not hungry?"

I shake my head. It is a lie, and I will most likely get punished for it, but the arch of Ghost's lips as he stares into my eyes has me forgetting every action has a consequence. They have me wanting to kneel in front of him again like it would be more about pleasure than punishment.

"Well, okay then..." He works his jaw side to side before he strays his eyes across the room.

I think I've won this battle until the clattering of cutlery on pricy dishes rumbles over the thud of my heart in my throat.

Without speaking a word, the room is emptied of patrons, leaving only Ghost and me in a space big enough to house fifty.

After watching the slow bob of my throat, Ghost raises his eyes to my face. "I can hear your stomach grumbling, yet you lie and tell me you're not hungry."

"I am not lying. I'm not hun—"

Quicker than I can finish my sentence, he lunges for me across the table. Dishes go in all directions when I'm plucked out of my seat and yanked across the large chunk of glossed wood. I blink in rapid succession when Ghost's grip on the neckline of my nightie pops several threads, but the blows I'm expecting when we meet eye to eye never come. I'm not hit by his fists or his weapon of choice. I'm slapped across the mouth with a piece of juicy steak.

"Open your fucking mouth." Ghost growls out in a low, dangerous tone. "Before I force something more than steak down your throat." His threat forces flashbacks of me on my knees in front of him into my head, and they have me obeying him as readily as I did then. "Now chew," he demands after ripping off a chunk of steak with his teeth and pushing it between mine.

I don't need to chew. The steak is so soft, just maneuvering it around my mouth with my tongue softens it to the point I can swallow it.

"Open again."

This piece is three times the size of the first piece, so I have to chew a handful of times before swallowing to ensure I don't choke.

"Was that so hard, *маленький ягненок?*"

When I shake my head, my dignity too low to argue, he plonks me onto the seat next to him, pulls it over until the armrests on our chairs touch, then drags over the entire serve of mashed potatoes as if it was made just for me.

"Eat, *маленький ягненок.* I won't repeat myself again." When I pick up the serving spoon and career it to my mouth, a hint of amusement plays at Ghost's usually straight lips. "And the little lamb is spared from slaughter again."

9

KATIE

*A*s I'm guided down the hallway of the sleeping quarters, I overhear a conversation. "The Petretti women are all groomed the same way. Tight cunts paraded around in white nightgowns with no panties or bra lines to be seen."

"They're dressed that way to entice you and have you believing their innocence," adds a second accented voice.

My ears prick when the nickname I was given years ago breaks out of the room two doors down from the one Ghost just entered. "*Раб* doesn't need gimmicks, though. That little lamb has gained the eyes of every wolf, including the pack's leader."

I assume they're referencing Ghost until a third voice mocks, "Do you think that's why Ghost killed Grigori? He wanted him to debunk Rudd's claims she's a virgin so he could keep her for himself." A ruckus occurs before he murmurs, "What? Did you fucking see her? I could see the lines of her cunt through her nightgown and every teeny tiny bump of her areolas. What I wouldn't give for a lick."

The man who thrust me into Ghost's office earlier today doubles the lengths of his strides, but other than that, you'd be none the wiser he heard the men's conversation.

That is until we reach Ghost's room. "The line is thin, Ghost."

Although this room is far bigger than the ones I was marched by during our long walk from the dining room, it is still compact and cramped. Even more so when Ghost's spikes are hackled from his number two's insinuation. "About as thin as my patience? *Не издевайся надо мной, Alek. Это не закончится для вас хорошо.*"

Not speaking another word, Alek dips his chin before leaving the room.

Ghost commences barking orders only seconds after he leaves. "You are not to walk these halls without panties. If you do, I will kill you. Interact with the likes of them..." he nudges his head in the direction of the men I overheard, his ticking jaw announcing he heard them too, "... I will kill you. Give them *any* indication they're in with a shot, I will kill you. Disobey my orders—"

"You will kill me. I understand."

He doesn't look happy about my interruption. If anything, he appears displeased. That is so unlike other men in this industry. Submissiveness is all they crave.

"Yes." He gestures his head to a small, shiny door on the right. "Shower then bed. Clothes will be waiting on the dresser when you're done. They are yours to keep." He hands me a silver key. "Lock the door anytime you leave this room. If I find it open..."

You will kill me.

I grow panicked that I said my reply out loud when his eyes snap to mine. I don't know what happened between the dining room and here, but his hooded gaze is murderous, and no amount of banter will bring his mood close to a manageable level.

"Lock the door when I leave. Don't open it for anyone."

I nod in understanding before shadowing him to the door. The lock is flimsy, but the power it fills me with is immense. My room has not had a door in years, much less one with a lock.

My bewilderment grows when I enter the bathroom. This door has a lock as well, and the shower has proper running water. I don't have to have a sponge bath.

In my excitement to wash off the doctor's blood from my skin the splashes from the ocean didn't take care of, I slip out of my nightgown, switch on the faucet, then step under the spray before the water is close to pleasant.

I jump out with a scream, then just as quickly, my bones leap out of my skin when the bathroom door is kicked open, and Ghost races in with a gun in his hand and an angry blood-smeared snarl.

After pulling across the shower curtain to make sure the cubicle is empty, he moves for the door he busted down, then the linen cupboard.

When he fails to find whoever he's searching for, he shifts his focus back to me.

He doesn't utter a word, but his bowed brow speaks volumes.

"The water was cold."

He already looks set to kill, but the glint in his eyes darkens when a voice from outside the bathroom asks, "Is everything okay?"

Ghost's narrowed eyes snap to my naked breasts, to the man outside, then back to me in two painfully quick seconds before his hand shoots up to my throat. He pins me to the only solid wall in the bathroom before I can utter a syllable, then gets up close to my face. "What did I tell you?"

"He-he didn't see me," I wheeze through the minute gap he left for small parcels of air to slip down my windpipe. "Ho-how could he? You're standing in the doorway."

"But that's why he's here, isn't it?" The tips of my toes struggle to maintain contact with the floor when he tightens his grip, which inevitably brings me closer to his height. "He wants to look."

"No." I try to shake my head when my voice is barely a squeak, but it is impossible with how hard he is gripping me.

"Do you know what he'll do to you if he finds out you let them look?" He doesn't wait for me to ask who he is referencing, much less think of an appropriate answer that won't get me killed. "He will gift you to them all. At once. Forty, fifty, sixty men all vying for the same hole at the same time." He leans in closer, bringing his mouth to within touching distance of my earlobe. "They'll tear you to fucking shreds before leaving you to bleed out. Is that what you want, Little Lamb? Do you want to be fucked to death?"

"No." Even in my breathless state, you can't miss my reply.

"Then listen to what I say. Do as I tell you to do." He weakens his grip before tightening it once more. "Because once you piss him off, no one will be able to save you." He tilts his head until every painful detail of his scarred face is exposed. He is a handsome man with devastating looks, but you can't hide the ugliness of the world he lives in when you look directly at his scarred face. "Not even me."

He waits for me to absorb the absolute truth in his eyes before he frees me from his grip and exits the bathroom with the same dramatic edge he undertook to enter it.

———

ALMOST AN HOUR LATER, I'm sitting near the closed window at the foot of the bed, admiring the moonlight peeking through the salt residue buildup on the window. It isn't the sun, and only dark temperamental waters swirl beneath it, but when you've looked at nothing but bland walls for what feels like an eternity, it is more captivating than you could ever comprehend.

I'm a bird trapped in a cage, but Ghost's response would have you convinced I'm the only one left on Earth.

My emotions already have my head in a tailspin, and his teetering moods aren't helping. He raced in to save me before almost ending my life. That makes no sense. How can you act as if my worth is invaluable but then treat me as if I am worthless at the same time?

With a shrug that adds a tinge of pain to my neck, I flop my legs off the mattress, then take a long, lazy cat stretch. I'm about to slip beneath the sheets when a shadow casting from the cloudless night captures my attention.

We're in the middle of the ocean, and excluding the moon, the sky is empty, so what caused the shadow?

Too curious for my own good, I balance on my knees and squash my face to the cool glass. My breath hitches in my throat when, for the second time, a dark object zooms past my window. It is bulky and large, but descending so fast it makes a splash before my eyes can follow its descent.

It is chased by another black object.

Then another.

What could they possibly be dumping into the ocean in the middle of the night?

Surely, they wouldn't have enough waste yet?

Once I started eating, I didn't stop until my stomach was bulging and the dining table was almost empty.

I sink back onto the balls of my feet when reality smacks into me.

I've seen those black bags before.

Normally, they were far too big for the petite bodies placed in them.

This time, the material looks strained under the enormity of the weight stuffed inside it.

I shouldn't feel relief knowing the people inside the body bags are too chunky to be female or a child, but I do.

I crank my neck to the side when muffled voices enter the corridor shortly later. They're not the first I've heard tonight, but one is recognizable.

Ghost is back.

"Ensure this mess is cleaned up by the morning." It sounds like he walks away before spinning back around. "And make sure word gets out. They won't be a ghost if I overhear shit like that again. I won't even leave them with a soul."

When his shadow appears under the door, I seek somewhere to act inconspicuously.

Just as my backside lands on the chair that was positioned under his desk two seconds ago, I recall his earlier order for me to shower then go to bed.

I scarcely make it under the sheets in time. As Ghost enters his room, I slant my head to the side, snap my eyes shut, then slightly gape my mouth. This trick always worked when I wanted to sneak out to visit Blaire during a school night, and it had Master Rudd convinced on more than one occasion that I was asleep so he could masturbate next to my sleeping form.

Thinking about Blaire makes my ruse more believable. It shallows my breathing and slackens the furious beats of my heart.

I miss her so much.

I pretend the wetness pooling in the corner of my eyes is sleep when Ghost mutters, "You need to sleep on my left."

As I rub the 'sleep' from my eye, I ask, "Sorry, what did you say?"

His miffed expression exposes he knows I heard him, but he humors me. "I said you need to sleep on my left." He removes his suit jacket, a two-gun holster I didn't realize he was wearing until now, before unbuttoning his dress shirt that is dotted with blood.

They weren't there when he pinned me to the wall by my throat.

"Did you kill them because of what they said about me or what they said about you?"

His glare is icy-cold, and it freezes me in place. "My left, маленький ягненок."

He waits for me to bob my chin before he enters the bathroom. He leaves the door ajar. Not by choice, and I don't think he would have, even if he had a lack of trust. He can't lock it since he bent the locking mechanism when he kicked in the door.

It takes me several seconds to move to the left side of the mattress as requested. It isn't solely Ghost's guns resting on his desk stealing my focus. It is the mirror on top of his dresser. It reflects straight into the bathroom and shows that Ghost's scars don't just affect his face. They cover most of his body. They appear to be shrapnel wounds or the effects of being caught in a dangerous blast.

However they occurred, they must be painful, and some are fresher than others.

Sorrow fills my eyes when Ghost peers over his shoulder and busts my watch. He returns my stare for several heart-thudding seconds before he steps into the spray and pulls the shower curtain across, hiding his marks from my solemn glare.

10

KATIE

Ghost slept with his T-shirt-covered back to me all night. He either isn't one of those men who roll a hundred times during their sleep like my mother complained my father did, or he barely slept a wink like me. I dozed off sometime in the early morning, but if my pounding head is anything to go by, it wasn't long before the sun began rising.

I'm not surprised to discover I am waking alone. However, I am stunned when my tiptoe to the door discovers it is unlocked, and my key is still in the spot I left it.

Does that mean what I think it does?

Am I free to roam as I see fit?

I mentally kick myself when reality dawns.

I'm on a cargo ship in the middle of the ocean. I can't go anywhere.

Still, I might be able to see the sun.

The hope alone gets my feet moving at a million miles an hour.

Accustomed to wearing one outfit until it hangs off my limbs, I stuff my feet into boots by the door before pulling open the weighted door and entering the corridor.

Holding my breath, I wait to see if I'm being tested.

Several long minutes pass in silence before I build the courage to let go of the door handle and slowly encroach down the hallway.

Each step I take is liberating, and it lifts my shoulders to heights they've never reached before.

My almost skip screeches to a stop when I reach the door the men were hackling behind last night. The door is closed, but there is evidence of what went down while I showered. The glossy wood has been scrubbed clean, but the bullet holes haven't been patched up yet.

"He had to make a point."

As my hand shoots up to my chest, I accidentally squeak out a curse word.

Alek smiles, oddly amused by my unladylike nature. Usually, a response like that would have seen me whipped three times with a horse crop. "If he were to take disrespect from bottom dwellers, he wouldn't have the respect of those we need to stay alive."

"I understand." I skirt by him before remembering he caught me at my worse. "I'm sorry. I should not know the words I spoke, much less speak them out loud."

"Shit is not a swear word, P—" He stops, angles his head to the side, then arches a dark brow. "What is your name?"

"Um..." *Is this a trick question?* "Everyone calls me *Pa6*."

"I know everyone calls you *Pa6*, but that isn't your name. What is your real name?"

His question shouldn't concern me as much as it does, but I'd be a liar if I said I wasn't on the verge of peeing my pants.

Madame Victoria said Katie Bryne no longer exists.

That she is dead, and any attempt to bring her out will end the Bryne existence for eternity.

I snap my eyes to Alek's murky blue pair when he murmurs, "They worked you over good, didn't they?" Although he is technically summarizing more than asking a question, I bob my chin. "Then shouldn't you know better than to ignore me when I ask a question?"

There's no malice in his tone, no anger, but I still jump on command like a dog performing tricks for a treat. "Um... Kat-Katie. My name is Katie."

I flinch from the slightest movement, and it frustrates Alek more than it entertains him. "No man here will touch you, Katie. You're safe on this ship." The stern work of his jaw doesn't give me any indication that he will issue the same guarantee when we reach our destination. As he lifts my chin to peer at my neck, he murmurs, "Ghost just has a hard time... *expressing* himself."

Ha! He had no issues yesterday displaying how much he loathes me.

Needing to get my focus off my annoyance, I ask, "Where are we going?"

Alek licks his lips, alerting me to how plump they are. Most of the men I've met the past eight years have thin, snively lips, but he doesn't. They're as large as his smile when he asks, "Ghost didn't tell you?"

I shake my head before recalling Ghost's lips are just as plump, but his scars often deter your eyes away from his mouth. "No."

"Then he must not want you to know." He continues down the hall like he didn't leave our conversation in limbo. "Enjoy the sun, Katie. Although, you may need a coat. It is a little windy today."

I watch him disappear into a room several spots down from mine before continuing my voyage. I'm not exactly sure where I'm going. It's one maze of corridors after another, but eventually, I find an unlocked door that leads to a deck gleaming in the sunshine.

This is ludicrous of me to say, but I swear the instant the sun hits my cheeks and soaks up the wetness my eyes can't seem to live without the past twelve hours, the last eight years seem nowhere near as bad as they once did.

I'm alive.

That is way more than most of the women taken hostage with me.

My cheeks are as red as my hair by the time my name is called several hours later.

Not my real name.

My captive name.

Раб.

When I turn my head in the direction of the voice, I am confronted by the man who sat across from me last night at dinner. Not Ghost. The man at Ghost's left.

"Come." He opens the door I exited a couple of hours ago before nudging his head inside. "Brunch is served."

As I stand, I wipe the sweat his reply caused my hands onto my nightgown. I'm usually responsible for making brunch, and I'm not eager to find out the repercussions of forgetting my obligations.

"Food and shelter are not free!" Madame Victoria regularly yelled while swinging her broom through the air. *"You are to work for everything you are given. Even scraps."*

I'm still shuddering at the reminder of her ways when I'm guided into the same dining room we ate in last night. The table is brimming with an assortment of foods, and I didn't prepare a single dish.

"I'm sorry," I murmur under my breath when Ghost's eyes lock with mine across the room. "The sun... it was—" I stop before I dig my hole even deeper. Greed is not a commodity I am allowed to hoard, not even when it corresponds with my happiness. "It won't happen again."

I don't wait for Ghost to dip his chin. The knowledge that I broke the rules won't change anything. I'll still be in trouble.

With my head dipped down low, I follow a woman wearing a stained apron into the kitchen at the side of the dining table, pluck a semi-clean apron off the shelf, then tighten it around my waist.

"Where do you need me?" I ask a lady with wiry gray hair and a wrinkled face. The kitchen is the only place age is respected. The elder of the group is usually the hierarchy.

She peers at me with a long gray hair on her chin wiggling in the breeze. "Блюда." When I look at her, lost, she places her hands on my shoulder, guides me to a sink full of bubbles, then makes a scrubbing movement with her hands. "Блюда. Yes?" When I pick up the first dirty dish and scrub it, her smile adds to the kindness in her eyes. "Yes."

GHOST'S MEN and a small handful of women were fed first, then we moved on to the crew before eventually setting our focus on the women downstairs.

Their rooms have locks too, but they're on the outside of their doors, and they don't have access to any keys.

They were me eight years ago, except they are on a cargo ship instead of a plane.

"What time tomorrow?" I ask Vera.

With breakfast crossing into lunch before it eventually encroaches on dinnertime, I've done nothing but cook, wash, and serve all day.

I am exhausted and ready for bed.

"Five a.m."

I inwardly cringe. I've never been a morning person. "Okay. I'll see you tomorrow."

I remove my apron and place it on the stack some unfortunate person will clean overnight before trudging back to my room. My feet are aching, and I'm reasonably sure I have a blister the size of my big toe on my little toe.

I almost curse for the second time today when my entrance into my room has a grumbling voice shuddering through my chest. "Close the door behind you."

"Gh-Ghost. Hello." I shut the door as requested, suck in a big breath, then spin around to face him. "About this morning—"

"Lift your nightie," he interrupts, his eyes locked on my hips.

"Wh-what?"

"First, you snub my invitation to eat, then you have the hide to steal from me." He lifts his eyes to my face. "And now you act ignorant. Take. Off. Your. Nightie."

When he stands in preparation to force the removal of my clothes, I do it myself. I whip it over my head so fast, crumbs from bread rolls I stuffed under my nightie float off my sweat-dotted skin and land on the floor between us.

Ghost's voice is deadly when he snarls out, "You stole from me in *front* of me."

"No." I shake my head so fast my hair slaps my face. "They were the bread rolls no one wanted. The half-eaten ones." My reply seems to anger him more, so I may as well be honest. "There isn't enough food for everyone, so instead of wasting the bread rolls that were barely touched, I collected them. They're hungry, Ghost. Hungrier than you could ever imagine."

A quiver almost hits my knees when he takes a step closer to me while asking, "They?" When I suck in a sharp breath, he snaps out, "Lie to me and I won't feed them for a week."

"The women," I blurt out, aware they won't last a week. Not in the condition they're in. "The women in the orlop." When surprise overtakes his anger, I murmur, "My father liked ships." I freeze when I realize my error. "*Likes* ships. He likes them." I breathe out the familiar pain in my chest memories of my family forever instigate before confessing, "There wasn't enough to go around, so I gave them the bread no one wanted." When silence prevails, I ignore the screams of my aching feet and head back for the door. "I'll go make extra bread for tomorrow. We have plenty of flour."

I freeze when Ghost mutters, "Flour that is not for you nor them. It is not yours to distribute how you see fit, *Раб.*" I hate that he's resorted to the nickname everyone else calls me, but I won't let him know that. "Shower and bed. Your penance is no supper."

My stomach's loud grumble should announce my penance is already being served.

I haven't eaten since last night.

Before I can escape into the bathroom, Ghost's hand shoots out to seize my wrist. "Don't steal from me again." His angry eyes bounce between mine. "Especially in front of my men. Don't force me to make an example out of you because I guarantee you will not like the results."

He pushes me away from him like he can't stand the sight of me before he leaves our room in a hurry.

11

KATIE

"*E*xcuse me," I apologize to the gentleman I'm currently clearing his setting. "It has a mind of its own."

He grunts in response to my apology about my grumbling stomach before he pushes back from his chair, leaving me to scrape his plate brimming with a range of delicious breakfast treats. He didn't touch his pancakes. He only ate the slices of bacon he loaded next to them and left the rest of his meal untouched.

It is such a waste, but who am I to talk? I did the same thing this morning when I left the bathroom and discovered a plate stacked high with pancakes, butter, maple syrup, and a generous serving of blueberries on one side. The smell alone was so enticing my resolve almost buckled, but I held on strong, mindful I am no better than the women living off scraps in the lower level of the ship.

I refuse to eat until they do.

We are currently on day three of a hunger strike.

When my stomach grumbles for the second time, I raise my eyes to make sure no one is subjected to its noisy protests. I don't understand its issue. It ate more my first night here than I have in my life. It should be content for a few more days, but instead, it's acting like I'm about to die of malnutrition.

My throat works through a hard swallow when I lock on Ghost's watch across the room. He is eyeing me like a hawk, conscious I'd give anything to bundle up the wasted food and deliver it to the women downstairs but aware I'll never not follow the rules.

I am a sheep, and I've never felt more ashamed.

It hurts scrapping the unnamed man's food into the bin Annika wheels into the dining room so we can clear away the mess—both physically and emotionally.

"Is that it?" Annika asks, her eyes scanning the room.

I nod. "Only Ghost's plate to go." Like a coward without a spine, I shift my eyes to hers. "Are you right to get that?"

"Um..." She looks terrified. "Sure."

Her smile is fake, but I race out of the dining room like my backside is on fire.

My reprieve lasts for barely a minute. Just like he snuck into our room the last three nights, Ghost enters the kitchen, slams down his untouched plate in front of me, then dips down low so we lock eyes.

On closer inspection, I realize his plate isn't food he loaded himself. It is the dish I dumped into the bin in the hallway outside our room this morning. The meal I believe he had delivered for me.

While staring at me with flaring nostrils and narrowed eyes, Ghost doesn't speak a word. Everything is relayed by his eyes—his anger, his frustration, and perhaps even his disappointment about my cowardly ways.

When I chicken out first, his glare too hot to continue staring at without the fear of being burned, he pinches my chin and guides my eyes back to him. "Did I say you could move?" Even though everyone in the kitchen appears busy, I feel their eyes on us. "Answer me, маленький ягненок. Did I give you permission to look away?"

"No—"

"Then why did you?"

My voice is shaky when I reply, "Because you scare me," I confess before I can stop myself. "I don't know what you want from me. I was taught to obey, but you seem to want the opposite."

My brows furrow in confusion when he murmurs, "Taught to obey who?"

"My owner."

I can't hide my bewilderment when he whispers, "And who is that, *маленький ягненок*?"

"Y-you," I reply, stating the obvious.

I don't know which way is up when he scoffs. "But that's not the right order, is it, my queen?"

His hold is cruel, demoralizing, and full of anger, but I have no clue what I've done to make him so mad. I wasted food by the bucketloads, was in the kitchen before anyone else the past three mornings, and I make sure I stay on my side of our bed.

I've done everything he has asked of me, yet he still seems to hate me.

"Tell me what you want, and I'll give it to you," I whisper when the tension reaches breaking point.

The torment in his voice sends a chill down my spine. "The one thing I want, you can't give me." He releases me from his hold as if it was nothing before shifting on his feet to face Vera. "Scrap today's menu and start again. It appears as if it isn't appetizing enough for *anyone* to eat."

"But, sir, we will have too many leftovers."

It only takes one sideways glare for Vera to back down.

"Very well, but what shall we do with all this food?" She fans her hands across the heating stations keeping the pancakes, bacon, scrambled eggs, and hash browns warm.

My dry throat suddenly returns when Ghost shifts his eyes to me and says, "I'm sure you can find someone hungry enough to accept it."

My entrance into my room tonight is done in silence. There are no grumbled comments or demands for me to remove my clothing. My room is empty, and despite loathing silence for as long as I've been captive, I'll take it over the sobs and whimpers I usually hear.

Tonight, the boat is silent since everyone's stomachs are too full to entice anything more than sleep.

Vera took Ghost's comment as literal, so she made sure every dish that left her kitchen tonight was of a chef's standards. Ghost's men and his crew ate like kings, and not a single morsel of food was wasted since Vera gifted the unwanted breakfast dishes to the women in the orlop.

After easing my feet out of the gumboots I shouldn't be wearing without socks, I cover the gigantic blisters on my toes and heels with Band-Aids Vera supplied me. I should put them on after I've showered, but I'd rather they be covered to lessen the sting of the water pelting into them.

As I enter the bathroom, my eyes lift to the vanity mirror. I look gaunt and pale, and I feel dirty, so instead of the hurried shower I've had the past three days, I take my time lathering my skin with the products in the shower stall, and wash my hair.

Since my nightie only has the smallest stains on it from the dirty suds while washing up, I spot-clean it before hanging it on the railing in the bathroom. I saw a second set of clothes on the dresser this morning, so I don't need to wait for the thin material to dry or wear it wringing wet.

When I exit the bathroom wrapped in a towel, I startle. Not just from the detection I'm being watched but because of the large feast displayed on Ghost's desk. I'm not exactly sure what the meat is that's still on its bone, but it is plonked onto a generous helping of mashed potatoes and drizzled with gravy. It looks and smells delicious, and I've not even taken the time to appreciate the large assortment of crusty bread in the basket next to it.

I drift my head to Ghost when he murmurs, "The lamb shank is for you, and the bread is yours to do with as you wish..." He pauses for a beat to ensure I am aware in no circumstances are his terms negotiable. "*After* you've finished your meal. Do you understand?"

"Yes." I nod to get across my point.

He smirks, appreciative of my swift reply before he stands from the chair in the corner of the room and stalks to the bathroom.

The hairs on my arms bristle when he brushes past me, but it has nothing on the response of his deep exhale when I murmur, "Thank you."

His hot breaths fan my wet hair when he replies, "You should not be thanking me, *маленький ягненок*." My brows furrow in confusion when he adds, "Those women are not your friends. They're your competition. You step out of line once, and you will be replaced by them." My stomach gurgles for a completely different reason than hunger when he says, "Except you won't live off scraps. You'll be the feast for the grubs and the worms in the garden of the compound."

12

KATIE

The next few days follow along the same path as my first seventy-eight hours here, except the bread rolls and pastries are delivered directly to the women instead of to my room along with my meals. I've gone from eating every couple of days to eating three times a day purely so the women won't know the hunger I experienced during my first years of captivity.

If I eat, they eat. The guidelines can't be any simpler.

Although I've enjoyed a range of meals the past three days, my stomach feels a little gluttonous. It twists and turns all night, and tonight is no exception. I need to use the bathroom, but Ghost is still asleep, and I'm not brave enough to climb over him.

The cabins on the ship are small, so the double bed we've shared the past six nights is squashed up against one wall. I'm usually in bed hours before Ghost, so we haven't faced any awkward shuffles on a bed far too short for a man of his height.

When my stomach flips for the third time, I bite on my lower lip and breathe through the pain. This is what I get for being piggish. I should have stopped once my stomach was full instead of acting as if it may be my last meal.

"Ghost..." I talk through the bile burning the back of my throat. My meal's exodus from my body doesn't want to occur the normal way. It wants to escape how it entered—via my mouth. "Can I please use the bathroom?"

Silence.

"Ghost," I try again, desperate.

This time, I add a nudge to my murmur, hopeful it will wake him.

It does, but he responds nothing like I anticipated. Faster than I can blink, he rolls over, snatches my hands above my head, then pins me to the mattress with his big, imposing body. "Don't fucking touch me."

I try to respond, to tell him the heaviness of his body against my stomach is far worse than anything I can do to him, but a second after opening my mouth, the contents racing up my food pipe rush through the minute crack.

"What the fuck?" Ghost scampers back, smacks on the cabin light above my head, then grimaces when he spots the second rush of vomit fountaining out of my mouth. "Christ, Little Lamb." He adds to the churns of my stomach when he bands his arm around my waist and hoists me off the bed. "What did you eat to make you sick?" He marches me into the bathroom, switches on the shower faucet, then places me inside the stall. The cracks in the drain are big enough to handle the product expelling from my stomach, but what it misses, Ghost's enormous feet take care of. "Vera was told to give you the fresh foods."

"It's not the food." I vomit again when the steam returns the ghastly scent to my nostrils.

"Get it all out first, then we will talk."

Ghost more whacks my back than rubs it soothingly, but it is effective, nonetheless. Within a handful of slaps, my stomach is emptied, and the scent of my recently washed hair replaces the horrid smell of vomit in the tiny shower stall.

My stomach hasn't been the only gluttonous commodity of late. I've taken to washing my hair and shaving every day as well.

My circumstances changed in a blink of an eye, so who is to say it won't switch back even quicker?

"Stay here. I will have clothes brought in for you."

Ghost's drenched boxer shorts and T-shirt leave a puddle of

wetness in his wake when he steps out of the shower stall and paces into the main room. The slap of them hitting the fake wooden floors bellows into the bathroom shortly before there's a knock at the main door.

"Leave them by the door. I will fetch them in a minute," Ghost barks out, his voice commanding. As quickly as a "yes, sir" creaks through the opening, Ghost recalls the reason I need a change of clothes. "Send someone from housekeeping. We need new sheets."

This reply is far longer than the female's first response. She sounds stunned like a greedy stomach couldn't possibly be the cause of needing fresh sheets at four in the morning.

I jump when Ghost's shirtless torso suddenly fills the bathroom door. For a man who stands at a little over six foot four, he shouldn't be so agile. But he is. Very much so.

He smirks at my skittish response for barely a second before his eyes lower to my thin white nightgown clinging to my body. It is drenched through, so it leaves nothing to the imagination.

He's seen it all before, but you wouldn't know that from the angry glare burning across his face when his eyes stop at the apex of my thighs. After a quick swallow and a brief lick of his lips, he returns his narrowed eyes to my face. "When did you shave?"

You could believe his question is in response to my glistening legs, but I know that isn't the case. His eyes didn't drop lower than my vagina.

"Yesterday," I answer, aware I have no choice but to be honest. "Should I not have shaved?"

My question ticks his jaw to the point of manic. "I don't care either way, but he would have preferred you to remain natural." He enters the bathroom, switches off the faucet, then shoves a pair of sweatpants, a white T-shirt, and plain cotton panties into my chest. "I don't want you serving today. If you are sick again, you'll face more rumors than you already do."

Rumors? What rumors?

He steals my chance to ask my questions out loud by leaving the bathroom as quickly as he entered it.

By the time I'm dressed and dried my drenched hair, the sheets on our bed have been replaced, and Ghost is nowhere to be seen.

What am I meant to do if I don't work?

I hang in our room for a couple of hours before the silence gets to me. Ghost said he didn't want me serving, but he said nothing about me being required to stay in my room.

I begin to wonder if I'm really not under lock and key when my exit from my room has me quickly bumping into Alek. He either wanders the halls at all times of the day and night, or he's trying to make his watch inconspicuous.

"Good morning, Kate. Late start for you today." For a man who has the grip of a wrench and the stern voice of a drill sergeant, his smile is awfully friendly.

"Katie," I correct, assuming he misheard me the other day.

He didn't. "Ghost asked me to call you Kate. He said Katie is too immature, and it will add to the men's wish to explore how innocent you truly are." When my face whitens, Alek's grin enlarges. "Aah... so you truly don't notice how the stares double depending on how tight you fasten your apron. On the sea, an apron is the equivalent of a corset."

"I'll be sure to keep that in mind," I murmur, unsure of a better response. "Is there anywhere you need me to be?" When he shakes his head, I dip my chin before farewelling him with a smile. "If Ghost needs me, I'll be—"

"You don't need to tell him where you're going. He knows."

He walks in the opposite direction as me, but I still feel as if I am being watched even hours later on the stern of the boat.

I've sought the cameras I regularly spotted around the compounds I've been captive in. There have been none to see.

They're either microscopic, or I'm being watched by means other than electronically.

I peer back at a stack of container ships when Alek calls my name. "Kate." He waits for me to shelter my eyes from the low-hanging sun before finalizing his reply. "Ghost wants to see you."

Like our first meeting on this ship, our meeting commences with

Ghost seated behind his big desk in the captain's office, except this time, there isn't a woman kneeling in front of him, sucking his dick.

Regretfully, the leftover residue of white lines remains on top of his desk.

A small tremor racks through my body when Ghost gestures for Alek to leave.

"He asked me to stay."

Ghost glares at him over my shoulder. "And I told you to leave. Pick whose wrath you want to face first."

My heart thuds against my ribs for several long beats before Alek eventually dips his chin, spins on his heels, then leaves.

It takes another set of thuds before Ghost eventually speaks. "Why were you sick this morning?"

I halfheartedly shrug. "I don't know."

He leans forward and balances his elbows on his desk. "How many times have you been sick?"

"This morning was the first." When his eyes narrow, I murmur, "I've had an upset stomach, but it is the first time I've vomited."

His next question pushes me off balance. "How many men have you fucked?"

"None," I answer immediately.

"Lie to me—"

"I'm not lying." I know what happens to women who lie in this industry. "I haven't... *been* with anyone."

Ghost takes a moment to ponder before firing off another question. "How many men have touched you?" When my eyes flicker as I mentally calculate the number of times I've been manhandled, he corrects, "How many men have touched your cunt?"

"One," I answer before swallowing harshly. "Actually, two." My voice quivers when a murderous gleam flares through his eyes. "The doctor you killed was the second."

"Who was the first?" He doesn't give me the chance to answer. "Rudd?"

I shake my head so fiercely my waist-length hair swishes against my back. "No. He never touched me."

He slants his head and arches a heavy brow. "Then who?"

This reply is the hardest to deliver. "My-my original owner."

The bend of his brow doubles. "Col?" I can barely breathe when my headshake shifts his expression to furious. "Then who?" he repeats, louder this time.

"Vladimir P—"

"Popov," he interrupts while slouching low in his chair and running his hand along the tick in his jaw. "You were taken by Russians?" I lift my chin, prompting him to continue his interrogation without interruption. "When?"

I stammer out, "Seven to e-eight years ago. I'm not exactly sure how much time has passed."

"Do you not think it is strange you've been untouched for so long?"

I nod before switching it to a shake. "I was auctioned to lure someone. To force them away from New York. Perhaps he only likes..." I can't think of the right word, so I mumble, "... people like me."

I stop talking when Ghost bangs his fist onto the desk. He looks furious, almost murderous, and all his focus is on me. "He was there for you?" He clenches and unclenches his fist three times in a row. "While they were setting us up for their fucking shit, he was there for you!"

His roar when he uproots his desk sends me stumbling backward. It lands feet away from me, so I'm not afraid of being hit by the thick wooden material. I'm petrified of Ghost's stomps as he makes a beeline for me.

"I didn't do anything," I murmur with a sob when he crowds me against the door with his frantically thrusting chest. "I was sold—"

"So we weren't in New York when they ratted us out? They fucking used you because they knew you were *exactly* his type." He grabs my face and forces it to align with his. "Milo is dead because you lured him to that auction, but instead of blaming himself, he blamed me. I wanted you, and he's reminded me of that over and over and over again the past four years." His laugh is manic, and it releases my heart from my ribcage. "Yet here you are, about to be his Virgin Mary." His expression turns stoic as his hand moves from my hips to between my legs. "*If you're even a virgin. He doesn't believe your claims. He thinks you were sick this morning because you're pregnant. He wants the doctor to check again." He cups my sex, his fingers digging in firm enough to make me squeak. "But we both know that can't happen. That the doctor is fish food with the rest of the men who thought they could question my loyalty." He exposes part of his shadowed face by realigning our eyes before muttering, "So maybe I should check for myself."

Our chests compete for air when he slips his hand under the waistband of my sweatpants and narrows his middle finger toward my vagina, but that is the only sign of a protest. I don't clamp my thighs together or loll my head to the side. I return his stare as if my stomach isn't twisted in knots before breathing out the pain his intrusion causes when he pushes his finger deep inside me.

His breathing changes when he leans his body in closer, bringing his lips to within an inch of mine He's so close, I hear his faintest murmur when he swivels the fat digit he stuffed inside me. "Fucking Christ, you're tight."

A shuddering breath ripples through my lips when his thumb attempts to arouse my clit. Unlike the doctor's attempt, his is effective. His briefest touch sends a zap through my body and almost buckles my knees, but before I can question how something so simple can feel so amazing, Ghost yanks his hand out of my sweatpants, then spins around so his back faces me.

"Go, маленький ягненок. Go now before I sully you so much, we all join the doctor on the bottom of the ocean." I remain still for barely a second before his roar kickstarts my legs and heart. "Go!"

I race out of the room as fast as my quivering legs will take me.

13

GHOST

"*H*ow can you be sure?"

As I stare at the door I had Katie pinned to not even ten minutes ago, the front of my pants tighten. "Because she is too scared to lie." *And I am a fucking prick who didn't take her word for it.*

You have no clue how hard it was for me to stop when her thighs swept open instead of clamming shut like in the footage from the doctor's office. There were no tears rolling down her face, no requests for me to stop. She liked my hands on her as much as I'd love the scent of her arousal surrounding my cock.

"I don't trust these men. I want a more thorough investigation. She was sick—"

"Because her stomach is not used to sustenance," I interrupt, my voice almost on the cusp of dictating. "They starved her for years. She is a bag of bones." That's why it was so fucking hard to follow his orders that she not eat for stealing. She went without supper before ignoring my peace offering several days later.

It pissed me off to no end, but I can't disclose that, or more bodies will be dumped overboard, and not all of them will be insolent fools. At least three of them will be innocent bystanders of my inability to keep my focus on the task at hand.

Katie is still the beautiful, ripe woman I bid on and won four years ago—I've changed more than her—but she barely weighs a thing, and the light in her eyes I once thought would never be snuffed is only a glimmer.

My back molars crunch together when Kirill mutters, "We will fix that when she is swollen with my son." Hearing the groan I wasn't meant to release, he adds, "Do you need a reminder of what occurs when orders are not followed?"

As I catch sight of my reflection in the blackened monitor on my left, I shake my head.

I know too well the consequences of my actions.

My face holds the stories of my betrayals.

As does hers.

"I will make sure the tests are completed myself."

Kirill hums in approval. "If she is saintly as claimed, continue on course. If not..." He stops to ensure I can't miss his evil smirk, even with him being thousands of miles away. "Gift her to—"

I disconnect our call before he can finalize his reply.

I know his orders.

He doesn't need to repeat them.

Because the exact thing he wants to do to Katie will happen to my sister if I disobey him.

The buzzer on my desk cracks under the pressure of my hit when I press the intercom button. Intercoms are wired throughout the ship, but mine only goes to one room—Alek's.

"Bring her to Grigori's chamber." He knows who I'm referencing as he is the only man beside me that I trust with Katie. That's why she is sleeping in my room. She is the ultimate representation of virtue, and every man on this ship wants to break her. "And knock before entering," I add after spotting Katie's entrance to our room. She must have sprinted because this cargo ship is a city on the sea.

"Grigori isn't there."

The lack of empathy in Alek's voice tugs my lips on one side. He knows of his fate because he cleared away the mess before assisting me in eradicating the scum who foolishly mocked me. I didn't kill them solely to force the rest of my men's respect. I did it because they looked when they were instructed to keep their eyes to themselves.

I don't have a look-but-don't-touch rule.

You bow your fucking head when royalty enters the room.

You don't gawk like the possibility of more is in your realm.

It isn't.

After another line of snow to keep my attitude high but my wish to kill low, I fetch my gun off my desk, store away the barely touched brick, then make my way to Grigori's room to set up.

Alek's men work fast. There won't be an ounce of evidence of Grigori's passing, but he was a sick fuck, so I need to ensure the instruments I'm about to use on Katie are sterile.

If you lie in a bed with strays, you're bound to get fleas.

The same can be said for the women Grigori 'inspected.'

14

KATIE

*M*y steps shudder when the familiarity of the rooms we're passing smack into me. I've only been down this corridor once, but it was so horrifying I don't see myself forgetting it anytime soon.

Like a reoccurring nightmare, Alek stops us outside the unmarked door Ghost did seven days ago. This time, he knocks before twisting the lock. I shouldn't exhale in relief when I spot Ghost inside the room, but I do. He's alone, and despite the odd smell in the air, the doctor's room doesn't look as grubby and unsterile as it did last week.

After lowering his eyes to my sweatpants, Ghost spears them to Alek. "You didn't request for her to change?"

"I told you, man, I don't know this shit like you do." As he waves his hand around the room, a strand of blond hair falls into his eye. "I handle weapons, distribution, and that shit dusting your nose." While dragging the back of his hand under his nose, Ghost sniffs. "This shit is not for me."

"It's not for me either, but some of us don't have a choice." Ghost glares at Alek while gripping my arm, yanking me into the room, then plopping me onto the hospital bed now covered with clean sheets.

"Stay," he barks out when Alek twists toward the door. "His trust is low. He will want proof."

"Your word should be enough." Alek's reply is cut off by the low, throaty groan rumbling up Ghost's chest. With a shrug, he folds his arms in front of him, leans his back on the door, then drops his eyes to his boots.

I drift my eyes from his slumber-like stance to Ghost when he murmurs, "Lie down, *маленький ягненок.*"

I wait for further instructions. When they don't come, I place my head on the pillow and straighten my legs. After what feels like a lifetime but is barely seconds, Ghost lifts my T-shirt to sit under my braless breasts then tugs down the waistband of my pants.

"You need to go lower than that if you want to see anything."

Ghost grumbles a Russian curse word under his breath before doing as Alek suggested. He tugs down my pants until they sit just above the opening of my vagina.

"What is that?" I ask, my curiosity too high to discount when Ghost rolls over an odd-looking television on wheels.

Not speaking, he pulls out a gray wand and loads it with a jelly-looking substance.

"Where are you going to put that?"

Ghost remains quiet, but thankfully, Alek is more forthcoming. "This one remains outside your body. It is the long skinny one you need to be wary of."

After shutting up his husky chuckles with a vicious glare, Ghost presses the now-slippery contraption onto the lower half of my stomach. He swivels it around a handful of times while looking at the black and white image on the monitor.

Once almost all the lower half of my stomach is covered with sticky residue, Ghost shifts on his feet to face a camera dangling in the top corner of the room. I didn't notice it the last time I was here. My focus was on surviving, not surveillance.

Barely a second later, a ping dings from inside the pocket of Ghost's pants. His jaw spasms when he yanks out a thick brick-like cell phone and flips open the screen.

"There's nothing," he bites out after squashing the phone to his ear. "Alek will tell you the same." I can't hear what his caller replies, but whatever he says, it doubles the tightness of Ghost's grip on his cell. "Very well." He snaps his cell shut, tosses it onto the doctor's desk, then picks up the device I'm reasonably sure Alek was referencing earlier. "Give me a condom."

A condom? Why does he need a condom?

My silent questions are answered when Ghost demands I remove my sweatpants and underwear.

"But..." I blink while recalling how quickly Madame Victoria and Master Rudd reacted when I questioned their authority. If you exclude the narrowing of Ghost's eyes, I'm not punished with anything but unspoken words.

After ensuring Alek's eyes have returned to his shoes, I shimmy my pants and underwear down my thighs while Ghost rolls a condom down the long, gray wand.

Almost robotic-like, Ghost spreads my thighs with his elbow, places the instrument between my legs, opens me with his fingers, then gently slips the wand inside me.

Due to the excess amount of lubricant Ghost placed on the end, the intrusion doesn't cause much discomfort.

Embarrassment, though, is in abundance.

"What are you looking for?"

Ghost doesn't take his eyes off the monitor while replying, "They used you as a ruse before, so who's to say they're not doing it again."

His reply stuns me for almost a minute. "I haven't seen Col since the day of the auction."

Ghost freezes, making it painfully obvious there's a foreign object inside me. I'm still not experiencing any pain. It is how dangerously close his thumb is to my clit. "That was four years ago."

"I know." It is ill-advised of me to speak freely, but my shock is too high to ignore. "I was told my owner was coming to collect me 'soon' for every week of those years. You never showed up until this week."

When Ghost's eyes snap to Alek, he shrugs. "First time my eyes landed on her consignment slip was after I'd collected the rest."

The rest?

I realize he means the women in the orlop when he adds, "Instructions were to deliver her to you. Special order. The rest are for the trade."

The deep vibration of Ghost's voice rumbles through me when he asks, "Then why is he paranoid?"

Alek's brows furrow in sync with mine when Ghost pulls the wand out of my vagina and houses it on the hook next to the monitor. "When isn't he when it comes to you?" He shifts his eyes to the monitor before slanting his head. "There's nothing in there. She's pure." I stiffen as quickly as Ghost when he adds, "As purchased."

It dawns on me that this is about more than me when Ghost grunts in response, but he tries to act as if I am the bane of his existence. "Supper is to be served by eight." He heads for the door Alek is holding open for him before spinning back around to face me. "If you are late, the scraps will be served to the fish, and the women will live off nothing but the men's cum for a week."

GHOST'S THREAT was more in frustration about his beef with a man whose name is only ever referenced as 'he,' but I arrive at the kitchen two hours before requested, eager to ensure no one faces the wrath of my insolence, and I've done so every day for the past three days.

I don't mind working in the kitchen. The women are pleasant, the crew keeps to themselves, and Ghost's presence is forever notable.

The last fact should scare me, but it doesn't. Ghost ensures everyone on the ship gets fed, including the women in the orlop, and although he barely speaks a word to me, he makes sure the rowdiness of his men doesn't affect the staff's ability to serve them.

The women only get manhandled once he leaves the table.

Since that isn't until after me, it is a rare occurrence of late.

I am usually the last to leave.

"It's tomato soup," I announce to a gentleman with a large face tattoo when he leans in to sniff the bowl balancing on my hip. "Would you like some?"

As he jerks up his chin, I spot Alek approaching Ghost. His expression is frustrated, and his shoulders are hanging low.

I don't eavesdrop on their conversation. More because I struggle with Russian in general, much less when it is spoken in harsh, angry tones.

Ghost's eyes lock with mine when I move to the gentleman seated across from him to serve him the first course of his meal. The worry in his eyes is for me, but his words are for Alek, "Watch her."

I follow his trek across the room when he vacates his seat and makes a beeline for the hallway that leads to his office. His moody stalk out of the room gains the attention of many sets of eyes. Most of the female eyes admire his dominating walk and structured back and backside. The males are mainly searching for an opportunity to act up.

"I wouldn't," Alek warns only a second after Ghost disappears down the hall.

When I shoot my eyes to his, my breath catches in my throat. He's pointing his steak knife in my direction but mercifully, slightly to the right.

"Unless you want this knife to slice off your cock." The man with his hand an inch from my ass yanks his arm back before straying his eyes to the other side of the room.

Alek snorts in his face. "Do you always have to ruin my fun, Artyom?"

When Artyom fails to answer him, Alek shifts his focus to me. He doesn't speak. His eyes simply give me permission to continue serving without the fret of being sexually assaulted.

Thankfully, his silent pledge isn't just for me.

All the female kitchen staff makes it through dinner untouched—some more disappointed than others since they crave the men's touches.

Alek is quite popular, and Ghost forever has admiring gazes locked with him. I've never seen Ghost accept an advance. I can't say the same for Alek. He stalks the halls with a different woman on his arm each night.

After a long shift, I enter my room, not surprised by the spread laid out for me on a serving tray. I eat like a queen every day, three times a day. It's added a bit of cushioning back to my breasts, thighs, and backside, but I'm not so sure that is a good thing. I get ogled more now than when I wore see-through nighties and sheer panties. Just no one is game to touch me since they'd face Ghost's wrath if they did.

Recalling how well he has protected me the past nine days, I gather up the serving tray and head back out of my room. Alek is lingering in the hall again, except this time, a pretty blonde is nibbling on his ear. I don't recognize her, but that's not saying I don't know her. Her face is so sheltered by the strands of hair fallen out of Alek's manbun, none of her features are displayed.

Confident I can sneak away without being detected, I carefully close my bedroom door, then take a right instead of my usual left. I've become accustomed to the many hallways and nooks and crannies of this ship. I know my way around. I've just not wandered at this hour of the night.

"I-I'm sorry," I stammer out when my trek down one corridor has me stumbling onto a couple in an intimate interlude. A brunette is on her knees, and a man with tattoos snaked up his arm is ramming his cock in and out of her mouth.

With the tension between them too hot to pay me any attention, I slip past them before crossing through a stack of shipping containers. The corridor Ghost's office is in is quiet. Not a peep can be heard—not even the moans of a woman enjoying herself until it is too late.

I enter without knocking and once again discover a woman on her knees. Her eyes connect with mine past the thighs of the man whose back is mostly facing me, but the bobbing movements of her head persist without fault.

She carries on unraveling him while I remain frozen like a fool.

Ghost didn't return to the dining hall, so I stupidly thought it would be nice to share my dinner with him. I didn't want him to go hungry since he ensures every stomach on the ship is filled each evening.

Clearly, his hunger had nothing to do with food.

I don't know how to explain the emotions that bombard me, but they make my jaw tight and my palms sweaty. I can't breathe through the unexpected anger enveloping me, but before I can fathom a reason for my odd behavior, my watch gets busted.

A man with eyes as icy as Ghost's glares at me, except he isn't Ghost. He's the brute who tried to grab me earlier.

"I knew you wanted me." My eyes dart down to his penis hanging out of his pants when he pulls back from the woman kneeling before him before they snap back to his face. "Come, *Раб*."

I shake my head.

It is stupid of me to do.

I'm not allowed to deny any man's demand, not even when I'm certain I'll die if I don't defend myself.

I dodge the knife he sends flying across the room with only an inch to spare. It stabs into the wall behind my head and spills some of the tomato soup down the front of my clothes.

Spit flies in all directions out of his mouth when Artyom sneers out, "I wasn't fucking asking. Come. Now!"

Even conscious my life is dangling on a thread, I shake my head again while shuddering like I'm in an ice bath. Alek said no one on this ship would hurt me, and although the pain of watching who I thought was Ghost in a sexual act hurt me, I doubt it will be anything on the pain Artyom wants to rain down on me.

I didn't glance at his penis because I wanted to look. It was because it's covered with blood—blood I doubt came from him.

When Artyom growls a menacing snarl, I drop the serving dish and hightail it down the corridor. I'd rather face Ghost's wrath than kneel before Artyom, but regretfully, I'm not given the choice when he catches up to me near a tall stack of containers.

He slows my sprint by grabbing a fistful of my hair, then he uses his painful grip to flatten me against a cool, salt-riddled surface.

I fight and squirm when he crowds me against the steel container before stuffing his hand between my legs. I'm wearing sweatpants so his access isn't as easy as it would have been with a nightie, but within seconds, he's cupping my sex and attempting to strum my clit with his thumb.

"Get off." My voice is weak and pathetic, yet somehow, someone hears me.

Artyom is yanked off me with brutal force. The pull of my savior is so powerful, Artyom skids across the rusty metal floor before crashing into a container across from the one he had me pinned to.

Ghost's wild eyes dart between Artyom and me for several terrifying seconds before they eventually lower to the big blood-looking blob smeared from my midsection to the top of my thighs.

"You..."

He doesn't say more. He simply pounces at Artyom with his fists blazing instead of his guns. He pounds into him relentlessly, his knuckles bloody and split in less than thirty seconds.

He doesn't stop once Artyom's face caves in, though. He beats into him with everything he has, and then his focus shifts to me.

Blood drips off his hands when he rises from his crouched position. It splotches on his now-stained shoes and forces me to make my second mistake of the night.

I run into my captive's arms instead of away from them.

Ghost is stunned, but he soon takes it in stride. He pulls me in close to his blood-dotted chest, his hold so firm my feet lift from the ground. "Shh... маленький ягненок."

When he spins to face the footsteps creeping up behind us, I burrow my head into his pecs. Artyom is no longer recognizable. He doesn't have a face.

"What the..." Alek swallows his curse word before breathing it out slowly. "*Fuck.*"

His focus must shift to me because Ghost's grip tightens before he demands Alek take care of Artyom. "And don't give him a bag. That fucker doesn't deserve a proper burial."

Alek doesn't strain while flopping Artyom onto his shoulder and heading for the stern of the ship. He walks as effortlessly as Ghost does when he makes his way back to our room.

"It's soup," I murmur when he places me on my feet in the bathroom. "I was... I thought..." I must be in shock because I can't form sentences. "I thought he was you." Out of all the concerns I could express, I go with my hurt of believing he was with another woman. "They were in your office. I thought... I wanted to make sure you ate—"

I stop blubbering when he squashes his index finger to my lip. The saltiness it rubs into my mouth alerts me to the fact I'm crying. I shouldn't be so stunned. I've been through many horrid things in the last eight years, but tonight's event truly scared me. I've felt safe the past few days, but Artyom stripped that away in less than a nanosecond.

Ghost carries me into the perfectly tempered shower, still dressed. He steps us back until the water careens down my tear-stained face and flows over my T-shirt. I'm drenched from head to toe in under a second and free to let my tears escape without fear.

Once my fright is replaced with determination, Ghost takes a step back. "Up." He grips the hem of my shirt and pulls it over my head before his snapped command leaves his mouth. I follow, forever willing to obey but also wanting to. The way he protected me is tainting my fear, messing it up so ruefully, I'm seeing it as endearing.

Once he dumps my shirt on the floor, his focus shifts to my sweat-pants. He pulls them down, growling when he notices the tomato soup soaked through to my underwear.

"It's just soup," I remind him when his anger deprives the bathroom of sufficient oxygen to maintain life. It is muggy and steamy, and another thing I can't quite explain.

"He shouldn't have touched you." Ghost words are so low I don't believe they are for me.

However, I still answer them. "He didn't..." His eyes lift to mine when I mutter, "Thanks to you."

His eyes are so tormented. Before I can consider the repercussions of my actions, I raise my hand to his face—the scarred side.

Ghost snatches up my wrist before my fingertips can get close to the mottled skin, and although his grip is firm, it has nothing on the pain in his eyes when he realizes the scarred side of his face is un-shadowed.

He is as exposed as me.

"Shower then bed, *маленький ягненок.*" My shoulders slump when he exits the shower, taking my dirty clothes with him, but they don't hang low for long when he adds, "I'll have some food brought here. We will eat together."

15

GHOST

*A*s Vera enters my room with the tray of food I ordered for Katie, I slant my head, squashing my satellite phone in closer to my ear before growling down the line, "You're watching her as closely as me, so how the fuck did you miss what Artyom did? He didn't penetrate her."

He's fucking lucky because I would have risen him from the dead and beaten him over and over again if he had.

I'm pissed.

Annoyed as fuck.

And exhausted.

There's only been one time in my life I've sprinted as fast as I did when I saw Artyom chasing Katie. It was the night a little girl entered the world as cruelly as I did. Her cries for help were as weak and pitiful as the ones Katie released when I entered the corridor at the speed of light, but they displayed the same thing.

A wish to live.

She is the reason I'm talking Kirill off the ledge instead of letting him believe Katie was violated. Katie is Lera's ticket out of this life, and I can't give it up, no matter how angry I am. *Or how fucking hard.*

"I was dealing with other matters." The creak of Kirill's office chair trills into my ear before he says, "So I need you to check."

"Again," I say in my head at the same time he speaks it out loud. "Do you have an issue with my request, Ghost?"

A childish whimper in the background snuffs the reply I want to give him. Instead, I say, "I'll take her to Grigori."

Vera's huff is barely noticeable, but it pisses me off all the same. I glare at her so sternly, she races out of the room as I expected Katie to do when I smashed Artyom's face in. I never thought she'd run to me in a moment of crisis. I'm not that type of guy. I don't offer comfort. I issue reasons you need it.

"No need. I trust you," Kirill murmurs, his voice hitching during his last two words.

I push the phone in close to my ear, certain I heard him wrong. He doesn't trust anyone—not even men with the same blood as him.

"Report the results directly back to me," he directs before disconnecting our call.

His wish to leave me hanging is fast but not quick enough for me to miss the feminine voice greeting him. I'd recognize it anywhere, and it switches my anger to annoyance.

Luckily for me, I have someone to take it out on.

Katie's eyes lift to mine the instant she leaves the bathroom. Her hair is damp and sweet-smelling, her clothing nothing but a teeny towel, and she's peering at me like I'm her savior.

I'm not.

To save her, I'd have to destroy them.

I'm not willing to do that.

But I'd be a liar if I said the visual of her standing before me drenching wet doesn't make my cock twitch. She's so enticing. Looking at any woman after her isn't the aphrodisiac I regularly sought only days ago. It is cock-softening and adds to the frustration heating my blood.

I'm sick of jumping on cue, but even more than that, I'm sick of spineless women doing the same thing.

They lick when I tell them to lick.

They suck when I tell them to suck.

And they moan when I tell them to moan.

Except Katie.

The marks on her body reveal she had the rules beaten into her, yet she's still willing to push the boundaries.

That alone makes me tempted as fuck to do the same.

I just can't.

Simple as that.

So instead, I be the prick I was born to be. "Lay down, *маленький ягненок.*"

A surging pulse zaps through my body before pooling in my groin when Katie repeats the pledge she made in the shower. "It was the tomato soup I was bringing to you to share."

When I angle my head to the side and arch a brow, the fight in her eyes ramps up, but she folds only a second later.

Regretfully.

After flattening her back to the mattress, she drops her arms to her sides.

"Now open your towel."

"I—" She stops, swallows, then pries open the cotton material from her navel down.

"More. I want nothing in my way."

It is the fight of my life to hide the twitch that hits my lips when she shoots daggers at me before doing as requested. She is as scared as fuck to disobey me but wants to.

The knowledge hardens my cock to the point it's painful.

I'm not the only one feeding off the tension. The folds of Katie's cunt can't hide the wetness shimmering between it, and her nipples are pert and erect.

A less arrogant man would say her glistening folds are leftover residue from her shower. I know better. I could smell her cunt when I bent down to take off her sweatpants. It was begging for me to touch it, and it took everything I had to step back.

I probably wouldn't have if Katie hadn't tried to touch my scars. I hate being touched in general, but when it comes to my face, I fucking loathe it.

Katie's eyes pop when I demand, "Show me what he did to you."

"Wh-what?"

My growl shudders her thighs more.

"Show me what he did."

With her brows furrowed and her eyes holding my gaze, she cups her pussy.

"Then?" My tone is gravelly, more in frustration of her hand hiding the enticing visual of her cunt from my thirsty eyes than anything.

"That's it. That's all he did," she snaps out in a hurry.

"What about your clit? Did he touch it?"

She shakes her head.

"Are you sure?"

It switches to a bob.

"How can you be so sure? I thought you said you haven't been touched by a man there before."

I'm backing her into a trap, and she knows it. "I know because I was taught the anatomy of my body in the sixth grade." The fear that usually clouds her eyes returns stronger than ever before she murmurs, "Sorry. That was out of line."

She accepts my head bob with more credit than she should.

She thinks it puts us on an even playing field.

That isn't close to the truth.

"Why did you kill him?"

"Because he touched what isn't his to touch." Since my reply is honest, it sounds that way.

A twitch inflicts my eyelid when Katie murmurs, "Is that why you won't touch me? Because I'm not yours?"

I'm confident she sounds more disappointed than hopeful, and it has me shutting down our conversation immediately.

"Scoot."

"I—"

"Don't make me repeat myself because I'm sure you won't like the consequences of my repetition."

Confident she will obey as taught, I remove my suit jacket, then slide off my gun harness. The strain of my cracked knuckles feels good when the worn leather straps roll over them. I'm usually a quick-bullet-to-the-head guy, my kills as swift as my moods, but I had too much adrenaline to disperse, so I used my fists on Artyom.

The crack of his cheekbones under my fists will ensure I have a restful night, not to mention the scent of Katie's cunt since she left her towel at the foot of the bed.

Once my weapons are stored on my desk, I bring over the tray of food Vera arrived with. Katie's eyes light up, but she won't dare to eat first.

She was taught to obey.

I'm forced to.

16

KATIE

"*T*hey should be arriving at any moment," Annika advises while thrusting a large banquet full of meat into my chest. "Place this out while I check the cutlery." We polish the cutlery three times a day, but it is still given a final once-over before the dining room doors are opened.

We freeze partway into the lavish dining space when Vera shouts, "Change of plans. Festivities are being held in the rec room."

Like magic, silver food service trays are wheeled into the kitchen, and the staff transfers the dishes onto them at lightning speed before stuffing them into an elevator I didn't know existed until now.

"Three decks up, mid-ship," Vera announces before she squeezes her plump frame between the rows of food and presses the close door button.

"First time?" Annika asks when she spots my wide eyes and gaped mouth.

The dining room is exquisite, but it has nothing on the opulence of the rec room. Twinkle lights adorn the roof, making it appear as if you're outside like the plastic stars in Ghost's room, and oversized leather sofas take up much of the space. A billiard table is to the left, and retro arcade games are to the right.

Smoke from cigars fills the air, but the aromatic food being spread across a long row of tables makes it appear more woodsy than lung-harming.

"They serve themselves during banquets like this," Annika advises while floating to the side of the room. "We just hover close by in case they need anything."

While dipping my chin in understanding, I scan the room. Scrumptious food isn't the only thing up for offer. Drugs, alcohol, and half-dressed women are available for the taking as well.

Alek has a handful of a brunette's backside, whereas the man who is usually seated at Ghost's right is snorting a line of cocaine off a black glass tabletop.

The unease twisting in my stomach slackens a little when the female faces register as familiar. They're not the women trapped in the orlop. They are the ones who usually dine with the men.

I could say they're partners, but that feels wrong when Alek's hand shifts from the brunette's backside to a blonde's. Her shirt is already removed, so he doesn't have to wait for her to pull it over her head to trap her nipple in his mouth.

"Have you seen Ghost?" I ask Annika almost an hour later.

The men have eaten, the women have grazed, yet Ghost is nowhere to be seen.

Excluding the night he left Alek in charge, this is the first meal he's missed all week. He doesn't eat with his crew, he waits to eat with me, but he is forever present to ensure I don't face anything like Artyom's attack again.

He's quite protective, even with it making him a little manic.

Sprouts of blonde curls topple down Annika's shoulders when she shakes her head. "He could be in one of the cubes. They're usually occupied by the hierarchies on the last night of voyage." She smiles when she spots the confused crinkle pops between my brows. "The cubes are where they..." She makes a hand gesture I have no idea how to decipher. "I told them there was nothing going on between Ghost and you. They didn't believe me."

If she is talking about prolonged glances and awkward thigh presses, then there's been plenty of stuff happening between Ghost and me.

Things changed the night he protected me from Artyom. However, it seems to be one-sided. Ghost only touches me when he thinks I'm sleeping, and it never goes any further than him curling my hair around his fingers.

His nightly routine ensures I wash my hair every evening. Sometimes twice.

I hate myself for my wish for attention, but as I said two weeks ago, when you're starved for attention as long as I have been, you strive to get it any way you can.

Before I can call myself a liar—Artyom was more than willing to sully me, but it isn't him I crave attention from—Annika balances on her tippytoes to whisper something into Vera's ear. Vera's eyes snap to mine for a brief second before she dips her chin in approval. It barely rests on her ample chest for half a second when Annika reappears at my side. She snatches up my hand and drags me toward the bow of the boat.

I peer at her as if she is insane when she hands me a floral lei dangling off a large set of wooden doors. The noise projecting from the concealed space reminds me of the nightclubs I badly wanted to visit but was never given the opportunity since I was snatched at such a young age.

"If you wear a lei, they know you're only here to watch," Annika explains while pulling her hair out from underneath the plastic flowers holding her curls hostage. "These events are purely volunteer. No one is forced here."

Images of Artyom pinning me to a shipping container flash before my eyes when I ask, "Forced to do what?"

I swallow my words when the first thing my eyes land on upon entering the disco-vibe space is a naked torso. A man has a woman bent over a desk in a cube with see-through walls. He's entering her from behind while another man stands at her front, stroking his cock a mere inch from her mouth.

As my eyes drift along the long line of cubes with similar activities being undertaken in each one, I ask, "Should we be in here?"

Annika stops me from leaving by grabbing the tops of my arms and spinning me back around. "It is *all* voluntary. No one is here against their will." When I give her a look, she murmurs, "I'd rather you learn now than with *him*." She snarls her last word, but it gives me no indication as to who she's referencing. It couldn't be Ghost because she's never sneered at him like she is now.

As we float from one cube to another with only two people in it, Annika asks, "Is it true? Are you his next pick?"

I shrug, but try as I may, I can't get my body to obey the other prompts in my head.

I shouldn't be watching a man with his head between a blonde's legs, but I can't tear my eyes away.

He's pleasing her.

Isn't that against the rules?

Our enjoyment is not ours. Women live solely to please men.

"Have you ever?" Annika asks, startling me since I didn't hear her sneak up on me.

I could lie, but the lofty peak of her tone announces she is as bewildered as me, so instead, I shake my head.

"What do you think it feels like?"

As I drink in the female's flushed cheeks, lusty eyes, and partly open mouth, I murmur, "Heaven."

Annika's quick exhale hits the back of my neck. "Heaven. That sounds like a good word."

An unusual sensation hits between my legs when the man ramps up his efforts. He grips the lady's bare backside hard enough to mark before he eats her vagina with the hunger of a starved man, and I do nothing but watch.

I'm not the only one hovering in close, certain they're about to witness greatness. Ghost is right there with the group of approximately thirty on the other side of the cube. Except he's not watching the couple clawing for a sense of normality. He's staring straight at me.

It is the same prolonged watch he's given me multiple times over the past three days, and it amplifies the frantic twinge between my legs. I'm desperate to writhe on the spot, but I don't dare move. Not just because I fear displaying any type of emotion but because I also don't want to risk losing the throb I've only ever experienced once before.

When Ghost stuffed his finger inside me before he thrummed my clit.

When a dangerous smirk etches onto Ghost's mouth, most likely in response to the unwilling curve of my knees, I press my thighs firmly together. He isn't solely smiling about the heat I feel creeping across my cheeks. He's hiding his grin about my mimicking ways.

When his tongue delves out to replenish his lips, mine copies.

When he rocks on his heels, I do the same.

I copy him because I am clueless as to what is happening inside me, and I'd rather he guide me through my confusion than anyone else in the room.

Is that wrong of me to admit?

He can be cruel and demoralizing, but he's also sheltered me the past two weeks and ensured I've been fed and clothed. He's treated me better than anyone has in the last eight years.

The woman's husky moans spur me to look down, to take in the visual that doubles the heat in the room in under thirty seconds, but Ghost's watch is far more gambling. He doesn't take his eyes off me for a second, not even when the woman breaks into a long, ear-piercing segment of moans.

Our eye contact only ends when Annika bumps shoulders with me and asks, "Do you want to go or stay?"

When my eyes snap back to Ghost, my training to obey too extensive to ignore, I suck in a sharp breath. He's no longer standing on the other side of the cube. He is nowhere to be seen.

"We should go," I reply after swallowing to relieve my suddenly dry throat.

I have a feeling my existence is about to become even more complicated.

17

KATIE

As I scrub my face in the shower, my mind drifts between when Ghost had me pinned against his office door last week and the sensation that roared through me when our eyes locked and held through the sex cube tonight.

I'm clearly starved of affection because I'm confident the sensation I experienced both those times was similar if not identical. It was slightly stronger tonight because of the edge of forbidden associated with it.

We were also in a room with naked women stretched as far as the eye could see, but Ghost only had eyes for one woman.

Me.

The rush of warmth the knowledge caused between my legs as I left the cube shouldn't have occurred. He's mentioned the requirement for me to be the picture of innocence multiple times, so I shouldn't be lusting over anyone, much less getting wet.

I fill my mouth with the torrent of water flowing out of the shower-head to stifle my screams of frustration. My thoughts the past few days are going to get me killed. They'll stuff me into a body bag and dump me overboard without any concern that my family will never know what happened to me.

I can't let that happen. I barely functioned during my first few weeks of captivity, wondering what Blaire was going through. I can't let my family suffer the same fate. I must play by the rules and project the innocence I was purchased for.

I guess I better start that by clearing away the evidence of my not-so-shiny ways before anyone finds out.

Droplets of water roll down my recently shaved legs when I step out of the shower stall to gather up the panties I stripped off in a hurry. Even while living in appalling conditions, I've never once felt as dirty as I did when I slid my damp panties down my thighs tonight. They were clinging to my vagina and were marked with more wetness than the minute droplets of blood Ghost's swiveling finger enticed.

I am ashamed to admit that I was turned on by his dominance that day.

Stockholm syndrome is real.

I am living proof of this.

"Where are you?" I murmur to no one when my hunt of the bathroom floor comes up empty. Ghost's boxers and T-shirt he stripped out of this morning are there, and my sweatpants and white tee, but my panties are nowhere to be found.

My eyes dart from the tiled floor to the minute crack in the bathroom door when a grunt sounds through my ears. It is similar to the one the man released tonight when the blonde ground her pussy against his mouth but more guttural and controlled.

A thrilling jolt bolts through my body when the adjustment of my head unearths a riveting yet concerning visual. Ghost is standing at the foot of our bed. His pants are huddled around his ankles, and his erect cock is rocking back and forth between his fisted hand.

His strokes quicken when he peers at something on our bed. I can't see who he's watching, the angle is wrong, and no amount of neck manipulation will correct it, but it clearly arouses him because the bead on the end of his thick cock doubles the longer he stares.

When he tightens his grip, I lower my eyes to the tiles. I shouldn't be watching, and he's obviously angry about something since he's taking his frustration out on his cock, but for the life of me, I can't command my feet to walk me back to the shower.

I saw Master Rudd being given head multiple times, but it never provoked such a stimulating response from me. My pussy is tingling, my breasts feel heavy, and the dampness between my legs has nothing to do with the water still pumping out of the showerhead.

I snap my eyes back to Ghost so fast I grow woozy when a long, grunted moan escapes his lips. "Fuck."

He rocks his hips faster, the glistening droplet at the end now dribbled down and around his hand.

I press my thighs together when he adjusts the span of his feet. His cock is impressive front-on, but it has nothing on the visual when you see its entire length. It is long, almost double the length of the man in the cube and fed by multiple throbbing veins weaved around the velvety smooth skin.

When his eyes pop open again, and he once again locks them to our bed, I'd give anything for an extendable neck.

Who is he looking at? And why did he bring them here instead of taking them to the cubes were Annika said most of these forays take place?

As his teeth graze his lower lip, Ghost tightens his grip on his cock. He looks close to the edge, but instead of his face morphing into a scary, demon-like state, the groove between his brows slackens, and his eyes flutter shut.

He strokes his cock at a frantic pace, his control remarkable considering how close to the edge I am by doing something as simple as watching.

I've never climaxed before. I kissed a boy I'd only just met as a dare. It didn't involve any tongue, and his mouth tasted like garbage, but I am reasonably sure that is the sensation growing in intensity in my stomach. It is tingling and enjoyable and making me feel incredibly hot.

My body temperature climbs when a handful of grunts emit from Ghost's sternly shut mouth. He seems to be trying to keep quiet, which makes me wonder why he decided to bring his date here. He would have had to hear the shower running. It's noisy, and the pipes rattle, hence my shower routine switching from morning to the middle of the day.

The tightness in the lower half of my belly augments when Ghost's thrusts become uncontrollable. He pumps his cock in and out of his hand before his free hand reaches for something on the bed. My stomach curdles at the thought of him groping a woman's breast, but before its churns can overtake the frantic tingles making my skin slick with sweat, he tugs up a pair of modest panties.

My modest panties.

After taking the quickest whiff of the mess his watch left behind, he lowers them to the head of his cock, and adds to the naughtiness by blowing his load over the small stains of my stupidity.

His rocks slow as the creamy cotton material absorbs the thick streams of cum pumping out of his cock until he eventually stills then pops open his eyes.

I bounce back from the door with barely a second to spare.

His head slanted, and I almost got busted.

With my legs wobbly, I scuttle back into the shower and pull the curtain to conceal my aroused expression.

Not even thirty seconds later, the faintest creak trickles into the bathroom. Ghost doesn't fully enter. He merely dumps my soiled panties on top of my sweatpants before requesting me to hurry up.

He waits like he's waiting for confirmation. When he gets it in the form of a murmured hum, his shadow remains in the doorway until I switch off the shower faucet and open a shower curtain far enough to see a new nightie hanging on the doorknob. It won't hang to my ankles like the ones I've owned over the past eight years. Its lacy edge will brush my knees, and the top half has a built-in bra. It is still white, but the material is thick enough to hide the pink shades of my nipples.

After putting on the delicate number, I stray my eyes to my soiled underwear before exiting the bathroom with only the slightest thud of my pulse. This is ridiculous to admit, but I feel kind of regal like I'm a princess of a dark realm.

Since Ghost is sitting on our bed, the cabin light above it shadows the scarred side of his face. He watches my approach for three strides before his eyes eventually drop to the scarcely covered area of my body —the object still thudding from his earlier stare.

"I... um... I don't have any clean underwear." I'm reasonably sure he knows I don't, but I'd rather let him know than be punished for walking the halls without panties tomorrow.

His voice is still husky from the grunts he swallowed while stroking his cock when he replies, "I'll have housekeeping bring you some tomorrow." He licks his lips before raising his eyes to my face. "You are not to leave my room until they arrive. Do you understand?"

I nod before drifting my eyes to my portion of the bed. I can't get to it without climbing over him, and he doesn't seem eager to move any time soon.

"Get in bed, маленький ягненок."

Again, I nod before sheepishly endeavoring to climb over him. It is no easy feat with how long his legs are, not to mention the fact he's not really sitting up. He's in a weird, slouched position that makes the connection of our bodies almost impossible.

When I slump on top of the bedding, he appears desperate to look at me, but he can't since the changeup will unshadow the scarred side of his face. "Goodnight."

"Night," I murmur before attempting to stay as still as possible.

That is more challenging than climbing over him. I'm still hot from our staredown across the cube, not to mention the riveting show after it.

After several long minutes, Ghost squashes his left ear to his pillow. It is a position he's never adopted in the past several days, and it sends my heart rate skyrocketing.

Whenever we've interacted, it is always when the right side of his face is hidden, and although the almost pitch-black night keeps most of his features on the down-low, I can see the faintest flutters of his thick eyelashes as he rakes his eyes down my still form.

The volume of his voice is so low I have to prick my ears to hear him when he asks, "Do you understand what tonight was about?" Confusion must cross my face as he is quick in his endeavor to fix it. "At the cube?"

I shake my head, unsure I can speak.

"It is like a last hurrah. A final display of the freedom we have on this ship." My throat dries when he drops his tone even lower. "Things won't be like this once we dock. No decisions will be yours to make. Not even whose man's head is between your legs." I can't tell if he is snickering about my quick balk or groaning about it. However, he doesn't seek clarification before pushing our conversation into dangerous, murky waters. "Have you ever?"

I wait, confident that can't be the entirety of his question.

When my pause adds to the tension burning between us, I ask, "Have I ever what?"

A jolt spasms through my pussy when he mutters, "Orgasmed."

Too stunned to speak, I shake my head.

"Then you should. Tonight."

I forget I'm talking to the man who controls my every move when I murmur, "With who?"

His growl is dangerous, and it prickles every fine hair on my body. "With yourself, *маленький ягненок.*"

"I-I can't do that." Although he made it look easy tonight, self-pleasure isn't something I can do.

"Why not?" I can't see his mouth since his interrogation forced my eyes to the ceiling, but I sense his challenging grin. He likes making me uncomfortable. I have no clue why. I'm not a bumbling idiot when I'm forced out of my comfort zone. I merely hide in my shell.

"Be-because it's against the rules."

His miffed huff fans my cheek with hot air. "Who said?"

"Um..." I swallow down the unease creeping up my esophagus. "No one, I guess. It was kind of implied."

"Implied by you or them?" When I slant my head to the side, he snaps out, "Eyes front and center, *маленький ягненок.*" Once they've returned to the bland and uninviting scenery, he asks again, "Implied by who?"

My stomach gurgles when I murmur, "Perhaps me."

"No, perhaps. *Who* implied it."

Uneased by his angry tone, I push out, "By me. It was enforced by me."

"Why?" His tone is back to friendly, and it gives me a severe case of whiplash.

"Because I have no clue what I'm doing."

"Then you should learn. *Now*."

I laugh at him. "How? By stabbing around in the dark and hoping I'll stumble onto what feels good."

His low, grunted tone activates fireworks in my stomach. "By asking someone who knows where to touch." He scoots closer. "Who knows what they're doing." A touch of harshness returns to his voice when he murmurs, "Self-stimulation is the only form of pleasure you'll get here on out, so you better learn fast what feels good before you die without experiencing a single orgasm."

Why does he say that as if it is a fact more than an assumption?

"Touch yourself, маленький ягненок. Eyes to the front!" His last roared sentence is a result of my eyes darting to his in shock.

He couldn't have just said what I thought he did.

He couldn't possibly want me to please myself in front of him.

"I'm not allowed," I eventually murmur when his breaths hitting my neck turn my brain to mush. "My pleasure is not my own. I am meant to obey—"

"Then obey me," Ghost interrupts. "I'm telling you to touch yourself." When my hands remain balled at my side, he murmurs, "Don't make me repeat myself, маленький ягненок. It *never* ends well."

My exhales add to the humidity in the room when I lift my hand to my breast and squeeze it. It feels okay, but it has nothing on the zap that roared through me when Ghost stuffed his finger inside me, so I travel my other hand down to the apex at the top of my thighs.

"Do you really want to ruin your new nightwear?" Ghost asks when I trace my fingertips over the opening of my vagina.

When I shake my head, he murmurs, "Then lift it out of the way."

I'm desperate to check if the curtain over the window is open, to work out how he can see me so easily when I'm seeing nothing but blackness, but since that means I'd have to look at him again, I can't. I must keep my eyes front and center.

"What was that?" he asks when a faint murmur purrs between my lips.

I bit my lower lip to hold back my moan when my finger rolls over my sensitive clit, but the sensation was too blistering to ignore.

"No-nothing. I didn't say anything."

"Mm-hmm..." His reply pushes him stroking his cock back into the forefront of my head, and it has my fingers venturing over my vagina with more eagerness. I roll my clit with my thumb while smearing the wetness below it with my index and middle finger. I haven't been brave enough to inch inside myself yet, but just the bit of attention on my clit is sufficient.

"Don't stop," Ghost demands when the quiver of my legs resurfaces my nerves. "It's meant to feel like that. Naughty, dirty, but oh so fucking good." He scoots closer until the heat of his body makes mine slick with sweat. "Think back to the lady in the cube. Her moans, her pleasure, then pretend it's happening to you."

I shake my head. I don't want those memories. I have a far more enticing visual keeping my blood hot. The images of Ghost stroking his cock while using my damp panties as his excuse to get off. I didn't think about it until now that the stares he gave weren't for a random woman. He was eyeing my panties, as mesmerized by the dampness as I was ashamed about it.

"Now dip your fingers a little bit. You don't have to push them in deep, but they'll give your cunt something to cling to while it builds the wave."

"Like this?" I ask, my voice husky from learning how wet his command made me. It feels as if I forgot to dry after getting out of the shower.

He scoots even closer, so close strands of my hair drying in the humidity cling to his facial hair. "A little deeper." The shakiness of my legs moves up to my stomach when he murmurs, "And curl the tips." When he hears the faintest moan creep out of my lips, he curses like he did earlier. "Fuck." Bedsheets shuffle as he barks out, "Keep your eyes to the front. You move them, I'll cut off your fingers so you can never experience such pleasure again. Do you understand?"

I only bob my chin once, but it fills Ghost with so much assurance that I will follow his every command, his fist whacks the touch light above our cabin bed, illuminating our room in an artificial glow.

"Use the pad of your palm, then you don't have to strain your thumb so much to reach your clit." His accent is thicker now, more husky. "Circular movements. You're not trying to push your clit back inside yourself."

A pleasing zap surges through my pussy when he stuffs his hand under my naked backside and lifts it off the mattress. It only adds the littlest tilt to my hips, but the pleasure it entices is unexplainable. I shudder uncontrollably as a blistering of lights form in front of my eyes.

"Don't stop," Ghost commands again. "Keep going."

When rustling bedsheets sound through my ears again, I break the rules. I look. Except I don't look at Ghost's face. I take in the hardness straining against his boxer shorts, the long thick ridge he's stroking like he didn't achieve release only minutes ago.

Knowing I've caused him to lose his self-control again has me pumping my fingers in and out of me faster. I move them in rhythm to his strokes, pretending they're his cock.

"Ohh…" I try to stifle my moan, to push it to the back of my throat, but Ghost grips my face and forces me to look at him before he drags his thumb along my top lip. It is damp with a salty product that ignites the fireworks developing low in my stomach.

They detonate without warning and send my moans skyrocketing to noisy, desperate grunts.

They could wake up the people sleeping on the same level as if Ghost didn't clamp his hand over my mouth. The fact his hand extends from one ear to the other augments the shakes tearing through me. I shake for several long minutes, the aftermath of my explosion as pleasing as the buildup.

"Fuck!" Ghost groans, expressing what I can't. "You… I…" He shunts my head to the other side when my dilated eyes lock with his. His eyes are just as glossy, but his scars are fully exposed, so I'm once again not allowed to look. "Sleep, *маленький ягненок.*"

With how fast my heart is racing, not to mention the pulse in my vagina, I think his command will be impossible to fulfill.

I'm wrong.

Within seconds, I'm dozing off, only waking again when I feel the faintest flutter of a soft material between my legs. Ghost is cleaning up the mess between my legs with a handkerchief, the shadows the moon casts on his face exposing I still have hours to rest.

"Thank you," I murmur faintly when he stuffs the handkerchief into his pants pocket before lifting the blanket to cover my exposed legs.

I'm still groggy and half asleep, but I swear he murmurs, "Don't thank me, маленький ягненок. I just signed multiple death certificates."

18

KATIE

*W*ith my body still reeling in the aftermath of a climax, I don't realize we've docked until I slip my legs off the side of my bed and stand with a pair of stable knees. There are no swaying movements I've become accustomed to over the past two weeks and no splashes of the ocean as the ship rolls along with its waves.

We're docked, and I am now even more panicked about Ghost's whispered comment last night.

Unsurprisingly, Alek is the first face my eyes land on when I crack open the door of my room. I'm still without panties and untrusting of my intuition when it stupidly tells me Ghost won't hurt me.

He will, and the lowering of Alek's eyes to the short hemline of my nightie exposes this.

"We have clothes coming, but you'll want to dress warm today. Conditions are fucking icy this morning." With it being summer, I take his comment as more the aura of the ship. It is choked with unease, and the mood is glum.

Alek doesn't hide the fact he's watching me today. After folding his arms over his chest, he leans back on the door across from my room and advises, "I'll let you know when your things arrive."

I thank him with a smile before closing the door and entering the bathroom. I don't really want to shower, but I guess I should. My purity has kept me alive for the past eight years, so I don't want my mishap last night having anyone believing I'm not pure.

By the time I've showered, washed my hair, and shaved, my room is a bustling hive of activity. Annika smiles sheepishly at me before placing a large breakfast tray between a woman sharpening eyeliner pencils and one searching for a plug for a curling iron.

"Who are these people?" I ask Annika when she butts shoulders with me.

"The brunette is Inessa." She nudges her head at a woman I missed during my first scan of the room. "She's worked with the Bobrovs for years. Has a brilliant eye but a heart of ice." She switches her focus to the makeup artist. "Anya is new. This is her first time, so expect her to be a little jittery." She gives me a look as if to say I should apply my mascara if I want to keep my eye. "And Polina is Alek's sister." I snap my eyes from the beautiful blonde to Annika when she murmurs, "Don't ask her for help, though. She's too loyal."

"And you?"

She ponders my question with furrowed brows before shrugging. "I wouldn't say I'm loyal. I am just..."

"Aware of your place?" I fill in when words elude her.

My words hurt her, but since they're not a reflection of the person she is but more a portrayal of the circumstances she lives, she dips her chin, farewells me with a rub on the arm, then leaves me to a hierarchy of women who look displeased about helping me.

Over the next two hours, I'm manhandled, grunted at, and squeezed into a dress with barely any room to breathe. My hair is glossy and hanging in ringlets down my back. My makeup is subtly beautiful, and for the first time in years, I'm wearing shoes that fit.

I should feel regal, but I've read *Cinderella*. I know the glam never lasts long.

The hairs on the back of my neck bristle when a familiar grumble rumbles into my room. "Is she ready?" Ghost speaks in Russian, but the simpleness of his question means I have no trouble understanding it.

When I spin to face him, my footing unsteady in the modest yet still knowledgeable heel of my stilettos, he shifts his eyes from the beading work of my white gown to Inessa. "Her dress needs to be white."

"It *is* white." Her scoff is barely audible. "Off-white is all the rage."

"It *needs* to be white. Pure. White!" he repeats, louder this time. He marches into the room, snatches up my arm, then drags me to the rack of gowns his bevy of women arrived with. "Pick again."

When I realize his narrowed eyes are on me, I murmur, "I like this dress. It's pret—"

His growl cuts me off. "Pick. Again."

When I snap my eyes to Inessa, certain she is the lesser of two evils, she rummages through the rack, searching for the whitest dress she has. It has nowhere near as much detailing as the dress I'm wearing, and it will require me to wear a lengthier heel, but it is still regal-looking.

"What about this one?" Inessa seeks Ghost's approval more than mine. "The tulle has slithers of the finest white silk. It will be picked up by the lights in the church. She will glow like an angel."

Church?

Before I can express my shock much less vocalize it, Ghost waves his hand in the air, silently agreeing with Inessa's suggestion before stepping back to give me room to change.

I've not held a moment of modesty since last night.

The room shrinks in size when Inessa and Polina assist me out of the first gown. I'm wearing panties, but they leave nothing to the imagination. They're sheer at the front and nonexistent at the back. My bra isn't much better. It has a small amount of lace edging, but the sheer material of the cups leaves my nipples fully exposed.

"Does she have a garter?" Ghost asks after my nipples are hidden by my new dress. After locking his eyes with me for barely a second, he shifts them to Inessa.

"Yes. It is here somewhere." Tissue paper flies in all directions as she hunts for a minute strip of material that announces my fate.

I am not Cinderella going to the ball.

I'm getting married.

Shit.

"Who?" I whisper to Ghost when he guides me down the hall a second after Inessa hands him my new shoes and the garter.

He doesn't speak a word. He merely assists me into a coat, walks me over the gangway, then slides into the back of an SUV where Alek is already seated.

"Kate," he greets with a kind smile.

When I return his greeting with a silent interrogation, he drops his hand to a platinum ring on his left hand. It isn't a wedding ring, but it has a similar symbol to the one Ghost's wears on his middle finger.

Nerves take flight in my stomach when I notice the strange writing on the street signs and buildings we whizz past. They're not in the alphabet most English-speaking countries use.

It is Russian.

I shift my eyes from the large, sterile building slowly merging with the countryside when Ghost asks, "Who is with him?" His eyes are locked with Alek's.

"Ogor. He can't shoot for shit, so if anything is going to happen, it won't be until after the ceremony." When Ghost demands he speak in Russian, he gives me an apologetic glare before murmuring, "*Если ты хочешь, чтобы она ушла сегодня невредимой, успокойся, блять.*" He drifts his eyes back to me. "You're blowing her cover more than her flushed cheeks and wide eyes."

Ghost calls him a bastard before leaning closer to the partition behind him and demanding the driver to hurry.

In ten minutes, we arrive at a large concrete-fenced property guarded by multiple security personnel and fang-bearing dogs. They're so aggressive, even the security guards controlling them appear worried they may slip their restraints.

"Take them straight to the chapel," the security officer in the black box near the gate instructs after locking eyes with Ghost in the back of the SUV. "*He* is waiting." The way he emphasizes 'he' has me swallowing harshly.

Ghost removes me from the SUV in the same manner he forced me inside with a quick pluck-duck-and-pull maneuver. Then he walks me up a set of marble stairs. The chatter coming from inside the chapel dulls to barely a hush when the creak of the door announces our arrival. The double doors separating the foyer from the main part of the chapel are closed, but it doesn't stop me from spying the man standing at the end of the aisle in a tuxedo.

It is the man from the auction four years ago. The one who handed over the cash for me.

I shoot my eyes to Ghost, seeking answers I know I will never get.

I thought he was my owner.

He bid on me.

He won me.

So why is he giving me to this man?

I spin barely a hair's breadth away from Ghost when he stops me in my tracks with a vicious snarl. "If you leave now, your sister will join your father and mother in the dirt of your family plot."

"What?" I can't think of a better reply. I am too stunned to speak.

Ghost forces me to look at him, ensuring I can't miss the honesty in his eyes when he murmurs, "This stopped being about you the instant you gained his attention."

"But what does that have to do with my family?"

Stupidly, I bang my fists on his chest when he replies, "They asked too many questions."

"So you killed them. You murdered my parents." I only get in two good thumps before he snatches up my wrists in a painful hold. "Let me go. Get your filthy hands off me!"

This entire time, I've been living for them. I've been fighting for them, so now that I know it's been a waste of time, I am fucking done.

I yank out of Ghost's hold and race for the exit doors. I don't have much meat on my bones, so I'll take my chances with the dogs guarding this property. I won't be appetizing enough for them to worry about.

My steps freeze partway out the door when Ghost orders, "Move in."

I snap my head back, gasping when I spot a small handheld device in his hand. It shows the university that was being built the year I was snatched and a beat-up Civic zooming into the parking lot.

"No," I breathe out with a sob when I spot the fiery red hair of the female behind the steering wheel. I haven't seen her in years, but I'd never forget her. It is my baby sister, Hailey.

"Please don't," I beg when a blacked-out SUV pulls in behind Hailey's car. It is a replica of the car we just traveled in, except this driver is wearing a balaclava and black gloves.

Ghost acts as if I didn't speak, forcing me to beg louder and more heartfelt. "Please, Ghost. She isn't a part of this. She doesn't belong here."

As a man dressed in black slips out of the back passenger side of the SUV, Ghost brings his eyes to meet with mine. "And you do?"

"Yes." I nod so forcefully I make myself dizzy. "I'll prove it. I will do anything you ask. Anything at all." I stray my eyes down the long procession of people waiting for the doors to pop open and for the bride-to-be to emerge. "I'll marry him and have his children. I'll do whatever he asks." My voice cracks when I realize the man is mere feet from Hailey. "Ghost, please!" I fall to my knees and grab his hand with mine. I need two hands to his one, but it gets across my point that I'm willing to obey. I always have been. "Don't do this."

I suck in a sharp breath when an abrupt "Stop" rumbles out of his mouth. I assume it is in response to my pleas for clemency but learn otherwise when the man approaching Hailey backs up, yanks off his balaclava, then proceeds to meld with the students around them.

I struggle to work out which way is up when I recognize the face of the man behind Hailey. It is one of the original men who kidnapped me.

I sound as rattled as I feel when I ask, "Why so long?"

I'm referencing the Bobrovs' obvious eight-year interest in my family, but Ghost doesn't realize that. "Because this dress was not made for you." He tugs me to stand before bobbing down to place on the heels needed so my dress won't swish against the ground. My thighs wobble more from his reply than the closeness of his breaths to my vagina. "She chose off-white, which meant she didn't make it to the end of the aisle."

As my eyes shoot to the glass doors separating the foyer from the main part of the chapel, my heart thuds in my chest. Behind the pipe organs at the left of the aisle is a black tripod. It houses a weapon I've only seen in movies.

Is that why half the congregation is wearing black?

They don't know if they're here for a wedding or a funeral.

I'm fairly certain it is both.

19

KATIE

*A*gainst the odds, I survived the ceremony.

My husband seemed pleased when the tulle of my dress caught the rays beaming through the stained-glass windows. He complimented the purity of my dress before instructing his guests to sit.

It was a brief five-minute sermon that gave no sign of my husband's identity or the grief I'm currently wading through. I must be in shock because I can't express a single emotion.

The aura of wealth in the room exposes my husband is a notorious man who is feared by many, but everyone refers to him as 'He.'

Even the priest.

An elderly lady with a wrinkled face she's trying to smooth with Botox stops waffling on about the sermon the priest gave during our nuptials when a scuffle at the side of the room captures our attention. Our 'reception' is being held in a ballroom next to the chapel. It is beautifully decorated but appears as if it was set up some time ago. The realistic yet still plastic flowers have dust on them.

My heart beats in my ears when I spot the cause of the commotion. Ghost is having a heated conversation with my new husband. My husband has him gripped by the scruff of his dress shirt, but that doesn't mean he is the clear winner. Ghost's snarl is enough to shake the scariest man's boots.

"You will do as I ask," my husband shouts when Ghost breaks out of his hold. "Or you know what the consequences will be."

I pray for a sinkhole when his threat forces Ghost's eyes to me. He looks at me as if he hates me. I want to say it is mutual, but for the time being, he still appears to be my only lifeboat.

"Come, *Раб*."

The snapped command is so demanding my feet leap into action before I can recall it isn't my husband barking orders. It is Ghost.

Not speaking a word, he walks me out of the reception room, across a gravel road, then into a mansion that seems too light and airy, considering how many armed men surround it. There are men stationed at every door and window.

When we enter a room on the second level, my breathing halts halfway to my lungs. It is brimming with men wearing white coats and holding scary instruments. They look more invasive than the instrument Ghost used on me last week.

Either sensing my unease or having his own set of bad memories, Ghost shouts, "Out!"

"We—"

"I said get the fuck out!" Ghost's roar already has them on the back foot, not to mention his reminder about what happened to the last doctor he crossed paths with.

News of Grigori's death clearly made it all the way to Russia.

Once we're alone, Ghost releases me from his hold before moving to a stainless-steel tray in the far-left corner. "Lay down, *маленький ягненок*."

Recalling the pledge I made only hours ago I move to the bed in the middle of the room and lay down.

I am doing this for Hailey and only Hailey.

The food I scarfed down for breakfast this morning creeps toward the back of my throat when Ghost spins around. He has a vial in his hand. It is filled with a cloudy white substance.

After pulling off the cap and cursing when it spills because he is holding it upside down, he requests I lower my panties.

"Now, *маленький ягненок!*" When the sheer material bands around my knees, he murmurs, "That is far enough."

I can't control the shake of my legs when the mattress dips under the strain of his weight. He sits next to my knee and pries it open before he lowers the vial so it presses at the opening of my vagina.

"What are you doing?" I murmur a second before he spreads me with his fingers, pushes the vial in, then squirts warm liquid inside me.

I'm confused as to why Ghost is doing what he's doing when it's obvious it makes him mad. Not even a second after the gooey substance is emptied inside me, he removes the vial and pegs it across the room before his hands shoot up to his hair. "Fuck!"

He tugs the blond strands until they stand on their ends before he leaves the room without so much as a backward glance.

SEVERAL HOURS LATER, I detect I'm being watched while leaving the attached bathroom. This room is far more spacious than the one I shared on the ship, but it is sterile and bland. The walls are white. The carpet is white. Even the tiles in the bathroom are a glossy white.

The door is also white and locked.

I tested it multiple times over the last four or so hours.

Ghost's face looks as red as mine when I finally lock eyes with him. I doubt his is from a torrent of tears from grieving his family. He probably doesn't even know a hurt like the one I'm experiencing.

How could he when he doesn't have a heart?

"I am here to escort you to dinner." With his accent thicker from the grogginess of his voice, I find it a little hard to understand him. "You are to gush about your new husband and tell everyone how perfect he is while ensuring you maintain your modesty." He walks to a wardrobe with glossed doors and pulls open the first door. "You are to *always* wear white and act pure." I feel ashamed when he murmurs, "You should never display signs that you are aware of ecstasy, lust, or wantonness. If you do—"

"You'll kill me like you did my family?"

My grief has arrived full force.

I am in the depths of utter despair and uncaring about who I take down with me.

"I did *not* kill your family." My hope lasts for all of five seconds. "I spared your sister."

My nails don't get the chance to add to the scars on his face—he grabs me and pins me to the glossy closet door before they get within an inch of his face. "Would you rather they all be dead, маленький ягненок? Would you prefer that than having her life hanging over your head for eternity?" He grips my cheeks so firmly his nails dig in deep before he forces me to look at him. "She's alive so you'll obey. That's how it works."

I must have a death wish because only someone who wants to die spits into the face of the man commanding every single move they make.

My breath comes out in short bursts when Ghost tugs a handkerchief out of the breast pocket of his suit to soak up the mess. I've seen it before—most notably when it was cleaning up the mess between my legs this morning.

It reminds me that our playing field is more even than originally thought.

That he has as much to lose as me.

"What will *he* do when *he* finds out *you* touched me?"

Ghost scoffs at me. "I haven't touched you. Not once."

"Your thumb was on my lips, and your precum was in my mouth... *twice!*"

He looks like he wants to slap me, but instead, he puts his fists through the wall next to my head. It dusts my shoulder with wood fibers and makes his eyes the most dilated they've ever been. "Then they're dead. *You* ordered their deaths. *You* killed them. Not me."

"Them?"

Guilt flashes through his eyes for barely a second before he unpins

me by taking a step back. "I will tell him you're not feeling well. That
you want to stay in tonight to double the chances of the insemination
working."

It isn't guilt on his face anymore when I ask, "What did you put
inside me?" It is remorse.

"Goodnight, *маленький ягненок.*"

"Ghost..."

I follow him to the door, but he is too fast. He's out of the sterile
room and walking down the hallway before my hand circles the dead-
bolt lock.

20

GHOST

"Дядя."

Lera races across the marbled floor to fling herself in my arms. She squeals when I spin her around before I bob down to her level. She is only four and short for her age, so it is a long drop.

"How is my favorite niece?" I ask her in Russian, aware her English isn't as good as mine since she's never left this compound. "Have you been a good girl for Momma?"

Tiny lines sprout out of the scar that runs down her forehead and across her right eye before stopping at the base of her ear when she screws up her face. "Momma is sick."

I peer up at her nanny behind us while asking, "What kind of sick?" I return my eyes to a pair identical to my sister's in every way. "Was it like she was when you went to build a snowman while you weren't wearing a coat?"

The muscles in my arms spasm when she shakes her little head. "No. She is sick like Alyna was—" I clamp my hand over her mouth to stop her words before signaling for Rusha to move closer.

"You can't tell anyone Momma is sick, Lera. Do you understand?" She doesn't appreciate my barked words any more than Katie, but she understands I'm only cruel to keep her safe. She is the reason I fall in line.

"I understand, *дядя*."

I ruffle her hair, doubling the drop of her lip before instructing for Rusha to give her as much ice cream as her stomach can handle.

"With *Зефир*?"

"You can have as many marshmallows as you want as long as you don't tell anyone Momma is sick."

"Okay," she mutters in English, willing to do anything for a sugar hit.

After tugging her in for a hug so my thigh blocks her good ear, I say to Rusha, "Keep her away from festivities for the next couple of weeks. She's too young to understand the consequences of her words."

She dips her chin in understanding before taking Lera's hand and guiding her to the industrial kitchen preparing tonight's feast. Kirill won't be happy when I announce his new bride isn't well enough to celebrate their nuptials, but I'm confident once I tell him we've begun artificial insemination, he will forget his anger.

To him, a virginal bride is nowhere near as vital to his plans as a virginal mother.

The bible says that we can learn from Mary how to be bolder in obeying the world of God.

Except in this world, Kirill is God, and we are his parishioners still seeking his ultimate Virgin Mary.

21

KATIE

*M*y head pops up from my knees when a whoosh sounds through my ears. On the ship, I wouldn't have noticed such a minute noise, but in the quietness of my room, I could hear a pin drop.

For the first time in hours, my heart beats with something other than heartbreak. There is a white envelope at the base of my locked door. It is addressed to Kate.

The scars on my knees when I was forced to kneel on tacks for hours creak along with my weary bones when I rise from my crouched position and make my way to the door. It is late. My body clock is alerting me to this more than anything, but I can't sleep.

Hailey's near kidnap keeps repeating like a movie in my head, then my thoughts shift to my parents.

How old were they when they died?

Was it a painful death, or were they taken out quickly as the men in Madame Victoria's compound often threatened?

Did they think of me when they died?

So many questions have swirled around my head in the past few hours, but I haven't been able to answer a single one of them.

The salty blobs I cleared away from under my eyes soak into the poorly made envelope when I gather it in my hands. The paper looks ancient and handmade. It almost crumbles under my weak touch when I pry open the seal and pull out the photographs from inside.

My breaths clog in my throat when I scan the first image. It shows Hailey graduating senior year. She is wearing her graduation cap and gown and posing between our parents. Her wolfish grin of satisfaction is huge but not as big as the people surrounding them.

My family was still suffering in this picture, but at least I know they survived my first six years of captivity.

The second image dries my throat to the point it is painful. It rattles my hands and my core.

"When was this taken?" I step back from the door before peering up at the monitor dangling in the corner of the space. Fresh blobs plop onto my cheeks when I spin around a photograph of a wreckage to the surveillance device. "Did you do this? Did you stage their accident?"

When my questions are answered with painful silence, I rummage through the rest of the photographs. They answer my questions, but they keep my grief high.

My parents are dead as Ghost advised, but he didn't kill them.

They were struck by a truck returning home from Hailey's high school graduation ceremony. It appears as if my father careened onto the wrong side of the road.

Hailey was the sole survivor.

A second after the lock on my door rattles, I lock eyes with Ghost.

"Why did you make out you killed them when they died in a traffic accident?"

He balks for barely a second before he enters my room to place a serving dish on a small table on the left.

"You said you spared Hailey's life, but you didn't." I toss down the photographs of newspaper clippings of the accident. "You didn't save her. You don't even know who she is!"

I swallow some of my sass when he murmurs, "Then how did I know how to find her today?" He opens the dish, exposing a meal fit for a king, then shifts on his feet to face me. "And I never said I killed your parents. I simply announced your sister would join them in the family plot if you didn't do as asked."

"Yeah, but that doesn't mean you 'spared' her." I'm confused, and it is heard in my tone. "You can't threaten someone then make out you're their savior when your threat works as intended."

My stomach was grumbling in hunger only minutes ago. Now it flips in devastation from Ghost's reply, "Do you think trafficked women are only used for sex, маленький ягненок? That there aren't other parts of their bodies people want." Bile burns my throat when he lowers his eyes to the images splayed across the glossy white table. "She wouldn't have survived without a transplant." He returns his eyes to mine. "We ensured she had one."

"Why would you save her? That doesn't make any sense."

The depths the Bobrovs go to make women fall into line is undeniable when he replies, "As I said previously, she is alive so you will obey. It is how things work around here." The tick on his jaw announces he isn't a fan of his reply, but he commences barking orders, stealing my chance to interrogate further. "You are to eat then rest until the morning. With your schedule corresponding well with our arrival, another insemination will take place in the morning."

"Insemination?" He mentioned it before, but with my grief too strong for me to comprehend, it is only sinking in now. "You're artificially inseminating me."

I'm not asking a question, more summarizing, but Ghost bobs his chin. "You will have another four rounds before the window closes."

"Window?"

He looks as ill as I feel when he murmurs, "Ovulation window."

"I don't... I can't—"

Everything makes sense when Ghost interrupts my quiet ramblings, "Hence the donation of organs."

I feel his eyes on me, but I don't return his watch. I'm too busy taking in the differences between Hailey's face in the graduation photograph and the video Ghost played at the altar. Her smile wasn't as large as the people around her, nor was her face carefree, but it was far more radiant and alive than the video footage. She's hurting—badly. I can't make matters worse for her.

"I will do as you ask." I don't want to see any dishonesty in Ghost's eyes when I plead, "Just leave her out of this." So instead of facing him while asking, I plonk my bottom into a seat around the dining table and stab my fork in the tender red meat.

THE FOLLOWING MORNING, Ghost arrives with two doctors in tail. They don't speak while setting up the procedure Ghost trampled over last night. They move around in silence, adding to the squirms of my stomach.

I'm not sick from being gluttonous with my food. I'm queasy from them raising stirrups from beneath the bed I barely slept a wink on last night. I never slept in silence before, and the quiet made the racks of my sobs even more noticeable.

I startle when a man with a thick mustache barks out, "Stirrups. Now."

Ghost mutters a Russian curse word under his breath but does nothing to stop their aggression when they grab my legs and force them into the stirrups.

He only moves when they restrain me to the bed. "*Почему ты ее сдерживаешь?* She is not resisting you." I can't understand what the man replies since he speaks Russian, but it angers Ghost more. "The door is fucking locked, and he has twenty men on her alone. How far does he think she will get?"

The man replies something about a sister, but 'sister' is the only word I understand.

"Stay still, *маленький ягнено,*" Ghost snaps out, his anger now directed at me.

His request is virtually impossible when the second doctor moves closer with a large silver instrument in his hands. It looks like a duck's beak, and he's coating it with lubricant.

"Be gentle." My Russian is basic, but I'm reasonably sure that is what the first doctor requests. "He wants her still virginal at birth."

I snap my eyes shut so fast when he raises the sheet maintaining my modesty, the wetness pooling in them has no choice but to careen down my face. Being beaten and tortured was so painful you were expected to cry, but this is different. It hurts my heart more than my body, and it shows my pain more freely than anything.

"Breathe, *маленький ягнено,*" Ghost demands, squeezing my hand.

When his fingertips brush the welts on my wrist from where I was restrained with barbed wire for four weeks straight, I pop open my eyes and connect them to his. Something in them has changed. They're still dark and dangerous, but they're also full of remorse.

"It will only be a minute of discomfort then the pain will be over."

He's lying. We both know it. But I nod my head, nevertheless.

Once the goop inside the vial has been inserted inside me, the doctor lowers the sheet, frees my legs from the stirrups, then exits the room, wheeling their tray of torture out with them.

"You need to stay immobile for a couple of minutes." When I stray my eyes to the breakfast dish Ghost arrived with, more because I don't want to look at him right now than in hunger, he asks, "Do you want something to eat?"

I shake my head, but he doesn't see me. After wheeling over a table you usually see in hospitals, he places the tray of food on top then opens the silver lid. "What do you want?"

I don't answer his question. Instead, I ask one of my own. "Why is he doing this?"

Don't get me wrong. I am grateful I'm not being held down and forced to have sexual relations with a man three times my age like many of the women I was taken with, but this process is just as violating, if not a little more concerning. I'm not being seen as a woman. I am an incubator.

Ghost places down the fork loaded with pancakes before muttering sternly, "He wants you to have his child."

"I understand that, but why like this?" I wave my hand to the stirrups still eradicating the air of sufficient oxygen.

My heartbeat is heard in my ears when he murmurs, "Because he believes it will ensure others that he is God."

"A god—"

"No," Ghost interrupts, his voice picking up speed. "Not a god. God himself."

My family wasn't heavy on religion, but even a nonreligious person knows what he is doing is wrong. "Mary didn't conceive by artificial insemination. It was via immaculate conception and the power of the holy spirit."

"Which is what everyone will believe when you become pregnant with his baby." Ghost strays his eyes to the camera in the corner of the room. "It is why surveillance is purely to insight fear. They're not monitored."

I should focus on the fact I'm not under surveillance for hours a day as I usually am, but his earlier disclosure that I have twenty armed men watching me from afar keeps my focus on other matters. "What happens if it works?"

Ghost's angry expression returns full force. "The infant's sex will be determined via ultrasound. If it is a boy, you will give birth at a nearby nunnery."

"If it's a girl?"

He acts as if I didn't speak. "Eat, маленький ягнено. You will be expected to make an appearance today."

22

GHOST

*K*atie's first appearance as Kirill's wife went well. She displayed her virtuousness with perfection and has everyone fooled. She shows no signs of lust or wantonness, not even when she looks at me, which pisses me off.

She is not mine to sully.

She is not mine to touch.

But she is my only hope.

Without her, my plan will unravel, and everything I've fought to achieve the past four years will come undone.

I can't let that happen.

No matter how delicious I believe it will be, no cunt is worth losing everything for.

So, instead, I curl my hand around my cock and stroke it to the beat of my heart, confident just the memories of Katie touching herself in the moonlight weeks ago will keep the fire in my belly burning longer than Kirill's wish to derail me.

I have what it takes to beat him, and it is all thanks to her.

As I remember her lips circling my thumb, I roll the same chunky digit over the head of my cock. I use the bead of pre-cum to lubricate my strokes. It is smoother than the water pumping out of the showerhead and slippery like her tongue when it darted out to lick up the salty blob.

A grunt rumbles in my chest when I tighten my grip. She's too tight not to strangle my cock and too virginal not to cause us both pain. I rock my hips, jackknifing them at speed until a familiar tingle forms at the base of my cock within minutes. Just now, the image of her stained panties comes to mind. It is closely followed by the scent of her arousal.

"Christ, Little Lamb," I murmur in Russian, confident the feeling of my hand pumping my cock will have nothing on how good she'd feel wrapped around it.

She'd suck at me and beg me to take her harder, all the while shuddering through orgasm after orgasm.

I grit my teeth when the images rolling through my head like a movie switch to ones I don't want to see. She's not meant to be lying in front of me, naked from the waist down, waiting for insemination. She's meant to be waiting for me.

"Come on." I grip my cock harder while endeavoring to get my thoughts back to the images of Katie stroking her clit in my bed. Her writhes were faint but present, and her moans were solely mine.

Not even staring at my scarred face could take her focus off her needs. She wanted to come, and she needed me to help her achieve that.

"Now I need you to help me do the same, маленький ягнено."

While pressing my thumb down on the vein feeding my cock, I remember the glint her eyes get when I enter her room with food the past three weeks and how she begs me to stay. She says she hates the silence, but I know it is more than that.

She thinks I'm her savior.

I know that is far from the truth.

If it weren't for me, she'd be free.

I did send the car to collect her from the auction. He was meant to bring her to the docks. Up until last month, I thought she was the consequence of friendly fire. I should have known better when Kirill ordered us to 'donate' a body to the hospital where her sister was taken after her family's accident. Organs on the black market don't go cheap.

Kirill lost over three hundred thousand that night but gained notoriety for his saintly ways.

It doubled his wish to be God and grew his manic behavior to an unmanageable level.

"Fuck," I roar when the remembrance of his ways softens my cock.

To function like a man without needs, I have to take care of the backlog, but he stole even that from me. Instead of blowing my load on the tiles in my bathroom, I switch off the faucet, climb out, and dry myself.

I'm partway into my room when my cell phone rings. The ringtone announces it is Alek, much less recognition that no one calls me. Kirill is old-fashioned. Most of our meetups occur in person.

"What?"

Alek takes my angry tone in stride. "He wants you to do Kate's insemination today."

The tick of my jaw is heard in my reply, "Why?" Kirill requested I be present during Katie's daily inseminations at their wedding, but this is the first time in the past three weeks he's demanded I undertake the procedure that will see her becoming his Virgin Mary.

The ruffle of a shrug sounds down the line before Alek's deep exhale. "The day I work out that man's inner workings is the day I'm dead."

I have an inkling to the reason he's fucking with my head, but I'd rather not disclose that. "Has she been fed?" I usually deliver Katie's meals, another request from Kirill, but this morning, my dick took priority over my obligations.

"No," Alek answers, his voice low.

"What is it?" I can read him like a book. He doesn't hide his worries well, not even when mass murdering as ordered.

"Sofia." My breath catches at the mention of my sister's name. "She is late." I work my jaw side to side when he announces, "The maids advised Kirill this morning that her sheets haven't bled for over two months."

"When?" I could say more, but I don't need to.

"End of the week." Before I can instruct to be advised an exact date and time by the end of the day, he adds, "I'll go with her."

"No—"

"You lose your cool, he will kill her. Is that what you want, Ghost?"

"You know that isn't what I fuckin' want," I reply, yelling.

"Then let me handle this." My silence agitates him. "Ghost—"

"Fine." I warn him in Russian that I won't respond kindly if Sofia is harmed before disconnecting our call, getting dressed, then heading to the kitchen to fetch Katie's breakfast.

My blood is still hot when I enter her room twenty minutes later. The guards don't look at me when I walk by, but I can smell their fear. It is leeching from their pores.

I'm not called Ghost for no reason. Most people are only in my presence for minutes before they become a ghost. That's how triggered my moods are. I can be calm and collected one minute, the next, I'm a raging lunatic.

Drugs don't help the matter, but I can't remember the last time I functioned without them.

My attitude doesn't know which way to swing when my eyes lock on a red smear on the right-hand side of Katie's bed. She's bleeding, and for some stupid reason, I'm as relieved as I am annoyed.

"Bring napkins and a maid," I instruct the closest man to Katie's room. "We need clean sheets." When he appears as if he is going to reject my request, I bark out, "Did I sound like I was asking a question?"

He shakes his head quickly. "No, sir, but He—"

"Doesn't talk on my behalf." I step closer to him, dropping his shake from his head to his body. "I told you to do something." My breath hits his cheeks when I sneer, "So fucking do it." I'm already pissed about the tightness in my balls I didn't relieve this morning. He'd do best not to test me.

"Yes, sir." He bows his head before scuttling away.

Two minutes later, I enter the bathroom where I hear water running. Katie is in the shower, washing her hair as she has done twice a day for the past month.

The front of my pants tightens when I follow the water careen down her tight and appetizing body. She has put on a few pounds since we arrived at the Bobrov home compound, and her tits have grown substantially. I may have ordered her mashed potatoes to be prepared with cream instead of milk solely for this benefit.

I'm glad, for once, my plan is working.

So accustomed to being degraded by vile pigs, Katie doesn't flinch when she spots me in the doorway of the bathroom. She also knows better than to hide from me, so instead of covering up, she lowers her head and acknowledges, "I got my period overnight."

"I am aware." I don't mention her stained bedding that is in the process of being removed. "Are you in pain?" I don't mean to take in the welts on her wrists when I ask my question. My eyes just naturally veered to them. Other than the burn-like marks on her wrist, her body's scars are mostly hidden by enticing curves and mouthwatering assets, unlike mine.

Water splatters on the glass wall of the shower cubicle when she shakes her head. "I was given paracetamol this morning."

Her reply angers me. "What did I tell you about accepting anything from any man in this compound."

She grabs a towel on the rail before spinning around to face me. "That I am not to accept anything unless it is given to me by you."

"Then why did you take it?" I'm not angry at her. I am furious that Kirill knows she is bleeding, yet he still demanded that I inseminate her today. She can't get pregnant. He just wants to fuck with my head.

"I didn't." She marches to the vanity to highlight the two white pills sitting on top of the marble. As suspected, they're not marked with a manufacturer's imprint. They're homemade and look like a mix of a pain relief medication and a hallucinogenic.

After flushing the 'drugs' down the toilet, I ask, "Do you require something for the pain?"

Katie shakes her head.

"Don't lie to me."

I'm looking for a fight, for a way to ease some of the tension, and Katie gives it to me. "I'm not lying. You asked if I require something for the pain, not *am I in pain*."

"It is the same fucking thing."

Before I can remind myself a hit of coke will give me the same thrill I'm chasing from a woman I can't touch, I curl my hand around Katie's throat and slowly back her toward the vanity mirror. The arch of her back gapes the front of her towel, exposing her bleeding cunt to my hungry eyes.

The thud of her fading pulse against my thumb makes me instantly hard, not to mention the sight of her glistening pussy lips. She's bare, her routine of shaving as regular as the number of times she washes her hair. "Why do you keep shaving? You know *he* hates it."

"How would I know what *he* hates? I've seen him three times and not once was it without clothing."

I tighten my grip, her voice not husky enough for my liking. Her attitude, though, I'm fucking obsessed with that. It's grown tenfold the past month. "You know because I told you what he likes. He wants you natural." *Unlike me.* With the need to come still rampant in my veins, I wedge my thigh between her splayed legs before stepping even closer. "Why haven't you touched yourself yet?" With the hand not circled around her throat, I tug down the front of her towel. "I've stroked my cock every fucking day for weeks, yet you've not once brushed a fingertip over your nipples that are begging for attention."

Part of the spark I saw in her eyes the day she was auctioned flares through her dilated gaze before she murmurs, "I've not had any incentive."

She means her words as an insult, and I take them that way. "Then maybe I should stop feeding you. Make you hungry enough you'll eat anything." I don't know if my grip is slipping in the steamy conditions or if she grinds down a little in response to my threat. Whatever it is, it has me pushing our exchange into dangerous territory. "You're still a virgin even if you suck dick, right?"

When I tug her onto her knees like I did the day she stumbled into my office, there's no hiding the effect she has on me. I'm strained against the zipper of my trousers, the pinch almost painful.

Fear doesn't highlight her eyes when she looks up at me. It never has once the past two months, but concern is in abundance and a whole heap of worry.

She knows what my cock doesn't want to acknowledge.

Having her suck it will get our sisters killed far sooner than it will us.

It takes everything I have to pull back, and it isn't done without the aggression I can't hold back when things don't go my way. "Dry yourself then get on the bed. Let's get this over with before I'm tempted to add to the blood on your sheets without using your cunt."

23

KATIE

$\mathcal{M}$y second period at the Bobrov compound has tapered to almost nothing. The small smears of blood on the sanitary napkins I'm allowed to use are more a light brown than red, but I see them growing murkier when Ghost instructs for me to lie down on the bed.

He doesn't use the stirrups like the doctors or the invading silver duck-beak tongs. He merely inserts the vial partly inside my vagina, then releases my husband's sperm inside me without looking at me or my face.

They'd have to know I can't get pregnant on my period. Even only having my period a year before I was abducted didn't exclude that knowledge from me, yet without fail, every day, I am inseminated with 'his' sperm.

Part of me thinks he's doing it to frustrate Ghost. His aggressive nature is paramount for all hours of the day, but it is even more noticeable during insemination periods the past two months.

I guess even a man with nothing wouldn't crave a woman with another man's sperm dripping out of her. This is my husband's way of making me unattractive to anyone around me. It ensures they will follow his every command no matter what.

"Did you bring it?" I ask when Ghost lowers the sheets to cover my wobbly knees.

He usually brings me treats to ensure I stay in bed for a minimum of twenty minutes. Yesterday, I asked for something different. It is foolish of me, but things have been different between us the past two months. He's pleased I am doing as asked and has been awarding my submissiveness in many ways.

Today, I want a recent photograph of my sister.

Next week, I may beg for my freedom. That's how confident I am that Ghost is starting to see sense through the madness.

"What did I tell you, *маленький ягненок?*"

I grimace when my squirm up the bed causes cum to dribble out of my vagina. I feel as damp and wet as I did five weeks ago when Ghost pinned me to the vanity mirror by my throat and wedged his thigh between my legs.

The tension was bristling. Excluding the night he showed me how to get off, it was unlike anything I'd ever experienced. But I also knew it could spell the end for us.

My husband doesn't share. He made sure I was aware of that during our first meal we shared together before he left the dining room with a pretty blonde draped over him.

His inability to keep his dick in his pants affected Ghost more than me. He left me to eat alone that night for the first time in ages and had me so desperate not to be left alone again, I've been obeying his every whim.

My submissiveness weakens the tension that's been brimming between us since our first meeting on the ship, but the bitchy attitude that comes with my cycle has returned it stronger than ever this week.

I'm one smart comment away from being punished, and for some reason, I push instead of rolling over and begging for my stomach to be scratched.

"You said I shouldn't ask for anything." Ghost locks eyes with me during the last half of my reply. "And that putting out demands will only double my penance."

"Then why do you push?"

I see his anger rising when I reply, "For the same reason you do."

"You know nothing about me, *маленький ягненок*," he spits out, his voice a roar.

"I know you wouldn't hold back if you weren't scared."

I said the wrong thing.

I took this way too far.

"Scared? You think I'm fucking scared!"

He may not be, but I am now.

"My father was the ruler of this realm. He was feared across the globe—"

"Yet you take orders like every other man here."

The silver tray housing the doctor's equipment sails across the room. It smacks into the wall with a thud before Ghost's furious frame takes up the bulk of its space. "Would a scared man do this?"

Before I can react, he hooks my ankle and drags me down the mattress. I kick at him and scratch at his arms, but within seconds, his belt is removed and wrapped around my ankles, and I'm pinned to the mattress by my stomach.

The fear shaking through me augments to something different when he cups me from behind. He doesn't stab his fingers into me like the doctors with no care for my soft and sensitive skin. He heightens the sensitivity by stroking my labia before he rolls his fingertips over my clit.

"Fuck, *маленький ягненок*." If his words had been spoken by any other voice bar the one he uses in ecstasy, I would have assumed he was mad about the wetness between my legs. "Your clit is throbbing with want."

He rolls the achy bud once, twice, then three times before giving it a mind-clearing smack. The briefest whack sends tingles all over my skin.

I moan into the sheets before increasing the spread of my thighs.

I should feel exposed.

I should feel violated.

All I'm feeling is euphoric.

"Please."

Ghost's growl is equally evil as it is enticing. Its vibration does damage to my brain and sends my head into a tailspin. "Pinch your fucking clit."

I do as asked but clearly not tight enough.

"Firmer. Make it hurt."

After showing me how, Ghost rocks his thick cock against the seam of my ass. He is hard and long and struggling not to take this from a PG grind up to an extramarital affair.

How do I know this?

I'm facing the same battle.

"When I tell you to let go, do so quickly and without question."

Moaning, I nod.

The tension is burning.

It is scorching me alive.

And I'm loving every minute of it.

"Ready?"

I barely nod for a second before Ghost leans over me to clamp my mouth with his hand. Then, just as my breathy moans seep through the cracks of his fingers, he instructs me to release my hold on my clit.

A nanosecond later, a hot droplet of goop rolls over my clit. It is Ghost's pre-cum. Except it wasn't placed there by his finger. He transferred it by rubbing the head of his cock over my clit.

The naughtiness of the image in my head is my undoing.

I come with a frantic breathy huff, my moans only silenced by the tightness of Ghost's hand clamped around my mouth.

"Fuck..." He hits my clit with another two swipes before he pulls up, grinds his cock against my ass, and shoots his load onto the back of my nightie.

"Fuck. Fuck. Fuck!"

These curses aren't ones of pleasure.

He's mad.

Really mad.

"For fuck's sake." He pushes me down by my back, unties my ankles, then flips me over as if I am weightless.

The pure anger on his face morphs when he locks eyes with my wide and massively dilated gaze.

I'm not scared of him. I'm fearful of how unhinged he makes me.

He is my captor, yet I crave him more than anything.

"Eat then shower." His jaw works side to side before he adds, "You smell *nothing* close to pure, and he will know that."

24

GHOST

I'm not surprised when Alek is the first person I lock eyes with upon exiting Katie's room. I told him to keep an eye on her, and he will do as asked no matter how much unease my request causes.

"Send someone to her sister's house."

Alek takes a step back. "What did you do?"

"Send someone to her fucking sister's house before we lose the only bargaining chip we have."

Not waiting to see if he complies, I sprint to the far west side of the compound. Despite releasing the heaviness of my balls on Katie's back, my legs feel the weight of concrete.

I fucked up.

I put myself first.

And now our sisters will most likely suffer the consequences of my actions.

I pause just outside my sister's wing, confronted yet not surprised by the number of personnel outside her door. They're no higher than low-ranked goons, but I fail to remind myself of that while removing my gun from the holster on my hip. I pop a bullet between one goon's head when he tries to stop me from entering before the second registers my approach.

He's dead just as fast.

"If one more bullet leaves your gun, you'll find one in your sister's head." Kirill shifts his gun from me to Sofia's temple that's covered with sweat. She's shuddering in the aftermath of whatever drug they forced her to take and staring blankly at her soaked-through nightgown. "We had an agreement. I don't want any more bastard kids. She..." He glares at the blood pooled between Sofia's legs, "... was not part of our agreement, so *she*..." he spits out his last word in disgust, "... was taken care of."

He stands, aware I'd give anything to put a bullet between his brows but confident enough to know I won't. There are thousands of men to my one, so as much as I want to get Sofia and Lera out alive, I can't. They'll be dead before we exit the west wing.

Fear doesn't award me the knowledge.

Facts do.

For a man who swears he once loved my sister, Kirill treats her like dirt when he demands she clean up the mess the doctors made. "And make sure *it* is taken care of. I don't want to return."

I ball my hands so tightly my nails dig into my palms when he walks by me.

He has me clutched by the throat, and he fucking knows it.

25

GHOST

*S*ofia healed so well over the past four weeks you wouldn't know she almost bled to death after a botched abortion. Kirill has no morality when it comes to daughters. His punishments are brutal and immediate, much like our father's.

No, Kirill's relationship with Sofia isn't incest. She has no Bobrov blood running through her veins. She was conceived after my mother left my father for the cruel way he made her birth me since he believed the lies of his wife. He cut me out of her stomach in front of his men to make a martyr out of her, not caring that his blade sunk deeper than the sac keeping me safe.

He scarred me in the same manner Kirill did his own daughter when our brother died. He no longer wanted a child. He wanted a replacement for Milo who was killed at the hands of his enemies acting as friends, a son to follow in his footsteps.

He changed that day, and everything in our lives altered as well.

Our father and brother were killed when the Gottles sought revenge for an act that was not solely ours, and Kirill grew manic. He turned on everybody, including those he loved. But there are rules that protect him, rules that keep him safe, and it doesn't matter how many lives he destroys, he will forever be protected by the entity that commenced his demise.

I'm feared in my own right, but since I am the spare who had to prove his lineage with DNA, I don't have the support Kirill does. He is the leader, and I am his puppet. There's no other truth than that.

"Why is she whining?" Kirill slams down his goblet of wine before narrowing his eyes at Lera. "She has everything she asks for, yet she still whines."

"She is a child, Kirill. She doesn't know—"

Kirill ends Sofia's reply by clearing the table of dishware. It clatters to the floor with a thud, startling Sofia so much she balks. "If she does not know respect, she should be taught it."

When he signals a goon to move for Lera, I stop him by rising to my feet. I don't speak, but the firm harshness of my lips and vicious snarl says plenty.

If he so much as touches a hair on Lera's head, I *will* kill him.

Kirill mocks me with laughter. "This is what I get for allowing you to name her after your mother." His eyes are for me, but his words are for Sofia. "He thinks he has to save her because he failed to save your mother."

I stab my steak knife into the dining room table.

It was either the slab of rustic wood or Kirill's neck.

I went for the one that won't get my niece and sister killed.

"I didn't save my mother because I didn't know she needed saving. Our father loved her enough to let her go. Your mother was the only one who had a problem with that."

"He disrespected her."

Our discussion is not for an audience, but since my anger is high, I let it continue. "As you have Sofia your entire marriage." The women seated across from Sofia don't even try to hide their snickers. They think they're the next Katie, that they'll soon be moved to a room with opulent furnishings and endless guards to ensure their safety. They have no clue she is being held captive against her will.

With a wave of his hand, Kirill clears the room.

The reason for his sudden wish for privacy is disclosed when he murmurs, "Your sister promised me a son, and when she failed to do that—"

"I promised to fulfill your demands on the agreement you would let her go once it was done." My jaw is so firm, it minces my words. "I know our agreement, Kirill. You don't need to keep reminding me what will happen if it doesn't come true."

My body wears the scars of the time I tried to renege on my pledge. It was shortly after Sofia's ultrasound revealed she was having another girl.

War ensued. I lost half my men and half my face.

"It's been two years—"

"And twenty-seven miscarriages." I air quote 'miscarriages' so he can't act as if they were natural.

He killed the children he didn't want.

All of them were girls.

"And she didn't fail you." I make sure Sofia isn't in the firing zone before adding, "You failed her."

Before I can leave having the last word, Kirill snatches up my wrist. I'm so very tempted to announce my dislike of being touched by blowing his brains out over his pricy antique table, but I hold back the urge when I spot a pair of inquisitive eyes peering at me from across the room.

Just like Katie, Lera doesn't show fear.

"I'm growing impatient. Improve the odds this month. Make sure she is adequately prepared before insemination." His mocking grin announces what his mouth won't speak. He wants Katie's cunt drenched before insemination.

"And how the fuck am I supposed to do that without touching her?" My words roll off my tongue so effortlessly anyone would swear touching Katie is the last thing I want to do.

"I'm sure you'll think of something." He stands so abruptly he startles Lera out of the room. "You have this month. If you fail, she will be discarded, and we will move on to other ways of getting me an heir."

He thinks I missed his quick inhalation. I didn't. He makes the same whimpering noise whenever he considers moving my sister back into the master suite.

In his own sick and twisted way, he loves Sofia. He's just too fucked in the head to acknowledge that love doesn't have to come with carnage.

It is a family trait.

26

KATIE

My eyes lock with Ghost's when he guides me into a room that is scarce of light but with humidity in abundance. Everyone is wearing masks, but they're not Superman's glasses. You can tell who everyone is despite a bit of cloth covering part of their face. Ghost is even more notable since he is the only man who is badly marked.

"This isn't a ball."

He lied to me this morning when he said I was invited to a ball. I should have realized he was scheming something when he walked in angry and left with a spring in his step. I thought he was happy because my period ended yesterday, so the doctors would once again take over the insemination process, but I now realize that isn't the case.

He was happy to force me out of my comfort zone, to remind everyone surrounding us that I am as naïve as believed.

If my cheeks glow any brighter, the spotlights highlighting the sex acts happening in each glass cube won't be needed.

The hairs on the back of my neck bristle when Ghost leans in close once we reach the first cube. I've seen this act before, so although it ignites tingles inside me, it doesn't dampen between my legs in the same manner it did when Ghost entered my room wearing a tuxedo and bowtie.

He's been steering clear of me for the past month, only eating with me once a day instead of the usual three. It hasn't weakened the tension burning between us. It just dulled it to a manageable fire instead of a raging inferno.

"Not your fantasy today, *маленький ягненок.*" Since he's stating a fact, not asking a question, I don't bother to nod. I merely stray my eyes to the couple in the cube Ghost is guiding me toward.

This one is a little more enticing. The man is gripping a woman's hair in a similar fashion Ghost used to tether me to my knees in front of him months ago, but instead of him pulling away, the instant her hands land on his leather belt, he encourages her to free his cock from his trousers before ramming her head forward until she gags.

The choking noises she makes cause a conflict of emotions inside me. It should be a concerning noise, but all I can feel is the same sense of arousal I experience when Ghost curls my hair around his fingers when he thinks I'm asleep.

That is one thing that's remained regular since we left the ship.

"Will she choke?"

I can only see half of Ghost's grin since the scarred side of his face is covered by the tilt of his head, but I can't miss the cockiness on it. "No." He guides me closer, ensuring I can't miss a single vein on the man's cock as he rocks it in and out of the woman's body. "But you might. It doesn't just come down to skill. Size must be part of the equation too."

When I shoot my eyes to Ghost's face, a twitch in the bottom of my peripheral vision doubles the heat in the room. He's hard, and even hidden behind the pleats of his tuxedo's pants, there's no denying his cock is bigger than the man in front of me.

It is definitely a choke hazard.

"Why am I here?" I ask, disturbed by my thoughts.

Ghost waits for the man to finish down the woman's throat before drifting us toward another cube. "Because you've done as I've asked. You've followed the rules."

"It isn't like I have a choice." I wasn't meant to say that out loud. I've just spent so much time alone with Ghost lately, I'm forgetting he's meant to be my enemy.

He's also made my body feel things it's never felt, and in a way, he's kept me safe.

I haven't been beaten once in the last four months.

That's an eight-year record.

"You have a choice." Ghost doesn't remove his eyes off the couple fucking like rabbits in the cube in front of us. "You either submit and live or deny and die."

"They're not the best choices."

I see his smile fade in the reflection bouncing off the glass. "They're the only ones we have." He steps in closer so I'm the only one privileged to his words. "Do you see how she's swirling her clit between her thumb and forefinger?" After my eyes stray to the woman pleasuring herself while one man enters her backside and the other pushes his cock between her lips, I lift my chin. "That's what you should have done last night." I fail to breathe when Ghost locks his eyes with mine. "You flicked, but you didn't rotate. Flicking alone isn't enough to get you off."

I don't know what to reply to first. The heat roaring through my body or his underhanded acknowledgment that he's been watching me. I go for the latter. "You've been watching me?" When his smirk reveals his secret, I push out, "You said the cameras aren't monitored."

"They're not." The woman's screams as the guy in her ass slams home almost conceal his words. *Almost.* "But I take the occasional glimpse to make sure you're okay."

"At two in the morning?" I understand the rush I'm aiming for now, but since I'm ashamed of my body's desires, I only give self-stimulation a try in the wee hours of the morning.

Even now, I'm more embarrassed about the prompts of my body than wondering how many times Ghost has spied on me.

He said he was making sure I was okay.

That sounds like more than a captor checking on his slave.

It sounds like he cares.

"Don't, *маленький ягненок*. I am not your savior." As he peers through the cube to a group on the other side, he murmurs, "And if he ever suspects any different, he will order me to kill you." Gone is the playful glint brightening his icy blue eyes, replaced with a pair that belong to a monster. "And he'll make sure there isn't a single body part intact enough to be buried."

I can't breathe when I stray my eyes in the direction he's facing. My husband is standing across from us. His evil glare exposes everything Ghost said is true, not to mention when he signals for two men to move in. Their flashy suits threw me off for a minute, but the demands they bark out are always the same, and they always involve the removal of my underwear.

27

GHOST

"Who are they?"

Alek joins me at the front of the compound, his eyes locked on the three redheads being ushered out of a van. "They're from the latest shipment. These are the only ones the new doc could approve."

"Pure?"

His sigh gobbles up the first half of his reply, "Would they be here if they weren't?" My jaw is already tight, but it firms even more when he adds, "One is for you. Two are replacements."

My eyes snap to Alek during his last sentence, "He said she had a month. It's only been three weeks." I don't know who the man is speaking when I say, "He can also keep his whore. I don't want her." Only four months ago, I would have never spoken such words.

"You either accept her or donate her to the trade."

"Donate her to—"

Alek's growl cuts me off. He's pissed as fuck, and not afraid to show it.

"Did I ask your opinion?"

A blond lock that's freed itself from his manbun falls into his eyes when he *pffts* me. "Nah, but if you had, I would have told you to keep her the fuck away from him." He's no longer looking at the latest baby-making machines for Kirill. He's watching my sister.

His stare startles Sofia enough, she closes the shutters, then returns to her room.

"Sofia is not a part of this."

Alek has the hide to mock me with laughter. If it were any other man, he'd be dead. "Time to take off the rose-colored glasses, Ghost." He pats my back before instructing the latest inmates to follow him. "Food and lodging is supplied, but you'll need to do more than chores to remain a tenant at our fine establishment." He picks out the woman with the closest features to Katie before hooking his thumb to me. "Except you. You only need to listen to him."

I won't lie. When she stops in front of me with pleading eyes, my cock twitches. Its throb only lasts as long as it takes me to slide my eyes down her body. She's shaking like a leaf and not an ounce of determination is seen in her eyes.

She's lackluster and boring.

I'd rather continue stroking my cock to the image of Katie sleeping than claim this woman's virginity.

"Go with him." I gesture for one of the guards at the front to join us. When he does, I instruct, "Take her to housekeeping. If she proves her worth, she can stay there for as long as she likes."

"Thank you," the woman whispers, her voice heavily accented.

She won't be thanking me when she realizes the housekeeping staff works eighteen hours a day. Not even a whore does those types of shifts.

KATIE'S EYES lift to mine when I enter her bedroom. She's curled up on a single couch like a cat slumbering in the middle of the day.

"Where are the doctors?"

She shrugs before stretching out. "I don't know." As quickly as relief crosses her face, it is replaced with hope. "D-did you bring it?" Worry flares through her eyes when she holds them to mine, but not once do they float to her shoes.

A smile that shouldn't be anywhere near as bright since we're in a windowless room gleams when I pull a photograph out of my jacket pocket and slide it across the two-seater dining table.

She leaps off the couch and snatches up the image before I can blink. "Where was this taken? She looks happy." Her eyes float over a recent image of her sister before they lift to mine. "Does she look happy to you?"

When she spins the photograph around to face me, I say, "She looks like you."

Unaware that isn't a good thing, she murmurs, "She does."

After drinking in the image for almost a minute, she hides it between her mattress and the bedside table. I almost reprimand her for being sneaky before I remember it could be the last thing she'll do.

"He is getting restless." She knows who I'm speaking about simply from how I pronounced 'he.' "He is seeking a new wife," I answer the question I see in her eyes. "If he finds one, you will no longer be required."

"You mean I'll be dead."

It is the wrong time for me to relish her spunk, but it can't be helped.

Her eyes shift from my mouth to my eyes when I reply, "Yes."

"What will happen to Hailey?"

"Nothing," I lie.

There are no guarantees with Kirill. Everyone is a mark.

My smirk returns when she murmurs, "You're a terrible liar." She plucks out the photograph she just hid before plonking her backside onto her bed. "At least she won't die a virgin." She's making light of the situation so she won't show fear. "She's in love. That's why she looks like this." Her eyes remain locked on the image when she murmurs, "Is that why you said she looks like me?" In the quietness of her room, her swallow is audible. "Do you think I'm in love?"

"Don't, *маленький ягненок.*"

"I don't want to die," she confesses, acknowledging the real reason she wants me to believe she is in love with a monster.

"That choice is not yours to make."

"But it is yours."

I shake my head before I can stop myself. It could be my choice if I were willing to put her above Lera and Sofia, but I have so many years to make up to Sofia, and so much hurt, I can't do that. I didn't know Sofia existed until I was sixteen and causing trouble that would have landed me in jail. She was fifteen and seeking the brother our mother told her about on her deathbed. Her confession brought out a lot of revelations about my lineage and why I was dumped in a boy's home as a newborn, but it also arrived with a heap of fucking shit that's had me in the firing line a lot more than boosting cars from billionaires.

When Katie spots my headshake, she begs, "Don't let him do this."

"I don't have a choice."

"Bullshit! Tell him no." She stands and approaches me. "Tell him you want me for yourself, and that you will buy me off him."

I laugh that she thinks that is possible.

Does she not know this way of life at all? She has lived it for eight years, so she should know better. I learned quickly that the instant you're in the bratva, nothing is in your control. Not even your life.

I realize her game plan when she cups my face on the scarred half. She thinks I'm a marked-up mutt who'll do anything for affection.

Even being played by a whore with an untouched cunt.

I move so fast a squeak pops from Katie's lips when I snatch up her wrist. "Did I give you permission to touch me?" When she remains quiet, her eyes watering, I ask again, "Answer the fucking question! Did I give you permission to touch me?"

"N-no."

"Then why did you?"

Her lips quiver before she replies softly, "Because I don't want to die, and you're my only life line."

With a grip on her face that rolls tears down her cheeks, I drag her forward until we meet chest to chest. I'm taking my anger out on the wrong person, but that isn't unusual for me. I've done that for over two decades. "I am not your life line, маленький ягненок. I am the sole reason you're captive. If it weren't for me, you'd be free." I push her away from me via her face. "So maybe you should remember that the next time you think you can play me for a fool."

Not speaking another word, I exit her room then track down the first whore I see.

"You, come with me."

28

KATIE

No matter how desperate I am, I shouldn't have tried to convince Ghost I am in love with him. He saw right through the ruse I'm not even sure is a ruse.

He controls everything I do, so why wouldn't he control my emotions as well?

I eat when he brings me food.

I sleep when he tells me to rest.

So when he said my time is running thin, I went with a ruse I thought would bide me more time.

I was wrong.

Ghost usually hangs in my room every evening until I fall asleep, then he brings me breakfast in the morning.

It's past noon, and I've yet to eat.

This is stupid of me to admit, particularly after he brutally rejected me last night, but I miss his presence more than the yummy food he arrives with. He's moody and a little hard for me to read, but there are sides of him I don't think people often see—a man as brainwashed as me.

I'm pulled from my thoughts when a knock sounds at my door. It is unusual. Ghost never knocks. He enters without an announcement, usually when I am in the shower.

My unease drops when I recognize the grin of the man entering. I've only seen Alek a handful of times the past three months, but his friendly grin is always welcome.

"I've come to escort you to lunch."

"Oh." My brain is as empty as my stomach. "Ghost usually brings my food here."

"Yeah, aah..." He scrubs a hand over his prickly jaw. "He's *busy* this morning."

I hate the way he says busy and how it twists my stomach.

"Aah..." He stops my exit of the room by blocking it with his large frame. "You should probably change."

When he peers down at my black slacks and off-the-shoulder sweater, I follow the direction of his gaze. "What's wrong with what I'm wearing?"

Air bubbles in my churning stomach when he replies, "You need to wear white."

"Oh..." I cringe at my lack of vocabulary today before spinning on my heels and heading for the closet. It is full of pure white clothes that don't match my virginal status.

How can you feel pure when you're sullied with a man's sperm every day for months on end?

Even after changing in the bathroom, Alek still blocks the path.

"They need to go." The consequences of my actions catch up to me quickly when he points to my bra and panty outline underneath my almost see-through nightie.

"Ghost said if I walked the halls without panties, he'd kill me."

Alek's reply is like a slap to the face. "We're not on the boat anymore, Kate. Those leniencies don't apply here."

Nodding, hopeful it will hide my grimace, I return to the bathroom to remove the cloak of protection I didn't realize I needed until now.

It is the fight of my life not to let my knees shake when I follow Alek to the dining room. I feel as naked as the day I was born and without an ounce of protection. It is also the first time I've felt vulnerable in months.

The dining room is brimming with people. There are as many seated around the table now as there were at my wedding. I spot Ghost before he notices me. He's seated near the middle of the table. A beautiful redhead is on his lap, her head buried in his neck.

Now I stumble, and every man in the room takes notice—including Ghost. He slants his head to the side before narrowing his eyes down my body, his watch lingering on my budded nipples and the apex of my thighs as well as many of his numerous counterparts. There's just one difference between their stares. Ghost's eyes slit when they return to my face. The others gleam with unhidden wants.

"Sit." This order didn't come from Ghost. It was from Alek, who plonks me into a seat across from Ghost and his female friend. They seem close, but not even the tablecloth can hide the shaking of her knees. She's scared.

"Kate?"

I drift my eyes to Alek, the person who spoke my name. "Sorry. What did you say?"

"I asked what you'd like to eat."

"Um..." The table is brimming with an assortment of food, but I'm not sure my stomach can handle any of it. "I'm not hungry." My eyes shoot to Ghost when the rumble of his growl reaches my ears. He thinks I'm lying. For once, I'm not. I truly don't feel like eating. "I think I should go. I-I..." As my eyes pop out of my head, my hand shoots up to my mouth. "I think I'm going to be sick."

I race out of the dining room as fast as my quivering legs will take me, narrowly missing my husband's late entrance.

29

GHOST

*W*hen Katie crashes into Kirill during her race out of the dining room, I tell the redhead quivering on my lap to return to serving our guests.

"Y-yes, sir," she whispers, as frightened now as she was when I unexpectedly pulled her to sit on my lap.

I'm surrounded by Kirill's top men, so the last thing I want is for them to suspect I was hard from watching his wife enter the room in a nightgown that was designed to entice any red-blooded man.

She may as well have entered the room naked, and my cock is in full agreement.

He was standing at attention, something he failed to achieve last night.

Katie played me like a fucking fool, but instead of teaching her a lesson, I added to her beliefs.

It won't happen again.

I add an extra something to my mug of coffee before slouching low in my chair. Everyone buys my act that I don't give a fuck about anyone but myself—everyone but Alek.

"Her sheets—"

"I don't fuckin' care," I cut him off, aware of where he is going. The head housekeeper told me this morning that she hasn't been called to Katie's room this month to change her sheets.

Alek leans forward to pop his elbows on the table. "What if she's..." He makes a gesture with his hand that would mean nothing to a man who hadn't witnessed the artificial insemination of a woman the past three months. "She could be... *pregnant*," he whispers his last word.

"Good." I sniff, hopeful some of the snow I had this morning is still lingering outside my nostrils.

He looks at me like I'm insane. "Good? You think that's fucking good?" He *pffts* when I nod. "Then why did that whore enter and exit your room in under ten minutes last night if it weren't for her?" He nudges his head in the direction Katie just went.

He shakes his head in disgust when I murmur, "It had been a while, so it was a bit quick-winded."

"Fucking bullshit, Ghost. You haven't touched a single cunt not associated with Kate since she arrived."

I act as if he never spoke. "And this is the fucking point, right? That's why she's here." I lock eyes with Kirill across the room. "To have *his* baby."

"I don't know, Ghost, is that the point?" He leans forward again to ensure I can hear him over the ruckus occurring around us. "Because from where I'm standing, this seems a little more about you." When my brows furrow in confusion, he doubles their stitch. "I was only asked to bring Kate here once you arrived. And they specifically stated she was to be dressed accordingly."

"By whom?"

I'm anticipating for his head to nudge to the left, so you can picture my surprise when he gestures it to my sister.

"Why would Sofia request that?"

Before Alek can answer me, we're interrupted by the last man I want to exchange words with. "Was that what I believe it was?" While stuffing his hands into his pockets and rocking on his heels, Kirill strays his eyes to the door Katie ran through. "Has she bled this month?"

"No," Alek answers on my behalf when I can't get my clenched jaw to unloosen.

Kirill acknowledges Alek's answer but keeps his focus on me. "Have we tested?"

"No." My reply is short and abrupt. "I'll have the doctors do the necessary tests on Monday."

"Do it today." He tries to hide his smirk. He fails.

"I'll send someone—"

"*You* do it today." As his eyes connect with my sister across the room, he murmurs, "And bring the results directly to me."

He isn't hiding his wish to have a child with another woman from Sofia.

He's rubbing it in her face.

"I'll do it now." My comment shifts his focus from Sofia to me, which gives her the chance to make a quick getaway.

"Good." After a final stare, he dips his chin in farewell, then joins the hierarchy we're gathered for at the head of the table. Mafia royalty is in town, so Kirill will be on his best behavior.

The knowledge makes my stomps less obvious when I exit the dining room and enter the industrial refrigerator at the side of the kitchen. This one doesn't stock food. It is where Kirill keeps his vials of sperm for his virginal brides and the supplies needed for pregnant women.

Over the past two years, we've had brides last between one day and two months. Katie is the longest recruit, and it has also taken her the longest to get pregnant. That could have more to do with the fact I'm not pumping her food with fertility drugs than a lack of fertility.

After grabbing an early pregnancy test off the top shelf, I head to Katie's room. Guards still mingle, but there are nowhere near as many today as there usually are.

Upon entrance, I hear water running. Katie doesn't usually shower in the middle of the day, but with the pungent smell of vomit mingling in the air, a changeup is understandable.

I prop my shoulder onto the doorjamb, stuff the pregnancy test under my arm, then rake my eyes down her body. She's gained at least twenty pounds since arriving on the compound but barely any of that weight gathered in her midsection. Her stomach is smooth and flat, giving no shelter to the visual of her bare pussy.

She's continued to shave every day, and I'd be a liar if I said at one stage I didn't believe she was doing that for me. We've discussed many things the past few months while she's lying in bed with *his* sperm inside her, and my preference for a bare snatch was at the top of my conversation pieces.

Katie's was her wish for hideous curtains.

When I detect I'm being watched while dragging my teeth over my lower lip, I raise my eyes from Katie's glistening pussy to her face. Her budded nipples announce she's aware of what caught my attention, but she shifts her focus in a direction I never anticipated.

Her jealousy.

"Who was she?"

I act ignorant. "She?"

"The woman at the table." The quickest furl of her top lip inches mine higher. "The redhead sitting on your lap."

"Who she is, is none of your business."

She has nothing to conceal herself with. The glass is spotlessly clean, and the water removed the suds she was coating herself with when I arrived, but she tries to act like her shield is the hardest it's ever been. "She just doesn't seem like your type." She steps out of the shower and curls a towel around herself before spinning to face me. "She was scared."

"And why does that matter to you?"

I hide my shock well when she replies, "Because you don't like them scared."

"Says you." My angry tone doesn't shake her knees in the slightest. They remain as sturdy as my prissy attitude until she spots the pregnancy test.

"Is that why you're mad at me?" I laugh at her insinuation I like her enough to be mad. It snaps her eyes to mine and doubles their wetness. "Nothing I said last night was untrue."

"There is a cup in the box you need to pee in."

When I toss the test into her chest, she catches but ignores it. "I went too far because I was scared, but that doesn't make anything I said untrue."

"You need to uncap the test and dip it into the urine. The results should come up in a minute or two."

"Why are you ignoring me?"

I respond more to the anger in her tone than her worry. "Because you're not here for me! You're here for *this*." I thrust my hand at the test. "And for *him*."

"Then why isn't he here doing this?"

She balks as if I physically slapped her when I snap out, "The fact you think anyone here cares about you is laughable. You're a nobody. A captive. A slave. You are here for one reason and one reason only, and if you can't give us that, you'll be buried in the same garden his last three wives were dumped in, so you want to pray that test comes back positive because it is the *only* thing keeping you alive."

I don't know if I am insanely turned on or ropeable when she snarls out in Russian, "Fuck you."

"What did you say?"

When I storm for her, she doesn't blink. She stares me straight in the eyes while repeating the words she would have been too scared to speak only weeks ago. "Fuck. You."

Katie sucks in a quick, long draw when my hand shoots up to the column of her neck, but that is the only protest her body displays when I commence punishing her ignorance. She doesn't fight me or claw at my hand with her nails. She holds my gaze, which shows no fear whatsoever, not even as her pulse fades from my hold.

Fucking fight, I want to scream at her. *If you bow now, you'll never get back up.* But I can't release the words from my mouth, and I can't look out for more people than I already am. The plate is full. Sofia and Lera take up all the room.

With a roar, I remove my hand curled around her throat and put it through the mirror behind her head. It shatters into a million pieces and circles the floor around her feet with dangerous shards of glass.

To ensure she can't mistake the cold-hearted bastard I am, I smirk at the nicks the falling debris caused her delicate skin before repeating,

"Dip the test into the urine and wait two minutes. I'll send someone to get the results later."

I stop partway to the door when Katie whispers, "Alek."

"No." I crank my neck back to look at her. "You seem to have attachment issues." I drop my eyes to her stomach. "I suggest you bring that to heel before you're severely disappointed."

30

KATIE

*M*y heart hurts more than my neck. Ghost's grip was painful, but his stare was more hurtful than anything. He glared at me as if he hates me and I'm the cause of all his worries.

If the two lines on the pregnancy test are anything to go by, maybe I am.

"Kate." I drift my eyes from the positive test to the doorway where Alek's voice projected from. "What the fuck?" he murmurs to himself when his eyes drink in the smashed mirror and my nicked feet. "Was this a result of that?" He locks his eyes on the positive pregnancy test, cursing when he takes in how strong the result is.

I shake my head, my brain too confused for a better response.

"What happens now?" I ask when silence is the only thing that passes between us for the next several minutes.

Alek shrugs. "I don't handle this side of the trade."

I want to vomit for the second time for the way he says 'trade.'

I truly am only a commodity here.

"At least this will give Ghost some time." I can't hold back the urge to release the little nutrients in my stomach when he murmurs, "They brought in your replacements yesterday. They were settled in last night."

So that's why I heard sobbing.

From my crouched position next to the toilet bowl, I ask, "Who... um... who's in charge of them?"

I shouldn't be jealous about Ghost's attention being shifted to another of Kirill's many brides. However, I am.

"The docs took care of them last night, but it is usually Ghost's job." Hearing the groan I couldn't conceal, Alek shakes his head to hide his grin. "The fact you think he has a choice in the matter shows you're as clueless as him." When I peer up at him, blinking and mute, he murmurs, "He's not here to torture you, Kate." I stray my eyes across the splintered glass for barely a second before the scrub of his hand over his chin returns my focus to him. "He is all she has. She would have been dead years ago if he hadn't stepped up to the plate."

Now there's no doubt jealousy is heating my veins. It makes me hot and clammy at the same time, which is utter lunacy since I'm in a bathroom surrounded by glass and with a bruised neck.

"Lera is four." His chuckles about my bulging eyes bouncing around the bathroom. "So the only competition you'll get from her is the wish to live."

Reading between the lines, I whisper, "I'm not playing Ghost to stay alive."

My eyes shoot up to Alek when he replies, "I know. But he has so many people doing *exactly* that, he can't tell the liars from the cheats."

"Aren't liars and cheaters the same?"

He shakes his head but doesn't relieve my curiosity in the slightest. "I'll send someone from housekeeping to clean up the mess." He spins on his heels before looking back at me over his shoulder. "Dinner will be served in a couple of hours. You should eat."

"I'll try."

Happy with my reply, he dips his chin, then exits my room.

AN HOUR LATER, I'm startled by the arrival of a guest in my room.

It isn't Ghost or Alek.

It is my husband.

He walks into my room with a regal edge beaming out of him, depriving the air of oxygen in only a second. He is a handsome man of similar age to Ghost, but his evilness hides behind a perfectly flawless face and thick, dark hair. If I had to guess, I'd say he was mid-thirties. His eyes are the same blue shade as Ghost's but not as icy since they're not fanned by thick strands of dark lashes.

After taking in the bed I made immediately after leaving it, he strays his eyes to me. "Do you not rise when your owner enters the room?"

If he had a broom, I have no doubt it would have been cracked over my head by now. That is how Madame Victoria issued her punishments for forgetting your place—with a stern and quick crack over your head.

When I stand from the single-seater chair I've been sprawled on the past hour, the corner of his lips tug into a rye smirk. "It is a little too late now." I swallow to relieve my parched throat when he mutters, "You've not bled this month."

His question is more a statement, but I shake my head, nevertheless. I don't need to give him more reasons to reprimand me.

He appears pleased by my submissiveness. "And your care. How has it been?"

"Good. Your staff is kind and considerate."

"Including Ghost?" My breathing barely alters, but he must notice my quick inhalation. "Is he kind and considerate as well?" I shake my head, but he doesn't believe me. "Get on the bed." I don't get the chance to follow his orders before he drags me to the bed by my hair. His mean hold rips strands from my scalp and adds to the throbbing of my temples.

I scamper back with a frightened gasp when he hooks my ankle and pulls it on the stirrup that hasn't left the bed in months. He does up the restraints tight before raising my nightie and ripping off the panties I tugged on the instant Alek left.

He doesn't prepare my body for the intrusion before he stuffs two fingers inside me. He just thrust them in deep, his moan a mix of annoyed and turned on.

"You're untouched."

I nod, confident it will please him.

It doesn't.

A second after he frees my legs from the stirrups, I'm yanked to his feet by a brutal tug on my leg, then he stomps on my stomach.

31

GHOST

*W*ith my schedule depleted and my mind fucking scrambled, I arrive early for dinner. The food isn't even prepped yet, and my presence scares the staff who will bring out the smorgasbord of dishes.

My scars make me the monster they believe I am.

My traits undoubtably prove it.

I'm a fucking asshole in every meaning of the word and a stubborn prick too. Even when I'm wrong, I won't admit it. It is a trait I inherited from my father, and a trait I'll most likely die with.

It is clear from my exchange with Katie earlier today that she doesn't think I'm a marked-up mutt who will do anything for a bit of action, but I can't concede that to anyone. Not even the woman who is on my mind at all hours of the day and night.

I've been working toward this goal for years, and just as it gets within touching distance, I'm tempted as fuck to toss everything aside and start again. But I can't do that to Lera. She needs me more than Katie, but I'd be a lying bastard if I said I didn't want to act like Lera is not my responsibility.

Sofia laid in Kirill's bed, but I'm the only fucker cleaning up her mess.

Maybe it's time to return the favor?

Maybe I should step back and let her take responsibility for her decisions.

I'm sure Katie would make the fallout worthwhile.

My cock strains against the zipper in my pants just thinking about all the filthy things I could teach her. She'd love it too—almost as much as me.

I'm pulled from my dangerous thoughts when Alek enters the room. As he struts across the still reasonably empty space, his eyes drop to the packet of cigarettes in front of me. I haven't smoked since the day half my face was blown off from a gigantic blast. I just carry them around with me as a reminder of what the consequences could have been if I didn't have a metal cigar canister in the breast pocket of my suit jacket when I was ambushed without warning. It was my great grandfather's on my mother's side. I liked its intricate design and that it had survived many wars.

It didn't make it out of the carnage that day, but I did.

Alek's face tells the story, but I silently ask for details anyway.

"It was positive. Bright too." He sits across from me before tugging a cigarette out of the pack, placing it between his quirked lips, then lighting it. "You sure she bled last month?" He talks around the smoke lingering out of his nostrils before screwing up his face. "They're as stale as fuck."

"As is your taste in women." I'm making light of the situation so he won't notice my ticking jaw and clenched teeth. This is the reason Katie is here, to give Kirill the heir he craves, but I'd be a liar if I said it didn't piss me the fuck off to know she's carrying another man's child.

He hasn't touched her—he won't—but it doesn't weaken my anger in the slightest.

I'm as jealous as fuck—just like Katie was in the bathroom this morning—and it is becoming increasingly hard to ignore that fact.

When Alek arches a brow, announcing I failed to answer his question, I slouch low in my chair and say, "Her bleed was light, but it was there."

"Do you think it could have been implantation bleeding?"

"I don't fucking know."

I'm a liar, and Alek knows that. "You've been his babymaker for years. You know everything there is to know about the female reproductive system."

I stare at him, silently goading him to speak to me in such a manner again. He won't make it out of the dining room alive if he dares to adhere to my spur.

Like a man with a brain, he huffs before stabbing his cigarette out into one of the ashtrays provided, then he scans the room slowly filling with the Bobrov men. "Isn't she?" He leans in closer like he needs his vision checked before finalizing his question with a shit-eating grin. "When was the last time you turned down a whore and actually meant it?"

As I drink in the redhead I gifted to the kitchen staff, I murmur, "She's a sheep."

"Exactly," Alek replies with roaring laughter. "So you make her part of your flock." He locks his eyes with mine. They're brimming with silent mischievousness. "Unless you don't want a flock anymore. You're more a one-sheep man now."

"Shut the fuck up," I snarl at him in Russian, my scold interrupted by a ruckus at the end of the dining room.

Kirill wishes for such silence, but he isn't respected enough for that. There's only one person who can quiet a room of rowdy men like this. A virgin in white, ripe, and ready for the taking. Except this time, the appealing lines of Katie's cunt isn't on display for the world to see. It's hidden by a vibrant red splotch of blood and a pair of wobbly thighs dotted with sweat.

"What the fuck?" Alek murmurs at the same time my eyes shoot to Kirill.

When he fails to make a move for Katie as she sways in the breeze like a dead leaf on a hot fall day, I shoot out of my chair so fast, the wooden trim smacks into the drywall behind me.

"Gh-Ghost," Katie faintly murmurs before she falls forward at a rate almost too quick for me to reach her.

I swoop down low with only a second to spare, catching her before her head connects with the rigid marble floor. When I lift her to my chest, her arms and head flop back. She looks like she's dead. The only reason I don't believe my intuition is because of the fast rise and fall of her chest.

Her body is in shock and fighting not to shut down.

"Come with me," I order one of the doctors when he enters the room where the blood dripping from between Katie's legs has caused a puddle of red on the floor. "Now!" I bark out when he peers over my shoulder to get permission to follow my demand.

He either follows me or dies, and I won't even remove Katie from my arms to do it.

As I weave through the many hallways of the Bobrov compound, my stomps echo in the silence. Every man has left his station, leaving only the doctor and me to assess Katie once we reach her room.

"Her blood pressure is eighty-two over fifty-one, and her heart rate is 113 beats per minute." He wheels over the gurney her room should now be without since the insemination was successful. "We will administer saline bolus before commencing laboratory tests." My guns feel heavy on my hips when he pushes down on Katie's stomach, and she whimpers. She is in obvious pain. "Her abdomen is gravid—"

"What does that mean?" I interrupt his the medical talk.

He swings his eyes to me. "It means she is pregnant." When Katie groans through the pain of him pushing down low on her stomach, he murmurs, "Or at least she was." I shrug when he asks, "How much time has passed since her miscarriage started?"

"I saw her a couple of hours ago. She was fine then." I am a lying prick. She was surrounded by glass and had a bruise on her neck. A bruised I placed there.

I stop curling an invisible noose around my neck when the doctor lifts Katie's nightie. I marked her neck and nicked her feet with glass, but my boot got nowhere near her stomach, and there's no denying the imprint stretched from one side of her stomach to the next.

For the first time in the years I've known him, the doctor sounds sincere while saying, "If she is retaining product from a miscarriage, she could go into sepsis." Every threat I've ever given feels weak when he murmurs, "She could die."

"Then fucking fix her."

The equipment on his trolley of torture litter the floor when I lose my temper. I'm not solely angry about the tiny whimpers still escaping Katie's mouth as her eyes roll into the back of her head. I'm fucking furious about the doctor's whispered reply, "I don't know if I have the equipment needed to do an emergency D&C."

"You kill my nieces every couple of months, but now you have the hide to tell me you don't have the equipment to save Katie's life." My gun is removed before I know what I'm thinking, and a bullet rips through his temple even quicker than that.

Katie doesn't flinch or scream. She does nothing but writhe in pain, and it fucking kills me to witness. It thrusts me back to when Lera was cut out of Sofia's stomach two months too early, and the wailing screams she omitted when I found her in the dumpster outside the compound I was dumped in three decades earlier. She was naked and tossed away like trash.

I almost killed Kirill that day. The only thing that stopped me was that I couldn't get to him without killing Sofia as well. She guarded him with her body.

Things haven't been the same for us since that day.

I've killed hundreds of men, possibly thousands, but they've never been slow and torturous deaths like Katie is currently enduring. I put them out of their misery as fast as possible. I don't stomp on them and wait for the internal bleeding to take hold.

This is a cruel fucking death to a woman not deserving of the pain.

Just as my desperation reaches an all-time high, Sofia enters the room. "You need to get her temperature down." She races for the detached bathroom. "Sepsis won't be a problem unless the fetus doesn't break down properly." She switches on the faucet over the bathtub before checking the temperature. "Her fever has more chance of killing her now." When she returns to the bedroom, she gathers towels and washcloths the maids left this morning before dumping them on a shelf next to the tub. "If she starts shivering, you need to increase the water temp or remove her from it entirely." After swirling her fingers through the full tub, she slings her eyes to me. "Now, Ghost. You don't have a minute to spare."

The confidence in her tone has me jumping into action. After lifting a flopped and lifeless Katie into my arms, I enter the bathroom and walk us toward the tub. It is far too big for her tiny frame, so instead of gently lowering her into the lukewarm water, I toe off my shoes and slip in with her held in close to my chest.

"Gh-Ghost," Katie whimpers again when the tempered water graces her burning skin.

"Shh... маленький ягненок. I am here." I unbutton the top few buttons on my dress shirt then rest her head on my pec before removing the strands of red hair sticking to her sweat-dotted face. "I'm not going anywhere."

It only takes three swipes of the drenched cloth over her temple for the pained movements of her eyes to lessen, but it will take a lifetime for my guilt to end—if it ever does.

She's on the cusp of death, but instead of seeking solace during her final hours from a deserving man, her mouth only mutters one name on repeat.

Mine.

32

KATIE

*I*t takes everything I have to lift my head.

I'm weak, thirsty, and my temples are throbbing.

Is this what it would have felt like to be hungover?

"It is an IV line."

When Ghost's acknowledgment of the object I'm grabbing offers little assurance, I shoot up to a half-seated position.

Wrong move.

I'm too dizzy not to vomit. Mercifully, this time around, Ghost is prepared for the deluge. He catches the slop spilling from my mouth with a bucket before wiping away the frothy dribble dangling off my chin with a washcloth.

"Where am I?"

It is a preposterous question but give me some leeway. I'm having a hard time remembering anything, much less that I'm a captive of a Russian mafia entity.

After giving me a moment to take in the bland palate of my room, Ghost asks, "What do you remember before you fainted?"

"I fainted?"

After scrubbing the back of his hand over his scruff that looks much thicker today, tracing the tremor there, he jerks up his chin.

"I don't remember fainting." A tinge of pain stabs my chest when I scoot up the bed so I can rest my weary torso on the headboard. I'm lying on one of those plastic sheets I was dreading meeting when I went to my mother's gynecologist appointment with her two weeks before I was snatched.

Dr. Leonard has rules about not assessing his patients until they're eighteen. I thought my captives followed the same rules until I noticed the youngness of the women purchased and returned. Hardly any were over the age of seventeen.

The pain in my chest augments to a tightness when Ghost mutters, "You stopped bleeding yesterday. The doctor is confident you didn't retain any product. An ultrasound backed up his claim."

"Product?" I hold my hand out between us when his eyes lower to my stomach. His expression tells me everything. I'm no longer pregnant.

"What does that mean for me now? I'm tossed aside and disregarded like an unwanted toy." *Killed.* I don't voice my last concern because I don't want to give him any ideas. I'm also not sure if I should be grieving a child I never had the chance to acknowledge or my livelihood.

I peer at Ghost with lowered brows when he replies, "For now, you are to rest."

When he steps closer, I realize I'm not the only one showing signs of exhaustion. His clothes are crinkled, his eyes are circled by dark rings, and he looks gaunt like he hasn't eaten in days. "Why didn't you leave?" I ask when I realize the jacket tossed over the single couch in my room was the one he was wearing when I found out I was pregnant. It is hidden under two to three days' worth of clothes. "How long was I out?"

"Three days," he replies, answering the easier of my questions before moving onto the big hitter. "And I stayed because you asked me to."

Huh?

"I asked you to stay?"

He nods. "Multiple times."

I slice his smug expression in half by murmuring, "I don't remember that. The last thing I remember is my husband—" I stop talking when my heart falls from my ribcage. Forgetting that my every move is being scrutinized, I raise the hem of my nightie and peer down at my stomach. My bruise has healed some, but it fills my heart with pain as rapidly as it doubles Ghost's angry glare.

"He trod on me," I murmur through a hiccup. I'm lost as to why he would do that. I'm here to have his children, but the instant he finds out I'm pregnant, he forces me to miscarry.

"Who?" Ghost asks, for once in the dark. "Did Kirill do this to you?"

I don't know who Kirill is, so I shrug.

"Answer me, Katie. Did the man you married hurt you?"

It takes me a few seconds to get over my shock that he called me by my name, but eventually my bewilderment ends, and I bob my chin.

It dangles an inch above my chest for a nanosecond before Ghost curses a Russian curse word, yanks his gun out of his hip holster, then storms for the closest and only exit.

I don't know if it is fear of being left alone after being stomped on or something far more sinister, but seconds after he stalks down the hall, leaving my door wide open, I yank out my IV, almost vomit in the process, then take off after him on foot.

Ghost knows the floor plan so intimately, we reach an office on the other side before an ounce of breathlessness hits me. I gasp like my lungs are desperate for air when I recognize the face behind the big, mannish desk. It is my husband.

"Why the fuck would you force her to have an abortion?" Ghost thrusts his hand to his left, proving he's spiraled so deeply into his anger, he hasn't noticed me on his right. "She's here to give you an heir."

"Exactly," replies the man I now know as Kirill before he shifts his eyes to me. "An heir, not a whore."

I'm lost to what he means, but Ghost isn't. "You couldn't tell if it was a girl. She wasn't far enough along."

"Medical professionals would disagree with you."

When Kirill glares at me, daring me to go against his lie, I take a step back. I know my place, and right now, I'm not sure Ghost has the power to protect me. Don't get me wrong. He is steaming mad, and his gun is directed at my husband's head, but his focus is no longer on Kirill. It is to his left, to a small child and a woman I swear I've seen before. They're being thrust into the room by a goon with a watermelon head. He has a gun butted at the woman's temple, and he is cruelly clutching a child I'd guess to be three or four.

Mercifully, the little girl seems oblivious to the danger a woman with oddly identical features is facing. She wiggles to get out of her mother's captor's hold before racing across the room that's so stifling hot, I'm sweating as much now as I was when I woke up on the floor of my room in a pool of blood.

"дядя."

I don't understand the word the little girl speaks, but I'm reasonably sure it isn't Father. Master Rudd had many children. None of them referenced him that way.

My heart pains for Lera when she is demanded to let go of Ghost's leg. "Now, Lera!" When she fails to pay Kirill any attention, he orders one of his goons to move in.

"Touch her again, and I will kill you." Ghost's growled words leave no room for argument. He means every word he speaks, and it has me confident I am on the right team.

Against the pleasure of his boss, the goon steps back from Ghost with his hands raised in the air.

I realize part of Ghost's threat is for me when he gathers up Lera then uses his spare hand to guide me out of the room. He mumbles several curse words under his breath during the seemingly long walk back to my room.

Once we enter, he places Lera down, then shuts the door. "My left pocket," he murmurs in Russian.

Lera's adorable face lights up before she rushes for Ghost's jacket hanging over the couch.

"Do you always walk around with jellybeans in your pocket?" I ask when she pulls out four small packets.

He waits for the color on Lera's cheeks to cool a smidge before replying, "I do when home. Lera is diabetic. Stress can cause her sugar levels to drop."

He shifts on his feet to face me head-on when I ask, "Who is she to you?"

"She is my niece." I peer at him weirdly when a smirk I haven't seen him wear once the past four months notches his lips high before he nudges his head to the mattress. "Bed." My groan isn't audible, but Ghost hears it. "Now, *маленький ягненок.*" It dawns on me that his bossy nature is how he shows he cares when he snaps out to Lera, "One more, then put them away. *Слишком много сладостей заставит ваш желудок урчать, как медведь.*"

I slant my head to hide my smile with my hair when Lera pleads, "Two?" She holds two fingers in the air to amplify her request. "And one for Mama." I'm a stranger, yet I still recognize her lie a mile away. Her eyes are as gluttonous now as mine were months ago.

When Ghost dips his chin, she digs through the bags of candy until she finds three pink jellybeans, then she stuffs the bags back into his pockets and skips to my side of the bed. She peers at me in silent question before twisting her torso to interrogate her uncle in the same manner.

"Katie, this is Lera." After tugging her closer to my bed, Ghost adds, "Lera, this is Katie." His accent is thicker when he says Lera's name. "She is..."

When words elude him, I say, "Pleased to meet you." When I offer her my hand to shake, she leaps onto my bed and throws her tiny arms around my neck.

Her hug melts my heart and pricks my eyes with tears.

It is the kindest gift I've been given over the past eight years.

"Thank you," I murmur when she hands me one of her jellybeans. "But I thought that was for your mama?"

I realize her English isn't as strong as Ghost's when she shifts her eyes to him so he can translate what I said. When he does, she pops one jellybean in her mouth before tightening her grip on the remaining one.

"Oh, we're sharing?" She can't understand me, but my tone alone gets her nodding. "Okay." While ignoring the tears welling in my eyes, I slip the jellybean between my lips and moan like it is the most delicious thing I've ever tasted.

It very well could be.

"Yum."

Lera giggles like the small child she is before turning her begging eyes to her uncle.

"One more," he concedes only two pleading beats later.

I'm out of line with my questioning, but with it being the only thing taking my mind off my thumping head and aching insides, I run with it. "Where is her father?" It is obvious Ghost is her only male role model, so it has me curious as to where her father went.

"He is here," Ghost answers, his focus not on me. "But he doesn't want her." He returns his eyes to me. "He doesn't want daughters."

Putting two and two together, I murmur, "Kirill."

Ghost doesn't answer me, but his stiff jaw tells me everything I need to know.

The already stuffy conditions grow worse when he asks, "Did he do tests as stated?"

My teeth crunch together when I recall the test Kirill did before determining my pregnancy wasn't viable. "Um... he... ah... did a test."

"An ultrasound?"

As my stomach flips, I shake my head.

"Then what did he do?"

I'm saved by answering when a knock sounds at my door. It isn't Alek as suspected. It is a lady with dark hair and kind eyes.

Lera's head pops up when she asks, "Должен ли я взять, Lera?"

"Rusha!" She sprints for Rusha as quickly as she did Ghost earlier. After leaping into her arms, she rubs her candy-stained face over the collar of her maid's outfit.

"I'll come check on her later." Before Rusha can leave with a sleepy Lera, Ghost adds, "Check her sugar levels. She was pale before she scoffed down half a packet of jellybeans."

Rusha dips her chin in understanding before leaving my room, closing the door behind her.

With Ghost's attention fixated on me, I am afraid he is going to return to his earlier interrogation, so you can imagine my surprise when he asks me what I'd like to eat.

"I'm not really hung..." I swallow my words when anger hardens his features. "Grilled cheese?" We've shared grilled cheese sandwiches multiple times the past three months. It was a staple in my childhood years but more a luxury now.

I joked last week that if I ever get out of here, I will have a grill press placed in my stovetop and will have ghastly colored curtains throughout my house to ensure it would never represent the same bland palette I've faced every day the past four months.

"Pickles?"

When I nod, Ghost pulls his cell out of his pocket and dials a number he knows by heart. Once he's placed an order for two grilled cheese sandwiches and a jar of pickles, he dumps his cell onto the table then undoes the top couple of buttons on his dress shirt. It sparks a memory of my cheek resting over his heart and him whispering kind words into my ear.

I shake my head, certain it is making things up.

Ghost isn't as cruel as some of the men I've been associated with the past eight and a half years, but there's no way he comforted me in a moment of need. I don't think he has a nurturing bone in his body.

"Can I shower?" A good soak will clear up some of the muddled confusion in my head. "I feel gross."

Ghost nods, but his eyes don't lift from the floor. "Make it quick. A doctor will be here to check on you within the hour."

I grimace more than I feel grateful. The only doctors I've been associated with the past few years are the ones wanting to clarify my purity before sullying it.

Will that be the case this time around as well?

33

GHOST

"*S*omething isn't right."

Alek props his ass onto the table Katie usually eats at before straying his eyes to the bathroom still sounding with running water. "I've been saying that for a while."

"He couldn't have known she was carrying a girl. It was too soon."

He folds his arms over his chest. "Did you ask the doctor what test he ordered?" I give him a leering look. "Oh, that's right. Dead men can't talk." His chuckles are breathy. "Want me to ask her?"

"No." His eyes snap from the bathroom door to me when my abrupt reply leaves no room for misunderstanding. If he makes Katie feel as uncomfortable as I did earlier, he'll join the good doctor in the industrial freezer out back. "I'll find out." *It just won't be by asking Katie.*

She almost died, but she was more concerned about eating my sister's jellybean than acknowledging that.

We fucked her over good, and I hate that I'm the one who snuffed the gleam in her eyes I was so fucking desperate to relight.

"What do you want to do, Ghost?" Alek eventually asks, his tone as low as my mood.

"First, get rid of them." I nudge my head to the cameras in Katie's room. "Kirill knew I was coming. That's how he got Sofia and Lera there before I popped a bullet between his brows, so he's either watching me, or he has a nark shadowing my every move." Alek nods, agreeing with me. "Then bring me some blow like I fucking asked you to do days ago."

I'm jittery and in pain without drugs in my system, not that I'll ever admit that.

"If you want to cut your fuse even shorter than it already is, you can get that shit yourself."

Alek drags a chair over to a camera perched in the far corner of the room before removing a utility knife from his pocket. He won't leave a single wire intact, much less a microlens.

As he yanks down the first device to stomp on it, I enter the bathroom to check on Katie. She fell in love with showers on the ship, but they've never lasted this long.

I follow a wet track of footprints from the shower cubicle to the vanity when I discover it is empty. Katie is standing in front of the vanity mirror drenched from head to toe, and not a snick of fabric covers her body.

She is staring at her marked and bruised stomach, cradling the non-existent bump in her shaky hands. She's so emersed in her fear she doesn't realize I'm in the room until I say, "He won't hurt you again. I'll make sure of that."

I don't know where my pledge came from or why she's the only one who's been deserving of it for the past eight years, but I mean it.

"Now come and eat. You'll need your strength."

Not giving her the chance to ask what battle I'm about to force her into, I rejoin Alek in the main part of the room. "I need you to find out where he took the other women."

"Women? What other women?"

I glare at him like I know he isn't as stupid as he is portraying. "His new Mary's."

I wonder how far out of the loop I've been when Alek replies, "He sent them to the trade. I thought you were told that?"

"No one has told me anything." I take a breather to calm down before grinding out through clenched teeth, "I need a replacement brought in." This is a dick move, but when you're desperate, you run with anything. "If you can't find one, bring me the redhead from the kitchen."

"The whore you were gifted without taking her for a test run?" I give him a look. It has him backpedaling in an instant. "I'll see what I can rustle up. Virgins are fucking pricy." He nudges his head to the bathroom door Katie is exiting. "I'm sure you're aware of that." Confident she heard him, he greets her with a grin before exiting the room, taking the smashed surveillance cameras with him.

After locking her eyes with the holes the camera wires left behind, Katie mumbles, "I thought you said they weren't monitored."

"They weren't, but anyone can log in and look at them." *Believe me, I have multiple times the past three months.* "Now they won't be able to." I pull out her chair before demanding she sit. My command isn't unusual, but my chivalry is. I don't pull out chairs or hold open doors. I give a command, and you follow it, but I'm finding it hard this time around.

I need a line or three of coke.

I could blame my urges on the awkwardness. We've eaten together multiple times in the past four months, but it's never been this awkward.

"What has your mind, маленький ягненок?" It is an insensitive question after what she's been through, but I fucking loathe silence.

She places down half of the grilled cheese sandwich she has barely touched before locking her eyes with a section of carpet that was replaced since it was filled with the doctor's blood and brain matter. "Am I meant to grieve?" I'm lost as to what she means until she murmurs, "She wasn't wanted, but she was still a part of me." She returns her eyes front and center. "I feel like I should, but it also feels stupid." As she wets her lips, she fiddles with the hem of her nightie. "I also haven't had anything that was solely mine for a very long time. She would have been mine... well, for at least nine months."

Her eyes rocket to mine when I murmur, "She wouldn't have lasted that long. Not if she was a she. And if it was a boy..." I stop talking as anger steamrolls through me.

Mistaking my silence as me not having an answer, Katie murmurs, "I'd be dead the instant he was born."

Although she isn't asking a question, I jerk up my chin. "So, yes, grieve, but don't ask me what you should grieve, *маленький ягненок,* because I am as confused as you."

The truthfulness of my statement slackens the pain strained across her face. It also gets her eating. She should be starving. She hasn't eaten in days.

And neither have I.

34

KATIE

*T*he doctor did nothing invasive. He checked my pulse, took my blood pressure, then asked if I had any issues keeping down the food Ghost and I shared. When I shook my head, he gave me the all-clear to resume normal activities before sheepishly leaving my room.

He was kind, if not a little scared.

When he left my room, I asked Ghost what happened to my last doctor.

He didn't answer me. Instead, he merely smirked before telling me to rest.

The doctor had only just given me the all-clear, so the last thing I wanted to do was crawl into bed, but what else did I have to do? So bed has been where I've been the past several days.

Ghost hasn't left my room either, but he's been occupied with his cell and keeping the table in my room filled with an endless number of desserts and flavorsome breads. We've talked on and off, but the hour-long conversations we've had previously have been on the scarce side. I think that may be more due to exhaustion than anything. I can't imagine an armchair being overly comfortable to sleep on for one night, much less six.

When Ghost releases a long string of curse words, I don't think any of his messages he's sent this morning have been well-received. He's more agitated than usual.

"гребаный ублюдок," he roars before tossing his cell phone to the floor with such force it shatters on impact.

As his hands shoot up to his hair, he unshadows the scarred side of his face. He always sits a certain way, his head angled to hide his marks. But right now, he is exposed, and the image is more beautiful than I could have ever imagined. It doubles the vision in my head of him comforting me, which brings me to the brink of believing they're true.

The buttons on his shirt are undone, and he hasn't put on the shoes he toed off last night. Despite the carnage I feel brewing, he looks casual and relaxed.

When he grimaces in pain, my first thoughts are to run to him, but I hold back. Just. "What's wrong?"

"My head." He more rips at his temples than massages them. "It's fucking pounding."

Recalling the way Master Rudd's wives soothed him during one of his regular migraines, I slip off the bed and slowly pad Ghost's way. I hate the shake my hands have when I raise them to his face, but it can't be helped. I can't massage his temples without touching his scars, but he's made it obvious more than once that I'm not allowed to do that.

His hot breath hits my cheeks when I circle the throb at the sides of his forehead, but he doesn't snatch up my wrist as anticipated. He surrenders to my gentle touch, his head slightly flopping back.

Its drop tugs me forward, making us more aligned and adding to the bristling heat teeming between us.

An unexpected smile tugs at my lips when Ghost places his hand over mine and rotates my fingers in a circular motion. "Just like when you stroke your clit... swivels, not jabs."

Seemingly feeling my smile, Ghost's eyes pop open. They show he's in pain, but they're not as murky as they were on the cargo ship and more free than they've ever been the past three days.

My breathing shallows when he drags his thumb across the goose bumps dotting along my neck. He's tracing the effect he has on me while doubling the rise of the bumps.

I realize my error when he murmurs, "I shouldn't have marked you. You just..." He doesn't speak another word. Instead, he removes my hand from his left temple and glides it down his face—the unmarked side of his face.

My heart launches into my throat when he does the same to the right side, but instead of going straight down, he outlines the marks scoured into his skin with my fingertips.

He stops halfway down before yanking his hand away. He doesn't take mine with his though, and I don't remove it. I take in the mottled tautness of his scars with my fingertips before adding my thumb into the mix. I trace it over his brow that's doing a good job of disclosing how close he came to losing his eye.

The difference in the age of his scars is obvious. The one similar in length and size to Lera's seems old, almost the same age as him, but the smaller, darker ones are fresh. They've not been there anywhere near as long.

I knew this because of the difference in his face from our first meeting to our second, but I feel privileged to be given the chance to make my own assessment.

I lock eyes with Ghost when he asks, "Scared?"

"No." I shake my head to add to my short statement. "Not of you."

"Who then?" I realize his thumb is still on my neck, counting my pulse when I swallow harshly about his ability to read me. "Who, маленький ягненок?"

Although this will most likely get me in trouble, I murmur, "Lera." When his brows furrow, I push out quickly, "Not her scar. She is so adorable, I barely noticed it." I take a quick breath, relieved my confession lowered the agitation on his face. "I'm scared as to why she has it and why it is almost identical to yours."

"We were born by the same knife." He pulls my hand down from his face, bites the tips, then orders me back to bed.

"I don't need more rest," I whine. "That's all I've done the past week." He hits me with a stink eye that has me immediately backing down. "I prefer my imagination than reality."

It dawns on me that I said my statement out loud when Ghost replies, "What are you imagining, *маленький ягненок?*" I don't even get in half a shrug before he barks out, "Don't lie to me."

"You holding me." My heart patters along with my hands when the memory rolls through my head again. "We were wet, and you promised to take care of me. And—"

"I held you while you cried until you fell asleep."

I startle, my mouth falling open. "But not just now. You did it while I grieved my family too, didn't you?"

He doesn't answer my question.

That's okay. I know the truth.

He doesn't hate me.

He hates that he has to hurt me not to hurt himself, and proof of that arrives when the doctor from three days ago returns to my room with another man in tow.

My husband.

35

KATIE

The pieces of the puzzle were already coming together, but they're forced into place when Ghost rejects Kirill's request to inseminate me. "She's still recovering—"

"Statistics prove the chance of conception after a miscarriage is significantly higher."

"She didn't miscarry," Ghost bites back, his hands balled into fists. "You fucking stomped on her."

When Kirill's eyes snap to mine, as icy as death, I lower mine to the floor. He issued his voiceless threat after I had spilled the beans to Ghost, so how can I be punished for it?

I inwardly mock myself. *This man is a monster. He will never act rational.*

And that's proven without doubt when Ghost's third denial angers Kirill enough to harm his own child. He grabs Lera so firmly she whimpers before he thrusts her in front of multiple red rays that light up her chest like a Christmas tree. "I let her live because you pledged me a Bobrov heir."

My stomach gurgles when Ghost replies, "And I've gifted you many wives and multiple positive tests."

"That all turned out to be girls!"

"How the fuck is that my fault?" Ghost asks, his eyes never once leaving Lera. His voice is raised, but the calmness on his face promises her that she isn't in any danger. I also believe she is the reason he is speaking in English so she won't understand the brutality of her father. "I can't alter your sperm so only boys remain."

Lera can't understand them, but she can feel the tension. A big salty blob falls down her cheek a second before a painful sob whimpers from her mouth.

She's scared, and it affects me more than I can ever explain. I was fourteen when I was taken. That is a decade longer than Lera has lived. She should be playing with dolls and getting a messy face while making mud pies. She should not have her life threatened daily.

Especially not for me.

"Do it."

Ghost's eyes sling to me. They're full of shocked and bewilderment.

"My husband wants an heir, and I am here to give him one." Kirill seems displeased by my submissiveness. Ghost is just as ropeable, but he knows he doesn't have a choice—not if he wants to continue protecting Lera. "I know my place."

When I slip onto the bed and place my legs into the stirrups the doctors pulled up the instant they arrived, a man with a full beard and a round stomach steps closer. He's holding the vial I'm all too familiar with, but mercifully, it is without the duck beak that causes discomfort.

Just before he reaches the foot of the bed, Ghost shoots his hand out, gripping him by the lapels. "Let me." He shifts his deadly gaze to Kirill. "She's still bleeding, so isn't this where I'm meant to step in?" His reply proves he's overseen my care because he told me when I woke that I stopped bleeding a day earlier.

"Very well." Kirill waves his hand through the air like a king gesturing for the jester to entertain him.

I wait for Ghost to gather the vial from the doctor before pulling the sheet across my legs for modesty. Once I'm certain Ghost is the only one viewing me from the waist down, I tug my panties to the side, then slant my head away.

He's always super cranky when I look at him while he inseminates me.

The mattress dips under Ghost's weight, and he spreads me with his fingers like he does every insemination, but the warm liquid isn't squirted inside me. It dribbles a few inches in front of my backside before soaking into the bedding.

What the?

Kirill mistakes my shock as discomfort. After peering down at the empty vial Ghost dumps onto the stainless-steel trolley, he pushes Lera away from him with an unkind shove, then gestures for the doctors to follow him out.

I wait for Lera's nanny to collect her from my room before scooting up the mattress and staring at the murky blob crusting the sheets. Some cum spills out during the insemination process, but it is never that much, and there is no residue on me. I am cum-free.

On the verge of hyperventilating, I slip off the bed and enter the bathroom to pace.

He's going to get my sister killed.

She's going to die.

And Lera—God.

"What do you think you were doing?" I ask Ghost when he props his shoulder on the doorjamb of the bathroom. He looks pleased with himself. I have no idea why. "I have a week. One measly week and you ruined it by pressing his semen into the mattress." When he looks at me surprised, I *pfft* him. "I know what you did. The vial got nowhere near my vagina." I march toward him. "You need to tell them you inserted it incorrectly. Ask for another batch."

"Fuck no," he replies with a stern shake of his head. "I said I wouldn't let him hurt you. This will hurt you."

"You have to do it!" I'm yelling, but it can't be helped. I am panicked out of my mind. "He will kill Hailey." Nothing but pain radiates in my voice when I murmur, "And Lera."

"Lera is not your responsibility—"

"Yes, she is," I interrupt, still shouting.

"No, she fucking isn't," he fights back, stepping closer. "She is *my* niece, *my* blood, and that makes her *my* responsibility."

"You made her *my* responsibility when you brought me here."

I'm so angry, my hand raises to slap him across the face before I can comprehend how foolish I'm being. Ghost snatches up my wrist, but his grab only slows the movement of my hand. It doesn't wholly end it.

My slap is barely a fly swat across his cheek, but it doubles the redness of his face. "I'm trying to help you, маленький ягненок. I'm trying to save you, yet you hit me."

"I don't want you to save me! I want you to... to..." I no longer know what I want, especially not with him standing inches in front of me. His breath is hot on my skin, his touch burning. I'm lost in the tension, bewildered by every inch of him—his fit, taut body, beautiful eyes, and handsome face. I am trapped. "I want—"

Ghost answers the fiery request I'm too afraid to say out loud with his lips. Our teeth clash when he seals his mouth over mine then spears his tongue between my lips. His kiss is rough and unhinged, painful and blistering.

It represents him to a T.

"Fuck, Little Lamb," he murmurs over my mouth before dropping his lips to my ear. He bites on the fleshy skin tag before laving it with his tongue. "Is this what you want? Is this what you fucking need?"

Not waiting for me to answer, he crowds me against the now-closed bathroom door and lifts me until my legs curl around his waist, his lips never leaving mine. He kisses and licks the soft skin under my earlobe before his focus shifts to my thrusting chest.

"Tell me to stop." He's not looking at me, so he can't see my head shake, but his finger traces the lace on my bra peeking out the top of my nightgown, nevertheless. "He will kill you if you don't."

"He's going to kill me no matter what." Ghost's eyes lift to mine when I murmur, "This way, at least I'll die happy."

I touched myself the night he stormed out in anger, hopeful it would prove it wasn't his touch I craved.

My efforts didn't arouse a single tingle.

Nothing can replicate the sparks his attention shoots through me, not even when he is doing something as cruel as gripping my throat.

When Ghost spots the honesty in my eyes, he mutters, "Then I better make it worthwhile."

Before I can comprehend what he means, he hoists me up the door, drags my panties to the side like I did only minutes ago, then rubs his stubble over my aching slit.

My thighs tremor when he growls against my heated skin, "*We'll* die happy."

I don't reply. I can't. I can do nothing but clamp my thighs around his head in response to him spearing his tongue inside me. I gasp, then jump a little, shocked by the sensitivity bombarding me. I feel hot and cold at the same time, and a blistering of stars is forming in front of my eyes.

A smile shines through Ghost's eyes when he peers up at me over my erratically thrusting chest. His lips arch high before he devotes the focus of his tongue to my clit.

"Ohhh…" I bite the inside of my cheek, fighting like hell not to reach the high notes. His attention has me wanting to sing, but I can't hold a note to save my life.

I crawl up the wall when my endeavor to bite back my moans triples Ghost's efforts to unravel me. He pushes his thumb down on my clit before swiveling it. His hands on me feel ten times better than my own, not to mention the stabs of his tongue as he rams it in and out of me.

Some of the blast must have ripped through his mouth as his tongue is calloused on one side. It adds to the sensation making me a giddy, sweaty mess.

"Gh-Ghost," I stutter, feeling out of control and worried. "I'm… I can't… I'm meant to please you."

"Then please me, *маленький ягненок*. Come on my face like a good little slut."

I don't know what turns me on more, his filthy mouth or the finger he pushes inside me. Slowly and painfully, he stuffs the fat digit in deep, furls the tips, then hits my clit with rapid-fired licks of his tongue.

"Ohhh..."

I rake my fingers through his hair and hold on tight until my knuckles go white. I'm burning all over, singing internally. I am mere seconds from detonation even though I'm not really sure if it is something I am meant to be cashing. Out-of-control fires are damaging, blasts are dangerous, so why the hell do I feel like I'll never breathe again if I don't give in to the sensation burning me alive?

As the butterflies take flight in my stomach, I buck against Ghost's finger and mouth.

Heaven. I was right. That is what this is.

I close my eyes, giving in to the overwhelming rush bombarding me.

Then it happens.

I come—loudly.

Except this time, Ghost doesn't clamp his hand over my mouth. He lets my moans ring through the compound, sealing our fate as brutally as mine when I was snatched without warning.

The recollection weakens my shudders and opens my eyes, but they also confirm I don't want this to end. Our fate is sealed, we can't alter it, so I plan to go out with a bang.

"Please..." I beg, writhing. "I want—"

"Me." Ghost wipes his drenched mouth with the back of his hand before standing so we're eye to eye.

He's stating a fact, but I nod my head anyway.

I do want him. Badly.

His lips tug into a smirk before he murmurs, "Then take what you want, маленький ягненок. I am your whore for the taking."

My mind goes wild, but not once does it veer toward my freedom. I think back on all our exchanges, and every memory leads me in the same direction.

To me on my knees the first day we officially met.

"Fuck, маленький ягненок," Ghost mutters when I push him back far enough I can wedge myself between him and the door. My body is still achy, particularly after the violent shudders it just endured, but the last thing I experience is pain when I bring myself to my knees.

Ghost is hard and straining against the zipper of his pants, and my mouth is salivating at the thought of tasting him.

I just wish I didn't lack confidence. I have no clue what I'm doing. None whatsoever.

"Take it out," Ghost demands, his voice as rough and commanding as ever.

When I do, the last of my confidence is pinched. He is much thicker and longer up close.

There's no way it will fit in my mouth much less anywhere else.

"Don't worry, маленький ягненок. You were designed for me. I'm sure you can take it." Ghost strokes his cock with each word he speaks, and it drives me wild with desire. "Now open up like a good little cum slut and flatten your tongue. I want as much of my cock in your mouth as possible."

His thighs twitch when I do as asked, but they don't remain clenched until my tongue takes matters into its own hands. It swipes across the crest of his cock, gathering up a bead of pre-cum there before it can be absorbed by his boxers.

Ghost curses in Russian before lunging forward, forcing his big cock into my mouth.

It feels foreign to start with, then gagging before it eventually settles on exciting. He doesn't ram himself in so deep that tears spring in my eyes like Master Rudd's wives or rip my hair from my scalp when he weaves his fingers through the glossy locks. He merely rocks his cock in and out, growling when my tongue swirls along the vein throbbing at the bottom.

"Your mouth feels so fucking good wrapped around. It is better than I imagined."

Loving that he's thought about this as much as me, I take as much of him into my mouth as I can, moaning that he's filling me like no one else could. He's so big and thick I barely get more than his knob in, but his grunts and moans keep the temperature in the bathroom scorching and the wetness between my legs saturated.

Accidentally, I bite down on Ghost's cock when a cool smoothness hits between my legs. Ghost adjusted his footing. Instead of both legs being on each side of my thighs, he's forced one between them, the toe of his boot a mere inch from my throbbing clit.

I should feel dirty when I grind down on the shoe that's been dotted with blood more than once, but I don't. Ghost's filthy mouth as he praises my skills makes me feel wanted and sexy, and if the saltiness pumping out of Ghost's cock is anything to go by, he's enjoying the naughtiness as much as I am.

"Grip me at the base, маленький ягненок. Stroke me while fucking me with your wicked mouth."

"Like this?"

Ghost's head falls back with a moan when I circle my hand around the bottom of his cock and pump him. I almost got to second base the weekend before I was kidnapped, and Blaire and I joked often about how we're meant to pretend we are making butter to get a guy off.

We had a field trip to a farm before summer break. All of our grade was joking about the butter-making experience the entire summer.

Seems as if it wasn't a joke.

"Your hand feels so much better than mine." Ghost slows the movement of my hand. "Just slow down a little. You're meant to suck the marrow from my bones like a dirty whore starved of cum. Not extract it with your hand."

I don't get embarrassed. His moans don't allow room for shame. He's being playful, and since it is a rare treat, I drink it in as much as his pre-cum.

After a few more minutes, Ghost orders me to sit on the vanity next to us. The glass has been replaced, and not a single shard remains on the tiles.

"But..." I stop myself. Questioning someone's objection is a habit I will never fully let go.

So is the obedience that was beaten into me.

My temperament changes in an instant, but mercifully, Ghost seems to miss it. After plucking me off the floor and planting my backside onto the vanity, he positions himself between my splayed thighs then rubs the head of his dick through my folds.

A zap bolts through me when a warmth hits my clit. It isn't spit or a foreign product invented to lube me up. It is a string of cum pumping out of Ghost's cock. He coats the outside and inside of my pussy, top to bottom, ensuring I am wet enough to take him before he returns his still-throbbing head to my opening.

When he peers down at me before breeching the perimeter that will change everything, I wonder if he's having the same thoughts as me.

"Are we being selfish?"

I realize I expressed myself out loud when Ghost replies, "Yes. But that's okay. We're allowed to be selfish every now and again."

In an instant, it dawns on me that his captivity has been as long as mine—if not longer—meaning he has every right to be as selfish as me.

"Hold me, *маленький ягненок*. This is going to hurt."

Pain splinters through me when he rams in a couple of inches without additional warning. It shreds through me like a wildfire burning and destroying everything it touches.

But it also comes with relief.

I've been tormented, taunted, and ridiculed for my virginity every day for the past eight years.

Now they can no longer hold it over my head.

"You're so fucking tight." Ghost breathes out heavily before the hand not gripping my hip darts up to my face to brush away my tears. "*Дышите сейчас, маленький ягненок.*" I don't realize I'm not breathing until he grips my throat so firmly my body instinctively sucks in a large gulp. "Fucking breathe."

When he frees my throat from his hold, I gasp in air like I've not taken a single breath in years.

It is released with years of torment and even more tears.

"Fuck." Ghost's curse this time isn't in pleasure. He's either angry or hurt. I don't know his emotions well enough yet to decipher them.

As he grumbles a string of Russian words under his breath, Ghost pulls his blood-stained cock out of me, gathers me in his arms, then moves for the shower.

Unlike the time Artyom attacked me, he doesn't wait for the water to reach a perfect temperature before stepping us under the spray. He stands us under the bitterly cold water, allowing me to hide my tears as well as he'd love to hide his scars from the world.

"*Дыши, Маленькая Овечка. Вам нечего бояться,*" he whispers in Russian, his voice almost drowned out by the water pumping out of the showerhead. "*я буду держать тебя в безопасности. Я освобожу тебя.*"

"They weren't wishful thinking." I lift my head off Ghost's pec to peer at his face. He can't hide in the shower. The light is directly above his head. "You spoke those words before. In here." The shocks keep coming when I recall the grumbled comments he made while twirling my hair around his fingers on the ship. "You—"

Ghost ends any chance of interrogation by whacking the shower faucet off, stepping us out, then wrapping my shuddering frame in a towel.

"Dinner will be served in an hour." He doesn't look at me, but the worry swirling in my gut weakens a smidge when he adds, "I will return then to eat with you. Don't open the door for anyone."

He leaves before a syllable can escape my lips.

36

GHOST

*K*irill pushes his chair back from his desk when I toss a black body bag onto the large, glossy material. It isn't filled with a body, regretfully. It is every cash, bond, bill, and IOU slip I had in my possession. Since it was too much for a duffle bag, I used the body bag I've been saving for him.

The one I plan to bury him in once I get my sister and niece out of this mess.

"Five point three million." I nudge my head to the bag. "None of the bonds are traceable. The cash is in random dominations, and the serial numbers haven't been recorded. I have another two million Alek will deliver this afternoon—"

Kirill cuts me off by slicing his hand through the air. After taking in my sweat-dotted chest and wild eyes, he snarls, "Is that all your sister is worth to you? Seven million and some change."

Of course, he wouldn't add Lera into his assumption. To him, she's worthless.

"This is not for Sofia." His interests are piqued, but he remains quiet, leaving me to fill in the gaps. "It is for Katie."

A twinge impinges his jaw. Anyone would swear he is annoyed, but

I know him better than that. He's scheming. "She is not for sale." He smirks. "Well, not anymore."

"She was four and a half years ago when *I* purchased her. *I* paid for her. You merely signed the contract." He wanted to look good in front of the Popovs and Petrettis. Since I didn't give a fuck about what they thought of me, I let him puff out his chest and act macho.

It was stupid of me to do.

"This is more than double what you paid, and it won't alter our agreement at all. I will give you an heir, just not with Katie."

After balancing his elbows on the desk, he makes a tepee with his hands. "She is *my* wife."

"In your eyes, not the eyes of the law."

"She is *my wife!*" he reiterates, shouting. "And she will stay my wife until the day she takes her final breath."

He doesn't give a fuck about Katie. He simply hates sharing. Has since the moment he found out his father birthed children with women he wasn't married to. He's always been a spoiled brat. That's why I was so surprised at how badly he reacted to Milo getting killed. He finally didn't have to share the podium. The glory was all his. Yet now he acts as if Milo was his best friend.

"Fine." My quick change in stance shocks him. He won't announce that, though. "I'll save myself a few million and take your gift for a whirl."

I leave before he can respond. That will annoy him more than anything. He hates not having the last word.

"How'd you go?" Alek asks while removing the body bag from my grasp and storing the cash bundles back into the floor safe in my office.

"Not as I thought it would, but not surprising either. Kirill is a loose fucking cannon." My cock twitches when I drag a finger under my nose. I haven't touched cocaine in a week, but old habits are hard to kill. I can smell Katie on my hand. "This isn't solely about an heir to him. He's got something else going on. It is got to be big for him to turn down seven million in untraced currencies."

With the Bobrovs being kicked out of trade in the US over four years ago, we've struggled to make headway in the smaller, less profitable markets. That's why I was on the ship during Katie's collection. I can't step foot on US soil.

Don't get me wrong, our ban doesn't mean we're not broke by any means, but money has been Kirill's bottom-line for a long time, so I know his wish for an heir has something to do with money. I just have no fucking clue why he's so adamant his plans must include Katie, besides that I want her, and he's a selfish prick.

"Do you think he's jealous?" Alek pushes across a brick of snow that's almost as enticing as the scent of Katie's cunt on my hand so he can fit in a folder of bonds I've been holding onto in case we ever trade in the US again. With the Yurys owning most of the organized crime turf in Russia, the US East Coast was our biggest earner before it was stripped from us.

"Of what? My late arrival to festivities because I didn't know who my father was until I was sixteen or my stellar good looks?"

"I was gonna say your cock, but what would I know."

I give him a leering look. Now is not the time to fuck around. I have three lives floating precariously in the wind and only two dumb fucks stupid enough to go against thousands to save them.

"Are you sure this is the team you want to be on, Alek? I can't guarantee we're not going to sink with the ship."

"I'm sure." His grin doesn't match the sentiment of our conversation. "And the mermaids will save me when they see the imprint of my dick."

"For fuck's sake."

He waggles his brows before telling me he's going to take Katie some dinner.

"I told her not to open the door to anyone but me."

My jaw ticks when he murmurs, "And when has anyone around here listened to you?" He intends for his comment to be playful, but my mood is too low to take it that way, even more when he shuts the safe with the coke I was admiring on the other side. "You're only just breathing again. Don't let that shit steal the air from your lungs."

WHEN ALEK RETURNS to my office an hour later I shouldn't grin like a smug prick, but I do. He's balancing a tray on his hand and raking his teeth over his lower lip.

I slant my head more to hide a smile I shouldn't be wearing than my scars when he murmurs, "Maybe she was in the shower."

"Or maybe she knows better than to defy me."

He *pffts* me before dumping the tray onto a filing cabinet and slouching low it the chair across from me. "Whatcha working on?" His amusement shifts to fret when he scans the photographs splayed across my desk. "You clearly think there's some shady shit going on if you're taking this off the table." He tosses down an image of Hailey being flanked by four FBI agents before tracing the tick in his jaw with his hand. "What did you call in?"

"Nothing." When he mocks me with an arched brow, I bark out, "A threat was made against her life—"

"Months ago." He sits up straighter then places his forearms on my desk. "We've not had a reason to utilize her since the wedding."

"Maybe the Bureau's files are as backed up as..." I almost say 'me' but stop before I make an idiot of myself.

I get why Katie froze. I understand it has nothing to do with my scars, but when you've been jumping on cue for years, it gets a little hard to remember not every fucker is out to get you. Some just want to be a part of your life.

It was Alek twenty-three years ago.

Now it is Katie.

I was also probably a little bit too vocal. I'm not usually the talkative one during sexual activities. I'm there to get off, and usually, I didn't give a fuck if the woman I was using reached the same level of hysteria, but I couldn't hold back with Katie. I wanted her screaming, moaning, and thrashing against me, and when her juices dripped from my hand when I called her a slut for the first time, I knew exactly how to achieve that.

Katie is the picture of innocence, but my fucking God, she is nothing close to naïve once she comes out of her shell. I'm hard again now, recalling the way she peered at me while flattening her tongue.

What I wouldn't give for another taste.

Alek pulls me from my vivid imagination. "Anyway, chitchats are for pansies." He stands, runs his palms down his thighs, then nudges his head to the tray of food. "She needs to eat." He drops his eyes to mine. "So do you, so why not take advantage of the situation?"

Not looking up, I gesture for him to fuck off with a wave of my hand. I mainly utilize the middle finger. I'm having enough issues keeping my ass planted in my seat, so I don't need him giving my cock ideas.

He laughs as if amused before doing as ordered, only to step back around two seconds later. "Oh, before I forget, I was thinking about something you said the other day—"

"Did it hurt?"

He gives me his best peeved expression before he continues, "Why does Kirill risk his Marys by impregnating them with straight-up, untouched sperm? Why wouldn't he just give them the boys juice?"

"You can do that?"

Alek scrubs at his chin to hide his grin. "Fuck yeah. Designer babies are all the rage." He rubs his hands together, a telltale sign he's thinking. "I heard it's pricy though, but for him to turn down seven million, he can't be living off pennies." His brows screw up as he purses his lips. "Unless he's banking on his male heir to bring in the bacon?" He appears confused. "Fuck. Forget it. I need to do a little more research."

"You could be onto something."

He won't ever admit it, but I can tell he is pleased by my unexpected praise. "You think?"

I jerk up my chin. "Dig a little deeper and see what you can find out."

"His financials or his swimmers?"

His breathy chuckle shifts to a groan when I reply, "Both."

He doesn't look impressed, but he lifts his chin and murmurs, "All right," then exits for real this time.

It's for the best. My patience is stretched thin. Kirill has always been unhinged, but his possessiveness has never extended past my sister. Wife or not, if they didn't give him what he craved, his Marys were killed within days.

Some didn't even make it down the aisle.

So I need to work out why he's so attached to the idea of having a child with Katie.

ALMOST AN HOUR LATER, when my stomach growls, I recall the number of times Katie's stomach grumbled while drifting in and out of consciousness. She barely sampled her breakfast this morning before I demanded every ounce of energy she had to give.

My cock shouldn't tighten at the thought of her passed out from exhaustion, but it does. Her warmth wrapped around me... fuck, I've never felt anything more magical. It had me forgetting the noose hanging around Sofia and Lera's head. Nothing but my needs were on my mind.

Now the plate is overflowing, leaving me no choice but to burn the candle at both ends.

I've put steps into play to ensure Katie's will to fight remains high. Now I need to make Sofia do the same. She once fought for Lera. I have no clue who she's fighting for now.

As I sink back into my chair, preparing for an all-nighter, I hit the speed dial for the kitchen. While waiting for Vera to answer, I scan my eyes across the pictures of Hailey. She is very much a replica of her sister with the same fair skin and big oval eyes. She just lacks one thing —the aura of innocence.

Even while being sullied by a monster, Katie's flushed cheeks, glossed-over eyes, and sweat- dotted skin still resembled the picture of innocence. I could taint her to hell, and she'd still convince Kirill she's his Virgin Mary.

The thought weakens the knot in my stomach, but it doesn't wholly end it.

The bit of leeway my confession gave is undone when I realize I'm an image short. Peter is anal. He always sends in multiples of two. He never delivers an odd number of stills—some shit about it being bad luck.

"Fucking Alek," I grumble under my breath when I recall what image is missing. It is the one of Hailey entering Bureau headquarters. She is flanked by agents, but it is clear they're guarding her. She isn't being arrested as I'm sure they'd love to do with Kirill.

Milo's death instigated a bloodbath that involved both federal agents and multiple gang associations, but since the Gottles weren't willing to listen, we were shunted back to Russia, where we've lived under embargo for over four years.

Not even the CIA can touch us here.

Part of me wonders if that's why Kirill took so long to announce Katie's location. Is he scared of the authorities hunting us or what my reaction would be when I discovered she was alive? I've been his puppet for years, but the desire to change things up has been dramatically different since Katie showed up. I'm walking the tightrope, aware I am one step away from disaster but still willing to take the risk.

I am fucked in the head.

After telling Vera to ensure she takes a cell with her so I can grant Katie permission to open the door, I stray my eyes to the safe hidden under the large Persian rug in my office. I'm so fucking tempted for a line or two of snow, but I need my head clear.

For years, I haven't cared about who I hurt to ensure Sofia and Lera's safety. You fucking do as asked or suffer the consequences. I can't run that route this time around. Katie has slithered under my skin, and when she fights back, she grips more than my cock.

I'm fascinated by her and dying to have her beneath me, but I need to fix this first. My mother died in this world, and my sister and niece are on the brink of following the same fate. I can't rest for nothing.

Not even the throbs of my cock.

37

KATIE

My heart beats in my ears when the faintest dip hits the mattress. It is late, well past midnight, but like he has almost every night I've been here, Ghost is sneaking into my bed. He probably thinks I drank the juice that arrived with my meal hours ago.

I didn't.

The message on the back of the photograph slipped under my door was abundantly clear.

If you want to remain lucid tonight, don't drink the juice.

I should be annoyed Ghost has been slipping something extra into my drinks each night, but when I consider how well I've been sleeping the past four months and how drastically fast it lessened my migraines and body aches, my frustration didn't linger for long.

I also couldn't be angry with how the message was delivered.

Hailey is safe. She is protected from the monsters.

Now I need to work out how we can do the same for Lera.

Yes, you heard me right. *We.*

I'm not leaving her care solely to Ghost. He brought me here to help Lera, but he made his job ten times harder by freeing Hailey from the torment.

He put my family first, so now I need to do the same for him.

"Fuck, *маленький ягненок,*" Ghost murmurs when I roll over and straddle his lap before his fingers can get close to my hair. I'm not wearing any panties, and although my nightie hangs past my knees, just the span they must take to connect our groins wiggled it up to my midsection.

When I grind down on the length rapidly growing between Ghost's splayed thighs, his hands shoot out to secure a hold of my hips. He doesn't hold me firm enough not to be able to rock against him, but his fingertips dig in firm enough to leave a mark.

I don't think he knows he is being brutish. He's rough because it is all he knows.

"How sore are you?" he asks after another three long grinds.

"I'm not."

He growls a low flat rumble that makes me forget tonight is meant to be about him. I want to thank him for what he did, and the only way I could conjure up doing that was by giving him the one thing he's wanted since the start.

Me.

"I'm not lying. I had a bath. Vera suggested some oils to ease my aches, and it worked like magic." I grind down hard, then moan, proving not an ounce of pain can be felt. Nothing but shimmers are darting through me.

"Fuck." This curse word is in Russian and comes with the gentlest roll of his hips. "I don't know how to be gentle. I'll fucking tear you."

It seems as if he's turning me down, but his actions are on the other end of the spectrum. He overtakes the rock of my hips, ensuring the sensitive bud at the top of my pussy flicks past the rim around his knob. It doubles the tingles in the lower half of my body and has me acting as if I'm not so naïve.

I meet the rolls of his hips grind for grind, moaning every time the friction is greatened by the intense pulse between my legs. "Who said you need to be gentle?"

His cock throbs, sending my head into a tailspin. Within seconds, I'm teetering on the edge of what I know will be orgasmic, but something feels off. Different.

Ghost must feel it too because he stops rocking then tosses me off him.

My eyes dart to the nightstand I've hidden the numerous photographs I've been gifted of Hailey the past few months. I was certain I made sure no unturned corners were peeking out, but what other reason would Ghost be stopping other than thinking I am only offering myself to him for freeing my sister?

Although I want to offer him my thanks, that isn't the sole reason for my boldness. He makes me feel like I can fly with broken wings and my knees won't buckle despite the weight placed on my shoulders.

He makes me feel alive.

"Ohhh..."

My moan shifts to a long, windy grunt when the reason for the changeup makes sense. Ghost isn't tossing me aside like a discarded toy. He's settling the rumbles of his tummy by burrowing his head between my legs. He doesn't devour me like dessert, though. He stares up at me with the worry he took off me blazing through his hooded eyes. "I want to wipe the innocence from your eyes, taint it so black, no one will ever doubt who claimed you." His words should tighten my thighs instead of loosening them. "But if I do that, he will know, and you won't make it to the end of the week."

I hate that he is right, but I can't deny the truth.

Kirill will know purely for the cruel way he checked my purity. Except there's one thing Ghost isn't considering. He already penetrated me.

"It's too late. You already..." It isn't as easy to speak the words out loud.

Ghost's smile is barely seen, but it is enough for the heat he's trying to snuff to return hotter than ever. "I was barely halfway in, маленький ягненок. You still had inches to go." My gulp takes care of his ghost-like grin. It makes it a full-hearted smile. "But when I claim you as mine, I'll be sure to grip your throat so you can feel just how deep I go." He snickers about my wide eyes and gaped mouth before returning to his usual bossy self. "Now, sleep. You need your rest." He forces me onto my side, then drags me back until his cock is nestled between my bare butt cheeks.

It is only minutes before his fingers find their way to my hair.

They suffocate the panic seeping into my veins in a way I can't explain, but regretfully, even cocooned in his warmth, I know it will be short-lived.

38

GHOST

*"W*hat the fuck crawled up your ass and died?"

Alek dodges the stapler I peg at his head. He isn't fast enough for the letter opener. It nicks his cheek, drawing out the droplets of blood I've been seeking for days.

My fists are itching for a fight, but no prick is game to take a bite out of the bait I'm dangling in front of them. Things are quiet, and I hate that even more than how I'm letting a soft-cock like Kirill control me.

I might have had more gall if I could get Sofia's suicide attempt out of my head. It was only four days ago, but I swear it has played on repeat in my fucking head a million times already. She was smiling at me like she did when she told me she had met someone six years ago. Then, out of nowhere, she yanked my gun off my desk and pressed it to her temple.

Thank fuck my reflexes don't slow down for anyone. I dove for her with barely a second to spare. The bullet only grazed Sofia's nose during its race for the ceiling, but it tore my fucking heart to shreds.

She thought her death would return my freedom. She failed to remember I'm in this as much for Lera as I am her.

And Katie.

Don't even get me started on Katie.

You have no idea how hard it was for me to turn her down the night Sofia attempted to take her life. Every inch of my body craves her. I want to feast on her until the churns of my stomach finally silence, but I'm being held for ransom, and the frustration has me wanting to pop a bullet in my head.

I remember Alek is still in the room with me when he murmurs, "Thought you said Sofia was getting help?"

"She is." I slouch back in my chair and scrub my jaw with my hand. Help is putting it loosely, but when you live in an industry that sees women as commodities, you don't have many options. "This isn't about Sofia."

"Kate?" When I slowly raise my eyes to his, the daggers endless, he holds his hands out in front of himself. "I get it, all right. I just don't understand why you torture yourself every night. There's no way I could sleep in the same bed as the girl I want to bed and not touch her. Fuck that. I'm not strong enough for that."

"I know. Hence my request for you to stay the fuck out of Sofia's room when we first met her."

I have no reply when he mutters under his breath, "Who would you have preferred? Me or him?" The way he growls out 'him' announces who he is referencing. I thought I only had to protect my baby sister from my friends. I had no clue my brother would sniff around.

An unusual twinge hits my jaw when he leans forward like our conversation is about to take a one-eighty. It does when he asks, "Is a lack of blow fucking with your head?" When I shake my head, the craving still prominent but not the catalyst of my wants, Alek murmurs, "Then maybe you should get laid." When I search for my gun, he blubbers out, "Not with Kate. Just some random whore. Work Kate out of your system until you're given the green light."

This makes me sound like an ass, but so be it. I considered his suggestion. I even got as far as flicking through a catalog of Bobrov women. Then somehow, I ended up in Katie's bathroom, stroking one out to the visual of her washing her hair in the shower.

I don't want another woman's warmth wrapped around my cock. I don't even crave it anymore.

I only want Katie's cunt sucking at my dick, begging for my spawn.

It took everything I had not to order Katie to her knees when she busted me. The only reason I held back is because my resolve is weakening. One taste and I wouldn't have stopped. I would have smeared mud over the plans I've been drawing up the past week. So instead, I blew my load on her panties, then made her wear them to bed.

She obliged without an objection.

I loved that almost as much as I do the defiance in her eyes.

"How'd you go with those other matters you were looking into?"

Before Alek can answer, something in the corner of my eye captures my attention. Kirill is stalking the halls, but instead of it being on his side of the compound, he's trampling my stomping ground.

"Where the fuck is he going?" Alek questions, speaking the words screaming inside my head.

I have no trouble finding my gun when I notice what is in his hand. He's clutching a vial of sperm and heading in the direction of Katie's room.

Alek overtakes me when we reach the east wing, but instead of barging into Katie's room and telling Kirill to get the fuck away from her, he blocks my entrance with his wide frame before he pushes me back three spaces. "Step back."

"What the fuck are you doing?" I sneer, up close and in his space. "He's in there with her." When my shove doesn't give him the hint to step the fuck back, I let my gun get across my point. I push it in close to his temple before telling him in no uncertain terms that I will walk into Katie's room with his brain splattered on my shirt before I will ever walk away.

"Better my brains than hers."

My jaw cracks when it tightens. I'm not fuming mad about his denial. I'm ropeable Kirill's number four is 'babysitting' Lera. She has no clue the big black gun wedged between Feo and her bookcase is earmarked with her name. Rusha conceals her shakes so well with her dance moves, Lera most likely thinks he's their special guest to their dance recital.

"He's playing you, Ghost. He wants any excuse to take away her lineage, and you're giving him plenty of reasons."

"He's..." I can't fucking say it. I refuse to consider what Kirill is doing to Katie right now. "He..."

"He won't touch Kate. Not how you're thinking. He never does."

"She's different from the rest," I blurt out before I can stop myself.

"Because you care about her."

I try to deny his claims. I try to brush off the pull I've felt for Katie since the day my eyes landed on her long before she was put up for auction, but no amount of denying can hide the truth.

She is different.

Sensing that my anger is calming, Alek promises, "Kirill will get what's coming to him. We've just got to finish laying the foundation. Without proper groundwork, our build will tumble within seconds of the first brick being laid."

His words are honest, his eyes a promise, but I am still fucking ropeable.

I want to maim.

I want to kill.

And I know just the man to take it out on.

"Go to Katie." I don't need to give him the same do-not-touch instructions I give every other man who crosses her path. He knows it well since I read him the riot act the first night on the ship.

I grin like a smug motherfucker when he asks, "Where are you going?"

Not stopping, I reply, "To take out the trash."

My grin is still tugging at my lips when I reach Lera's room. She freezes mid-hip wobble before racing across the room to greet me like she always does when she spots me.

Regretfully for Feo, Lera's room only has one entry point. There's not even a window for him to weasel out of.

"Uncle, are you here to watch me dance?" she stammers out quickly in Russian, her cheeks awfully white for how hard she is panting.

"Soon," I reply. "But I found the treasure we were seeking. The ones with jewels and gold bars. Do you want me to show you where it is?"

She nods so quickly more color drains from her cheeks. "Okay. I just need to speak to Feo real quick. Can you wait for me in the pantry?" Her eyes adopt a sleepy look as she peers at me in silent begging. "Two." I hand her a packet of jellybeans. "But only if Rusha says it's okay."

Rusha sees this as her out. After scooping Lera off my leg, she inconspicuously nudges her head to the corner Feo has crept into. I don't need her help. I can sniff out a rat from a mile away, but it is nice to know whose team she is on. Her allegiance reminds me there are more people on my side than just Alek. I simply need to free the fighters from the weeds strangling them.

I will find them—*after* I've eradicated one of the main offenders.

A grin pulls my lip high at one side when a red dot highlights my chest upon entrance of Lera's room. I must give it to Feo. He has more balls than I realized.

Despite my brother's puppeteering, I am mafia royalty.

You don't fuck with me and expect to come out of the carnage with your life intact.

Feo is about to learn that the hard way.

39

KATIE

"Open up for me, *маленький ягненок*, give me something enticing to work with." I'm rolled over with a groan before the faintest brush of a hand down my breasts prickles my skin with awareness.

I'd startle as I obviously did when Kirill entered my room earlier today if I didn't recognize the pants of a man in ecstasy. I've only heard two men come. Master Rudd didn't make a peep when he stared into space.

Ghost is as vocal when he comes as he is while climbing to the summit.

His breathy grunts and naughty words spur something deep inside me and have me acting as if I'm not half asleep and groggy. I roll my hips in rhythm to his timed moans, shuddering along with his breaths as tingles activate low in my stomach.

"Yes, *маленький ягненок*," Ghost hisses between clenched teeth when I splay open my thighs. "Now part those lips like my tongue is begging to do."

It is pitch black, so I should have no idea what is happening, but Ghost's shallow pants and the rustles bouncing between us paints everything in glorious detail.

He's stroking his cock again, but instead of hiding the fact he's using my body for inspiration, he's announcing it out loud.

The thought has me forgetting about how invasive it felt having my husband conduct today's insemination instead of Ghost. He's done the last four inseminations, but today was different, not solely because it wasn't done by Ghost but because the vial of semen didn't get pushed into the mattress.

It was freed inside me.

I was worried that was the reason for Ghost's lack of appearance today. Even with him turning down my attempt to seduce him, he has eaten with me morning and night for the past seven days.

But on the day my husband takes charge of my insemination, he misses breakfast, lunch, and dinner.

I bet it is screwing with his head that I have another man's sperm inside me.

It is mine.

Although you wouldn't know that for how loud I moan when hot spurts of cum jet out of Ghost's cock. I can't see a damn thing, but the heat that roars through me is warmer than a fire in winter. It has my thumb rolling over my clit at the same frantic pace Ghost's hand rubs the still-warm liquid into my neck. He smears his cum from my neck to my pussy and ass. He even goes as far as pushing some inside me with his pointer and middle finger.

His growl shoots rockets of ecstasy through my veins when I spasm from his thumb brushing over my clit. I'm so wound up only the faintest brush will send me toppling over.

"Fuck, маленький ягненок," Ghost murmurs again, his voice nowhere near as pained as when he first woke me up. "You're dripping down my fingers like a dirty little slut." He pumps in and out of me in tempo with my pulse before he places the perfect amount of pressure on my clit.

After the events of the day, it should take a mammoth effort for me to come. I was violated and humiliated, but with only three rotations, I'm arching my back and moaning Ghost's name into the frigid night air.

"One more," Ghost demands when my shudders only last thirty seconds.

It was a quick but brutally draining orgasm, so instead of lifting my ass as requested, I shake my head. "I can't."

"One. Fucking. More." He punctuates each word he speaks by hitting my clit with quick-fired flicks of his thumb before he wholly upends any attempts of me denying him again. After whacking on the bedside lamp, he tugs his boxers to his knees, fists his reforming erection, then gives it a long, firm tug. "I want him out of you, Katie. I don't want him anywhere near you. You are *mine*." The possessiveness in his reply squeezes my vaginal walls around his finger and thickens his cock like he didn't recently achieve release. "Yes, like that. Squeeze him out, then I'll replace his semen with mine."

The cum he rubbed into my mid-section already has me smelling like him, but he ups the ante by smearing his pre-cum over my lips.

As I lick my lips, desperate for a taste, I lock my eyes with Ghost's. The excitement blistering through me dulls a little when I realize how dilated his pupils are. And don't get me started on how bloodshot his eyes are.

He's using again.

I'm certain of it.

"How much did you snort?"

Ghost acts as if I didn't speak. "Raise your ass. Let my fingers in deep."

"Alek said you were quitting—"

"Alek doesn't know shit." He swivels my clit with his thumb, optimistic it will shift my focus off his whispered confession. "He also doesn't understand my pain."

My clit will forever beat under his touch, but it is my heart talking now, not my libido. "That stuff isn't good for you, Ghost. It won't help you heal."

"You don't think I know that?" He yanks his hand away from his cock and drags it under his nose before sinking back to balance his ass on the balls of his feet. He's still hard, and his fingers are still in my vagina, but his focus is shifting. "I know what's fucking good for me and what's not." It feels like a thousand knives are stabbed into my chest. "You're not good for me, but you keep drawing me back in, begging for fucking more. Your cunt is so goddamn fucking hungry, you don't care who gets killed just to get it filled."

He catches my hand before it gets within an inch of his face, then he uses his painful hold to pin me to the mattress. He wants me scared, but I won't give him the satisfaction. "Do it. Degrade me and defile me. See if I care."

I thrash, hit, and scratch him with my free hand when he shreds off my nightie as if it is tissue paper before he forces my left hand to join my right hand.

My hips buck when he swivels his tongue down my stomach. I'm angry as hell but more frustrated at myself than him. His most basic touch sets me on fire, and he knows it.

After stopping at the apex of my thighs, he glances up at me. His eyes are lifeless, he is snowed under, so the last thing I want him to do is any of the wicked thoughts streaming through my head.

I don't know this man.

I don't like him either.

"Get off me."

"Get you off? I can do that." Before I can utter a syllable, he curls his lips around my clit, swivels his tongue around the nervy bud, then sucks it into his mouth, uncaring that he was smearing his cum on it only seconds ago. "I bet I can get you off better than *he* ever could."

"This isn't what I want."

My body can't produce the same lies as my mouth. Every fine hair is prickled with awareness, and there are more fireworks being lit in my stomach than a New Year's Eve party at Times Square. I just don't want it like this. Fueled with jealousy.

"Ghost..." His name sounds more like a moan than a plea for him to let me go.

The more he bombards my pussy with teasing licks and sloppy kisses, the more I sweat, shake, and fight my eyes not to roll into the back of my head. Try as I may to fight it, I'm about to come, and there's nothing I can do about it.

"Yes, *маленький ягненок*." Ghost growls against my heated skin when my body sinks into the mattress a mere second before a hazardous blaze races through my veins.

I come with a hoarse cry, but in a last-ditch effort to maintain my dignity, I swallow Ghost's name every time it tries to surface.

He knows that too.

My defiance doubles the flicks of his tongue and sees him stuffing two fingers inside me.

He fingerfucks and eats me until I have no choice but to relent on my earlier stance.

I scream his name loud enough for the world to hear before I collapse from exhaustion.

The next morning, I wake in an empty bed.

40

GHOST

*M*y gun highlights Alek's chest before he's halfway down the corridor. To anyone else, I look like I'm asleep. My pounding head and heavy eyelids are the only things telling another story.

I haven't slept more than an hour in days, and the exhaustion is taking a toll on me more than the shit I snorted without checking the seal to ensure its quality. There are some fucked drugs on the market, and three nights ago, I dove in headfirst.

I've regretted it ever since.

I didn't just relapse into the man I was four years ago. I made my biggest mistake to date.

I made Katie scream my name.

"Anything?"

While pushing my feet off the chair butted against Lera's new room with his boot, Alek shakes his head. "Not a single rumble." He looks as suspicious as I feel when he adds, "Which is real fucking surprising considering I heard her, and I'm nowhere near this half of the compound."

He's stirring, and although I appreciate his attempt to weaken my annoyance with humor, now is not the time for jokes. I didn't move

Lera to another room solely because I took my time with Feo. I did it because it was either Katie or her who will face the wrath of my insolence, so I brought them to an area where I can protect them better.

If anyone comes for them, they'll have to take me down first.

I've been camped outside their rooms for three days. Alek and Rusha are the only people permitted to come and go as they please.

"What about Sofia? Any news?"

I haven't heard a peep from my sister since her suicide attempt. That isn't unusual. We shunt away our embarrassments as readily as Kirill does his daughters, but Alek usually has his ears close to the ground when it comes to Sofia.

Alek screws up his nose before once again shaking his head. "Vera did mention an extra set of dishes coming from Kirill's wing." He looks green at the gills when he murmurs, "You'd think she'd know better."

"The fact you think she has a choice is laughable. She doesn't want to be here anymore than Katie."

"Are you sure about that?" I assume we're still talking about Sofia until he strays his blue eyes to Katie's door. "She's known her sister is out of harm's way for over a week now, yet she still gets up on the bed every morning to help you."

"She's not helping me." *Why would she after I forced myself onto her?* "She doesn't want Lera to get caught in the crossfire."

I lift my head so my chin is no longer balancing on my chest when Alek mutters, "Same fucking thing." When he spots my stitched brows, he shakes his head. "You are so fucking clueless, so let me help a brother out..." He stands, shoves the food tray for Katie into my chest, then heads down the hall, his strut undeniable. "Feed your girl. She's hungry." I wish I had my gun still pointed at him when he cranks his neck back and murmurs, "If you want that to be your cum, I'm sure she'll be down for it. Women don't scream like that when any fool's head is between their legs."

I wait until Katie's porridge is on the verge of being uneatable before I man the fuck up and enter her room. Unsurprisingly, she is in the shower. Shockingly, I let her shower in peace. I could leave altogether, but Katie is a stubborn fuck. Alek has threatened her every day the past three days to eat, and half the time he left with more food on him than in Katie's stomach.

"No tantrums today, *маленький ягненок*. I'm not in the fucking mood."

Katie freezes in the doorway of the bathroom before shooting her eyes around the space, searching for an answer as to how I knew she was approaching when her footsteps were soundless.

I know when she is near because I can smell her.

Her scent isn't unique, every woman in this compound uses the same shampoo and conditioner. Katie's is the only one with extra added ingredients. I thought having her smell like me every time she washed her hair would be enough to get over my anger that Kirill's sperm was inside her after me, but I needed more.

I wanted my cum coating her head to toe, so what her conditioner wouldn't take care of, I fixed by smearing my cum into her breasts, stomach, and thighs. I wasn't meant to wake her, but the little moans she released when I rubbed her nipple through her nightie made my urge for her stronger than the sedatives I slip into her food to knock her out.

Excluding her hair, I don't usually touch her when she is asleep.

But as I said earlier, I fucked up momentously.

"They made your fav—"

"I'm not hungry."

Slowly and angrily, I raise my eyes to her face. My lips twitch when I realize she's washed her hair, but not an ounce of pleasure is heard in my tone when I say, "It may be a little much, but I'm not leaving until you've finished at least half of what I've arrived with."

"I'm. Not. Hungry."

My fuse is short, but only Katie can make it the size of an ant.

She doesn't flinch when I send the salt and pepper shaker across the room. Why would she? I pegged them nowhere in the direction of where she's standing. "You *will* eat." I stand, silencing any reply I see firing in her eyes. "Or I'll force it down your throat with my cock."

Katie smiles a grin that would make any man's cock twitch before she saunters across the room. Her skin is glistening, her hips are swinging, and even though I can smell my cum intermingled with her conditioner, the smell of her cunt is even more prominent.

It takes my focus off the task at hand—her malnourished frame when she first arrived—long enough for her to flip the tray on the table, spilling all the contents onto the floor. "I'm. Not. Hungry."

I blame my reflexes for my quick grab of her throat, but in reality, it is my drug-fucked head. I say I can't think without them, but it is more that I hate the responses given, so I drown them out instead of acknowledging them.

As Katie's pulse thuds the length of my hand, I drag my thumb over her lip. It is swollen like it's kiss-swollen, but on closer inspection, I realize they're grazed from the number of times she's run her teeth over them. "Why are you fighting me?" When her lips remain still, I slant in so close there isn't a wisp of air between us. "I shouldn't have forced myself onto you. I fucked—"

I stop talking when the slightest ruffle hits my ear. It isn't Katie's struggling for breaths. My hand is curled around her throat, but I'm not applying any pressure. She's speaking in hushed whispers.

When I lean back, certain I didn't hear what I think I did, she stares straight into my eyes before slinging them to the heater vent. For a man with no reason to be suspicious, nothing is out of the ordinary. Only someone who lives their life under the spotlight would notice that the screws don't match. Two are white, and two are silver—shiny and new.

Katie's pulse thuds when I shift my focus back to her. Her sneer has returned, but nothing but silent begs beam from her eyes.

"Fine," I reply before stepping back, unpinning her from the wall. "Fucking starve. See if I care."

She slides down the wall and huddles her knees into her chest, playing the part well for whoever is watching on the camera they hid in the vent.

41

KATIE

I have been so confused of late, four weeks pass in a blur.

I've been given regular inseminations by Ghost, fed like clockwork, and asked a range of questions by both Ghost and Alek, but today is the first interaction I have had with Ghost where he's back to acting like he hates me.

The way he raced out of here last month when I told him Kirill said I should fight him if I want Lera to eat more than porridge with glass splinters in it had me convinced he would loathe me—they're trying to force him to pick between Lera and me—but today is the only day he has treated me differently.

He hasn't looked me in the eye since he arrived. Not even when my shocked gaze shoots to him on confirmation that I'm pregnant.

Ghost squeezes the vials into the mattress, so there's no way I can be pregnant.

Unless that one insemination he missed was successful.

Oh God.

"Now what?" Ghost asks the doctor, still ignoring me.

He packs away the positive test into his bag before shifting on his feet to face Ghost. "We will conduct an ultrasound in a couple of weeks.

If the results are positive, we will have to wait for further instructions. We've not moved past that stage previously."

"There's always a first time," Ghost replies, dropping my stomach further. For the first time in weeks, he strays his eyes to me. "Pack your things. Someone will be here to collect you within the hour."

"Where am I going?"

He usually appreciates the inquisitiveness years of abuse couldn't snuff.

Not today.

"I said to pack your things."

When he marches me into my room, I notice Alek suspiciously mingling around. He wouldn't look so suspicious if he didn't cover the vent I pointed out to Ghost weeks ago with his thigh the instant he spots us.

"Pack everything you need. You won't be coming back to this room." After waiting for me to nod, Ghost shifts his focus to Alek. "Do you know where she's going?"

He jerks up his chin. "Same wing. Different suite."

"How many men are en route?"

Alek traces a tick in his jaw. "Four, but he's got a dozen here, though."

When I stare at them, hopeful something on their faces will explain what the hell is going on, Ghost inconspicuously drops his eyes to the photographs I stuffed between my mattress and the bedside table.

Certain I heard his silent disclosure for me to collect them, he returns to the bathroom where the doctor is located. "I think you should test again. I told her to get midstream urine, but you know what some of these Marys are like. They'll do anything to get a windowed room."

He isn't lying. My heart rate kicked up a beat just at the assumption I may end up in a room with a window.

With Ghost keeping the doctor occupied and Alek's thick thigh covering the camera no one's touched since my husband placed it in there, I carefully pluck Hailey's photographs from their hiding spot and shove them down the front of my nightie.

My already stuttering heart gets another surge of blood when I notice one of the photographs has a torn edge. I've always been super careful with them. I'd never manhandled them like a man with no clue of their sentimental value.

Alek's Adam's apple bobs up and down when I slant my head in his direction. He knows why I'm pissed, so it discloses that he is the culprit of my ruined images. The only thing I can't work out is why he would touch them. They mean nothing to him.

The cloak of danger slips when I flip over the damaged photograph. Something is scratched on the back, but since it appears to have been done with an inkless pen, I have to shimmer it in the light to see what it says.

Play along. This is the only way I can guarantee your safety. G.

This handwriting can't be Ghost's. It is the same cursive style that was on the envelopes slipped under my door that housed the photographs he was shocked to learn came into my possession.

Unless he was the person gifting them to me all along, and he didn't want me to know because he would hate for me to believe our teams are equally stacked?

I don't get the chance to work through my bewilderment. Minutes after a second positive test is recorded, I'm walked out the door by a steaming mad Ghost and guided outside the compound.

I might have believed his anger more if his grip on my arm was a little firmer. He's barely touching me, but to every man we walk by, he looks like he's clutching me for near death.

The sun is blinding when I'm guided to a long line of SUVs. When Alek said four, I assumed he meant guards in total, not four SUVs full.

"Watch your head." Ghost places his hand on my head before dipping it down so it doesn't bump into the car's roof. He slides in next to me, and Alek and another man sit across from us.

We don't wear seat belts as our driver careens us down a hilly terrain. We weave and bob so badly, I'm glad I didn't eat much of the breakfast Ghost arrived with this morning.

"What's wrong?" Alek asks, staring my way. "Feeling queasy?"

I move my head only an inch before he cuts off my reply with a stern glare. After scratching the area on his body where I stuffed my photographs, he murmurs, "Pregnancy will do that. Just don't vomit on my shoes. I only purchased them last week."

His game plan dawns on me when the driver says, "Don't fucking puke. The interior was recently detailed."

Alek gives me a praising smile when I shoot my hand up to my mouth. My gag is unladylike and so authentic, Ghost demands, "Pull over at the church coming up on the left."

"He—"

"Do you want fucking puke in your car?" Ghost interrupts the driver, his voice heart-shuddering. The driver stares at him in the rearview mirror for three terrifying seconds before he shakes his head. "Then pull the fuck over." As the driver follows his demand, Ghost speaks into the cuff of his suit jacket. "Taking a detour. Keep an eye out for the Yurys. I'll secure Mary."

I realize I'm Mary when he grips my arm a second after the driver stops at the back of an old church, and he tugs me out. The men in the cars following us pile out as well, but only Alek shadows Ghost's angry stalk.

We only just break through the threshold of the bathroom when Ghost's demeanor immediately changes. He crowds me against the door, his aura forever brooding, but his hold is gentle since he cups my jaw instead of gripping my neck.

"I need you to listen to me and do everything I ask." My chin barely graces my chest when he adds, "There are canisters of urine in the top drawer of the bathroom of your new room. Anytime you use the toilet, pour some of the liquid from the canisters into the bowl before flushing."

"Why would I—"

He silences me by squashing his index finger to my lip.

"We don't have time." Even with his statement sounding one hundred percent honest, he still waits for me to nod in acknowledgment before continuing, "If anyone asks to examine you, tell them *he* said no, and that *he* wants his Mary to remain untainted. If they argue, ask one of the nuns to contact me. I will only need to take down one insolent fool for the rest to fall into line."

My stomach gurgles at the thought of being poked and prodded again, but I tuck away the flare of doubt, confident Ghost will protect me as well as he does Lera.

"He will want to parade you around. Go along with it for an hour, then say you're tired." I feel nothing close to pure when he murmurs, "And always wear white. *Pure* white. It will make him less suspicious that your pregnancy is fraudulent."

"I'm not pregnant?"

Relief and worry flood me at once when Ghost shakes his head. "Little hard when you haven't been inseminated with his semen in over a month." I feel his frustration when he mutters, "But this is the only way he will lower his suspicions enough for us to get the info we need. I don't want to send you away, but for the moment, it is for the best."

I don't get the chance to ask how long he thinks our separation will last. Alek bangs on the door, alerting us that our time is up. "We've got three heading our way."

"Out of everything I said," Ghost mutters, drawing my focus back to him. "The first point is the most prolific. They regularly check HCG levels, and although the main doctor there is on my payroll, five others aren't."

My eyes bulge. *Why the hell do they need six doctors?*

"I said don't get vomit on my shoes," Ghost shouts, startling me. I grimace when he kicks up the lid with the toe of his boot before he dumps a handful of the jellybeans he carries for Lera into the bowl. "For fuck's sake." His grip on my arm is firm, but it won't leave a mark. "Let's go before you puke on me some more." After we exit the bathroom, he shakes his foot, sending the three goons stumbling backward. "I'm never eating scrambled eggs again."

It is the fight of my life to hide my smile, but I manage—somewhat.

Any amusement from Ghost's show is squashed when we enter a

large, heavily-manned gate several miles later. The compound we just left was massive, but this residence is beyond huge. It is a mansion fit for a movie star.

"This is where he brings all his Marys," Ghost advises, his voice barely a whisper. "You will be safe here until..."

Like the worst cliffhanger of all time, he leaves his reply hanging when the SUV's door is pulled open, and a nun gestures for me to follow her. "Come, quickly."

When I sling my eyes to Ghost, he jerks up his chin, wordlessly demanding that I follow her orders. "No one will hurt you here. I promise."

Despite his pledge, my legs shake when I follow the nun into a residence far too opulent for the number of armed guards surrounding it. The windows aren't boarded up, the walls have pops of color with multiple paintings, and even the bedspreads aren't bland and white, but it still feels more like a graveyard than a home.

When I enter a room at the end of a grand staircase, my eyes naturally veer to the edges of the bed.

My heart beats triple time when I realize there are no stirrups.

"Lunch is served at noon. You'll have chores to complete but nothing too strenuous." The nun with kind eyes shifts on her feet to face me. "We can't be exhausting you in your condition."

"Especially *if* she's carrying the future heir of the Bobrov realm."

That didn't come from the nun. It came from outside my room, and although his accent is as thick as Ghost's, it is too tainted with haughtiness to mistake them as being the same person.

I genuinely want to be sick when my husband enters the room. He walks with the same arrogant strut he used the time he stomped on me, but there's something different with his expression this time around. I grow worried he's not looking at me as if I'm pure, but on closer inspection, I notice he appears more pleased than annoyed.

My thighs involuntarily shake when he murmurs with a smirk, "Perhaps we should conduct another test? We don't want you here under false pretenses."

"The doctor already did two tests."

"What was that?" he asks, mocking the weakness of my reply.

"I said... the doctor already did two tests." This reply is louder but still shaky.

"And what does that mean for me?"

When I shoot my eyes to the nun, seeking help, bile scorches the back of my throat.

We're the only two people in the room.

I slowly return my eyes to Kirill when he mutters, "Although tempted, miscarriage rates are higher with old-school methods, so perhaps we should just use one of these." A brick lodges in my throat when he holds up a pregnancy test. "We wouldn't want any mishaps like last time, would we?"

Like a coward without a voice, I shake my head.

"Good." His smirk is evil. "Then get a wiggle on. I have other pressing matters to handle."

I almost hyperventilate when he guides me into an attached bathroom before taking up station outside the door, but as quickly as my panic rises, it is wiped out from beneath me when I spot the top drawer in the vanity. It is positioned right next to the toilet, within easy reaching distance but blocked by a tiled wall.

Kirill can't see me.

After removing the pregnancy test from the packet, I sit on the toilet, then pull open the drawer. I breathe in relief when I notice rows of sample cups full of urine.

With a wad of toilet paper, I pick up the first one, remove the cap, then dip the pregnancy test into it.

Two lines display almost immediately.

I almost store the sample cup away before remembering Ghost's request for me to pour some of the urine into the toilet bowl each time I use it. I'm not exactly sure how much is needed to give my urine traces of the HCG, but since there are approximately a dozen cups in the drawer, I pour half of the one I used into the bowl before storing it away, flushing, then exiting the bathroom.

The corners of Kirill's lips lift when his eyes drop to the positive test in my hand. "Very good."

I slump onto my bed in a sweaty heap when his approval is quickly chased by his exit out of my room.

42

KATIE

*G*host's assumption that Kirill would want to parade me around wasn't a lie. Although he hasn't told people I am pregnant, he's introduced me to high-up dignitaries in Russia, political personnel who happily turn a blind eye to the illegal activities happening right in front of them at the club we visited, and he has taken me to eat at an actual restaurant twice.

I'm being paraded around for the world to see. It just appears as if no one is looking for me. They're polite and say hello, but other than that, they keep their focus on Kirill.

I drift my eyes from my fingers entwined in my white, free-flowing dress to Kirill when he asks, "How much longer until she starts showing?"

"She is only a few weeks along," the doctor announces while removing the blood pressure cuff from my arm. "First pregnancies take longer. But she is encroaching the safe zone, so we won't need to be as worried about miscarriage soon."

"And the gender?" Kirill doesn't sound happy.

"It is usually determined at twenty weeks gestation, but there are blood tests we can do—"

"Do them," Kirill interrupts, clicking his fingers before he shifts his focus to Nun Ellery. "Then organize events according to the results. If she is carrying my son, she should be included in the celebrations. She is, after all, my wife."

This is the first-time possessiveness has been in his tone when referring to me. He certainly didn't have any issues forgetting I am his wife when he entered a back room at a strip club to pick the three strippers he wanted to take home with him.

He doesn't have an ounce of respect for women, and it has me wondering why Ghost thought this would be the best place for me to lay low.

I haven't seen him once in the past month, and it is hurting me more than I thought possible.

My pain turns physical when the doctor jabs me with a needle. The pinprick is the most I've been poked and prodded in the past month, but it has me out of my mind with worry.

Urine can be tainted.

Blood can't.

"How long will it take for the results to come back?" I ask, my voice as low as my pulse.

"Usually a week. I can ask for a rush order."

"That's okay. We don't need it yet."

"Get it done as soon as possible." Kirill locks his eyes with mine. "I already have one unworthy mouth to feed. I don't want another."

"I'll see what I can do." The doctor pulls out the syringe, labels the vial so it won't get confused with the other pregnant ladies who live here, then stands. "I need you to rest before our next checkup. Your blood pressure is a little high, and you have a small trace of protein in your urine." When my eyes shoot to his, he smiles. "It is minute, but it would be best to lower your stress as much as possible."

That's easy for him to say. His every move isn't scrutinized by men brandishing assault weapons.

Kirill doubles the unease surging through my veins when he murmurs, "I'll take care of her." He locks his eyes with mine. "Come, *Раб*."

He doesn't give me the chance to object. He yanks me up by my arm before marching me down the stairs and veering me toward a section of the mansion I've not been granted permission to venture down. It is just as guarded—if not more—as the rest of the house.

I internally curse when Kirill guides me through an expansive bedroom before stopping our rushed tour at the attached bathroom. The over-the-top opulence doesn't scare me, it is his murmured comment when he switches on the faucet of the large claw-foot tub. "A bath with oils works wonders for overworked bodies, right?"

My time on the ship with Vera had me forgetting who she works for. She is not my friend. She is Kirill's head service person.

"I don't have oils, but perhaps they won't be needed since it's your stomach I want swollen this time instead of your cunt."

"I was in pain after the miscarriage," I lie, saying anything to keep me alive.

I've never wanted to die, but my desires are even stronger since my time in the bathroom with Ghost last month.

My life is nothing close to ordinary, but it could be worse.

"My periods have always given me hell."

Kirill checks the water's temperature like he's a doting husband before shifting his focus to me. "Then it's lucky for you, you won't get them anymore, isn't it?"

His reply startles me more than it fills me with panic. I've not had a period since coming to this mansion. I should have had two by now.

"Not too hot as per the doctor's instructions." He doesn't look at my face while barking out his next set of orders. "Now in you get."

"I—"

"*In!*" His roar shudders my heart out of my chest. "Before I find a better use for a bathtub full of water."

When he steps closer to me to ensure I can see the threat in his eyes, I gingerly step into the tub. I'm clothed, but my nightgown clings to my skin the instant it soaks up the first sloshes of water. It exposes my nipples and the lines of my vagina to a man I was assured would have no interest in them, even with his eyes not leaving the apex of my thighs for almost a minute.

"Don't forget your head."

Kirill pushes down on my head until it's fully submerged, then holds on tight.

I don't wiggle until the screams of my lungs demanding air releases the last snippets of oxygen in them. Then I thrash and kick violently.

The pain is intense. It burns through me like a wildfire and reinvigorates my wish to live.

I didn't come this far to give up now.

Just as black blobs form in front of my eyes, Kirill frees me from his hold. I burst through the water gasping, crying, and on the verge of hysteria. I can't take in enough oxygen even while being surrounded by it. My panic won't allow it.

Kirill appears amused by my coughing splatters, but no humor is heard in my tone when he snarls out, "Give orders to any of my men in front of me again, and we will come back here and finish what I started." His evil eyes bounce between mine when he adds, "You have no power here. None whatsoever. Remember that."

He tosses a towel into the bath that's now half empty because of my violent thrashes before he exits the bathroom.

I shudder when I step out of the tub. I'm not solely scared. The bath water wasn't close to a pleasant temperature. It was freezing cold—as bitterly frigid as Kirill's heart.

Today proves I won't survive in his presence much longer. His anger is growing each day, but this is the first time he's acted on his frustrations.

When I exit what I assume is Kirill's bedroom, my soaked nightie leaves puddles in my wake. If I thought I had a chance, I would sprint for the door Kirill and several of his men are zooming through. Since I know my every move is tracked by over twelve men with orders of shoot to kill, I trudge to my room, then replace the frigidly cold water clinging to my skin with hot, scolding water.

With my mind blank with shock, I use the facilities, dress, then climb into bed without touching the tray of food laid out for me.

I'm exhausted, both mentally and physically, so within seconds, I fall fast asleep.

IT IS dark when I'm woken by the squeak of the mattress springs.

When I scamper back, frightened, the voice I've been searching for the past month finally floods my ears. "Shh, *маленький ягненок*. It's me."

Too angry to think rationally, I bang my fists on Ghost's chest before giving in to the tears that have been threatening to stream down my face for the past eight-plus hours.

He takes my beating until the sob I can't hold back overtakes my thumps. He curls his hands over my fists before using his hold to pull me into his chest.

"He tried to kill me. He..." *Hiccup.* "He wants me dead."

"No." Ghost rubs my back, soothing my shakes with a roughness I've become accustomed to before he presses his lips to my ears. "He wants you scared. That's how he likes them. You're too strong for him, so he'll try and break you."

"He did break me."

"Speak shit like that again, *маленький ягненок,* and I'll do more than hold your head under water for thirty seconds." I can't see him, but I imagine his jaw working side to side when a grinding crunch sounds through my ears. It is like he's fighting for his mouth to produce his next lot of words. "You are too strong for a weak, pathetic man like him to break, so remember that the next time he's playing tricks on you to have you thinking otherwise."

His reply suits him to a T.

He is a brute who can still be kind.

Ghost must have eaten his carrots when he was a child because the accuracy of his touch when he pulls the strands of hair stuck to my cheeks behind my ear without a wayward poke makes it appear as if he can see in the dark. "We're close, and it's making him panic, but instead of taking it out on me, he's focusing his anger on you." His deep exhale hits my cheeks before he mumbles, "It is a bad trait he learned from my father, but he won't hurt you any more than it takes to scare you."

Although curious about the first half of his last sentence, something he said earlier has my sole focus. "Close to what?"

Tears prickle my eyes when he replies, "Getting you home."

"What?" That's the best reply I can come up with. I'm too shocked to say more.

I would give anything to see his face when he replies, "You lied to me." He doesn't sound angry, but his tone rarely changes. Even when he is being playful, his voice remains stern. "You said you were made for this life." As I recall me throwing my life on the line for Hailey before my 'wedding,' he repeats, "You lied to me, didn't you?"

I want to shake my head. I want to continue fighting, but my exchange with Kirill today is playing tricks with my head. It has me scared. So much so, I'd rather face Ghost's wrath for lying than have another run-in with Kirill. "I thought I was, but I'm not—" Footsteps sounding down the hallway outside my room interrupt me before I can tell Ghost I only feel fearless when I am with him.

I can't understand a word our interrupter speaks, but I know it is Alek. I would recognize his deep timbre anywhere.

"I have to go, маленький ягненок."

I act as if I haven't faced the last eight and a half years by myself by gripping Ghost's shirt for dear life. I don't want to be left alone. "Stay with me."

"I can't tonight," he replies, his angry tone returning full force. "But I will be back."

He slips out of bed, then either straightens his clothes or the bedding.

My assumption goes in another direction when he advises, "You need to eat. I brought over some of Vera's ragu for you."

His unexpected but craved generosity thrusts me straight back into Kirill's bathroom. "Vera—"

"I know, маленький ягненок, and it's okay." I stare at his shadow like he is insane when he discloses, "I asked her to tattle." He drags his calloused thumb over my lip before murmuring, "Don't look so worried. I finally know what needs to be done. It is just taking longer to implement. You just need to trust that I'm doing everything I can."

"I do trust you." *Stupidly.*

"Good girl." He rubs at my lips for the second time like he'd rather it be anything but his thumb touching me before saying in a grouchy tone, "Obey as you've been taught, and you shouldn't face any more issues."

In other words, don't talk unless given permission to do so. That was the first lesson beaten into me by Madame Victoria, and the first rule I broke when Ghost pushed me to bite back.

He seems to like me feisty, and Kirill knows that. He wants us to fail because it doesn't just mean the end for me. Our attraction will cause Ghost's demise as well.

When a second lot of footsteps sounds through my door, Ghost growls a menacing tone that activates every one of my fiery buttons before he hotfoots it to the door.

He doesn't open it. He vanishes into thin air, which shouldn't make sense but kind of does since my door is deadbolted shut every night.

My eyes dart to the door when a loud bang sounds through it. I stop having a near coronary that Alek was taken down for my foolish sobs when one of Kirill's guards shouts, "Check in."

"Check in," I reply, well-rehearsed on the men's nightly routine.

Showering or not, if you don't reply in a timely manner, your door gets kicked in for a visual check.

The goon's next question is new, though. "Are you alone?"

"Why wouldn't I be?" I curse my snappy attitude to hell before replying more courteously. "Yes."

I lean over to switch on the bedside lamp when the guard mutters to himself, "I thought I could smell ragu."

He chuckles out something about snorting too many lines before he stomps to the next room to make sure Kirill's other brides are still present.

Just as quickly, I race for the tray of food that was delivered to my room between the doctor leaving and Kirill's attempted murder. The usual brothy soup isn't under the silver dome. It is Vera's famous ragu smothered in parmesan cheese and a generous dollop of sour cream. It is warm too, like it was just removed from the stovetop.

Feeling a little gluttonous, I snatch up the bowl and fork, plonk my backside onto the bed, then devour the serving big enough for two without coming up for air.

I pay for my foolishness only an hour later.

Half the ragu ends up in the toilet bowl, the other half in the shower stall.

It doesn't taste anywhere near as good coming up as it did going down.

My already sluggish steps into the main part of my room slow even more when I detect I'm being watched. It isn't a good feeling bombarding me, and when it arrives with a snickered, "I didn't think you'd want to wash again today," it is nothing close to virtuous.

Recalling Ghost's pledge, I dip my head before murmuring, "I was unwell."

"I heard." Kirill steps closer to me, his walk arrogant. "It's about time." He pulls my hair out of my eyes then raises my chin, alerting me to the fact his face is bruised. "Perhaps the doctor was right. Maybe boys don't cause morning sickness until closer to the second trimester."

It would be a lot harder to smile at his comment if his face didn't look sore. His right eye is blackened, and there is a large gash that goes from his left ear to his cheek.

"Are you okay?" I don't give a shit how he feels, but I'm curious as to why he is so badly marked only hours after hurting me.

Did Ghost do this in retaliation for him hurting me?

My stomach gurgles with worry instead of happiness when Kirill replies, "Why wouldn't I be?"

The familiarity of his words startle me so much I end our conversation instead of pushing it. "Goodnight."

"Before you go, I brought you something." I hate that my first thought is to gleam with excitement. It is hard to learn that affection doesn't come in the form of objects when you're being starved of attention. "It is on the bed."

I lick my suddenly parched lips before sidestepping Kirill and moving deeper into my room. A shiny box with a large pink bow sits near the folded blanket at the foot of the mattress. It looks expensive.

"Open it," Kirill encourages when I hesitate.

Everything comes at a price.

Even my freedom.

"What is it for? It isn't my birthday." *Is it?*

I truly don't know.

"No reason. I just saw it and thought you'd like it. Open it." Don't misconstrue his words. They were spoken with a vile, incensed tone. He's angry about my line of questioning.

Not wanting to give him a reason to punish me, I undo the bow, then flip open the lid. My already queasy stomach doubles its churns when I spot the lace detailing on the nightie beneath the tissue paper. It is identical to the one Ghost gifted me on the ship.

I swallow down the lump in my throat before murmuring, "It is beautiful. Thank you."

"Put it on." His tone doesn't leave room for leeway, much less how quickly he snatches up the delicate material and hands it to me.

It is virtually impossible to get dressed without exposing myself, but I do my best. I keep my back faced to him and slip the material over my head instead of stepping into it. This way, I only need to tug off my sleeping pants once the material is ready to float to my thighs.

"A perfect fit. You just need one last thing." The acid of my empty stomach scorches the back of my throat when he pulls out a pair of modest panties from the bottom of the box. They're stained with a similar white murky liquid that was in the vials he used to inseminate me and so damp, I'm confident the mess was only recently made, and more than one vial was used.

"I'm already wearing panties." I loathe the weakness of my reply. I absolutely hate it.

Kirill angles his head and cocks a brow. "What was that?"

He silently dares me to repeat myself, to give him the opportunity to strike while the iron is hot.

Although I've felt sparks of myself regenerating over the past couple of months, I'm not brave enough to defy him when it is only me standing at the plate, swinging by myself.

"That's what I thought you said," Kirill mutters when I slip my hands under my nightie to remove my panties.

My chin quivers when I slide the soiled pair he hands me up my thighs. They're saturated with cum, so soaked, goopy blobs drizzle down the smooth plains of my vagina.

I've continued my shaving routine for the past month. I have no idea why. I like how it makes me feel, but it was also my last-ditch effort of defiance. Ghost told me Kirill hates women with shaved vaginas, so I've shaved every day since.

"Perfect," Kirill murmurs a painfully long thirty seconds later. "Now into bed."

I want to run to the bathroom for a shower. However, I only promised Ghost tonight that I'd obey as I've been taught, so I dip my chin, then scuttle into bed.

My heart beats in my ears when Kirill tucks me in. It isn't just his unusual show of chivalry that has my tongue thickening. It is the words he whispers, "Goodnight, Little Lamb."

He doesn't free me to stew over his use of Ghost's nickname until I alleviate my breathing and gape my mouth. And even then, his exit appears to be done under protest.

43

KATIE

*P*retty sure it's not the ragu that made me sick. I've been throwing up every morning for the past month, and my clothes are becoming more fitted. My breasts feel heavy, and I've been sleeping like I didn't get an ounce of sleep the past nine years.

In a way, I should consider myself lucky that I don't have to pretend I'm pregnant anymore, but I'm also scared shitless. The gender of my child doesn't matter when it comes to my fate.

I'm dead either way.

Most of my concerns center around what Ghost's reaction will be. He left me in the care of my husband for the past two months, unaware that I've yet to have a period since the last real insemination. I'm petrified he will think I've done more than obey to get back into Kirill's good books.

"Come, Miss. We need to get ready." Nun Ellery's whizz into the bathroom slows to a trot when she spots me kneeling near the toilet. "Again?" When I nod, she wets a washcloth, then dabs up the spillage dribbling off my chin.

"I feel terrible."

Nun Ellery appears torn. I understand why. Tonight, I am meant to be attending a function with Kirill. He won't be happy if I try to get out of it. By obeying his every command, I've flown relatively below his radar the past month. "I'll pack some mints. They might help."

She assists me to my feet, then ushers me into my room. The drapes are closed, but I can tell it is dark out. The room gets super icy when the sun disappears behind the mountains.

"It needs to be white," I tell Nun Ellery when she pulls a beautiful baby pink dress out of the closet. "Pure white."

With a groan, she stuffs the dress back into the bursting closet, then selects a dress with a flowing skirt and fitted bodice.

"Oh, dear," she murmurs when the bodice hugs my breasts so firmly they spill out the top of the boned material. "That's not what we would call pure."

Since I agree with her, I ask, "Is there anything else?"

"With the weight you've put on the past two months, I don't think so." She moves to stand in front of me, then pushes down on the flabby skin popping out the top of my dress. When her shoves do little to hide my cleavage, she suggests, "Perhaps you could wear a coat?"

"That's a good idea." I have a large white feathered coat Kirill has requested I wear multiple times when we go out. He thinks the feathers make me look like an angel. "What do you think?" I ask after placing it on.

"It is good. He will be pleased." Although her habit will have you convinced she is referencing God. I'm not so easily fooled. She is speaking about my husband.

"Good." I'm such a liar. I still loathe Kirill with everything I have, but I'm living off the hope that my time with him will be short. Ghost said he was striving to get me home, and I trust that is still the plan.

"I placed mints in your bag." Nun Ellery stuffs a plain white purse with a strap into my chest before fetching my shoes from the bottom of the closet.

At this stage, most people heading out for the evening would commence a makeup and hair routine. I don't. Kirill said makeup makes me look trashy and that I am only ever to wear my hair down and add a small dab of gloss to my lips.

He'll probably be wishing he wasn't so boring when he spots the dark circles under my eyes and my pale skin. My room has a window I sit at for almost sixteen hours a day, but it isn't the same as standing directly under the sun's rays.

"I will see you when you return." Nun Ellery never says goodbye. She thinks it is a bad omen. Not often do the women who leave here return breathing.

After farewelling her with a smile, I make my way downstairs. Don't let the naivety of my reply fool you. My walk is flanked by the four men who regularly check my room, and there are another four at the end of the stairwell.

Their suffocating presence has had me convinced multiple times in the past month that I imagined Ghost's middle-of-the-night visit. How could he get through an army unscathed?

He must truly be a ghost.

After dismissing the men shadowing me with a wave of his hand, Kirill steps back to drag his eyes down my body.

He isn't checking me out. He is approving my choice of clothing.

I breathe again when he spins on his heels and walks outside. He doesn't need to demand that I follow him. He is anticipating I will obey him or die.

In the back of the stretched town car, Kirill reminds me of the rules he enforces anytime we're in public together. I am not to speak unless spoken to, I am to explain that my English is poor in a foreign accent, and I am to gush about him as often as possible.

Clearly, his ego isn't as big as everyone thinks.

"We have special guests attending tonight, so I expect you to be on your best behavior. I will not offer any leniency. If you act out, I will retaliate."

"I understand." I choke on the last half of my reply when the driver signals to turn right. We always travel left. Left is into town. It leads us toward society. Right only takes us to the Bobrovs' private compound.

Does Ghost know of Kirill's plans tonight? Is he aware I'm coming with him?

I'm highly doubtful when my exit from the car has a stern pair of eyes burning my skin. Ghost is standing on the second-level balcony.

His hands are balled into fists, his lips are stern, and he's shooting daggers.

Mercifully, they're not at me.

Well, not until Kirill assists me out of my coat in the entryway.

There's no hiding the tiny pop in the bottom half of my stomach, and don't get me started on my excess cleavage. Every man in the room notices it, including Ghost, who is making his way down the stairs. He's dressed to the nines like tonight's feast is more a celebration than a standard Friday night get-together.

"Shall we eat since our special guests have finally arrived?" Ghost asks in Russian, his gaze holding mine for a fleeting second.

"In a minute." With a wave of his hand, Kirill announces for everyone to head into the dining room. "I have a final surprise to set up." His suspicious-filled eyes bounce between Ghost and me as he demands us to follow his men into the dining room. "I will collect you shortly." Ghost's jaw ticks when he leans in to press his lips to my cheek. "Behave."

It dawns on me what tonight's celebrations are about when I spot a sign dangling above the mantel in the dining room. I understand little Russian, but I know one word, and it is the most detrimental.

Son.

When my eyes shoot to Ghost, he heads to the bar to pour vodka into a long line of shot glasses. "Can you believe it? He's finally getting the son he craves." He hides his twitching jaw by raising a shot glass full of vodka in the air and shouting, "To the Bobrovs."

I balk when the men echo his sentiments. "The Bobrovs!"

They clink glasses before downing their vodka. The only man who doesn't drink is Ghost. He stares at me before he places his still full shot glass down on the sticky bar top, then leans his elbows on the railed edge.

His watch tells me everything I need to know.

He knows what every man in this room doesn't.

That my pregnancy is no longer a ruse.

Before I can wordlessly plea for the chance to explain that it may be a result of the insemination he didn't do months ago, Kirill returns from setting up his surprise.

"Come. It is in the other room." I stand on a wobbly pair of legs when he shifts his focus to Ghost and says, "You too."

I shudder like the night he tried to drown me when our entrance into the room next to the entryway has my eyes locking with a piece of equipment I've seen before. It was when Ghost scanned me on the cargo ship.

"Blood can't lie, Kirill," Ghost says, his voice as rough as the swirls of my stomach. "She is carrying your son."

As untrusting as he is corrupt, Kirill replies, "Then there will be no harm checking, will there?" He locks his narrowed eyes with me. They're as unhinged as they were in the seconds leading to him holding my head under the water last month. "Get on the bed."

When my eyes instinctively shoot to Ghost to seek permission, Kirill grabs a fistful of my hair and yanks me to the makeshift hospital bed a doctor is standing next to. He is a doctor I've associated with a handful of times in the past two months, the one who told me I should reduce my stress.

I mouth, "*Lera,*" to Ghost when no amount of pain could have me missing his reach for his gun. He's mad and confused but sane enough to understand there's no way he will make it from here to Lera before all hell breaks loose.

"Does he look familiar?" Kirill asks, diverting my attention from the doctor to him.

I shake my head, but he doesn't believe me. "That's surprising, considering he's been working with you two the past several months."

I freeze like a statue when he ends his insinuation by shooting the doctor in the head.

Dr. Marc remains standing for two heart-clutching seconds before he flops to the floor in a contorted position that leaves no latitude to believe he isn't dead.

"One liar down." The scold of Dr. Marc's death is felt by me when Kirill pushes the end of his gun into my stomach before growling, "Two to go."

When he gestures for Ghost to move forward, Ghost growls out, "It's your fucking kid. I haven't touched her."

"I know." Kirill sounds more annoyed than pleased. "That's the fucking point. Scan her." A whimper seeps through my lips when he stabs his gun in so firmly it will leave a bruise. "Now!"

"All right. Fuck." Ghost snatches up the wand, coats the end with the special gel, then asks me to lift my dress. Only the slightest quiver hits his jaw when the flabby bulge at the bottom of my stomach is exposed before he pushes down on that exact spot. "If you want proof of the sex, you're shit out of luck. I can't tell the difference between a head and an ass with these things. You should have kept the doctor alive until after the..." His words flow into silence when an image pops up on the screen. I don't know what I'm looking at, but Ghost seems knowledgeable. "I guess that is pretty obvious." His eyes flick to mine for the quickest second before darting back down to my stomach. "That's his head."

"He?" Kirill asks, his voice shocked.

"I think so." Ghost swivels the wand around a handful of times before Kirill's impatience gets the better of him.

He snatches it out of his hand before conducting his own set of tests. He doesn't glide the wand over my stomach gently like Ghost did. He digs it in deep and jabs it against my pelvic bone before freezing it on an image that seals my fate.

I only have months left to live.

"It's a boy."

Ghost sounds as shocked as Kirill when he replies, "I fucking told you blood tests don't lie." He hides the sweat beading on his top lip by dragging his tongue along it before murmuring, "I also told you that you need to stop being so paranoid. I'm not out to get you."

Regretfully, I'm not offered the same courtesy.

Seconds after Kirill yanks his cell out of his trouser pocket to snap an image of our son, a beautiful blonde breezes into the room unannounced. She's wearing a flowing red dress and a sultry grin that's enhanced by red-painted lips.

"Honey, are you ready? Our guests are waiting."

My stomach drops to the floor when Ghost answers her instead of the man I was anticipating. Blondes are Kirill's top pick. "I'll be there in a minute." As he scrubs at his jaw, he peers down at the goop spread across my midsection before shifting his attention to Kirill. "Anything else? We have guests waiting." During the 'we' part of his statement, he nudges his head to the unnamed beauty who doesn't balk at the fact there's a dead man on the floor and that my dress is tucked under my breasts.

"No." Kirill doesn't look at Ghost while dismissing him from the room.

He must have learned a trick or two from Ghost, who curls his arm around the blonde's slender waist and exits without so much of a glance in my direction.

44

KATIE

Tonight's celebrations aren't solely about Kirill's future heir. It is also honoring the soon-to-be nuptials of a couple who found love on the crazy and fast route.

Ghost is engaged.

From information I've overheard from the serving staff and a handful of the guests as out of the loop as me, Ghost only met Anastasia last month. After a whirlwind affair that barely saw them coming up for air the past four weeks, he proposed in front of everyone at brunch yesterday.

Allegedly, Anastasia cried while sobbing 'yes' on repeat.

That tidbit had me wondering if Ghost regrets his proposal. I barely shed a dozen tears the night he comforted me after Kirill almost killed me, but it appears as if that is all it takes to be shunned by him.

I had a good reason to cry, but it appears as if his wife-to-be is the only one who is allowed to cry and live to tell the tale.

I won't lie. Even unsure what the hell is going on and terrified I only have a few months left to live, I am as mad as hell. Ghost asked me to trust him, and I gave it to him without hesitation.

I was an idiot.

For the umpteenth time this evening, I startle when the goon with a watermelon head cheers the Bobrovs again. "To the Bobrovs!"

They've been doing the same cheer all night like greatness is just around the corner.

I wonder how close they are when Kirill leans into my side and whispers in my ear, "Be ready to leave in ten. We have an early start tomorrow."

Goose bumps rise over my skin. I'm not turned on by his hot breath hitting my neck or the closeness of his lips to the shell of my ear. I'm responding to the glare his nearness throws me from across the table.

Despite his gushing fiancée spending the entire meal on his lap, Ghost has been watching me all night. He looks as angry as I feel.

Two hours ago, I could understand why.

Now, I am clueless.

When Kirill's phone rings, he gestures to a man to follow him outside before he mutters, "I need to take this. I'll be back to collect you in a minute."

I nod, unsure why he is suddenly updating me on his whereabouts. He never has before, and quite frankly, I don't care what the hell he does as long as it takes him away from me.

The daggers being tossed across the room greaten when he presses his lips to the edge of my mouth before he stalks outside. Ghost looks ropeable, and his glare is so white-hot I excuse myself to use the restroom. I don't really need to go, but anywhere will be more comfortable than sitting directly across from Ghost.

I make it halfway down the hallway the washroom is located in when my elbow is suddenly clutched, and my speed is unwillingly doubled.

After shoving me into the bathroom and locking the door behind him, Ghost slowly spins around to face me. He doesn't speak a word. He merely rakes his fingers through his hair, leaving it standing on end while breathing erratically.

I could let him stew, but I've never been one to pause on the dramatics. "I—"

"Don't," he interrupts, his Russian accent the deepest I've heard.

"Because I am this fucking close..." He holds his index finger and thumb out an inch to show how close he is from losing his cool. "To doing something I am sure you will *not* like."

"Like learning you're engaged isn't bad enough."

I realize I said my last comment out loud when he mutters under his breath, "You'd be praying that was the worst of it."

We're interrupted by a knock on the door. Ghost only cracks it open far enough for a pregnancy test to be pushed through by a heavily veined hand before he denies Alek's request to calm down by slamming the door in his face.

After ripping open the test and pulling out the tiny plastic cup inside, he tosses it to me. "Pee."

"I don't—"

"Pee!" He looks seconds from emptying my bladder with a knife until I walk to the toilet, drop the lid, then lower my panties down my legs.

"I've not had a period since I went to the mansion."

He scoffs but remains quiet.

Regretfully, I can't do the same. "You missed that one insemination."

"You're blaming this on me?" He doesn't give me the chance to answer him. "There were no traces of HCG in your urine the night Kirill..." He stumbles over his next two words. "Bathed you."

Bathed? Ha!

"Yet now, you turn up a month later, looking swollen with child." He looks downright murderous when he mutters, "But I haven't fucking touched you in over a month."

"Because you were too busy screwing your new fiancée."

He acts as if I never spoke. "So if this test comes back positive, I'll know you've been stepping out on me."

Stepping out? Are we in high school? "You did the scan. You know this baby is from the insemination you missed. Maybe they just stuffed up the test last month."

"It was the fucking demo video that comes with every machine!" Ghost glares at me like he has no clue who I am. "Do you really think

I'm not one step ahead of that prick? That he wouldn't want confirmation of the blood test Dr. Marc forged."

I freeze. Mercifully, I finish peeing before his shocking revelation is absorbed by my blurry head. "I'm not pregnant?"

While snatching the plastic cup full of urine out of my hand, uncaring that some topples out, he mutters, "I guess we're about to find out." He rips open the pregnancy test with his teeth as I'd imagine he would a condom if he ever used one, pulls off the cap, then dips the end into the urine.

I won't lie. I feel as if I am kneeling on tacks again. I've been sick almost every morning this month, and my breasts went up a cup size. I'm not anticipating a good result, and I am not exactly sure how to process that.

Ghost angles the test so I can't see the result screen, but I don't need to see it to seal my fate. His deep huff tells me everything I need to know.

"I didn't step out on you. I swear to God."

"God?" He huffs out a chuckle. "Good choice of words." With his anger so hot to send a bead of sweat rolling down my back, he throws his fist into the vanity mirror, smashing it to smithereens.

It barely brings his anger down to a manageable level. For several long seconds, he sucks in ragged breaths while clenching and unclenching his fists, then with nothing but a degrading tsk, he once again leaves me to pick up the pieces.

45

GHOST

*A*lek's eyes lift to mine when I enter my office at the speed of light. He grins at me hopeful a bit of banter will have me failing to notice that he moved the bulky wooden chair from under my desk to the middle of the room.

It's too fucking bad for him that I know the reason for his sudden wish to redecorate.

The brick of snow I haven't touched in three months is in the safe in the floor, under the very spot Alek positioned my office chair.

"Move."

"Gh—"

I cut him off with a vicious glare.

I am ropeable.

Fucking unhinged.

Now is not the time to mess with me.

"Move!"

He curses under his breath in Russian before he steps back with his hands held in the air. He doesn't remove the chair or the thick Persian rug hiding my once most-valued possessions from the world, so I have to dump Katie's positive pregnancy test onto my desk and the whore I found wandering the corridors onto the couch to do it myself.

"Fuck..." Alek breathes out slowly, his hands in his hair when he spots the positive result. "You know—"

I cut him off for the second time. Now is not the time for words, sympathies, or fucking limp-dick excuses.

It is time to get shitfaced.

Being drugged out of my head might be the only way I'll be able to show my face again.

"Two months. Two whole fucking months I've been working to get her out, and for what? For her to switch her focus from me to him."

"Ghost..." Alek's excuse trails off when he fails to find one. "She's not like..."

I stare at him, silently goading him to finish his sentence, to thrust my sister into my line of sight again. I am as desperate to kill as I am to lose a handful of brain cells, so I'm praying like fuck he will take a nibble out of the bait I'm dangling in front of him.

Like a fool without a wish to live, Alek finishes his sentence, although he leaves Sofia out of it for the first time in months. "You need to step back and look at things properly. Something isn't right. You've been saying it for months."

"Because you've been fucking with my head!" *And her. Her more than anyone.*

While growling about my accurate inner monologue, I pull open the thick safe door, lift out a brick of cocaine and toss it onto my desk, uncaring that the white puff cloud left in its wake is worth a couple of thousand. It is so fucking pure it will only take a line or two to have me forgetting the idiot I am.

That alone is worth a hit in revenue.

"I ain't watching you go down this path again," Alek mumbles while heading for the door. "You want to give that fuck face exactly what he wants by fucking yourself over, go ahead, but don't expect me to watch."

"Did I ask your opinion?"

"Nah," he replies, spinning around to face me. "But if you did..." he nudges his head to Katie being guided outside by Kirill, "... you would recognize that she can't stand sitting next to that fucker. He fucking stomped on her, so why the fuck would she lie with him?"

"Because she wants to live."

He pffts me then blows me off with a two-fingered salute. "You're fucked in the head."

The air forced into my office from my door being forcefully shut juts out the lines I'm cutting on my desk, but I snort them, nonetheless.

By the second line, pure euphoric pumps through my veins.

Third—fucking heaven.

There is nothing more exultant than this.

Except her.

Needing to drown out my thoughts, I look over to the redhead seated on the couch. Not my rough grab nor my exchange with Alek has rattled her knees.

She'll be a good distraction to the tightness my balls have been experiencing the past two months.

"On your knees."

After a long lick of her painted lips, she stands from the couch, saunters my way, then drops to her knees. When she peers up at me, I angle my head to ensure she can't see my scars before demanding, "Take it out."

My dick is flaccid, but it'll still be bigger than any she's handled. What I lack in empathy, I make up for in cock size.

As she undoes my belt, confident she will need to lower more than my zipper to free me from my trousers, I yank off the stupid-ass tie Anastasia suggested I wear to our impromptu engagement party, then unbutton the three top buttons of my dress shirt.

I figure my dick's lack of interest means I'll be here for a while so I may as well get comfortable. What I am not expecting is the reminder of the last time I undid my shirt while with company. It wasn't with Anastasia, and it most certainly didn't involve a woman expecting to be paid for a service.

It was when I slipped into the bath with Katie and promised I'd never let anything happen to her.

"Hurry the fuck up," I grumble out in a rough tone, annoyed by the memories flooding my head.

I'm a grouchy cunt in general, but I am worse when I haven't been laid in months.

Anastasia is gorgeous, but I'm not fucking interested. Not only would Alek cut off my balls for mowing the grass he never stopped watering even when she left him years ago, my cock still isn't interested in anyone but Katie.

Just like Katie's pregnancy, my engagement is an act, a ploy to unearth where Kirill's interests lay. Is it an heir anyway he can get it, or does he want Katie for more than the fact I want her?

After today's revelation, I have no fucking clue which way is up.

"For fuck's sake. How long does it take to remove a fucking belt?"

As I push the redhead away from me with my boot so I can remove the strap of leather myself, Alek's shouted words hit me on repeat.

"He fucking stomped on her."

He stomped on her.

He. Fucking. Stomped. On. Her.

With my mood obliterated and my understanding shut down, I do more than remove my belt. I upend my desk, sending it flying across the room as if it belongs in a dollhouse. My roar is animalistic, my veins hot. I'm seconds from doing more than smearing the redhead's lipstick, then I'm greeted by the last people I expect to show up at my office without notice.

Sofia and Lera.

"You did it," Sofia whispers, her voice a sob. "He's going to let us go." She hugs Lera in closer while muttering, "We're months from freedom."

46

KATIE

*M*y hand shoots up to clamp my mouth when my entrance into my room has a squeak popping between my lips. "Holy... Alek, you scared me half to death."

"Sorry." Don't let him fool you. His grin says the opposite. "Figured I'd come check on you." He fights his eyes to drop to my stomach for almost three seconds before they eventually win. "Things are a little..." He leaves his comment for me to work out.

"I didn't..." My speaking skills are as poor as his. It is a lot harder to fool someone when you're truly lost as to what is going on. "Ghost just..."

He looks sympathetic about my lack of vocabulary. "He'll come around."

"If not, I'm sure Anastasia will bring him around."

Anger about my statement hardens Alek's features with as much fury that rains down on me when I recalled I'm not the bad guy, but he steers our conversation in another direction. "I brought you something to eat. It's not ragu, but I still think it is the bomb."

When he lifts a silver dome off a dish I didn't notice on my drawers until now, an idiotic tear slips from my eye. He bought me grilled cheese sandwiches.

"Hey... jeez... fuck." We really shouldn't communicate when we're confused. It doesn't make a lot of sense and only adds to the bewilderment. "Don't cry, Kate. It is just some bread and cheese slapped together."

"I'm not crying about that. I just..." I squeal my frustration into the cool night air before trying again. "I don't know what the hell is wrong with me."

I shoot daggers at Alek when he mumbles, "I have an idea." He chuckles, bringing the temperature in the room to a manageable level. "I know you didn't, but I've got to ask—"

"I didn't sleep with Kirill."

"I know." His voice sounds nothing but downright gospel. "But did he do anything else?" I shake my head when he asks, "Inseminations? Weird doctor's visits?" I freeze and glare when he murmurs, "Warm baths with added lotions?"

"What?"

He scrubs a hand along his prickly jaw. "I've been researching swimmers way more than I ever fucking should, and you'll be amazed how long those suckers can last. If the temperature is right, they can survive days."

I take a moment to get over my shock so I don't sound like a brain-dead idiot before saying, "I haven't been in Kirill's vicinity the past month. Other than him stopping in the night..." My eyes widen as a memory I tried to bury floods my head. "He gifted me a nightie and new underwear."

Unease remains captive on his face until I dig the underwear from the bottom of my underwear drawer. "What the fuck?"

"They were stained like that when he gave them to me," I push out, wanting to ensure he is aware I am not responsible for their crusty, gross appearance. "Could they have?"

He screws up his nose. "I honestly don't know." He looks on the verge of being sick when he asks, "Can I keep these?"

I nod. The only reason I stuffed them into the bottom of the drawer was because I didn't want Kirill to have an excuse to gift them to me again.

"Thanks." He pushes them into his jeans pocket before checking his phone. "I need to go." He locks his eyes with mine. "You good?"

My nod must be pathetic as he grins a halfhearted smirk before he pulls me in for the quickest hug. "It's only fair I ruffle his feathers a little since he's been shaking the shit out of mine the past month."

I have no idea what he's referencing, but I relish the warmth of his hug for a minute before walking him to the door. "Try and eat and get some rest. Some shit appears to be going down. Sofia and Lera were moved here an hour ago."

"Lera is here?" My question should include her mother, but since I'm not exactly sure whose side of the fence she is on, I left her off. Something seems off with her. I just can't quite put my finger on it.

"Yeah." Alek's smile makes the need for moonlight unnecessary. "She usually raids the refrigerator for sweets around nine. It'll be a good time to catch her."

I point to the locks on my door. "There's no sneaking out for me."

My heart thuds against my ribs when Alek murmurs, "Do you really think he chose this room for no reason?" I assume he is referencing Kirill with how low his voice lowered during the 'he' part of his reply but am proven wrong when he mutters, "He couldn't sneak into your room every night if he didn't have access to the keys."

When he pushes on an empty bookshelf next to the door, my mouth falls open. *There's a secret passage.* "Where does it lead?"

"To the kitchen." Suddenly uneased, Alek steps into my path. "This isn't an escape route, Kate. If you run, it will cost more than your life. Do you understand?" His tone isn't threatening, but what other way can I take his warning?

"I understand."

My reply must not come out as confident as I was aiming for.

"Kate..." He drags out my name as if it has more letters than it does.

I lift my eyes to his. "I won't run." I made a pledge to Lera, and I plan to keep it, even if I have to do it without Ghost. "Thanks for checking on me."

"You're welcome." He bumps me with his shoulder, flashes me a quick grin, then exits the normal way.

I last an hour before my inquisitiveness gets the best of me.

After the festivities tonight and the multiple shots of vodka, the house is quiet. I doubt anyone will notice my feeble footsteps

The secret corridor is lit, so within minutes, I enter a massive walk-in pantry. As Alek advised, Lera is sitting at the island bench, scoffing down a handful of marshmallows. She isn't alone, so I am cautious to approach her, but she leaves me no choice when she spots me. "Katie!" My name sounds adorable in her Russian accent.

"Hello, Lera." As I walk out of the pantry, I smile at Sofia. "Should you be eating so much sugar this late at night? The bears might roar in your stomach." I speak my last sentence in Russian, making her giggle. I learned it from a nursery rhyme I recited at Master Rudd's. Her response makes me wonder if she has read the story.

She replies something in Russian that I don't understand before peering behind my shoulder. "*Дядя?*"

"He's not here," I reply, my tone dropping. "But I bet he will come see you soon."

When she peers up at her mother to translate, her brows knitted, Sofia smiles before saying, "It is time to wash up. We have a big trip in the morning."

She realizes she said too much when I ask, "Are you going somewhere?"

Lera returns her eyes to me. They're gleaming with excitement. "*Хороший. Мы едем на большой самолет.*"

This time, Sofia translates. "She said we're going on a big boat."

I balk at the end of her reply. My Russian is average, but I know what *самолет* means. Jace refused to bathe without his *гидросамолет*. Finding his favorite toy seaplane was the only way I could get him into the bathroom. I also had to pretend he was a plane to get him out of the dirt-stained tub.

Acting daft has kept me alive for the past eight and a half years, so I give it another whirl. "That'll be fun. I hope I can come with you."

Sofia interprets my reply for Lera before she clutches her hand and tells her it is time for bed.

"Goodnight, Katie," Lera whispers faintly as she is carried toward the exit. When I wave, she once again looks over my shoulder and farewells, "Goodnight, *дядя*."

Aware his hidey spot has been given away, Ghost replies, "Goodnight, Lera."

When I spin on a wobbly pair of knees, I discover Ghost in the walk-in pantry I only exited minutes ago. His eyes are wild, his clothes are disheveled, and I'm suspicious not all the white powder on his fingertips is the powdered sugar coating the marshmallows he's holding.

Despite the hope in my heart, I know he isn't here for me.

If Lera goes anywhere, Ghost is not far behind her.

I hate that I have to skirt by him to return to my room, but with multiple deadlocks on my door and just as many guards manning the hallway, I have no choice. I must return to my room before check-in or more than my life will be at stake.

It seems more than cocaine was on Ghost's hit list when I attempt to slip past him. He reeks of alcohol and perfume.

I take it his engagement party was a raving success.

I'm almost in the clear when Ghost's hand darts out to seize my elbow. His grip isn't painful, but I'd have to rip my arm out of its socket to get away from him, so I do nothing but freeze.

The hairs on the back of my neck prickle when he leans across to suck in my recently washed hair. It is the fight of my life not to sway into him. I'm hurt and confused, but my body craves his touch. I want it no matter the cost and would rather give up my freedom than lose it again for months on end.

"Ghost..."

He drags in a big breath that whistles through his teeth before pushing me toward the hidden stairwell. "Go, *маленький ягненок*, before I destroy you more than I already am."

"But—"

"Go!"

I race up the stairwell so fast the angry tears welling in my eyes almost pop free.

Their threat to spill is heard in my tone when I reply to the goon's request for me to check in.

"Check in."

I made it back to my room with only a second to spare, meaning my door remains intact.

My heart is another story.

47

KATIE

"*Shh, маленький ягненок, I'm here.*"

I jackknife into a half-seated position before straying my eyes around my room. When I see a shadowed figure at the end of my bed, I whack on the lamp so fast it topples to the floor.

"Jesus..." I breathe out the curse word I really want to say before slumping my head back onto my pillow. A shadowy being isn't standing at the foot of my bed. It is the suitcase I was requested to pack by the goon last night and my winter coat hanging in front of the freestanding closet.

It is lucky I packed early because I zonked out within an hour of eating last night. I haven't done that in weeks. I guess knowing Ghost isn't hating on me as badly as I thought loosened some of the heaviness on my shoulders. I just wish it could do something about my jealousy.

He's engaged. I'm not meant to want a taken man.

But I want him.

Ugh!

After checking that it is light out, I toss off the comforter wrapped around me like a burrito then trudge into the bathroom. I usually wake two or three times throughout the night to pee, but since I slept through last night, my bladder is on the brink of bursting.

Once I've done my business, I wash my hands in the vanity sink, grimacing when I catch sight of my reflection in the mirror. One side of my hair is flat as a tack, but the other has faultless curls framing my pale face.

After shrugging off my wish for something to hide my fatigue, I head back into my room to gather the clothes Nun Ellery left out for me last night. They're white but modest.

My hand shoots up to muffle my scream when I am startled by a large black figure near my stack of drawers. "You really need to stop doing that," I scold Alek, mumbling through the fingers clamped over my mouth.

"Sorry. I knocked. You must not have heard me since you were in the shower." I don't get the chance to tell him I haven't had a shower yet. "We're heading out in five."

"Heading where?"

Alek clicks his tongue against his top teeth. "The day I figure out that man's inner workings will be the day I'll take my final breath." He lowers his eyes to my nightie. "Do you want to wear that or get changed?"

"What do you think?" My nighties leave nothing to the imagination, which is highly annoying when you're trying to hide unwanted flab in your midsection. As I gather up the clothes personally selected for their purity, portions of my exchange with Lera pop into my head. "Lera mentioned she's going on a plane. Do you think that is what this is about?"

My throat gets scratchy when Alek's reply comes out shocked. "A plane?" When I nod, he asks, "Does Ghost know?"

"I don't know." It's my turn to shrug. "He was in the pantry when she said it, so he might have heard her." Although his whereabouts shouldn't bother me, I can't help but ask. "Did he stay here last night?"

I'm disappointed when Alek shakes his head. "He comes here every night, though."

"To check on Lera."

I realize I mumbled my highly ridiculous comment out loud when Alek laughs. Lera is not my competition. She is a child, for crying out loud. "Lera was only moved here last night." When my brows furrow, confusion evident on my face, his laugh ramps up, almost making his next statement inaudible. "You, however, have been here for months. If you were two seconds later, you might have passed him in the secret stairwell." While chuckling at my shocked expression, he nudges his head to my clothes spread out on the bed. "I will wait for you outside while you get dressed."

I smile in thanks before walking him to the door. The importance of our move is unmissable when I peer down the hallway. All the pricy paintings are being removed and placed into crates, and the antique hallway tables are being protected with white sheets.

We're not going on a weekend getaway.

The same heavy sentiment hits me when I dress and follow Alek to a long line of SUVs outside. The mansion is being placed into lockdown, and all of Kirill's top goons are filling the SUV I'm loaded into.

"We're going to the docks," I murmur to no one in particular when the landscape registers as familiar. It was several months ago I traveled through here, but I drank in every inch of the landscape since I had been starved of visual stimulation for so long. I'd never forget it.

My heart falters when I am proven right. Not only do we arrive at the original dock I was delivered to over six months ago, but Ghost is here as well. He's standing at the side of the gangway. A machine gun is strapped to his chest.

"Stay close to me," Alek murmurs, his voice barely a whisper.

Nodding, I follow him halfway to Ghost before all hell breaks loose. Gunfire rings from the hills behind us, forcing the Bobrovs to respond. They scramble in all directions, panicked yet somehow familiar with being ambushed.

"Keep your head down." Alek hides me behind a shrub before yanking a gun from the back of his jeans and returning fire on the people hiding in the dense bushland.

From my vantage point, I spot the vehicles of the people littering the docks with bullets. The front SUV's keys are tossed onto the driver's seat, and the door is hanging open.

With all the commotion being focused in the opposite direction I'm facing, I could make a break for it.

I won't, though.

Hailey is free because Ghost placed my family first, so I must do the same for him despite my heartache.

My plans falter when I crank my neck in the direction Ghost is standing. He is returning enough fire to keep the focus off him, but I can't miss the inconspicuous nudge of his head. It is the same gesture he did at the auction years ago, the head bob where he pointed me in the direction of freedom.

He wants me to run.

I shake my head.

I can't leave.

Not now.

Not until Lera is free from danger.

I also don't want to leave him.

"Now, маленький ягненок!" Ghost shouts, his voice loud enough to project over the booming gunfire.

When he spots my second headshake, he curses before he demands Alek to move me, which he does a nanosecond later.

He doesn't direct me toward the cargo ship, though.

He races me to the concealed line of SUVs.

Regretfully for them, like a choreographed stunt in an action movie, Bobrov men flood the shipping yard from all angles. They're heavily armored, geared up for a fight, and outnumber the insurgent of their enemy ten to one.

"Get her onto the boat," Kirill orders, blocking the path Alek was just racing me down.

Before Alek can respond to his demand, the goon with a head the size of a watermelon tosses me onto his shoulder then veers me past Ghost, his steps thunderous.

I'm dumped into a locked office, my worry only intensifying when the door is flung open over forty minutes later. Ghost is standing in the doorway. His veins in his arms are bulging, his jaw tight.

He appears furious.

"Why the fuck didn't you run?" His voice is a vicious snarl.

"Be-because..." I don't speak another word. How can I be expected to speak when he crowds me against the only solid wall in the room before gripping my neck in a firm I'm-going-to-kill-you hold? His skin is hot, and he smells insanely mannish since gunpowder residue has been added to his already alluring palette.

"You were meant to go. It was your way out. That whole fucking fiasco was set up for you!"

I'm stunned he'd go to such lengths so soon after believing I betrayed him, but the truth can't be hidden. "Lera—"

"Isn't your responsibility!" He bangs his fist into the wall behind me before tightening the grip of his other hand. "But you are mine..." I take his comment as possessive until he adds, "And I said I'd get you home." He means I am his responsibility, not that I am his. "That was our only fucking chance." His wild eyes bounce between mine. "I have no jurisdiction where he is taking you. No say. I have no power there." I wonder if I have his emotional prompts mixed up when he mutters, "I also promised I wouldn't let him hurt you again. I wanted to get Sofia and Lera out, and we've done that." My eyes widen when I realize Lera wasn't lying last night. She is going on a plane. "But not like this, маленький ягненок. Not by putting your life back in his hands."

"He hasn't hurt me." Gosh, the heartache in his voice cuts me raw. He believes that I didn't lie with Kirill, but since I am pregnant, he's reached another conclusion. "Not in the way you're thinking. He—"

We're interrupted by the goon who threw me into the office with no concern for my 'status.' "Well, well, doesn't this look cozy?"

After flashing me the quickest apology solely using his eyes, Ghost steps back. "That was about her." He nudges his head toward the docks we're sailing away from. "We were fucking ambushed for a whore with an untouched cunt!" He licks his lips then snarls at me like he hates me. "Kirill might not have the balls to tell her how it is, but I fuckin' do." He looks me up and down before speaking words I am all too familiar with. "You have no power here. None whatsoever."

"Yeah, yeah, save it for the boss, big boy." After gesturing for us to follow him, he announces, "Kirill wants to see you." He locks his eyes with mine. "Both of you." Before I can blink, he flattens his gun to my temple like he knows I am the only bargaining chip Ghost has left to barter with. "I'll take those," he murmurs, gesturing his head to Ghost's gun holster he's wearing on the outside of his clothing today. When Ghost's teeth grit, he adds, "And the one strapped to your ankle."

"I'll have your fucking head for this," Ghost sneers in a vicious tone as he removes his holster before lifting the cuff of his pants. He doesn't hand his weapons to Watermelon Head. He tosses them onto a desk before ensuring he knows he will be coming back for them. "Because I'm gonna shove them into every fucking orifice you own before releasing the trigger. You'll be eating shit and brain matter at the same time."

The goon smiles. It is foolish for him to do because it doubles Ghost's determination. He's furious, downright ropeable, and his wish to kill doubles when we reach the stern of the boat. We're not the only duo Kirill has summoned. Alek and Anastasia are here as well.

"You want to have a good fucking reason for dragging me out here after that showdown." He nudges his head to the carnage left for the dock workers to clean up. "Sniper bullets can travel miles."

Terror rains down on me when Kirill murmurs, "That would have been handy to know." It isn't the viciousness of his words that has me choking back a sob. It is the gun he pulls out from behind him that he arrows onto Ghost's chest. "Would have saved me the cleanup."

"I'm your fucking brother, you can't touch me."

My shock that Ghost and Kirill are related doesn't get the chance to sink in. "No!" I scream in a frantic roar when three bullets shred through Ghost's midsection. They hit him in rapid succession, pushing him back so forcefully, he hits the salt-eroded floor with a thud.

As Anastasia's eyes shoot to Alek in panic, I dive for Ghost. Splatters of the blood Ghost is choking on as he fights to live dots my cheeks when I shield him from additional carnage with my body. "Hold on. Please."

He could survive.

He's still breathing.

It is low and wheezy, but he's not close to dead.

"No," I scream when an arm wraps around my waist, and I'm dragged behind a large stack of shipping containers. It isn't just the image of Ghost lying lifeless that's shutting down my emotions. It is the direction Kirill aims his gun next.

He is pointing it at Alek's head.

I'm paralyzed with fear when a bullet being fired ricochets throughout the containers only seconds later. It cruelly informs me I have nothing to live for anymore and absolutely no hope.

Not a single iota.

So, with my mind shut down and my heart shattered, I ram my elbow into the goon's rib, throw back my head, then start my sprint to hell with a grunt.

I'll dive into the frigidly cold waters without an ounce of hesitation this time around.

"Get her," Kirill shouts, doubling the length of my strides. "But don't hurt her. She is with child. *My* child."

His possessiveness makes me sick. I can't be pregnant with his child. I'd know if I was growing the devil's spawn.

When I round a corner too fast for my skittish legs, I skid into someone coming from the opposite direction.

Regretfully, it belongs to the one person who shouldn't be here anymore than me.

After taking in my wide, wet eyes and colorless face, Sofia pushes past me and sprints into the opening. When her gut-wrenching scream booms over the lifeless splash of a body being dumped into the ocean, the world crumbles beneath my feet.

I collapse to the floor with a sob, my reality now worse than hell itself.

48

KATIE

"You need to eat." Kirill's anger is so apparent half of the tomato soup in the bowl he slides across the table sloshes over its rim and lands on the battered wood wedged between us. "You look unkempt. Like no one cares about you. I won't fucking have it."

I wipe away the sneaky tear that falls from my eye when Vera places a grilled cheese sandwich and a jar of prickles next to the cracked soup bowl. It was once my favorite meal.

Not anymore.

"I'm not hungry." My voice sounds robotic. It matches my aura to a T. I am on autopilot mode. Breathing, sleeping, and occasionally eating, but not living.

I am dead on the inside.

"I didn't fucking ask if you were hungry," Kirill roars. The vibrations of his voice could have rattled my heart out of my chest if it was still there.

I am empty—both heartless and soulless.

When his aggression gets him nowhere as it has the past two days, Kirill takes another direction. "What do I need to do to get you to eat? Magic. A threat? T—"

"Bring him back."

He throws a wedge of grilled bread onto his plate before rubbing the grease from his hands on his napkin. "Who back?"

"You know who." For the first time in days, my fighting spirit emerges. "You killed him. You fucking killed your brother." He backhands me so forcefully my teeth crunch together, but it doesn't slow me down. "You're a murderer."

He stands from his seat and flattens his palms onto the tabletop, his face as red as a beetroot. "Because he deceived me! Because he went behind my mother's back! I should have killed him years ago." I'm lost as to what he's referencing but am not given a chance to seek clarification. "And I'm over spoiled fucking princesses who think their bloodline is more important than their status." His angry breaths fan my stinging cheek when he snarls, "So how about I teach you a lesson." When he jerks up his chin, Watermelon Head snatches my wrist in a painful hold and drags me to kneel at his feet. I snarl at him, baring teeth when he murmurs, "Barbed wire, right? That's your favorite form of restraint."

With the last of my energy, I spit at him.

My defiance only doubles his grin. "Let's see how long that attitude lasts."

With a second head nudge, I'm plucked to my feet by a rough grab of my hair and yanked out of the room.

―――――――――

My first stay in the orlop lasted four days.

My second was a little shorter, coming in a day short.

My third is by far the shortest, only lasting a little over twenty-four hours.

I'm not giving in. I just don't have the energy to fight the goon forcefully returning me to the dining room where my initial punishment began.

"Eat."

I'm thrust onto a seat across from Kirill by Watermelon Head. Well, I think it is Kirill. My hunger is so apparent my vision is blurry.

For the first time, I look in Kirill's direction with something other than disgust on my face when he compromises. "If you eat, I will feed the women in the orlop along with you. If you don't..." I should have known there was more to his compromise than he led me to believe when he ordered my return to the dining room, "... I will kill one woman for every meal you refuse."

"What?" My voice is brittle and weak.

He smirks, grateful he forced me to respond. "Starting with her."

My heart falls to my shoeless feet when Anastasia is brought into the dining room by two goons. We've bonded the past week, and I learned things between her and Ghost weren't as perceived. Up until his death, he was striving so much to get me free that he didn't have time to eat, much less fool around.

The meals Ghost, Alek, and Anastasia shared in his office added to everyone's belief that Ghost was doing more than burning the candle at both ends, so they pushed their beliefs to gauge Kirill's reaction.

It wasn't as anyone expected.

I'm drawn from my thoughts by Kirill asking, "What will it be, Kate?"

My head naturally shakes, my stubbornness hard to overcome until the briskest movement sees Kirill waving his hand through the air like a king granting a kill shot. "Okay," I shout, my voice brittle and in pain —both physically and mentally. "I'll eat. I will do as you ask."

Kirill doesn't believe me. I'm not surprised. It sounded dishonest even to me.

To prove my point, I pluck a bread roll out of the basket, tear it apart, then push a massive chunk between my lips. My mouth is so dry since none of the food scraps are delivered with water, and it is hard to swallow the bread, but I manage—eventually.

"More."

Once I finish my bread roll and move on to the pasta dish Vera places down with a rattled hand, Anastasia is returned to the orlop untouched.

"It's okay," Vera whispers as quietly as a church mouse. "I'll make sure they're fed." She squeezes my hand, her kind gesture concealed by the tablecloth. "I promise they'll be okay."

Her pledge confirms what I already suspected. Our meals were designed to look like scraps, but they were much more generous than previously served and not rotten.

I thank Vera with a halfhearted grin before shifting my eyes to Kirill. His ticking jaw has me worried he overheard our conversation, so I steer him away from Vera before he can reprimand her. "What now?"

He keeps his eyes locked with Vera for three painfully long seconds before he eventually drifts them to me. "You are my wife, so it is about time you act like you are."

When he gestures for me to follow him, I swallow down the food I just scarfed before shadowing him to the side of the ship where the cabins are located.

My steps would be heavier if I hadn't snuck the bread knife off the table. It fills me with even more power than a room with a lock. It makes me feel alive for the first time in over a week.

It can't issue Kirill the same guarantee.

49

KATIE

The last half of our voyage was long but thankfully uneventful. Kirill wants a wife, but only in title. He walked me to my room, which stabbed my heart a million times, but proved some of Anastasia's theories were right. This stage of my captivity was as much about Ghost as it was me.

Kirill wants to taunt me.

I won't give him the satisfaction.

My fear is not his to barter with.

Even if it is the only thing of value I have, I own it.

I think I celebrated a birthday a couple of days ago, but don't quote me on that. The calendar in Ghost's cabin was several years old, and one day is constantly melding into the next at the moment. I was free to roam the ship as I wanted, but since the women in the orlop only had Vera and me looking out for them, I couldn't grieve by curling up like a cat in the circular window in my room and sobbing until my body ran dry of fluids.

I cooked for Kirill and his men, purposely making double the amount needed so there were plenty of leftovers, then tried to sleep away my grief.

It didn't work.

I am so tired it takes me several long moments to recognize my surroundings. I'm not sure how I forgot it. My father brought me here multiple times in the summers before my kidnap, and it's hardly changed since Alek walked me onto the cargo ship over four and a half years ago.

When I huff, Watermelon Head murmurs, "It is easier to hide in plain sight than start a new identity in a new town. People are accustomed to seeking things out of the ordinary. If it fits in, you don't give it a second glance."

I roll my eyes at his snooty tone. I've been obeying as taught for the women in the orlop, but I have no incentive now they've been bundled into the SUVs surrounding us. "If you're stupid enough to bring me to a town that borders my hometown, I doubt you're smart enough to realize I'll be recognized."

My stomach gurgles when he replies with a grin, "Maybe that's the point."

Thick, hot blood filters through my veins when our SUV is stopped for an immigration check by a local department. I realize the surge of adrenaline it arrived with could have been saved for a better use when the quickest exchange of funds has our fleet pushed through customs without a single officer peering into my SUV.

I've changed a lot in the past almost nine years, but they would have aged my kidnap fliers, surely.

Watermelon Head is a wealth of information today. "Over half of Hopeton PD are on the mafia's payroll. It's why we dock here."

"It is also where I saw you for the first time." Kirill has been so quiet I didn't realize he slipped into the same SUV as me. "Fire-red hair, untouched skin, and attitude in abundance." His haughty smile gleams off the windshield. "I should have taken you then, but Ghost said you were too young. That you'd be dead within a year of being put in the trade." He cranks his neck back so he can witness my disgusted expression without hindrance when he snickers. "You proved him wrong, didn't you?" He doesn't wait for me to answer before exposing I would have ended up in this exact predicament no matter the decision I made the day I was barely fourteen. "Sergei was meant to bring you to the docks, but he let Colum Petretti whittle in his head." He drags his eyes down my body. "I found you, though. Eventually."

"You didn't find me," I fire back before I can stop myself. "They lured you to me because even they know you're too pathetic to find a woman willing to procreate with you the God-given way." He launches for me, his grip on my dress firm enough to pop threads, but it doesn't stop my vicious tongue. "You're not a god. You're a limp dick fraud—" He ends my rant by backhanding me so fiercely my brain rattles against my skull, and several teeth loosen.

Regretfully, that is only the start of the retaliation. Guns are drawn, words are exchanged, and a weapon is jabbed into my stomach. "Do it," I mock with a blood-stained grin. "Kill the child you so desperately want."

When my rile has the gun digging in so deep it brings a whimper to the base of my throat, Kirill growls out, "You even think about it, and I will blow your fucking brains out all over your ugly shirt."

One vicious snarl is all it takes for the goon to remove his gun and raise his hands in the air. It is too late for him, though. A second after he slumps back in his chair, hopeful his silent apologies are enough, Kirill blinks once. I assume it is a natural occurring reaction when fear is induced, but I soon learn otherwise when Watermelon Head inflicts a large gash to the goon's neck. It squirts blood on my face and reminds me that I am nothing but a commodity to these men.

He was taken down as warned, and Kirill shows not an ounce of remorse. All that projects from his face is anger when he locks his narrowed eyes with me and snarls, "New rules."

With a flick of his wrist, the fleet of SUVs stops, and a goon in the car in front of us slips out of his seat. He isn't alone. He is clutching a frail blonde's hair, dragging her from her seat as remorsefully as Kirill wishes he could handle me.

My unborn child is the only thing keeping me alive.

"You act out..." He doesn't finalize his threat but simply does a meager wrist flick, and once again, someone else suffers the consequences of my actions.

After knocking her off her feet with a backhanded slap, the goon seemingly reading Kirill's thoughts pops a bullet in the blonde's head, stilling her movements immediately.

While grinning like a man without a heart, Kirill shifts his focus back to me. "Do I make myself clear, *Little Lamb*." He looks like he ate raw liver while muttering my nickname. "Or shall we go another round?"

Despite the wish to continue rebelling, my chin quivers when I recognize the blonde they choose next.

Anastasia.

"I will do as asked."

"What was that?" He heard me, he's just being a jerk.

I wipe the blood from my teeth with my tongue before repeating, "I will do as asked."

He waits a beat before dipping his chin then righting himself in his seat. "Very well. Continue."

The goodbye wave I give Anastasia when our SUV careens around hers is pathetic, but since it is all I have to offer her in reassurance, I don't keep it from her.

It could be the last gesture we exchange.

THE MANSION we arrive at forty-five minutes later isn't as large as the one in Russia, but it has ample bedrooms with sturdy locks and thick walls. It means only the quietest of whimpers will ripple through the wallpapered walls instead of the moans, groans, and sobs I heard on the ship at all hours of the day and night.

I doubt I'll have time to unwrap what happened earlier today until tonight.

A second after being pushed through the entryway, I'm shoved into a room, told to unpack, then informed dinner will be served within the hour.

Since my door has the most locks on it, I assume my meals will be brought to me, so you can picture my shock when someone knocks on my door a short time later and says, "Dining room in ten."

I stare at the shadow under my door, certain it is a trick, before sheepishly replying, "I eat in my room."

"Not tonight you're not. Dining room in ten." My mood is so unbalanced, I almost argue. The only reason I don't is from the unnamed man's reminder that I am nothing but an incubator for Kirill. "And he wants you in a fitted white dress. You'll find it in the wardrobe."

While building up the courage to open it, I peer at the closet. If it is anything like the one in Russia, it will be filled with pretty things I'm not allowed to wear.

Shockingly, I'm wrong. One dress is dangling in the middle. It is similar to the one I wore at my 'wedding' except it is minus the tulle that lit up in the church's many lights.

Once I've squeezed into the dress two sizes too small, I brush my hair, dab my lips with gloss, then walk to the door to wait for someone to collect me.

When twenty minutes pass without a single knock, my inquisitiveness gets the best of me. I test the lock, gasping when it opens without the usual clang of locks. My tour through the mansion was quick, but I caught sight of a dining room at the bottom of the stairwell, so I head in that direction before realizing my walk isn't shadowed by the usual goons who follow me. They're still present but mingling toward the back like they're not documenting my every move.

My hope that a MIB neuralyzer wiped the memories of every man in this mansion is dashed when my arrival at the bottom of the stairs sees me greeted by Kirill as if I am his wife. "Here she is. The lady of the hour."

When he steps away from a man I've never seen before to hold out his hand in offering, I take it before acting the part I only had to play in public in Russia. "Sorry I'm late. I had a little bit of trouble fitting into my dress."

Our guest's eyes shoot to my stomach before they return to my face. "I see." He has dark yet kind eyes, and his accent is a mix of many. "And how are you, Katie?"

His use of my name throws me off character for a second, but Kirill's firm grip on my hand pulls me back into line just as swiftly. "I am very well. Thank you. I'm not loving this humidity, though. It does crazy things to my hair." It is flat and lackluster since Ghost's fingers haven't entwined in it for weeks.

I also haven't washed it, but that is a story for another day.

"I think your hair is lovely."

The stranger's praise sounds genuine, and it heats my cheeks. "Thank you."

He takes a moment to assess my reply before dipping his chin. "Shall we eat?"

"Yes, please. I am starved."

That is a lie, one of many I've issued the past month, but no one in this room would know that.

When the gentleman with the black hair and pricy suit gestures for me to lead the way, Kirill's eyes silently warn me to behave. Although I don't have much to lose, I will obey as taught. Not because I'm the coward every man in this room thinks I am, but because I recognize a handful of faces mingling in the dining room. Particularly the little cherub already seated at the table.

Lera has arrived stateside, and the knowledge almost breaks me.

Her freedom was meant to be Ghost's legacy.

Now he has nothing.

"Katie," Lera exclaims excitedly when she spots me.

The heavy lines of suspicion on the stranger's face soften when I bob down to greet her with a cuddle. "Hello, Lera," I whisper in Russian. "Did you have fun on the plane?"

When she nods, I drag my index finger across her ruddy cheeks before returning to a standing position. Not willing to let me go any more than I am her, she wraps her arms around my leg like she always did to Ghost. She smears her jellybean-stained face into my dress with no concern she'll defuse my cloak of purity before she peers over my shoulder. "дядя?"

When her brows furrow while her tear-filled eyes bounce from man to man to man, I lie so I'm not the one forced to break her little heart, "дядя is still on the ship. He will be here shortly."

Before the wetness welling in her eyes angers her father, I guide her back to her seat then plonk onto the vacant chair next to her, our hands never losing touch. It exposes to Kirill that he has more chips than he realized when it comes to controlling me, but so be it.

I have enough strength to fight for us both, and I won't give up until we both make it out of here alive.

DINNER GOES WELL, but a second after our guest leaves, Kirill orders me back to my room.

"It's okay," I assure Lera, although certain she still can't understand me. "I will see you again soon. I promise."

I wipe away the sneaky tear that escapes her eye before heading for the stairwell that is once again brimming with goons and their angry snarls.

"I'll take her," a man offers when my elbow is suddenly clutched by Watermelon Head. I still haven't learned his name, even with him watching me for months on end.

My heart drums in my ears when I sling my head in the direction of the badly accented voice. We've met before. He was at my auction, and at one stage, I believed he was on my team.

"Get the rest ready for my return." His snicker doesn't match the gleam darting through Watermelon's hooded gaze. He didn't order for his sheets to be turned down. He gave Watermelon Head dibs on the throng of women the Bobrovs are rarely without.

Mercifully, they're not the same women I was locked in the orlop with.

Once we clear the landing of the stairs, Aaren drops his hand from my elbow before he walks ahead to open the door for me. It would be a more chivalrous act if he didn't greet me into my room with the same horrid accent he used downstairs.

I'm aware some of my anger resides from his false pledge to help years ago—if he had kept his word, I may have seen my parents again before they died—but most of it is my wavering mood swings.

I am so hormonal.

Also, he can't punish me, so I bite without the fear of being smacked over the nose for disobedience.

"Your Russian is horrendous."

Aaren follows me into the bathroom so I can wash my face of the dirt I feel coating it anytime I am in Kirill's vicinity. "Sorry? How can it be terrible? It is how I speak."

I shoot my eyes to him, my fear not as apparent as normal. "There are no 'I'-sounding words in the Russian vocabulary. They're pronounced 'ee.' Big is *Beeg*. This is *theese*." His shocked expression encourages me to continue expressing the differences I adored about Ghost's accent. "And you don't roll your R's enough. A real Russian flicks his tongue along the roof of his mouth almost the entire time he speaks. You do not." I could leave our conversation there, but my grief is still too deep for me to pull myself out of it. "You also didn't have an accent the last time we spoke."

As he looks at his shoes, his tongue darts out to replenish his dry lips. "You remember that day?"

"It is a little hard to forget the day you were sold."

I twist to face him when he mutters, "That is what he wants everyone to believe." When he nudges his head to the door, a blond lock falls in front of his face. He has a similar mannish manbun as Alek, but his hair is more platinum blond than dirty. "He wants everyone to believe that you are here of your own free will. That you choose to be with him."

I huff before I can stop myself.

The chances of blowing Kirill's cover are doubled when Aaren adds, "And that you begged him to birth his child."

"Begged." My laugh is more manic than authentic. "I don't recall it quite like that."

When I move into the main part of my room to wash down some headache tablets with a glass of water, I look at Aaren in a completely different light. It isn't solely his offer to pour the glass on my behalf, it is how he raises it into the light and swirls it around.

More than water is in my jug.

Specks of white powder can't be missed in the swirls of the light.

"It's a lot harder to drug you when you pick your own place to sit." With his accent forgotten and his wink a little too cocky for my liking, Aaren wishes me goodnight before he exits my room, leaving me speechless.

50

KATIE

A parcel of air escapes my mouth in a hurry when I'm suddenly clutched at the side.

Kirill drags me into a room next to the entryway before pushing me toward a desk a bank of monitors is spread across. "Who is he?" He shoves my head so close to the monitor, I can't make out a single image before asking again, "Who the fuck is he?"

"I can't see who you're referencing, but if they're anyone associated with me, he is one of your men."

"One of *my* men?" He laughs a condescending chuckle. "None of *my men* are brave enough to go against me." He pushes my head in so close to the monitor it almost cracks under the pressure. "They know what happened to the last fool who betrayed me." He tosses me across the room as if I am a ragdoll, uncaring of my 'condition' as he often refers to my pregnancy. "Get the fuck out of my sight and stay away from him."

He doesn't need to tell me twice. I scamper to my feet, then race for the door, narrowly missing the man who has Kirill's panties in a twist for the fourth time this week.

"Katie, what's going on?" Aaren asks, following my race up the stairs.

He's become the equivalent of Alek to me in the past four weeks. Nothing more. We are friends, but it appears as if I can't even have that.

"Hey, slow down, talk to me." Aaren grabs my arm before spinning me around to face him. Blood floods his face when his eyes bounce between mine before he snarls out in a fake Russian accent. "What did he do to you?"

"Nothing. I'm fine. He did fucking nothing."

"This doesn't look like nothing?" I feel giddy when he lowers his thumb from my hairline. It is coated with blood. But that isn't my sole concern. I swore, and Kirill just disclosed he has more than men watching me. "Whoa. Don't go fainting on me."

Before I kiss the floor, Aaren gathers me in his arms then walks me into the closest bathroom. It happens to be mine since I almost made it to the safety of my room before he caught up to me.

"In the second drawer," I announce when his hunt for the first-aid kit starts on the wrong side of the bathroom.

"Used this more than once the past month?" he asks, assuming the cuts in my wrists are recent since Kirill's rough grab reddened them up.

I shake my head. "This is the first time."

Aaren uses my shock against me. "What about the bruise on your cheek your first night here?"

"I raced onto the gangway a little too eagerly."

He arches a blond brow, unknowingly showing off his icy blue eyes. They're the same color Ghost's were when he didn't shelter them with an angled chin. "You still running with that?"

"It's the truth."

Aaren's lips tug into a grin. "Sure, it is." When I hiss from him dabbing iodine on my cut, he murmurs, "Sorry. I'm used to handlings thugs. Delicateness is not my forte."

His reply thrusts Ghost into the forefront of my mind again, which also grants him my first genuine smile in weeks.

"Hey, I much prefer that than the sad look your eyes are rarely without. How come you hardly smile?"

Recalling an altercation months ago, I murmur, "I've not had much incentive."

"What about him?" He nudges his head to my stomach, slackening my grin. If you didn't know my circumstances, you wouldn't know I'm pregnant. My stomach appears more flabby than round, but that doesn't stop Kirill from announcing to anyone who will listen that I'm pregnant with his son.

When I remain quiet, Aaren negotiates, "Truth for a truth?"

There's only been one man who has ever seen through my lies, so I jerk up my chin.

"My real name isn't Aaren."

I try to act shocked.

Aaren doesn't buy it.

"It is better than me telling you I'm not Russian." He chuckles under his breath while waggling his brows.

I wish I could appreciate his humor, but I can't. My life is not fun.

I am inquisitive, though. "What is your real name?"

He arches a brow, wordlessly announcing I have to tell him a secret before he will disclose any more details.

I have a million lies at the ready, but my heart pulls me in another direction, "Kirill killed his brother."

I stare at Aaren in shock when he snaps out, "Milo?" His shocked expression augments when I shake my head. "Then who. He doesn't have any other brothers." When I curve my brow, giving him the same mocking response he issued me when I tried to interrogate him without paying my dues, he murmurs, "I'm..." His pause doesn't flood me with the promise that he is telling the truth, but the lack of deceit in his tone has me on the fence. "Grayson. My name is Grayson, but you have to call me Aaren, okay?"

"Okay." Aware I am digging his hole deeper for every second we spend together alone, I slip off the vanity then pad to the door. "We probably shouldn't hang out anymore, though. Kirill is getting mad."

"You don't need to worry about Kirill. I don't work for him. He has no say in my time here."

Just before I reach the door, I pivot to face him. "Then who do you work for?"

I don't know if I should be relieved when he drops his eyes to my stomach or panicked. "For the man who wants to authenticate Kirill's claims you want to carry his son." Realizing he said too much, he lowers his eyes to his shoes before saying, "Have an early night. I'll tell everyone you passed out from exhaustion."

"I'm not tired."

A smile twitches on my lips when he replies, "I didn't ask if you were."

He's as bossy as Ghost.

Well, as Ghost was.

With grief weighing heavily on my chest, I murmur, "Goodnight, Grayson."

My almost smile lands on his lips before he whispers, "Goodnight, Katie."

51

KATIE

"*Circular movements, маленький ягненок. You're not trying to push your clit back inside yourself.*"

As my teeth rake my lower lip, I recall more of Ghost's teachings.

"*Now dip your fingers a little bit. You don't have to push them in deep, but they'll give your cunt something to cling to while it builds the wave.*"

I slide two fingers inside myself before furling the tips. A shudder hits my thighs when I find that sensitive spot that loosens the tight band strangling my chest.

"*Don't stop. It's meant to feel like that. Naughty, dirty, but oh so fucking good.*"

While imagining his hot breath hitting my neck, I use the pad of my palm to stimulate my clit. First contact sends a surge of electricity through my body, reminding me for the first time in months that I'm alive.

"*What was that?*"

"Nothing," I reply to the voice in my head. "I didn't say anything."

A smile breaks across my face when I recall how angry lying made Ghost and how his fuse was even shorter than his ability to make me come.

One swipe of my clit, and he sent me spiraling over the edge of orgasmic bliss.

I haven't felt that type of euphoria in months.

"Please," I beg, needing my memory to last longer than my grief. "I need this." *I need you.*

Tears form in my eyes when the faintest whisper hits my ear, *"Keep going."*

"Ghost."

"I'm here, маленький ягненок, *but you need to swivel your clit too. Flicking it isn't enough."*

"Like this?"

I pump my fingers in and out of myself while rolling my thumb over my clit.

"Fuck." I choke back a sob when my imagination pretends he's scooting closer for a better look before doubling my efforts. I want to come. I deserve it. *"Yesss,"* Ghost hisses, his voice right at my ear. *"A little deeper,* маленький ягненок.*"*

I can't hold back the sensitivity splintering through me when I recall how he grabbed my face and forced me to look at him when I came. He hid his scars from everyone, but that night, he let me see them.

I climax with a silent moan, the soundless thrashing arriving with a handful of tears. My heart and body are torn. They're at war with each other, and the person they're fighting over is dead.

It is a ridiculous fight, but one I can't control.

"Katie." I kick up the covers and scamper beneath them when Grayson calls my name a second before he enters my room. Alek knocked. Grayson hasn't learned that politeness yet. "You up? I wanted to show you something." He flicks on the light, then stops partway to my bed, his brows lost in his generous hairline. There's no way he has the balding gene. "You all right?"

"Yes," I lie. "I was just a little tired, so I thought I'd have a sleep-in." I look at the windows, grimacing when I notice it is still dark out. "What time is it?"

"Around five."

"Five in the morning?" Surely, I must have heard him wrong.

I didn't. "You can't catch the worms if you're not up before the sparrows." I stare at him strangely when he shifts his focus to the camera in the corner of my room I forgot about when my libido convinced me it was too dark to see anything.

After staring at it for what feels like an eternity, he finally shifts his focus back to me. "Can you tell me how many men in this picture you recognize?"

He hands me a glossy photograph with multiple headshots spread across it. They look like mugshots, but they're minus the mugshot board.

Needing to keep the field even, I ask, "What do I get for my participation in your event?"

Grayson scrubs a hand across his face, hopeful it will hide his smile, before he replies, "How about I wipe whatever you were doing from the servers before he sees it?" He doesn't need to say Kirill's name for me to know who he is referencing, and I don't need additional information as to what event he's referencing.

He looks back at the camera when I mutter, "Sounds fair."

Too embarrassed to look at him and unwilling to leave my bed since I am minus any panties, I scan the image. There are several familiar faces, but I don't point out the obvious. Grayson already knows who they are since his presence agitates them to no end.

"That's Vladimir, although he's aged a lot since I saw him."

I peer up at Grayson when he asks, "How long ago?"

"Five or so years."

I wonder just how deep his research goes when he asks, "So the Popovs didn't kidnap you?"

"Um..." I'm truly unsure how to answer. "They were Russian, but I don't believe they were the Popovs." Kirill said he organized for someone named Sergei to abduct me but that Colum got into his head and changed their plan, and although I trust Grayson, it isn't reliable enough to share that with him just yet.

Grayson nods, knowing I'm holding back but not going to push me. "What about anyone else? Do you recognize anyone else?"

"That's Colum, Mr. Watermelon Head." He's amused by my comment but doesn't respond with anything but a smile. "I think he was at the auction." I stop breathing when my eyes land on a face I will never forget. Ghost's face only has the original scar he had at the auction, although it is barely seen since his head is angled. "That's Ghost."

"Ghost?" Grayson checks, shocked.

I jerk up my chin. "Kirill's brother." I brush away the blob on my cheek before he can see it. "If you will excuse me, I need to use the bathroom."

Forgetting I am without underwear, I scoot off my bed and make a beeline to the bathroom.

Mercifully, Grayson is gone when I exit thirty minutes later.

52

KATIE

*M*y stomach is squashed into the buffet table when Kirill sneaks up on me unaware. His breath reeks of alcohol, but his attitude is the most pungent of them all. "Why the fuck are people asking questions about Ghost?"

"Whatever do you mean?"

The orange juice in my hand wobbles when he grips my face to forcefully make me look at Grayson, who is in conversation across the room, oblivious to Kirill's rough handling. "He wanted to talk to me about Ghost." The juice splatters on the pristine white tablecloth and soaks into my dress when he snarls, "Not a fucking ghost. Ghost, a person." He stares me dead set in the eyes. "How could he know about him if you didn't tell him?"

Lying will get me nowhere, so I go for the truth. "I didn't know we were meant to keep his existence a secret."

"Existence?" He mocks me with laughter. "He would have to exist to keep his existence a secret." He pushes me forward by my face, moving the table forcefully enough for others to pay attention. "You really should be more careful with what you're doing." His smile is as fake as they come. "You've gotten juice on your dress." He dabs at the blobs he caused with a napkin before saying with a false frown. "Go upstairs and change. I'll send someone from housekeeping to fetch it for dry cleaning." He uses my tears to his advantage. "Don't cry, my love. It is just a little bit of spilled juice. It's not hurting anyone."

When he leans in, to others it looks like he is whispering reassurance in my ear.

The only reassurance I get is that this man is going to be the death of me.

"First, you touch your cunt while moaning his name. Now you're ratting out a family business you will *never* be a part of." He presses his lips to the shell of my ear before growling out, "Keep your mouth shut before I find something far more enticing to stuff it closed."

He jackknifes back when I whisper, "Do you really think your limp dick will be up to the task?"

I don't think my teeth will survive his strike this time around, but I brace myself, nevertheless.

The hit I am anticipating never comes. Kirill chuckles like I said something funny before he shifts his focus to someone I hadn't noticed entering the room until now. "Lera, come to Daddy. I think we should play a game with Katie."

Fear rains down on her as quickly as it does me.

"I won't mention him again."

Kirill angles his head, then pricks out his ear. "What was that?"

"Ghost—"

"Ghosts don't exist. Hasn't anyone ever told you that?"

To ensure he gets across his point, he walks Lera out of the room with a rough tug on her arm that instantly springs tears down her face.

"Don't," I bark at Grayson when he joins me at the table. "I spilled some juice. I'm fine."

"Katie—"

"I said I'm fine." After waiting for the focus to shift off me, I murmur, "But it would be better if you weren't here."

Stealing his chance to reply, I disregard the hungry grumbles of my stomach and return to my room, where I spend the next three days in solitary confinement.

I am starving and thirsty but untrusting of everyone.

Grayson said he would remove the footage of me self-pleasuring myself. He clearly lied because there was no way Kirill would have known about that if he had done as offered.

He lied to me, and that hurts as much as knowing I could be hurting more than myself with my refusal to eat this time around.

My head slings to the side when an odd vibration sounds from my feather coat. It isn't cold enough in this part of the world for such a large coat, but since it is Kirill's favorite, I'm forced to wear it anytime we go outside.

Don't misunderstand what I am saying. We haven't had any ventures outside the house yet, but there have been two events in the expansive garden. They all seem to be celebrating the same thing.

The Bobrovs' resurrection in the United States.

My breathing shallows when I discover the reason for the noise. It is the smooth, sleek cell phone Grayson gave me after the altercation in the dining room days ago. It was a peace offering I clutched to until I realized I don't know the lock code.

I hid it away when my attempt to unlock it saw me locked out for five hours. I couldn't risk a permanent lockout.

After digging it out of the breast pocket of my jacket, I debate whether I should answer the call for what feels like a lifetime. My head is one hundred percent against it, but my heart slides my finger across the screen and squashes it to my ear before I can contemplate how dangerous I am behaving.

First, goading Kirill.

Second, going on a hunger strike amongst men who don't give a shit about me.

And third, this.

"Hello," a deep yet still boyish voice says down the line. "Grayson, are you there?"

"Grayson isn't here." I swallow a handful of times, hopeful some spit will ease out my next lot of words. "I haven't seen him in days."

"Katie?" I pull down the phone to make sure it is not recording before squashing it back to my ear. "It's you, isn't it?"

"I have to go."

"Is Grayson okay? That's all I need to know." He sounds genuinely concerned. "You don't need to tell me anything else."

I peer up at the camera in the corner of my room before angling my torso so my back faces it. "He's okay, but he needs to go. Kirill isn't happy."

"What do you mean? Why isn't Kirill happy?"

My neck snaps to the side so fast when a thick Russian voice booms through my closed bedroom door. "Did someone order room service?"

Grayson's phone slips from my grasp when I recognize the voice.

Alek.

53

KATIE

*J*ust like the time Ghost protected me from Artyom, I don't run from Alek when I notice his split knuckles and bloody face. I run to him.

"Hey. It's okay, Kate. You're all right."

I clutch to him for dear life, certain he is going to vanish at any moment.

"It's okay," he assures me again before pulling me back to arm's length. "But I need you to listen to me, okay? I don't have long." It dawns on me why he is whispering when his hand clamps my mouth as a shadow moves under my door.

No one is aware of his visit.

He is a ghost.

My throat sounds scratchy when I ask, "How? I saw you get shot." When I shake my head, hating its reminder that I didn't witness Alek's punishment, tears topple down my cheeks. "Ghost... did... he... um..."

I can't say the words.

Even more so when I see the remorse in Alek's eyes.

As he licks his lips, he locks his eyes with the tray of untouched food on my dinette table before flipping our conversation on its head. "Why aren't you eating, Kate?"

Although confused by the changeup, I mutter, "They've been drugging my food." It is the response that won't add bruises to his face. Alek is as protective as Ghost was. He proved that during our time in Russia. His responses weren't as violent as Ghost's, but he certainly portrayed that he wouldn't take shit from anyone.

"And? They've been doing that from day one." He laughs at my peeved expression. "Ghost wanted to lay with you every night like he did in the ship, but he couldn't let you know that."

"Why?" For such a simple word, it is extremely hard to articulate. I can barely breathe through the knowledge that Ghost was more attached than perceived. I was beginning to wonder if my feelings were one-sided.

"Because it would have placed the target on his back even sooner."

His reply reminds me that I'm not the only one who has shed tears for Ghost. "Lera. She's here—"

"I know," he interrupts. While dragging a hand over his clipped beard, he curses, then mutters, "Sofia is..." He curses again before working out his reply through a tight jaw. "Still a work in progress." His brows pull together above his mannish but perfect-sized nose for his face. "That's why it's taking so long to get you out. We have no fucking clue who our enemies are."

"We?"

The word has barely left my mouth when my bedroom door shoots open.

Grayson enters my room, his gun at the ready.

"What the..." Alek stands to his full height, which is almost a head taller than Grayson. "Who the fuck are you?"

I dart between Alek and Grayson before either of them can react to the violence teeming in the room, my arms outstretched. "Alek this is G... aah... Aaren. He's been helping me."

"Helping you?" Alek rubs his hands together in a non-threatening manner, but the wish to kill still blazes in his eyes. "Right. Now it all makes sense." He sits on the end of my bed, then balances his elbows on his knees. His reach is so long, he can pluck a breadstick out of the basket I refuse to touch without needing to stretch. "You're the douchebag making Kirill manic." After ripping off a chunk of bread and chewing it, he says, "I don't know if it is this shit you've got going on." He swivels his hand around Grayson's face before dragging it down his body. His highlight of Grayson's form alerts me to the fact that he is a lot more handsome than I realized. I wasn't looking at him as any more than a friend, so I didn't take in his untouched skin, platinum blond locks, and well-structured jaw. I just saw a man who appeared as desperate as me to get out from beneath Kirill's nose. "Or that." Alek locks his eyes with Grayson's weapon. "That isn't genuine."

"This is a Makarov, the most widely distributed pistol in Russia."

"And neither the fuck is that." Alek wiggles his finger in his ear like Grayson's horrid Russian accent caused him pain before he yanks a gun out of the back of his jeans. "This is the most widely distributed pistol in Russia." His I's sound like double E's. "It doesn't have a trademark or brand. It was also banned from sale four years ago." His narrowed gaze is deadly. "So they won't find any serial numbers, manufacturer details, or any of that other fucking shit the Bureau will wade through when they dig my bullet out of your head." Grayson doesn't cower at his threat. His stance strengthens. "They'll have nothing but the knowledge you were taken down by a *true* Russian gangster not the fake-ass motherfucker you are."

Alek stands again before tugging me behind him. "So you've got two options. You listen to that voice in your ear telling you to stand down, or I'll take you down."

"I don't know what the fuck your—"

I squeal when Alek fires. He doesn't hit Grayson, but his shot is so close, it whips out the lock curled around his ear, and if he has an earpiece in place, as Alek suspects, the person's ear on the other end will be ringing as loud as Grayson's. "Did I sound like I was negotiating?"

"Fuckin—" Grayson doesn't finish his sentence, angles his head, and grumbles out, "I fucking heard you," then drifts his sorrowful eyes to me. "I will get you out. I swear to God, I will."

"No, you won't." I'm still reeling over the fact Grayson is an undercover agent, that I can't take in the rest of Alek's reply with the diligence it needs. "Because she's got you so fooled, you're like every other dumb fuck out there." He nudges his head to the hallway. "You think she's carrying Kirill's kid."

When Grayson's wide eyes ask a range of questions, I do nothing but return his stare. I don't deny Alek's claims or express that I am as confused as him. I stand as frozen as a statue, only moving when a squawk coming out of Grayson's ear is loud enough for me to hear.

"You won't make it back to Russia," Grayson threatens, glaring at Alek.

Alek takes his threat in stride. "Says you."

After an intense standoff, Grayson flicks his eyes to mine for a nanosecond, dips his chin in farewell, then hotfoots it outside.

His cologne is still lingering in the air when Alek shifts on his feet to face me. "There is no way that snowflake is Russian. What's his real name?"

I shrug before stammering out, "I-I don't know."

Grayson was nice to me, so he doesn't deserve the wrath of the Bratva coming down on him.

Also, he was doing his job—just like Ghost at the start of our interactions.

For the first time in a long time, I feel fear when Alek asks in a low, gravelly tone, "Are you lying to me, Kate?"

"No." I should be given a doctorate in deceit with how easily lying is coming to me lately.

After what feels like a lifetime, Alek finally relents. "All right." His expression turns miffed. "I'd ask you to walk me out, but that might be a little hard since you need to stay in their good books." When I unknowingly screw up my face, he grins. "As hard as it may be, try and remember what you were taught. It will make your time here pass a lot quicker."

"It would pass even quicker if you stayed." I loathe the desperation in my voice. Don't hold it against me. It is an extremely lonely life when you can't tell the difference between fear and excitement.

Dirty brown locks fall into his eyes when he shakes his head. "I wish I could, but I need to do a favor for a friend."

My brain instantly goes to Ghost, but my stupidity only lasts as long as it takes to remember that ghosts can't ask for favors.

Once he is certain the coast is clear, Alek cranks his neck back to me. "If anyone asks, the dead man across the hall died of a self-inflicted gunshot wound to the head."

He grins, winks, then leaves me gobsmacked.

54

KATIE

*W*hen Alek said good behavior would contribute to a faster transition, I thought he had plans in the works to free me from Kirill's clutches.

I had no clue that months would pass before I would hear anything again.

The Bobrov ties have strengthened in the US. Their bridging networks that were fractured years ago and creating ties with entities that weren't around during their previous tender in the US, and for some strange reason, I have a feeling their foundations are being built on my pregnancy.

A meeting rarely goes by that I'm not requested to sit in on, and some of the men speak to me with familiarity, like I should know who they are.

I'm clueless, but the role I was beaten to portray keeps them as unknowledgeable as I am free of Kirill's anger. He hasn't associated directly with me for months, preferring for his messages to be passed through his staff.

I don't mind. The conditions are bearable, and I'm left to myself most of the time.

I also haven't seen hide nor hair of Watermelon Head since Alek's visit. Rumors circulated that he left the sanction on his terms—by a self-inflicted bullet wound to the head—after a fallout with Kirill, but those in the know said he was executed.

Supposedly, it is unusual to self-mutilate certain regions of your body before committing suicide.

The knowledge has slimmed Kirill's crew greatly over the past few months. Even with a handful of new members joining from a mutual collaboration, the Bobrovs' notoriety isn't as strong here as it was in Russia.

The changeup means only on the rare occasion do I have to pretend the sun shines out of Kirill's ass.

Like now, at a doctor's office on the outskirts of town. Kirill said we're here to check on 'his' son's well-being, but my intuition is warning me to stay on high alert. It is why I denied Lera's beg to come with me today. She is as desperate as me to leave the house, but a horrid feeling in the pit of my stomach saw me shaking my head.

I think it was for the best.

The furniture in this office is so new, the carpet pile isn't indented, and it doesn't have that sterile, gross smell most doctors' offices have.

It is a new practice. I am certain of it.

Kirill also seems extra agitated. He's snapped at our chaperone a number of times, telling him his demands are ridiculous and that he expects an apology when his accusations are founded as untrue.

"In Russia, you would be castrated for such insinuations."

The blond man with a wonky nose doesn't balk at his angry tone. He merely stands when the doctor's nurse calls me into the examination room before snapping his eyes to Kirill. "Stay here."

Kirill's face reddens with anger. "She is *my* wife!"

"Then you should trust her with me fullheartedly, right?"

Kirill has not a single thing to say.

The direction of a second man's gun doesn't give him much choice.

For once, he is being held for ransom, and I can't help but smirk at the knowledge.

"That's what I thought."

The blond plucks me from my seat before walking us into the

office at the end of the hall. I'm already in shock about the lack of muscle to his maneuver, so you can picture my surprise when my eyes lock on a familiar face. "Dr. Leonard." He is my mother's gynecologist.

Well, he was.

"Katie." Dr. Leonard swallows harshly before shifting his eyes to the man seemingly running the show. "You can tell Henry he doesn't need proof. She is who they are claiming. She is the spitting image of her mother. A Petrov through and through."

I don't get the chance to ask who the hell the Petrovs are. The nameless goon speaks before I can, "The child's paternity is in question as well. We've heard from numerous sources she is not carrying his son."

Worry fills Dr. Leonard's eyes when he asks, "How far along are you?"

I shrug, but the goon appears more informed than me. "Seven months, give or take a week or two."

As Dr. Leonard stares at my stomach, he warns, "It can be risky doing an amnio at this stage of pregnancy. We usually suggest waiting until after the child is born."

"We can't do that. The Bobrovs are reforming under injunctions they're not entitled to if the lineage is not accurate."

"And you believe it isn't?"

"We don't know," the man replies, glaring at Dr. Leonard, unappreciative of his line of questioning. "That is why we are here."

Either oblivious to the man's anger or unthreatened by it, Dr. Leonard swings his eyes to mine and asks, "Do you want an amniocentesis to determine the paternity of your child?"

"She doesn't have a choice."

Dr. Leonard cuts off the stranger's snarl with a glare before muttering, "She does with me." He steps closer to the blond, his height suddenly appearing double. "You do not run the show around here. Neither do the Petrovs. Not anymore."

"Henry—"

"Leaves the approvals of this town to one man." In the most macho of showdowns, Dr. Leonard spits out, "He is *not* you." When the man says nothing, Dr. Leonard returns his focus to me. "Do you approve to have an amniocentesis, Katie?"

I wish my voice was stronger when I ask, "What is it?" Regretfully, it is what it is. I've sunk back to the scared, cowardly captive I was before Alek marched me out of Master Rudd's compound.

It has kept Lera and me alive over the past few months.

Dr. Leonard wheels an ultrasound machine closer to the bed decked out with sterile paper and those dreaded blue underpads every gynecologist uses. "After administrating local anesthetic, a thin plastic needle is inserted through your abdomen to collect amniotic fluid."

"Which will tell you the paternity of my child?" The 'my' part of my statement feels weird to say. The tiny curve in the bottom of my stomach has always been referred to as Kirill's. I've not felt any connection to it whatsoever.

Not even now.

"Yes. It is a relatively quick and painless procedure, but there are some complications."

My voice tremors when I ask, "Such as?"

Dr. Leonard's tongue clicks on his teeth before he replies, "Such as placental abruption, premature labor—"

"Death," I interrupt.

He believes I am referencing the baby. I'm not. I am talking about my demise that will occur within minutes of his arrival. "The odds are low, Katie, but still present."

"Then I don't want it."

As much as it frustrates me, I still want to live. If not for myself, for Lera. She needs somebody on her team, and at the moment, that person is not her mother.

"Then you don't have to have it." Ignoring the stranger's deep growl, Dr. Leonard steps closer to me. "But do you mind if I take a look?" I must balk because he is quick to free me from worry that he is going to poke and prod me like I was during months of inseminations. "Not down there. With the ultrasound machine." He looks more fretful about his next comment than worried. "Your stomach is very small for your gestation."

"I don't eat all the time." God, that makes me sound like a terrible person. "And I was tiny when I was born."

"Still, I would like to take a look." He smiles to reassure me. "It won't take more than a couple of minutes."

He has kind eyes, and he defended my right to choose even with it placing his head on the chopping block, so I go against my heart by nodding my head.

"Thank you." He assists me onto the bed before requesting that I lift my dress. "This will keep your legs warm while I scan you." He places a heated blanket on my legs. "Regretfully, I was only told about your appointment at the last minute, so I didn't have time to heat the gel."

He shakes the ultrasound gel until the goop inside falls into the nozzle, then he squirts it onto the flab at the bottom of my stomach.

"Sorry," he murmurs a few seconds later. "Some babies like to hide, so we have to push a little harder to make sure we don't miss them."

He waves the wand back and forth for ages before he eventually stores it away. When he gestures for the unnamed man to join him next to the ultrasound machine, I slowly sit up.

I should have remained lying down when the unnamed man shouts, "What do you mean there's no baby?"

Dr. Leonard peers at me apologetically before he brings up my scans on the monitor. "Her uterus is enlarged but empty. There are no signs of a gestational sac."

I can't tell one black-and-white image from the next, but the man has no trouble deciphering them. "Did you really think you could deceive us?" Something on my face must give away my shock as his anger soon shifts in another direction. "Henry only allowed the Bobrovs to stay because of his claims you have the Petrov blood. They debunked years ago, but Ravenshoe will always be their turf."

I'm too shocked to speak. Luckily, because Dr. Leonard fills the silence with mind-numbing facts. "Your mother was mafia royalty, Katie. She left when she met your father, but he still had to pay her dues. It was only a couple of weeks out of the year, but it kept them in good graces with her family. He worked inventory at the docks during your formative years. It was scaled down to one-off jobs once you went to middle school."

I am clueless as to what he is saying, except the part about my father working at the docks. "He didn't work in insurance, did he?" Dr. Leonard and the stranger both shake their heads, but I keep my focus on Dr. Leonard since he is the more upfront of the two. "What happened?"

"When you were taken, your family was told you had been killed. Shortly after, your father lost the ability to follow orders. That never ends well."

He's not saying what I think he is, is he?

He isn't implying my mother's family took them out for not following orders. Surely, I am reading his reply wrong.

"To Henry, you never take down family. They're protected by a covenant. So instead of killing his cousin, he withdrew his support. The Petrovs didn't last a year."

"Who is Henry?" Out of all the information I'm being bombarded with, his identity shouldn't be my focus, but my curiosity is too perverse for me to ignore. His name keeps popping up like I should know who he is, but I have no clue which way is up, much less the identity of a man I'm certain I've never met.

"Henry Gottle," the stranger answers. "The boss of all bosses and your great uncle." After straying his eyes to the door Kirill is seated behind, he adds, "He is also the man he's trying to play for a fool for the second time. Henry won't let the Bobrovs run back to Russia with their tails between their legs this time around. He will kill them all."

As much as I want Kirill to get his just desserts, Lera doesn't deserve to be taken down with him. I'm still on the fence about Sofia. "You can't do that. There are children involved." The man doesn't flinch in the slightest. "My child." Dr. Leonard stares at me like he doesn't believe me, but since I have no clue if he can read me as the liar I am, I continue on course. "Lera is my daughter. I gave birth to her shortly after arriving at Master Rudd's compound."

"Rudd?" When I nod at Dr. Leonard's question, he answers the stranger's silent question with words, "It is plausible. The baby farm was in full operation back then. Rudd let the women keep the defects." His reply makes me queasy. He isn't the saint I thought he was.

Then again, neither am I.

I wipe the riled expression off my face when the unnamed man asks, "What's wrong with her? They wouldn't have let you keep her if she was healthy."

My mind spirals for an excuse before the perfect one presents itself. "She's diabetic. Type one."

Once again, Dr. Leonard answers the stranger's unasked questions. After logging into his computer to scour prescriptions issued to the Bobrovs since our arrival stateside, he murmurs, "It works. One child had nostrils bigger than the purchasing parent wanted. He was given back to the birth mother."

When the stranger curses, I say, "So you can't go in guns blazing. Not while Lera is in the house. She is Henry's family, and he won't let you kill his family."

"As you are too, Katie."

Dr. Leonard's reminder shocks me. I thought the child I'm carrying would tie me to the mafia for life. I had no idea I was already embroiled in the controversy that follows the title.

I choke back a shocked huff when I realize how wrong my statement is.

I'm not pregnant.

Dr. Leonard said my uterus is empty.

"Why would they pretend I'm pregnant?" I stumble out, my shock too high not to seek answers.

Ghost's ruse made sense. It was the only way he could keep me alive. But after his death, why was it continued?

"Have you had any tests since you discovered you were pregnant?" the stranger asks, suddenly curious.

I shake my head before recalling the scan Ghost conducted. "I had a scan around six months ago and a positive urine test shortly after that."

"Urine is easy to taint," Dr. Leonard announces, drawing my focus back to him. "What did you see during the ultrasound?"

"That," I murmur when something on his computer monitor captures my attention.

His screensaver is an ultrasound video.

"That is a demo video that comes with all machines." As he huffs out a breathy laugh, I recall Ghost mentioning the same months ago. I was too panicked about his anger to absorb what his comment meant. "It's quite genius when you think about it."

"Says you. There are millions at stake, not to mention the discomposure this could cause the Gottles." After gripping my arm like every other man his height and size, he says, "I need to speak with Henry." He drops his eyes to me. "Until I get word from him, you are to remain pregnant. Understood?"

After swallowing the brick in my throat, I nod.

I've fooled Kirill once, so I'm sure it won't be hard a second time.

Kirill stands when the still unnamed man and I return to the waiting area. He looks worried, and it has me wondering if he knows my pregnancy is a ruse.

"It's your lucky day." The stranger nudges his head to Dr. Leonard who shadowed our walk. "He was Amelia's doctor, so an invasive paternity test isn't required. Your unborn child has a rightful claim to the Petrov syndicate."

Kirill grins as if all his Christmases have come at once. "As I already told you." He takes over the stranger's hold, his grip more cruel, before he leads me to a waiting car. "I won't hold my breath for an apology, though. Henry hates being proven wrong."

He's angry that they've been making him jump through hoops for months, uncaring that he does the exact same thing to everyone in his realm.

He's a hypocrite.

And so am I.

I haven't acknowledged my pregnancy once in the past several months, yet now all I want to do is crawl into a hole and cry. I'm grieving something I swore I didn't want. I guess a small part of me hoped by some miracle that my child ended up being Ghost's, and it would carry on his legacy.

See? I am a hypocrite.

I stop internally rationalizing my stupidity when a female voice murmurs, "Katie?"

When I sling my eyes in the direction the voice came from, I catch sight of a face I've never stopped scanning the crowd for the past almost nine years before my view is blocked by two of Kirill's goons. They slip out of their SUVs in an instant and attempt to push Blaire back.

"Katie!" she shouts for the second time when I'm bundled into the SUV idling at the curb by the stranger wanting me to continue faking my pregnancy.

"I wouldn't if you want to live." The stranger locks his eyes with the gun Kirill is brandishing before nudging his head to Blaire following our SUV down the footpath. "She has sanction."

"From who?"

My world continues being tossed on its head when the man answers, "The Popovs. She's one of them."

55

KATIE

*M*any hours later, I'm still working through my confusion as to how Blaire became a part of the association that kidnapped us but can walk free without goons shadowing her every move.

She followed our SUV for so many miles we had to lose her in a packed nightclub. And even then, it almost took a stampede to slow her down. The unnamed man caused a commotion by firing two shots into the air, then paid for his stupidity with a bullet to the knee.

His kneecapping proved that Blaire is part of the Russian Mafia, but I've not been given a single answer to any questions I've asked the past five-plus hours. I was bundled back into our SUV at the same time Blaire was dragged to the taxi she commanded, then driven to an unknown location.

My room is as dark and dingy as the one I was thrust into after I was sold, but they didn't cuff me to the radiator this time around, so my wrists are scald-free.

I'm also not alone.

I thought I was brought here in retaliation for sparking unease between the Bobrovs and the Popovs, who are head of the Bratva in the

United States, but within hours, Lera and Sofia were shoved into my room with me, where we've remained for the past several hours.

My wide-with-panic eyes shift to Sofia when she asks in a thick, whispered accent, "How did he find out?"

She doesn't scare me. I'm petrified that the man who got kneecapped didn't return to our SUV. Excluding Dr. Leonard, he is the only person who knows I won't be giving birth in three months.

Well, so I thought.

"How did Kirill discover you're not pregnant?"

"He didn't," I murmur, still unsure which team she is on. "They didn't tell him." My Russian isn't very good, but I wouldn't use it anyway since I don't want Lera to be a part of our conversation. "How do you know I'm not pregnant?" When she strays her eyes to her feet, I ask again, louder this time, "How do you know?"

My angry voice startles Lera, but she only responds by tightening her hands around her ears and burrowing her head into her knees. Her cheeks are awfully white. She doesn't have any energy to give, much less for a fight she should not be a part of.

My bewilderment increases when Sofia confesses, "I gave you hormones."

"What?" I could have misheard what she said because of a commotion occurring outside. There are raised voices and a handful of bangs. Standard noises on the ship when the crew got drunk, but unusual since Ghost's murder.

I'm not the only one grieving. Half of Kirill's men are as well.

"Hormones," Sofia repeats. "I told the staff to put hormones in your food and water." When I take a staggered step back, she mutters, "Ghost's plan would have only worked for a couple of weeks. Kirill knows the changes in a woman's body during pregnancy. He looks for it in mine all the time... *even when it makes him angry*." Her last sentence is a mumble.

"Why lay with him if you hate him?" I realize my error when she grimaces during my second to last word. "You love him?"

My stomach flips when she nods. "But I knew him before this. Before Milo's passing."

Her excuse sounds plausible until I recall Kirill's mocked comment that he organized my kidnapping. "He organized for me to be kidnapped *nine* years ago. That was *four* years before Milo was killed."

"Because he knew you could give him what I couldn't. That you could give him a mafia heir."

"He is head of the Bobrovs. He doesn't need my weak connection to a Russian entity. The Petrovs have *nothing* to their name. They don't even have the Gottles' support." Which I am slowly learning is more important to any mafia entity than anything. "So what the hell could I give him?"

I've never felt so confused when she murmurs, "You could seduce Ghost." I sit on the soiled mattress, certain I'll need to be seated for her next confession. "Kirill isn't a Bobrov. His mother strayed, then pushed her guilt onto our mother. That's why Ghost is scarred." Her pained sob arrives with a handful of tears. "And why they killed her when she told me the truth that I shared with Milo." She brushes away the salty blobs rolling down her cheeks before continuing, "I thought he was the brother I was searching for." A painful ripple escapes with her laugh. "He wasn't, but he promised to keep it a secret. When he didn't, Kirill was so angry, he lashed out." More tears fall. "He was paranoid Milo might have told someone else when the Gottles tortured him before his death. He was scared of losing everything, so I told him Ghost's lineage could give him a son who would have the Bobrov blood."

Her voice cracks along with my heart when she mutters, "I didn't think he would kill him, though. He just got so angry when Ghost remained loyal. No one could tempt him." A painful rattle rumbles through my chest when she murmurs, "Then Kirill remembered his instant fascination with you. You were just harder to secure since Henry banned us from the US." I stare at her like she is missing a few brain cells when she smiles. "It was risky to get you but so worthwhile. Ghost wanted you more than he wanted to save Lera from my fate."

"That's not true." When she dismisses my claims with a firm head shake, I shout, "Everything he did, he did for Lera." When she looks like she doesn't believe a word I speak, I say, "I stayed for Lera too, because I didn't want Ghost to lose everything because of me."

When I drag my hand under my nose to remove the contents spilling there, Sofia uses the breather to defend herself, "Then you understand why I did all the terrible things I've done?"

"No, I don't," I reply, shaking my head. I thrust my hand to Lera. "She's your daughter. Your flesh and blood, yet you let him mark her—"

"To save my family."

My angry voice reverberates around the room when I shout, "From what? A life of pain and devastation? Little good that did."

I swallow my harsh tone when she says matter-of-factly. "I either stayed with them or they killed my entire family... including Ghost. I was fifteen."

Them?

"You think you're the only victim they've taken? The only type they crave?" My heart breaks for her when she murmurs, "He said I looked exactly like my mother when he claimed her for the first time and that he couldn't wait to reminisce. Kirill stopped him two minutes too late."

Oh God. "Sofia, I'm—"

My sympathies are cut short when a loud bang overtakes the raised voices. It can't be concealed as a raucous group of men who have had too much to drink. It is explosive and loud and has me instantly moving for Lera.

When I realize Sofia is already sheltering her with her body, I cocoon them both. My life means nothing to these men, but if this is in retaliation for the shooting of the man I spent most of my morning with, perhaps it might mean something to the foreign accents pouring into the room.

A handful of them are Russian but most sound American.

"No," I shout, kick, and scream when I'm yanked away from Sofia and Lera a nanosecond after a door with multiple locks is kicked open.

A man wearing all black with a balaclava covering his eyes continues yanking me away while announcing there are two more victims in the room with me.

Victims, not perps?

"Go in light. One is a child."

As shock stills my legs and arms, my eyes dart to the dark pair peeking out of the balaclava. They're as black as the pits of hell but oddly familiar.

"Rico?"

I can't breathe when his eyes lower to mine. It is the teenage boy from the room. The one who had acid poured on his back shortly after I was kidnapped, except he is no longer a teen. He is a man who can hide his scars far more easily than Ghost since they're not covering his face.

Instead of summarizing how my life has come full circle, my focus is pulled to a commotion in the living room. Sofia and Lera are being carried out of the room by men dressed similarly to Rico, but instead of being grateful they're moving them away from Kirill, Sofia fights to get free before she skids to a stop in front of Kirill. He's hogtied on the blood-stained concrete floor and has a hessian bag over his head, but everyone in this room knows who he is.

His arrogance suffocates the room of oxygen.

When we make it outside, my vision is hindered by the headlights of many oversized vehicles as Lera is rushed past me. "Her pulse is dropping, and her skin is clammy. I think she's going into shock."

"She's a diabetic," I shout, aware of the warning signs Ghost constantly looked for whenever Lera was in his vicinity. "Her sugars drop when she's stressed..." My words shift to a shallow groan when one of a hundred men racing in all directions plops a bag of jellybeans into Lera's lap.

The axis keeps tilting when Lera murmurs, "дядя," before she groggily opens the packet to hunt for the pink jellybeans.

"Ghost?"

Unaware I am wiggling to be put down and not palmed off onto someone else, Rico hands me to a man with similar features as Ghost but with an unscarred face.

He is big, but his reflexes are slow. A second after I land in his arms, I shoot out of them like a rocket, then take off in the direction the shadowed figure went. There's a sea of black and devastation as far as the eye can see, but there's nothing more terrifying than looking into a pair of familiar icy blue eyes when a bullet whizzes past his head.

It isn't earmarked for a man who has oddly similar eyes to Ghost or me.

It is for Blaire, and her rounded stomach no one would ever believe is fake.

56

KATIE

Six months later…

"*A*re you sure you don't want to come with us?"

I raise my eyes to Hailey, smiling when I notice she borrowed the hideous white leather jacket she gifted me last Christmas. It is a flawless cut, designed to enhance all your desirable assets, and it would have cost her a pretty penny, but the color alone ensures I'll never wear it.

"I'm sure. I've got a lot to do."

I'm such a liar. I have an appointment with a therapist who is convinced my feelings for Ghost were nothing more than Stockholm syndrome and a metro card application to fill in.

Life has continued to remain boring even after I was freed from captivity by a joint mafia slash FBI sting. The only time my heart has galloped was when I stood outside the Bobrov safehouse across from a man with eyes as icy as Ghost's.

Since I was bundled into a blacked-out SUV a second after Blaire's ambulance roared down the street, I was never given the chance to hunt for Ghost. I searched for him later, but according to Grayson,

Ghost is exactly that, a ghost. There are no records of his birth or ties to the Bobrov and no archives of his death.

To the Bureau and the CIA, he never existed.

I stop reminiscing about the detailed reports Grayson shared with me three weeks after I left the hospital when Hailey pleads, "Please go to your appointment today, Kate. I know you think she has no clue what she's doing, but she was a godsend to me after Mom and Dad passed. She helped me a lot." When I nod, my heart not up to lying, she murmurs, "I left the travel pamphlets you requested on the counter for you. You didn't give me much to go off, so I grabbed a heap for every continent."

Her reply makes me smile. Blaire and I had some contact my first few weeks of freedom, but once she was discharged from the hospital for a gunshot wound to her stomach, it has been sporadic. She is traveling the globe with the man I believed was killed along with everyone else since his death was flashed across every news broadcast for weeks on end.

Blaire's adventures with Rico have been encouraging me to do the same—except I won't be visiting foreign nations with a ghost. His death wasn't primetime news. He didn't even get a proper burial.

When Hailey sighs about my downcast bottom lip, I remember that time away will also benefit her. I've inconvenienced her a lot in the past six months. I stole her only bedroom, a lot of time away from her boyfriend, and cried endlessly on her shoulder when reality dawned that I was never going back to Madame Victoria's or Master Rudd's compound.

I also grieved Ghost and the child I was never carrying.

Those tears were a little harder for Hailey to understand, but she supported me nonetheless.

Alek killed Master Rudd, so I was never overly threatful that he would find me again, but when Henry learned I'd been taken by one of my supposed 'own' and not killed as stated, he debunked more than the Bobrovs wish of a resurrection in the United States. He took down multiple organizations, then gifted the profits of their illegal activities to me.

I can't use that money. It is blood money, but I have some funds left from my parents' estate I plan to deplete by exploring the world without boarded-up windows stealing the scenery.

I sat at the window in Ghost's room on the cargo ship for hours on end, watching nothing but the swell of the ocean. It was the only thing that could settle the pain in my chest long enough to secure an entire breath.

The remembrance reminds me of why I told my therapist I want to travel once I've recovered.

"I want to see color. Lots and lots of color."

"Maybe you should go to Mardi Gras? There's plenty of color there."

Hailey laughs before ribbing her boyfriend, shutting him up. "Mardi Gras is color*ful*, but that is a completely different color than the one Katie is seeking." She peers at her watch before sighing. "We really need to get going, I don't want to be late. Rise Up is headlining today. It is their first major concert since Noah's accident."

"Then go." I shoo her away with a flick of my wrist. "Have fun."

When she remains as stubborn as ever, I walk them to the door before securing the locks, then I have a long heavenly shower.

Don't judge me, but I searched online for the shampoo I used at the Bobrov compound. I found the exact one. It cost me a fortune to ship it here, and it was a complete waste of money. There's still something not quite right about it.

Once I've showered and dressed in a bright pink shirt and skinny jeans, I make my way to the bus stop. I still haven't learned how to drive. I'm not sure I want to. I imagine it will be hard concentrating on the road and the back seat to make sure I don't have any unwanted guests.

I'm not scared I'll be taken again. I'm terrified of living the remainder of my life without an ounce of excitement. Blaire is living her life on the run, but I bet her heart is constantly racing. Mine has barely thudded over sixty beats a minute since I was freed from captivity. My hands haven't been clammy, and I've had no adrenaline spikes whatsoever.

I'm so bored. Just like my last four months in captivity, I frequently check my pulse to make sure I'm still living.

Jesus. Maybe my therapist is right. Perhaps I do have Stockholm syndrome.

As I walk along a footpath that follows the coastline, I stop to admire a new building that's been in construction since Grayson dropped me off at Hailey's building with a bag full of borrowed clothes and his phone number scribbled across a napkin. We've talked a handful of times since he assisted in my release, but it is more in reference to Lera and Sofia's ongoing care than me.

Sofia one hundred percent has Stockholm syndrome, but just like me, she denies it.

So immersed by the porthole-like windows in the foyer of the building, I don't realize I've walked inside until a woman greets me with a big smile. "She's a beauty, isn't she?"

"It's gorgeous," I agree, mesmerized by the aqua walls and pink-trimmed windows. It is so bright it should be hideous, but it makes me smile. "Is every apartment as colorful as the foyer?"

As she nods, her smile grows. "Would you like a tour?"

"Um..." I check the time. When I notice I still have thirty minutes before my bus arrives, I sheepishly bob my chin.

"This way." She rattles off details of the apartments still available for sale while we ride the elevator to the top floor. "This is the only apartment not available. It was purchased off the plan before the build began."

"The construction crew works fast. This was nothing but a pile of dirt when I..." I can't say freed, so I mumble, "... came home."

"College?"

Her question stumps me for a second. "Um... no. I was... traveling."

"Lovely. I've been wanting to go to Italy for years." She gestures for me to exit the elevator car first before she finalizes, "Even more so after seeing this apartment being decorated."

"Aah..."

The realtor laughs when the decor leaves me speechless.

It isn't in a good way.

The drapes are hideous, and not a single one matches.

"It's an acquired taste that grows on you." As she leads us into the kitchen, she rattles off a number of features. "All appliances are built-in, the flooring is heated, and the butler's pantry has three dishwashers." She displays how the tap mixer pulls out before she swivels to face the stovetop. "You also have a pot tap, which comes in handy for any little fire mishaps us working ladies have." I appreciate she is adding me to her statement, but I haven't worked a day in my life.

Well, that's if you exclude fighting to stay alive.

"What's that?" I ask, curious about the handle in the middle of the six gas burners.

"That is a..." Unsure, she yanks up the handle, then twists her red-painted lips. "A sandwich press?"

As the world spins around me, I take in all the odd features she pointed out—the hideous curtains, the bright blue carpet, the sandwich press in the middle of the stovetop that's big enough to make grilled cheese sandwiches for two.

There's just one thing missing from the features I told Ghost my forever home would have.

A pantry full of pickles.

Tears burn my eyes when my race into the butler's pantry has me stumbling onto row after row after row of pickles.

"Where is he?" I ask the realtor when my race through the spacious apartment fails to find another presence except her. "The man who bought this apartment, where is he?"

"It wasn't a man," she replies, shocked by my sudden meltdown.

I'm acting like a lunatic and stupidly feeding off her fear. "Then who the fuck is it?"

"It was designed by a woman." When she ruffles through her clipboard, hopeful she will lose my focus the instant she shifts it onto someone else, I'm anticipating for her to say my name, so you can picture my absolute devastation when she utters the one name I don't want to hear, "Sofia. It was purchased and designed by a Sofia Bobrov."

A ghost didn't design this apartment for me.

His alive-and-still-breathing sister did, most likely in penance for listening in on exchanges she wasn't meant to be a part of.

Kirill didn't authenticate my purity the second time because he assumed the night Ghost rubbed his cum over and inside me that we were having sex.

No one knew how strong Ghost's determination was to free Lera and me from his lifestyle.

Not even me.

EPILOGUE
KATIE

Six Months Later...

*A*ir-conditioned air blasts my face when I step onto the tourist bus at Procida, Italy. It was just like Blaire's photographs showed—bright, colorful, and full of life. I've spent the last several hours exploring, and my feet are aching. I can't wait to get back to the cruise ship to soak them in a tub.

Hailey laughed when I said I was taking a six-month around-the-world cruise. She said it was a vacation for retirees before they die.

Although ninety-nine point nine percent of the passengers are over the age of sixty, I've loved the first two weeks of my twenty of the most colorful destinations in the world tour.

Procida can't be accessed by a cruise ship, so it docked at a neighboring harbor, and guests were shuttled to town.

"Photographs don't do it justice."

"It doesn't," I agree with Jeanette before taking a seat behind her. She is also traveling solo, so we often sit together at dinner so we don't look like losers. She is fifty-five going on thirty-three. Her husband passed away from Parkinson's two years ago. He purchased this trip the month before he died. He didn't want her to stop living when he passed and thought this would be the best way to ensure she didn't.

His admiring features had me thinking back to my conversation with Sofia six months ago. She didn't eavesdrop on my time with Ghost. He mentioned to her my wish for hideous drapes and carpet when she was shuddering through a fifth botched abortion. That one saw her lose her uterus, and it was the reason Ghost was absent a lot during my first month at the mansion.

Sofia said he still snuck in to sleep next to me every night, though.

Her disclosure doubled my grief instead of easing it.

I'm still grieving now.

"Dinner tonight?" When I nod, Jeanette asks, "Six o'clock?" When I roll my eyes, she says with a laugh, "What? I like to go to bed early."

"Why?" I don't give her the chance to answer. "So you can wake up early and count down the hours until you can go back to bed?"

Travel was supposed to encourage me to enjoy life again, but I'm one early night from retirement. Don't get me wrong, the cities we've visited are beautiful, and the air is the freshest I've breathed, but something is missing.

Someone.

My interest is piqued when the driver murmurs, "Be careful when we arrive at the harbor. Despite what your travel insurance company tells you, pirates still exist."

"They're just called the bratva these days." Jeanette's comment gets the bus giggling. It freezes my heart, especially her final snickered comment, "We can only hope after the books I've been reading. Who wouldn't want to be held captive by a Massimo or a Nikolai?"

I muster up a fake grin to hide my hurt, then free a real one when I realize this is the exact reason I wanted to travel to exotic locations. No one here knows me as Katie Bryne, the girl who was abducted and held against her will for nine years.

They only see Kate.

"CAREFUL. VERY GOOD." The driver helps me step down from the bus before offering his hand to Jeanette. "Don't forget the souvenir bags you packed in the undercarriage, Jeanie. Don't want your grandbabies missing out on all those goodies you snaveled up."

"I'll grab it for you," I offer when Jeanette groans about another twenty pounds being added to her beautifully plump frame.

I lost a few pounds the hormones Sofia slipped into my food added, but the final ten refuse to budge. They're with me for good.

"Jesus, Jeanette. If you buy any more junk, you'll sink our boat," I murmur to myself when the removal of her bag has it tearing open under the strain.

When I bob down to collect the bobble-headed sea turtles and plastic snow globes, my heart freezes for the second time today. A shipping container dock is across a wide gravel driveway. Several ships are being loaded with stock, but one stands out more than the rest.

It couldn't be. Surely.

With my heart thumping out a tune it hasn't played the past year and a half, I absentmindedly make my way closer to the industrial dock on the other side of the harbor. It is secured from the public by a large chain fence, but there is a cut-out close to the rocks being sprayed with salty whitewash.

My head screams for me to turn around when my trance-like trek is concealed by dozens of men and a handful of scantily clad women, to return to the cruise side of the harbor before I stumble onto something I don't want to acknowledge, but my heart refuses to listen.

The cargo ship is beckoning me to it, and no amount of logic will stop me from crossing the gangway and gliding down familiar corridors.

It is exactly the same. A massive city on the sea with insides far too opulent for its rusty shell. The dining room is grand, and the rec room with its twinkling lights and boyish games could house dozens. The kitchen's multiple pantries are brimming with bags of flour and enough canned food to spend months out at sea, and there are men in almost every cabin except one.

Ghost's.

I know it's his room because it smells like him, and the bathroom door is still hanging off its hinges.

I snap my eyes shut so fast a tear springs down my cheek when a thick Russian accent says, "You think they would have fixed that by now."

"Alek." He balks when I throw my arms around his neck to hug him tight, but he eventually returns my hug, if not a little hesitant. "What are you doing here? Why are you in Italy?"

He props his shoulder on the doorframe far too casually. "Restocking. Supplies get low when you voyage from one butt-lit city to the next." My nose screws up like a rabbit when he traces the red tinge near the spaghetti strap of my shirt. "You really should have gone for the SPF 50+. The sun out here is brutal, especially for your pasty white skin."

"What?"

He laughs at the reply that would usually have had me smacked over the head with a broom before explaining, "Your sunscreen is SPF30. You need SPF50. I'll get some shipped to your room tonight. Room 8212, right?"

I talk despite my suddenly scratchy throat. "You know I'm on a cruise?"

"Of course I do." My heart whacks against my ribs when he says with a grin, "*He* knows everything when it comes to you."

He can't be referencing Kirill. He was sentenced for so long they may as well throw away his key. He's never getting out alive.

My voice is almost a sob when I ask, "Who knows everything?"

I would give anything to be brave enough to whack him in the gut when he replies, "You know who." And he knows it. His smile exposes this. "It's the same man who waits in his office for hours on end every time we anchor in case a special delivery arrives—"

If he says anymore, I don't hear him. I sprint like the wind. Maybe the Russian whispers I hear in the wind each night aren't my imagination. Maybe his smell isn't, either.

My race only ends when a voice I've only heard in my head for the past year and a half sounds through my ears. "Think before you leap, маленький ягненок. My lack of greed was a one-time-only deal." I gulp in a rugged breath when the big black chair behind Ghost's desk spins around.

It is him.

It is Ghost.

The man I've been grieving for over a year. His dress shirt is undone to the desired third button, his hands are resting on his pants-covered thighs, and his head is unnecessarily angled. "If you step over that threshold, come hell or high water, I will make you *mine*."

My heart pains for him when he leans forward enough for the shadow to move off his face. His new scar is extensive. It takes up a majority of his right cheek and is circular in its pattern.

It appears to be a bullet hole that mercifully lodged an inch or two below his brain.

The racing heart I've been seeking for years returns stronger than ever when Ghost mutters, "And I will *never* let you go again."

His possessive tone makes me dizzy, but it won't stop me from conveying my shock. "How? You got shot in the chest three times. I saw you go down."

"Alek." He curses a Russian swear word under his breath before he pushes back from his desk, walks around it, then plops his backside on the edge closest to me. He is still several feet away from me, but the tension is crackling with electricity. His new scars don't hinder his appeal. He is a ruggedly handsome man who could set any woman's pulse on fire. "He doesn't trust anyone, much less the Yurys. He made me suit up just in case they weren't playing fair, and Watermelon Head is a fucking shit shot."

"Thank God."

My response pleases him, and for once, he doesn't have to hide his appreciation. "I came to you as soon as I could. I wiped away the tears you shed for me." The twitch impinging his top lip piques my curiosity. "Struggled not to help you over the line when you dreamed about me." His smile drops into a snarl. "And I killed the men who grabbed you too hard or made you cry." He unshadows part of his face when he stares me in the eyes and murmurs, "I worked endlessly to get you and Lera out. You just didn't know it."

"Why?" The comments about him coming to me when I was asleep make sense—he often drugged me—but the rest I am lost about. "Why send Alek to calm Kirill when Grayson's presence frustrated him? Why didn't you come yourself? And why did you let me believe you were dead?"

He flips my interrogation on its head by commencing his own. "Why did you walk onto this boat, *маленький ягненок*? There are five in this harbor alone. Six if you include the hideous one I've been tailing the past two weeks."

I try to keep my tone neutral while replying, "I don't know."

It is virtually impossible not to squirm when Ghost grumbles out, "Don't lie to me, *маленький ягненок!* Why did you pick *this* boat?"

My heart speaks before my head can talk it out of it. "Because I want to live."

Ghost angles his head to the side while he assesses me in silence.

It is a painfully long thirty seconds that doubles the tension brimming between us.

"So you lied to me?"

My breaths come out in a quiver as I shake my head. "No."

I breathe in quick, rapid pants when Ghost moves for me so fast, I'm pinned against the wall next to his open office door and his brooding body in two heart-thrashing seconds. "You lied to me, *маленький ягненок.*"

I try to shake my head again, but his grip on my face is too firm. His thumb and forefinger are gripping my chin, and his other three fingers are wrapped around my throat. His hold is rough and unhinged, very much like him.

"You lied to me," he repeats again, his voice not as hot as the surge of electricity zapping through my veins from his closeness. "Because you said you weren't made for this life." As his eyes bounce between mine, their dilation easily able to expose that they're the clearest they've ever been, he murmurs, "That's why I let you go. That's why I let you believe he had killed me." His breath tickles my face when he whispers, "That's why I stepped back when you and Lera finally made it out unscathed." His voice is husky and pained. "That's why I walked away when you begged Lucianna to tell you who decorated *your* penthouse apartment."

It is ludicrous for me to be jealous that he knows the realtor's name after disclosing he's been watching me for over a year, but it can't be helped. "And that's why I'm following you around the globe instead of smearing my cum over every inch of you in each city we visit." His Russian accent is the thickest I've heard when he murmurs, "You said this life was not for you, so I let you go."

The aggression he is showing should have me running for the hills, but my clammy palms, racing pulse, and the insane thud between my legs has me doing the opposite.

"I lied," I reply before stepping over the threshold that will return me to a captive. "So now you have no choice but to punish me."

BONUS EPILOGUE
GHOST

Two Years Later…

"*F*uck, *маленький ягненок*." I tightened my grip on Katie's long, glossy tresses before slowing her pace. "You're going to suck the marrow straight out of my fucking bones."

She glosses up her lips with the pre-cum dripping out of my cock's head before she flashes me a quick smirk, then she gets back down to business.

We fucked like rabbits the first month she returned. We had a lot of time to make up for, but even now, two years later, I still act as if she owes me eighteen months of blow jobs since I went without physical stimulation for so long.

I force Katie onto her knees as often as possible, my urge to have her beneath me, above me, and all fucking over me never waning.

Three years ago, I resigned myself to the fact I had gotten them out, that I achieved what I had set out to do four years earlier, then she waltzed back into my life with a gleam in her eyes that almost knocked me on my ass for the third time.

We didn't make it out of my office before I claimed her as mine, and Katie never made it back to the cruise ship.

Her sister thinks she met a distribution clerk on the first half of her tour. She has no clue she's spent the last twenty-four months messing the sheets with the real heir of the Bobrov Bratva. The only person who knows that is Blaire.

Her ties with the Bratva are helping Katie return the Petrov name to the glory it once had—minus trafficked women, of course.

We won't go down that route again. I'll take a hit in capital before I ever contemplate if someone else's Katie is trapped in an orlop, living off scraps.

"Fuck, маленький ягненок. Don't stop." I roll my hips, the urge to come pulling my balls in close to my body. "I'm going to drench your throat with my seed before drenching your cunt." My painful grip on her hair doubles the dilation of her eyes. "Flatten your tongue like a good little slut. I want as much of my cock inside your mouth as I can fit before you swallow my cum."

I stuff my cock in deep, a growl rumbling up my throat when she takes me to the very back. Then I give her what she's desperate for three to four times a day. I blow down her throat with an unearthly groan, my thighs clenching when she stares up at me while swallowing me down.

As the pulse darting through my balls simmers to a pleasant throb, I pluck Katie from the floor, toss her onto the cabin bed too small for how flexible and adventurous my Little Lamb is, then demand she spread her legs for me.

"Wider, маленький ягненок. Don't fucking hide from me."

My hand falls to my rapidly reforming erection when the defiant gleam I crave more than cocaine blazes through her eyes.

She has me by the fucking throat.

So I do the same to her.

Her pulse thuds against my hand when I curl it around her throat and drag her to within an inch of my face. She isn't scared. Why would she be? I'm giving her what she craves.

Me in all my hideous form.

"Is this what you want, *маленький ягненок?*" I tilt my head so the cabin light above our bed doesn't shadow my face, then I roll my teeth over my lower lip to hide the twitch in my jaw.

If anyone raked their eyes over my scars like Katie does, they'd be dead, and I wouldn't even remove my gun from my holster to take them down.

But since it's Katie, my wife and fucking queen, I let her look.

"Yes." A moan vibrates through my chest when her voice is the husky purr I aim for every time I bed her. "I want you."

After cupping my jaw, her hold not as firm on the scarred side of my face, she kisses me with the last ounce of oxygen left in her lungs.

It is a desperate, unhinged kiss that strengthens her pulse instead of weakening it.

Incapable of holding back my urges for a second longer, I use my grip on her throat to pin her to the mattress before I lower my head between her legs. A hot breath of air escapes my lips when I notice how drenched she is for me. Her thighs are holding evidence of the juices her cunt frees when she sucks my cock, and since her pussy is bare, I can see her clit throbbing at the apex of her greedy cunt.

"What do you say, *маленький ягненок?*"

She squirms and thrashes before the faintest beg seeps from her lips. "Please."

As her hands find their way to my hair, my tongue finds her clit. I lick the swollen bud with a long, purposeful stroke before I swivel it around it, then suck it into my mouth.

Katie bucks once, twice, then with the third jerk, her hands fall to her sides, and a breathy moan simpers between us.

"Louder."

I suck, lick, and teeth her clit before slipping two fingers inside her to force her to follow my demands. I don't need gimmicks or threats for her to obey me.

I merely need her beneath me.

"More. Please. Gh-Ghost."

She fists the sheets in a white-knuckled hold before she lifts her ass off the mattress to grind against my mouth. She doesn't want kindness and compassion when she's being fucked. She wants to be manhandled and tossed around.

She wants to know she is being bedded by a man, not a pussy with a five-inch cock.

I work her harder. Faster. I drive her to the brink of insanity before I stop.

"Ghost... no... fuck." Katie freezes along with me when her last word reaches our ears.

I angle my head, my expression stoic. "What did you say to me?"

"No-nothing."

The wetness dripping off my fingers doubles when I mutter, "Don't fucking lie to me, Little Lamb. You won't like the consequences of your actions."

I try to continue with my ploy that I'm angry, but the damn furl of my top lip gives me away in an instant.

A nanosecond after she sees it, a gleaning grin stretches across Katie's face, immediately weakening my resolve.

"Scoot. If you want to swear like a man, you can do all the fucking work too."

I'm acting as if I am disappointed I'm forcing her to ride on top.

I am a fucking liar.

There's nothing sexier than my wife lining up my cock to drive home. And since she knows how much she can handle, I don't have to worry I'm hurting the bump that's real in her midsection this time around.

I had no clue Sofia was pumping Katie's food with hormones that would make a pregnancy test positive. She branched out on her own with that and a handful of other things I'm not happy about—most particularly learning that the vials inserted into Katie were only filled with female sperm. That's how Kirill knew her unborn child was a girl by checking her purity. But we're slowly bridging the gap, purely because Kirill would have killed Katie along with me if he had learned the truth.

Mercifully, neither of their ploys affected Katie's fertility.

She is five months pregnant, so it is finally time for her to go home to share the news with her sister. Since our daughter is a Petrov, I can go with her without the war I was planning if anyone dared to try and separate us again.

I had to kill daily to keep Katie safe during her captivity, but since it was best for everyone to believe I was dead, I couldn't let her know I was always there in the background, protecting her.

Although my tactics were inhumane, they've grown worse since I made her mine.

I'd kill on the second for her now.

We've built an unbreakable empire in Russia, but I'd be a liar if I said I wasn't interested to discover how far we can expand it with the US ties we will commence forming the instant Katie realizes we've anchored.

Mafia royalty has arrived in town to welcome her home with open arms.

Katie's unknown lineage with the Gottles is why Kirill held her head underwater. The Petrovs are ranked higher than the Bobrovs on the bratva rankings because of Henry's title, and Kirill wasn't happy when he was informed about that.

I don't give a fuck. Katie is mine, and rank doesn't enter the equation when it comes to my possessiveness.

The same can be said for Katie.

I came to tell her that we've arrived at Hopeton, but when she looked at me with hungry eyes, our plans altered in an instant.

I'll never say no to her, especially when it entails my dick in some region of her body.

I also don't give a fuck how important Henry thinks he is, he can wait.

There is only one person I answer to.

It ain't fucking him.

It is the redhead with my cock deep inside her.

The mother of my unborn child.

And the woman I dragged through hell when I had no fucking clue she knew the way out all along.

Katie is resurrecting the Bobrov Bratva to the glory it deserves, and its upsurge in reputation has nothing to do with her mafia lineage and everything to do with the attitude she displayed over a decade ago when she saluted the middle finger to two dock workers who wolf-whistled at her.

Kirill confessed last year that he organized Katie's kidnap while I was handling the Neanderthals who couldn't recognize mafia royalty in the making.

Since he was no longer protected by mafia code—how could he without an ounce of our blood—I hung Kirill from the rafters of the prison the CIA was hiding him in the same night.

Katie's long-lost uncle's hideout was my next stop.

Slowly but surely, the paupers are learning what they should have known all along.

When royalty graces you with their presence, you don't gawk like the possibility of more is in your realm.

You bow your fucking head like every man in my crew does when Katie approaches them.

If you don't, enjoy your last breaths because they will be limited.

I promise you that.

The End!

Love what you read? Want to read more? You should jump into Alek and Anastasia's story… yes, that Anastasia.

It will release sometime on April 25. You can preorder it here: Sinful Intentions

If you loved this book, please consider leaving a review.
Also, stay in touch. I love hearing from you.

Facebook: facebook.com/authorshandi

Tiktok: https://www.tiktok.com/@authorshandiboyes

Instagram: instagram.com/authorshandi

Email: authorshandi@gmail.com

Reader's Group: bit.ly/ShandiBookBabes

Website: authorshandi.com

Newsletter: https://www.subscribepage.com/AuthorShandi

ACKNOWLEDGMENTS

Those who know me know I am not a huge fan of the acknowledgment page. It isn't that I don't have anyone to thank. I have a ton of people. It is worrying that I'll miss someone.

The past twelve months have been so challenging with my wanting to write, but the publishing house pulling me in another direction. I barely get a moment to myself, so I made a huge decision early this week to stop all submissions and work only with the authors we currently have contracted with us.

It means forgoing on a dream I honestly didn't know I wanted until it popped into my head, but allowing me to continue the dream I secretly knew I always wanted.

We were so young when we met, but I used to whisper naughty stories into Chris's ear every time we had a sleep over. I never considered putting pen to paper. I merely liked making him squirm LOL.

Life requires us to go through many steps before we get it right. I got the perfect guy the first try, so I had to work harder to find the best career.

Writing is it for me, so although I am upset we've had to close one chapter of the publishing house, I am very much looking forward to getting back to what I love.

Lots and lots of words!

Oh, right, this is meant to be an acknowledgment page. Back to it.

As usual, thank you to my husband, Chris. He truly is my rock, and despite social media usually only showing the good side of a relationship, what you see on there is us. He can be a pain in my ass sometimes, but 99.99% of the time, I couldn't imagine life without him. I've told him on many occasions he needs to buy a coffin big enough for two. He isn't leaving without me. No peace for him.

To my mum, who still reads my books within a day of me handing them over. That is pretty damn impressive for how many I have.

To Lauren, your graphics.. girl, they make me squirm in my seat, and I wrote the damn words. Thank you for being there when I've needed to be talked down from a ledge. This industry isn't easy, and sometimes it seems easier to give up, but with people like you on my side, I think I can make a good go at it.

To my ARC readers, thank you for sharing your love of my books. If I didn't have readers bragging about my stories, they'd sit on a shelf gathering dust, so thank you!

And to everyone else, I hope you loved Ghost and Katie's story as much as me. It was a twisty, crazy ride but when aren't they.

Until the next release, which I am aiming to be a lot closer than my last two, stay safe and happy.

Cheers

Shandi xx

ALSO BY SHANDI BOYES

Perception Series

Saving Noah (Noah & Emily)

Fighting Jacob (Jacob & Lola)

Taming Nick (Nick & Jenni)

Redeeming Slater (Slater and Kylie)

Saving Emily (Noah & Emily - Novella)

Wrapped Up with Rise Up (Perception Novella - should be read after the Bound Series)

Enigma

Enigma (Isaac & Isabelle #1)

Unraveling an Enigma (Isaac & Isabelle #2)

Enigma The Mystery Unmasked (Isaac & Isabelle #3)

Enigma: The Final Chapter (Isaac & Isabelle #4)

Beneath The Secrets (Hugo & Ava #1)

Beneath The Sheets (Hugo & Ava #2)

Spy Thy Neighbor (Hunter & Paige)

The Opposite Effect (Brax & Clara)

I Married a Mob Boss (Rico & Blaire)

Second Shot (Hawke & Gemma)

The Way We Are (Ryan & Savannah #1)

The Way We Were (Ryan & Savannah #2)

Sugar and Spice (Cormack & Harlow)

Lady In Waiting (Regan & Alex #1)

Man in Queue (Regan & Alex #2)

Couple on Hold(Regan & Alex #3)

Enigma: The Wedding (Isaac and Isabelle)

Silent Vigilante (Brandon and Melody #1)

Hushed Guardian (Brandon & Melody #2)

Quiet Protector (Brandon & Melody #3)

Enigma: An Isaac Retelling

Twisted Lies (Jae & CJ)

Bound Series

Chains (Marcus & Cleo #1)

Links(Marcus & Cleo #2)

Bound(Marcus & Cleo #3)

Restrain(Marcus & Cleo #4)

The Misfits

Russian Mob Chronicles

Nikolai: A Mafia Prince Romance (Nikolai & Justine #1)

Nikolai: Taking Back What's Mine (Nikolai & Justine #2)

Nikolai: What's Left of Me(Nikolai & Justine #3)

Nikolai: Mine to Protect(Nikolai & Justine #4)

Asher: My Russian Revenge (Asher & Zariah)

Nikolai: Through the Devil's Eyes(Nikolai & Justine #5)

Trey (Trey & K)

The Italian Cartel

Dimitri

Roxanne

Reign

Mafia Ties (Novella)

Maddox

Demi

Rocco

Clover

Smith

RomCom Standalones

Just Playin' (Elvis & Willow)

Ain't Happenin' (Lorenzo & Skylar)

The Drop Zone (Colby & Jamie)

Very Unlikely (Brand New Couple)

Short Stories - Newsletter Downloads

Christmas Trio (Wesley, Andrew & Mallory -- short story)

Falling For A Stranger (Short Story)

One Night Only Series

Hotshot Boss

Hotshot Neighbor

The Bobrov Bratva Series

Wicked Intentions (Katie & Ghost)

Sinful Intentions (coming soon)

Made in the USA
Columbia, SC
22 March 2023